GW01117682

DEALING WITH KRANZE

Also by the same author

Fiction
Hunt for the Autumn Clowns
The Killing of Yesterday's Children
Lonely the Man Without Heroes
A Darkness in the Eye
Bridie and the Silver Lady
The Crucifixion of Septimus Roach
Crucible of Fools
Come the Executioner
Children of the North
Skating Round the Poppy
The Stalker's Apprentice
A Sheltering Silence

Non-Fiction
A Summer Soldier (with P. A. Williams)
As I Live, Dying

Dealing with Kranze

M.S. Power

MAINSTREAM
PUBLISHING
EDINBURGH AND LONDON

Copyright © M. S. Power, 1996
All rights reserved
The moral right of the author has been asserted

First published in Great Britain in 1996 by
MAINSTREAM PUBLISHING COMPANY
(EDINBURGH) LTD
7 Albany Street
Edinburgh EH1 3UG

ISBN 1 85158 771 3

No part of this book may be reproduced or transmitted in any form or by any means without written permission from the publisher, except by a reviewer who wishes to quote brief passages in connection with a review written for insertion in a magazine, newspaper or broadcast

A catalogue record for this book is available from the British Library

Typeset in Times by Pioneer Associates Ltd, Perthshire
Printed and bound in Great Britain by
Ipswich Book Company Ltd

*For Jimmy Rigden,
remembering, or perhaps forgetting,
those hilarious days in Perth, Dumfries,
and Lanarkshire*

What hinders me from smiting now?
Thee and thy monkey-sprites with fell disaster?
Hast for the scarlet coat no reverence?
Dost recognise no more the tall cock's-feather?
Have I concealed my countenance?
Must tell my name, old face of leather!

Faust, Scene VI
Johann Wolfgang Von Goethe

CONTENTS

Book One — 13

Book Two — 101

Book Three — 213

ROT IN HELL!

EXCLUSIVE

The Judge wasted no words as he jailed evil fiend Marcus Walwyn for life yesterday.

Mr Justice Packard said simply: 'Marcus Walwyn, on both counts of murder on which you have been unanimously convicted by the jury the sentence is one of life imprisonment, and if attention is paid to what I think you will never be released. You were a particularly privileged young man, well educated and wealthy. Yet you murdered two young people in the most brutal fashion, two young people who had never done you any harm and whom you barely knew.'

The Judge ordered prison officers: 'Take him down.'

As posh, Downside-educated Walwyn, 22, was driven away in a prison van, heart-broken mother of murder victim Sharon Hayes told of her agony over her daughter's terrible death.

Betty Hayes, 47, said: 'Sharon was such a lovely girl. She was kind and cheerful and loving. How that monster could use her to practise murder is something I will never understand.'

Asked about the life sentence passed on Walwyn, Mrs Hayes added: 'He won't really suffer. His type don't. **But I hope he rots in hell.**'

During the eight-day trial Walwyn denied brutally knifing Sharon Hayes to death as a practice run for another murder he was planning. He also denied murdering Darren Cornell by deliberately running him down having lured him to an isolated farm near Windsor.

Killer

As sentence was passed, the cold-blooded killer smirked and said: 'Thank you.' His lawyer, Harold Rutherford, said later: 'He is devastated. We will be appealing. Mr Walwyn is as much a victim as either of the two young people he is accused of killing.'

In his defence, Mr Rutherford claimed his client had become unbalanced following his father's suicide, and had been influenced by a book he was reading. But the Judge slammed this and said that he himself had read many gruesome tales during his life but had never found himself driven to act out any of the crimes they contained.

Obsessed

The prosecution said Walwyn had become obsessed with Karen Scott, the fiancee of Darren Cornell and best friend of Sharon Hayes and that he had murdered both Cornell and Hayes because they interfered with his plans to gain Karen's affections. Karen was also brutally murdered but police have not yet been able to identify her killer.

The evidence was horrifying enough. But the jury were appalled by Walwyn's gloating expression when extracts were read from the book it was said influenced him.

As sentence was passed the gallery erupted in cheering, and a huge crowd shouted at the van as the cocky killer was driven away to start his sentence.

'Murder can be a very pleasurable business'

Judge asks if books can make you kill

OPINION

NOW that the trial of Marcus Walwyn is over and he has been found guilty of the murders of Sharon Hayes and Darren Cornell, and been sentenced to life in prison, I find myself thinking that, indeed, Walwyn was, as his lawyer claimed, a victim, a victim of his privileged upbringing and affluence. Had he been a yob he would, in all probability, never have committed the crimes. Although Mr Justice Packard dismissed the Defence claim (somewhat hastily in my opinion) that Walwyn had been influenced beyond reason by the manuscript of a book entitled *A Letter from Chile* which he was editing, I cannot for the life of me see why a young person with a highly active brain – and one he is clearly willing to use – cannot be influenced by a violent book to the same extent that many impressionable minds are influenced by graphic violence on our television screens.

Although the manuscript of the novel was not produced in court, extracts from it were read and they were chilling to the extreme. Written as a novel with the author purporting to be a serial killer who has committed the perfect murder, it lays down the ground rules for murder. It is, in many senses, a handbook to murder, starting with the frightening sentence: 'Ever since I could think reasonably I knew I would kill someone.'

It does not, I think, require much imagination to see how such a statement could fire the mind of a lonely young man already traumatised by the suicide of his father, the eminent gynaecologist Douglas Walwyn. Nor should it be too difficult for the courts to appreciate the results of obsession, and Walwyn was clearly obsessed when he stalked the friend of the two victims, Karen Scott, and when he discovered he could not have her, he – quite logically to his way of thinking – decided to remove the obstacles that prevented him from so doing. This, of course, is no excuse for his cruel actions, but to me it represents an explanation and I cannot for the life of me see how sending this intelligent young man to prison is going to improve matters for him. He will, eventually, be released, and if past experience is anything to go by, the treatment he needs will certainly not be forthcoming within Her Majesty's prison system. Indeed, given the time to brood it is highly likely he will be released a much more disturbed and dangerous person.

A Letter from Chile has not been published. Its author, Helmut Kranze, has, I understand, withdrawn his manuscript from the publishers. Perhaps it is just as well. Or should it be published so that all of us can ask ourselves if we, too, could be influenced by it to such a degree that we also can understand, at least in part, what was meant by that other terrifying quote: 'Murder can be a very pleasurable business'?

BOOK ONE

ONE

I've no intention whatever of being so tedious as to start telling you all about life in prison. It's enough to say that it's no *Hi-de-Hi* land, nor is it some sort of hell-hole, so both those patronising do-gooders who think prisoners suffer irreversible mental damage and those moronic sadists who think inmates should all be flogged or castrated are wrong. Actually, it's just plain boring if you really want to know. That's if you go into prison with a functioning brain: if your little grey cells are already clotted up you'd probably find Her Majesty's Guest Houses pretty nice places since the one thing you certainly don't have to do is use your mind. In fact, that activity is vigorously discouraged just in case you give the screws an inferiority complex, which wouldn't be all that good for the system, would it? I suppose if you insisted that I describe the life in prison in just one word I'd have to say it's weird.

I don't know if you've ever been to Bombay. If you have you'll know what I'm talking about, and if you haven't you'll learn something – nothing that will change the course of your life, mind. Anyway, all along the pavements, squatting and grinning up at you, are ethnic gents called street dentists. These guys will do all the dental repairs you might need right there and then, so there's a fair bit of screeching mixing with the sound of traffic. And if you're short of the odd rupee or two, they'll yank out a few of your good teeth as payment, keep them in little cardboard boxes, and eventually insert them in the gums of someone else who can afford to pay cash for them, turning a healthy little profit. So, all over Bombay, all over the subcontinent probably, you get people smiling smiles with other people's teeth, smiling someone else's smile in a way. The reason I'm telling you this is because on visiting days in prison the same sort of thing happens: cons switch on smiles that aren't their own, smiles as phoney as Gunga Din's. As soon as the visits are over and the visitors have gone, those smiles are wiped away and stored until the next time. That's what I mean by weird.

Not that I got many visits, by the way. Ma came only once, and all she had to say for herself was, 'Oh, darling,' in a reproachful kind of way, as if she held me personally responsible for the state and smell of the place. Mind you, being Ma, she did have the odd preen when she noticed some of the cons ogling her: it's not too often you get someone as classy as my Ma coming to prisons. I even caught her giving one of her coy, don't-be-so-silly little smiles when Big Charlie Graham winked at her, but she soon came back to earth when I told her Big Charlie was definitely working class, and Scots, which was worse. She'd probably have passed out if I'd told her more about Big Charlie. Rampant though Ma is at times, I don't see even her bedding someone with a penchant for slitting people's throats. Actually, Big Charlie was all right, just a bit slow and easily led. Somewhere along the line someone, probably his daft social worker, had told him he had an Oedipus complex and Big Charlie was really proud of this though he hadn't a clue what it meant. He went off his food for a few days when I told him he had to kill his father and screw his mother to qualify.

Harry Rutherford, my lawyer, came in every few months, doing his duty and keeping on the sweet side of Ma. They were still 'seeing' each other even though he hadn't got me off. He was, he told me seriously, still working on my case, looking for grounds for an appeal.

'Thanks, Harry,' I told him. 'Any luck?'

'Not so far, I fear.'

'Ah, well, keep trying,' I said, just to encourage him.

'I intend to, Marcus.'

Which brings me to my only other visitor. Inspector Birt. He really did surprise me. Came to see me regular as clockwork once a month. And, being who he was, we could have nice little private visits in a small room away from the riff-raff. More civilised. The first time he came I was sure he was just there to gloat. 'Come to gloat, then?'

Birt shook his head and even looked a bit hurt. 'No, Marcus.'

'Why then?'

Birt just shrugged and, to tell the truth, I don't think he really knew why he had come to visit. Not at first anyway.

'I thought you'd got the shove?'

Birt smiled. 'Just suspended for a while.'

'Oh. So you're still out there catching all those wicked criminals?'

'Doing my best.'

'I bet.'

'You all right?'

'Me? I'm fine. Just love being banged up twenty-three hours a day.'

'I'm sorry, Marcus,' Birt said.

And you know something? I honestly think he meant it, but, 'Oh, sure,' I said. 'Must break your heart.'

Well, to cut a long story short, as they say, I'd just done three years, eleven months, three weeks and two days of my life sentence for murder when Harry Rutherford came to see me looking as if he'd been made Lord Chief Justice or something; but, being an eternal pessimist, he started with a dour warning. 'Now, I don't want you to get too excited at this stage, Marcus, but I do believe we may have found a flaw in your trial which would give us the grounds for appeal we've been looking for.' He sat back, beaming, waiting, I suppose, for me to tell him what a terrific fellow he was.

'Oh, yeah?'

'Yes,' Harry said, a bit deflated, but he soon recovered.

'Nice,' I told him, but even that must have shown too much enthusiasm since he immediately warned, 'Now, *please,* Marcus, don't let your hopes get *too* high. These appeals can be extremely tricky. The first hurdle is to get *leave* to appeal, and that is no formality I can assure you.'

'So why are you telling me all this then?'

'I'm sorry?'

'Why are you getting me all excited if – '

'Because I thought you'd want to – '

'Look, Harry. To tell you the truth, I don't want to know one sodding thing until you get me out. *If* you get me out. I don't want any bloody carrots, thank you very much.'

And that was that. Mind you, I did feel pretty good in myself because I knew Harry wouldn't really have said a damn thing unless he was fairly confident of success. But at the same time I wasn't about to hold my breath.

And then Birt came to see me again. About three days after Harry had been. He tried really hard to act his normal boring self but I could tell he was up to something. Not that I let on I was aware anything was different about him: I allowed him to ramble on in his usual way, just chatting, waiting for him to make the first move. Then: 'Ever thought about what you're going to do when you get out, Marcus?' he asked with a fair attempt at sounding casual.

'Naw. No point, is there? Be an old man when *I* get out.'

'But you must have thought about what you will do.'

'Claim my pension.'

'Seriously.'

'Don't think about it at all.'

'I see. Well, maybe you should give it some thought.'

I gave him one of my penetrating looks. 'Oh, yeah?'

He stared me straight back in the eye. 'I would if I were you.'

'Ah, but you're not me, are you?'

'You know what I mean.'

'Oh, I know what you mean, all right. Sounds to me like you're taking the piss, if you really want to know.'

Birt shook his head. 'I wouldn't do that, Marcus.'

And that was when he brought up Kranze. It was really strange to hear that name again because not once in all the time he had been visiting me had Birt mentioned it. Maybe on purpose. Maybe he'd been saving it so that when he *did* mention it the impact would be greater.

'I suppose,' he supposed, leaning back in his chair, swinging on the back legs and folding his hands behind his head, 'I suppose you've often wondered how you could get your own back on Kranze?'

And of course he was right but I wasn't about to let him know that. I said, 'What d'you mean – get my own back? Why would I want to do that, for God's sake?'

Birt grinned. 'Well, he put you here.'

'*You* put me here,' I corrected him.

'I'd never have been able to nab you if Kranze hadn't killed Karen.'

'You don't know he killed her.'

Birt gave a scoffing little laugh. 'Oh, I know that all right.'

'So arrest him.'

Birt said nothing.

'Too clever for you, is he?' I asked, quite enjoying the little jibe.

Birt's eyes went very cold. But he nodded. 'So far. So far.'

'You'll never get Kranze,' I told him. 'Not in a million years.'

Inspector Birt stood up suddenly and his chair fell backwards with a crash. He started to walk round and round the room. He stopped walking after about five minutes and stood behind my chair with his back to me, staring up at the window. 'I could if I had help,' he said. He turned then and stared at me, stared at the back of my neck and I could feel my hair start to tingle. I didn't look round. I waited.

But Birt had said all he was going to say for the moment – on that subject anyway. 'I must go,' he said brusquely, and before I could recover myself he was at the door, telling the screw he was ready to go. 'I'll come and see you again, Marcus,' he told me as a parting shot, and all I could do was nod.

And, true to his word, Birt did come in again to see me. Three weeks later he turned up, looking different: very businesslike.

'You're ahead of schedule,' I told him, meaning there usually were four weeks between his visits.

But Birt was not amused, or interested, it seemed. He sat opposite me, looking pretty grim, I thought, his hands on the table, palms down, his fingers sort of jerking like he was scratching the woodwork. Then, abruptly, he asked, 'Seen Mr Rutherford recently?'

'Harry? Not since you were last here, no. Why?'

Birt didn't answer that. He started breathing heavily through his nostrils and I could see the hairs in his nose quiver. It crossed my mind to tell him that a thing called scissors *had* been invented – can't stand hairy noses and ears on men. No need for it anyway.

'Why?' I asked again. Birt shifted uncomfortably in his chair, and went on fidgeting, driving me crazy. After a bit I said, 'Well, this is really interesting. Nothing I like better than a silent visit. Does my mind no end of good.'

Birt bucked up a bit. 'I'm sorry, Marcus. I just thought . . .' Then he stopped again.

'Like I said, really interesting,' I told him sarcastically.

'I just don't want to pre-empt – '

'Pre-empt what, for Christ's sake?'

'Anything your lawyer might want to say.'

'Like what?'

Birt looked away.

'You know something?'

'Just – ' He got up and started his patrolling. Then he pulled up in front of me and kind of shook his body like he was edging into a tight little parking space. 'Marcus, if I tell you something, can you keep it to yourself?'

'Oh, no. I'll probably take a stroll down Canary Wharf and shout it from the rooftops. Of course I'll keep it to myself if you want me to.'

Birt went round the table and sat down again. 'Let me ask you something first, Marcus.'

I waited for him to ask me something first. And waited. 'Is this going to take long?' I asked finally. 'I've only got another twelve years to go, you know.'

Birt managed a thin smile at that. 'I'm sorry, Marcus. It's difficult.'

'Must be.'

'All right,' Birt said at last, making up his mind, it seemed. 'Supposing – just supposing – you got out sooner than expected, would you help me to bring Kranze to justice?'

I had to laugh at that. I guffawed really. It sounded such an archaic expression – 'bring Kranze to justice'. When I calmed down I asked, 'This is all hypothetical, of course?'

Birt frowned. 'Not altogether,' he said hesitantly.

'You know something I don't?'

'You didn't answer my question. Would you help me?'

'I might.'

Birt shook his head. 'Not good enough.'

'Okay. Hypothetically, yes, I would,' I told him. I'd have told him anything he wanted to hear just to know what he was on about.

He nodded at that. 'That's all I wanted to know.'

I waited a few minutes. 'Well?' I asked.

Birt gave me a wicked grin. 'Well what?'

'Oh, for shit's sake! Look, I'm in no mood for your bloody little games. Just piss off and leave me alone if – '

'Calm down, Marcus. Calm down,' Birt told me, clearly getting a bit anxious that I might change my mind about helping him. 'There's not a lot I *can* tell you.'

'Well, tell me what you *can* tell me.'

'Just – well, your lawyer's going to lodge an appeal, I think.'

'I know that,' I said, which was a bit of a lie.

'And I think there's a good chance he might win it,' Birt added.

Now that *was* news. I hadn't given Harry a snowball's chance in hell of getting an appeal off the ground let alone winning it. 'What makes you say that?' I asked, trying to sound sceptical.

Birt sighed. 'Experience.'

'Oh – that all?'

'Plus – ' Birt began, and then the screw stuck his head in the door to say that Harry Rutherford was here to see me. He didn't say Harry Rutherford, of course. He said, 'Your solicitor's here to see you,' getting Harry's title wrong as per usual.

Birt stood up. 'I'll be off then,' he said, sounding pleased to have been given the chance to escape.

'But you'll be back, no doubt.'

'Oh, I'll be back, Marcus. I'll be back.'

'Thought you might.'

Well, all I can say is thank God for technicalities. I'm not about to take you through the whole rigmarole of legal appeals: suffice to say that Harry Rutherford, bless his cotton socks, had uncovered enough of those technicalities for the Appeal Court to find my conviction 'unsafe'. Mind you, he was helped by the fact that there'd been a couple of other unsafe convictions just prior to my appeal and the bewigged judiciary were pretty twitchy, and by the fact that the police didn't seem all that enthusiastic about keeping me locked up. Birt was particularly demure in the box, looking almost bashful, which was quite sweet.

So, one fine summer day, with the sun shining and the birds atwitter, I walked out of prison a free man again. Of course, the tabloids had a right go at me and at the Court, dredging up the whole story of my life and background, all the turgid details of the killings of Sharon and Darren and everything, and asking their moronic readers if any young woman was still safe in this day and age. Did I care? Did I fuck!

TWO

Ma had moved from Balham – something to do with her not being able to tolerate the way she thought people eyed her after my conviction: sort of accusing her of having suckled some sort of monster. She did try her Greta Garbo bit for a while (dark glasses, head bowed, sloppy clothes and all that jazz) and it seemed to help her cope temporarily. But then some freaks started putting weird, threatening notes and excrement through the letterbox, so it was time for her to vamoose. I really felt quite sorry for poor Ma: twice in her boring life she got the attention she craved, and both times it was for the wrong reasons: Dad hanging himself and then me getting banged up. Anyway, glorious Balham was abandoned and a bijou mews house in Chelsea was now home.

'Nice,' I told Ma when Harry had driven me from prison to the house, and I'd given the place a quick once over.

'Yes, dear,' Ma agreed.

Well, the address might have changed but Ma certainly hadn't. In fact, Ma hadn't changed in all the years I'd known her, or became aware of her, anyway. I always had this feeling that the Harrods

Beauty Department had some sort of magic mask of her tucked away in a drawer and that every time she turned up they peeled a layer off it and stuck it onto her face. And in all those years, too, her hairstyle hadn't changed: maybe Simon couldn't do it any other way, but I've a theory that changing her hairstyle would have been about as irrevocable to Ma as a sex change. And as for her clothes, well, Ma didn't give a fig for fashion. Style was her big thing, and she certainly had that. What she'd have done without Coco I've no idea. Simple little suits and frocks, and a minimum of good, expensive jewellery. Like now. A little black number with a small diamond brooch pinned on the shoulder. That was all. And she looked a million dollars, as they say.

'How did you find it?' I asked. 'This place?'

'Oh, Harry found it for us.'

'Ah,' I turned to Harry who was now shuffling in the corner. '*Very* kind of you, Harry. Thanks.'

Harry nodded his acknowledgement of my gratitude. Funny, now that I was on the outside again and he'd lost his power over me, so to speak, he'd returned to being that kind of naughty schoolboy, scared stiff I was going to take the piss out of him. Of course he knew that I knew why he'd selected this particular pad for Ma: just five minutes from his own place so he could nip round and lay Ma whenever the urge took him.

'Maybe you'd prefer to get a place of your own?' he asked hopefully. 'I mean – '

'Oh, no, Harry. This is really nice. Honestly,' I told him with a really generous smile and I pretended not to notice the small flicker of disappointment that passed between him and Ma. 'Not just yet anyway,' I added, giving them a straw to clutch at. 'Maybe when I've got back on my feet.'

'Of course, dear,' Ma said quickly.

'But don't worry, Harry. I'll keep out of your way.'

Harry went red and Ma gave a simpering little smile. Things clearly hadn't changed much in that area either.

'And,' I went on. 'If you ever feel that I *am* in the way, all you have to do is say so, and I'll move.'

'Don't be silly, darling,' Ma said. 'This is just as much *your* home as it is mine. Isn't that right, Harry?'

Harry grunted.

'No, I mean it, Ma,' I insisted, loading my voice with gentle understanding. 'I mean, I owe so much to Harry and you. I want you both to be really happy, and I certainly wouldn't want to – well, you know . . .' I let my sentence trail off into Ma's Joy perfume.

And that, apparently, was just what Ma wanted to hear, as I suspected. She came across and hugged me, and sobbed a bit onto my shoulder. I dutifully patted her back, and she brightened. 'Now,' she said. 'Guess what Mummy has in the fridge?'

'Ice?'

'*Champagne!*'

I nearly said 'That's fucking terrific', but managed to restrain myself. It was something I was going to have to watch. My language. My vocabulary had deteriorated somewhat through lack of exercise. After all, there's only about fifty words you need to get you through a life stretch, the good old F-word coming out top of the pops. And you have to use it so that the yahoos can understand you, and so they won't think you're some kind of nonce or pervert. 'Golly,' I said. 'That's just terrific.'

So, while Ma scuttled off to get her champagne I decided it was diplomacy time: time to thank Harry for everything he'd done and to try and sound sincere. And, to be truthful, even though I found him very hard to take and could never understand what on earth Ma saw in him, he had been very decent about everything, very professional, never even hinting that he disapproved of what I'd done. Mind you, it probably suited the old lecher to have me out of the way for a while, leaving him a clear run at Ma without having to wonder if he'd have to dodge past me every time he visited. And, because I'd asked him to, he'd looked after my money while I was inside, and the crafty old sod had increased what Dad had left me by a tidy little sum.

But now, for the very first time, when I thanked him, he let me know he didn't think much of me. 'I was only doing my job,' he told me tersely.

'Of course, Harry.'

'And, if the truth be known, I did it more for your mother than for you.'

'Still got the hots for her, have you?' I asked. I wasn't going to let him get too cocky with me.

Harry ignored my question. 'I trust you're going to – '

'Behave myself?' I interrupted. 'That what you were going to ask?'

'I – '

'Or maybe you're wondering if I'm plotting to kill someone else?' and I could see from his eyes that this was exactly what he'd been thinking. I gave it some thought, just to upset him. 'Shouldn't think so,' I told him finally. 'But you never can tell, can you?' I then asked, half-joking. Only half-joking because you never *can* tell what might happen, can you?

Ma came back in then with champagne glasses tinkling on a tray, and a bottle of Moët looking a bit unbalanced. 'There we are,' she announced. 'Champagne for my two very favourite men.'

Harry and I said, 'Thank you,' in unison and for some reason that gave me the giggles. Ma thought her idea of champagne had made me really happy.

'That's what I like to see, darling,' she said. 'Nice big smiles. Put all that horrible business behind us.'

'Yes, Ma.'

My room wasn't that much bigger than the cell I'd been in, but it was a hell of a lot prettier. Actually, it was much bigger but it was smaller than the room I'd had in Balham. Still, Ma had arranged it nicely for me, and she'd left all my personal things in boxes: not wanting to pry, as she told me later, and thinking I believed her. Ma not pry? Well, if you believed that, you'd believe anything.

It was funny, but once I got into my room and closed the door I had this urge never to come out again. I guess it was because in prison the only place you feel really safe is when you're locked up in your own little cell, knowing none of the psychos can get at you if they have one of their turns and go on a slashing rampage. And you'd think locked doors were the very last thing I'd want: not a bit of it. Practically the first thing I did when I got into my room was to lock the door behind me. Don't ask me why. And for weeks after my release I always locked that door when I was inside the room.

Anyway, I had a shower and changed, listening to a bit of Mahler's Fifth which was really great after years of crap by Guns 'n' Roses, bloody rap which the tinted folk all insisted on playing, and the squealing of the Minogue sisters who should never have been let out of the Antipodes.

As soon as I got downstairs again, Ma said, 'Now, what would you like to do this evening, darling?'

I hadn't given that any thought. 'Dunno, Ma.'

'Go out for a lovely dinner? My treat?'

I shook my head.

'Oh.' Ma sounded disappointed, like she'd been planning this lovely dinner ever since I'd been sent down.

'I'd really like to, Ma, but – look, why don't you and Harry go out and have dinner? To be honest, I'd really just like to stay at home and unwind. You know. Get my head together. It's a bit of a shock coming out and – '

'Very wise,' Harry said, looking pleased enough. He turned to Ma. 'Marcus will need some time to himself, dear. Prison can be so very – '

'Disorientating,' I said, taking my turn to interrupt.

'But of course!' Ma exclaimed. 'How silly, how inconsiderate of me. I'm sorry, darling,' she added, putting her arms about my neck. 'I wasn't thinking.'

But then Ma never really thought. 'Hey, hey,' I said. 'That's okay, Ma. No big deal. Give me a day or two to reacclimatise myself to the good life and there'll be no stopping me.'

Ma kissed me on the cheek. 'Of course, darling. Take all the time you need.' She stepped back a pace, still holding me, and stared into my eyes. 'Maybe we should all stay in this evening.'

Jesus! That was the last thing I wanted. 'Good God, no, Ma. You and Harry go out and have a good time. If you stay in just to be with me, you'll make me feel – well, you know – sort of in the way.'

'Marcus is right,' Harry said quickly.

'If you're sure, dear?' Ma said.

'I'm sure,' I told her.

I waved them off, watching Harry do his gentleman bit, holding the Jaguar door open for Ma to sidle her bottom onto the seat elegantly. He always drove a Jaguar. This one was better than the one he'd been driving when I was sent down. A better colour, I mean. Dark blue. Much more discreet than the silver job. Which reminded me: what had happened to my BMW? Have to check on that.

It seemed quite strange being alone in the house. The quiet was unbelievable. Nice, really nice, but strange. I went to make myself a cup of coffee. Old Pissquick, the cat, had come to Chelsea too. It lay in its basket giving me its usual disdainful looks. 'Hiya, Pissquick,' I said. 'Better buck your ideas up now that I'm back.' Pissquick ignored me and went back to sleep.

I took a sip of real coffee and thought of the poor sods drinking that chicory crap in prison. Then I noticed Ma had also brought that magnetic knife-holder with her from Balham. All the knives were neatly arranged in size. The one I'd used to dispose of Sharon was still there, second from the left. I felt a strange little tingle as I stared at it. When I eased it from the rack and held it I found myself starting to shake, shake so much I had to put my coffee mug down on the worktop. It was the most exciting feeling I'd had in years. Maybe ever. Really strange, like the knife was sending tiny electric shocks through me. When I affixed it back onto the rack the shaking stopped, just as though the electricity had been switched off at the mains. I felt myself ease the breath out of my lungs. Then the doorbell rang and I just about jumped out of my skin. 'Shit!' I said, and for a moment felt quite dizzy.

I padded along the hall to open the door, and I have to tell you that I did this with some apprehension although if you were to ask me why I was so nervous I don't think I'd be able to tell you. Maybe just not knowing who was on the other side of the door had something to do with it. Fear of the unknown or whatever.

'Hello, Marcus.'

'Oh. It's you,' I said, oddly enough feeling very relieved that it was just Inspector Birt.

'Yes. Me.'

I peered over his shoulder. 'Not got that moron with you then?'

For a bit Birt looked puzzled. He even turned and looked in the direction I'd been peering. Then: 'Oh, Sergeant Wilson? No. This is – well, let's just call it a social visit.'

'Social visits to this house are made by invitation only.'

Birt smiled thinly. 'Can I come in?'

I stood to one side. 'Down there. I'm in the kitchen,' I said pointing the way with a jerk of my head.

'Thank you, Marcus.' He walked towards the kitchen. 'All alone are you, Marcus?'

'As if you didn't know.'

Birt cackled.

'Probably been sitting outside all day waiting to catch me alone.'

'Not *all* day, Marcus. No, not all day.' He sniffed the air in the kitchen, getting the whiff of coffee, and then he sat down at the table with a look on his face. A longing.

'Want coffee, I suppose?'

'Ah. That would be nice, Marcus.'

Bloody Pissquick came out of its basket and started rubbing itself against Birt's legs. Ganging up on me.

'So, how does it feel to be a free man?' Birt asked, bending and rubbing the cat's ears, making it purr.

I shrugged. 'Okay, I guess. Haven't had a chance to get used to it, yet,' I told him pointedly.

'No. I suppose not,' Birt agreed, sounding a bit vague, like he was really thinking of something else he wanted to say.

'You take sugar?'

'Please. Two if I may.'

'You may.'

I put the sugar in the mug, stirred it and passed it to him. Then I sat down opposite him. For a few minutes neither of us said anything. I had nothing I wanted to say, and Birt was clearly taking his time to sort out what he wanted to say. Then I had an idea. I thought it was a pretty funny idea. 'You want a sandwich?' I asked, and when I saw Birt was about to refuse I added quickly, 'I'm going to have one. I'm starving.'

'Thank you, Marcus. I am a bit peckish. If you're sure it's no trouble.'

'No trouble at all.'

And so I set about making a couple of sandwiches. Ham and cheese with a spot of chutney. When I'd made them I cut them in half using the knife I'd used on Sharon and getting quite a little thrill out of that. I could hardly contain myself when Birt bit into his not knowing what I'd done.

'Okay?' I asked.

'Very good indeed. Thank you.'

I gave him another few minutes, and then demanded, 'Why don't you just say what you came for?'

Birt finished his sandwich and took a sip of coffee, savouring it like it was some kind of nectar. Then he eyed me and nodded. 'Very well,' he said, sounding very matter of fact all of a sudden. 'You remember our chat in prison?'

'About?' I asked, just to needle him.

'About Kranze,' he said testily.

'Oh, that,' I said dismissively. 'Yeah, I remember. Some scatty idea you had about me helping you to – '

'Not scatty, Marcus. I meant it.'

'Yeah, well, things have changed now, haven't they? I'm out and about, so I don't have to listen to your codswallop.'

Inspector Birt looked none too pleased at my comment, and even though I knew there was bugger all he could do to me, something about his gaze made me edgy. That long, smouldering gaze seemed to suggest that, okay, he couldn't do anything about the crime I'd been convicted for, but he sure could, if he felt like it, stitch me up for anything else he fancied. So, when he now said, ever so quietly, 'You agreed, Marcus,' I replied, 'Yeah, I did, didn't I?' and took the sandwich plates and went over to the sink.

'That's better,' Birt told my back, like some spaniel he'd been training had finally got the knack of some stupid trick. 'Now, will we start again?'

'Up to you,' I told him, putting the washed plates in the draining-rack.

'Up to us, Marcus. Up to us.'

'Whatever you say,' I answered, taking my time about washing the knife before sticking it back in its place.

I didn't much relish the prospect of being sucked into some sort of grim partnership with Birt, but there didn't seem to be a hell of a lot I could do about it just at the moment, so I decided I might as well play along. Maybe I'd end up enjoying myself. 'You want more coffee?'

Birt shook his head.

'Beer?'

'No. Thank you, Marcus.'

I made myself another coffee and then sat down again. 'Okay. I'm listening.'

So, Inspector Birt started to talk, and, to be honest, the more he talked the more intrigued I became. He started off, of course, by telling me that regardless of the success of my appeal, he still regarded me as a killer, but that he was generously going to put all that behind him.

'That's big of you,' I told him.

Then he said he knew I'd bumped off Sharon and Darren. Big deal. I'd admitted that much before the trial. Well, not admitted, maybe. I just hadn't denied it which, I suppose, is a different kettle of fish.

'But I also know it was Kranze, not you, who killed Karen,' he stated.

'You don't *know* that,' I pointed out.

'Oh, I know it.'

'So arrest him.' This all sounded vaguely familiar.

'I *know* it but I can't *prove* it.'

'Ah. Tough. Life's a bitch, isn't it?'

'And what is more – *you* know I'm right, Marcus.' He got up and started pacing about the kitchen, followed by Pissquick who wasn't about to give up on free affection all that easily. Then he went and poured himself another coffee which I thought was a bit cheeky. He tasted it. Tasted it again and carried his mug back to the table. 'Kranze used you, Marcus. You know that and I know it. He played you along so that he could commit the perfect murder – just to get his own back on me for getting him sent down years ago.'

Well, needless to say I wasn't all that thrilled at being accused of being so crass and stupid as to let someone string me along, use me. 'Kranze had nothing to do with – ' I began, getting a bit hot under the collar.

Birt gave a snorting laugh.

'I'd decided – you know – even before I ever met Kranze.'

'Sure, sure.'

'I'd only read his manuscript. Hadn't met him. Didn't know anything about him when I – '

'Quite,' Birt said tersely, and lapsed into a sort of meditative silence, looking grave.

All right. So Kranze had, in a way, influenced me. Or his manuscript had. That sentence – 'From the moment I could think reasonably I knew I would kill somebody' – had certainly got to me. Awoken something in me. But that wasn't Kranze's fault. All he'd done was write the words in his book, *A Letter from Chile*. And sent the manuscript to the publishing house where I happened to be working. Not his fault either that I'd read it and taken to it. Not his fault that –

'Didn't it ever strike you as strange that Kranze just turned up at your house the night Karen was killed?'

'I'd phoned him, for God's sake.'

'Oh, yes. Of course. That's right. Poured your little soul out to him, didn't you?' Birt asked, mocking.

I didn't want to get into all that. Phoning Kranze that night and telling him everything hadn't been the most intelligent thing I'd ever done. And to this day I don't know why I did it. I thought about that episode in prison. Thought about it quite a lot, and the only conclusion I could come to was that I was driven to do it by something outside my control. And if that's not crazy I don't know what is.

'– oh, Marcus, Marcus,' Birt was saying, 'can't you get it into your skull once and for all that Kranze used you. Not only that, but he was quite happy to see you go down for life just so he could have the last laugh. You saw him in court, didn't you? Smiling smugly away to himself as you got blasted?'

And that was true enough. Kranze had been in the gallery for the sentencing, and he certainly had looked pretty smug. But then, as I watched Birt across the table, it suddenly dawned on me what this was all about. Birt didn't give a shit about me. It had nothing whatsoever to do with Kranze using *me*. It was all about Birt's bloody ego. All this apparent concern for me was just so much crap. I found myself relaxing, feeling quite good, in fact.

'So, let me get this straight, okay? What you're really saying is that *you* want to stitch Kranze up so you can get your revenge, and you want *me* to help you? Right?'

It was Birt's turn to squirm a bit. Clearly he didn't like it put like that even if it was the truth. He didn't say anything, just gazed at me.

'So, what's in it for me?' I asked.

That was something Birt hadn't even considered. I suppose he thought I'd be so pissed off at Kranze that I'd fall in with any plan to do the shit on him.

'I would have thought – ' Birt began.

'That I'd be stupid enough to fall in with any crazy plan of yours just so *you* could satisfy your ego, eh?'

'I was about to say I would have thought you'd be pleased to make Kranze pay for what he did to you.'

He didn't sound very convinced, so I said, 'Kranze did *nothing* to me, mate.'

I was a bit surprised when Birt just shrugged, and stood up as if he had nothing further to say, as if the matter was closed. But already there were little niggles going on in my mind. Maybe *I* could use Birt while he thought *he* was using me. I didn't yet know in what way I'd want to use him, but I'd soon think of something, I was sure.

'Tell you what,' I said, getting up also and making towards the hall. 'Give me a day or two to think about it.'

Birt was pleased. I could see him trying hard not to let me see just how pleased he was, but the way he eased the breath out of his lungs and the little light in his eye made it pretty clear he was delighted. 'Take all the time you want, Marcus.'

Maybe a jolt would do him good. 'I might just call round and see Kranze and discuss things with him,' I said.

Birt froze and looked as if he might be contemplating strangling me.

'Not about what we spoke about,' I said. 'Just try and make up my own mind if he did, as you say, use me.'

'Ah,' Birt sighed. 'Yes. Do that if you want.'

When Birt had gone I leaned my back against the front door and stayed there for quite a while. Who'd have thought my first day out of prison would have been filled with such possibilities? Possibilities of what I wasn't sure, of course. Not yet anyway.

Then, suddenly, I was laughing. Laughing my bloody head off because something was telling me that somewhere down the line there was going to be the chance for *me* to commit the perfect murder, and that was certainly something to laugh about, wasn't it.

THREE

Three years isn't all that long, really. Well, it *seemed* long when I was locked up, but in the greater scheme of things, like they say, it wasn't very much. Yet, when I came to unpack my stuff, it was honestly amazing the number of things I'd forgotten I ever had. Opening the newspapers Ma had wrapped everything in was like one big Christmas splurge.

It was Friday morning when I did all my unpacking so Ma had gone off for her weekly makeover in Harrods, and I had the place to myself. Me and Pissquick, that is. Maybe it was senile decay creeping up on him but he was getting much friendlier towards me. Or maybe he just had a lousy memory and had forgotten just how much we really hated each other. By lunchtime all the boxes were empty, and my belongings were in little piles, ready to be put into their rightful places. I fixed myself a salami sandwich and a cup of coffee, and sat on my bed looking at everything. I was about to start tidying up when Ma phoned to say she wouldn't be home until late.

'Oh. Okay. What happened?'

'I spent longer at Harrods than I expected.'

'Had to get extra Polyfilla in, did they?' I asked, thinking that was quite funny.

Ma didn't think so though. 'That's not very nice, dear.'

'It was a joke, Ma.'

'Yes,' she agreed but made it clear she didn't find my joke funny.

'So what time will you be home?'

'Oh. I'm not sure. Five. Half past. Something like that.'

'Right. I'll see you then.'

I was going to hang up but I sensed Ma had something else she wanted to say. There was a bit of a pause before she asked, 'Are you all right, dear?'

'Me? I'm fine. Why?'

'I just – '

'Don't worry, Ma. I'm fine. Really.'

Then I did hang up. The last thing I wanted was Ma getting all motherly all of a sudden. What did she think anyway? That on my second day out I was going to bump someone off? I think she thought killing people was a naughty sort of habit, like smoking or biting your nails, that was hard to give up. Maybe she was right, come to think of it.

While I was at the phone I decided to give Harry a call and find out what had become of my BMW. Had to have wheels if I was going to get about, even if the Underground did have happy memories for me – mostly.

'Ah, yes,' Harry said, like he was trying to remember where he'd mislaid my car.

'You didn't sell it, did you?' I asked.

Harry sounded aggrieved. 'Of course not. Had I done so I would have told you and I would not have done so without your authority.'

'Yeah. Sorry, Harry,' I said to pacify the sod. All I wanted to know was where the bloody car was, not to get lectures on how proper and correct Harry bloody Rutherford was.

'I had it garaged for you.'

'Great. Where?'

'Fulham, actually.'

'Can I go and get it?'

'Em. No. No, I'm afraid not. It's garaged in my name. I'll have to get it for you.'

Typical. 'So could you do that?'

'Not just this moment,' Harry said, I suppose to give the impression he was desperately busy.

'When?'

Harry thought for a moment. 'Tomorrow morning.'

'That'll do nicely. Thank you, Harry.'

'You're welcome.'

And, true to his word, as you'd expect, the next morning Harry arrived with my car. They'd certainly looked after it well. It gleamed, looking almost as if it had just come off the assembly line. He handed me the keys with what I thought was a funny sort of look: like he was saying not to use the car for carting corpses around in. But I just said, 'Thanks a lot, Harry,' and took the keys.

But the funny thing was that now that I *had* the car again, I had no real urge to go out in it. Like I told you, I was still, for some unknown reason, none too keen about going out at all.

'Need it for anything in particular, dear? The car?' Ma wanted to know.

I shook my head. 'No. Just wanted to have it there in case.'

'In case of what?' Ma persisted.

'In case of anything,' I told her vaguely. Ma and Harry had a quick look at each other, and this really infuriated me. 'For God's sake Ma, give me a break, will you?'

'Oh, darling,' Ma said, seeing that she'd really upset me. 'It's just, you know . . . I'm desperately worried about you,' she finished lamely.

Well, never a one to miss a trick, I went over to her and gave her a cuddle. 'You don't have to worry about a thing, Ma,' I whispered to her. 'Honestly.' Then I held her at arms length. 'You see before you what the wise call a reformed character.' I now included Harry in my gaze. 'You've nothing whatever to worry about. Honestly,' I said again as if just saying it actually made me honest.

Ma believed me all right, but Harry didn't. I could see that. But, I thought, bugger him. Ma was all that mattered. What I had to do was deal with her and she'd soon deal with Harry.

Anyway, Ma and Harry were going out. They'd got tickets for the men's semi-final at Wimbledon. Ma would have preferred to be there for the final, of course, but Harry didn't have quite enough clout for that yet. Give him a year or two and he undoubtedly would, grovelling sod. So, as they left, as a sort of parting shot, I said to Harry, 'You want to take my car keys with you – just in case,' I emphasised. But Harry ignored that apart from a baleful look.

About twenty minutes after Ma and Harry had toddled off to be seen at Wimbledon, my ex-girlfriend, Heather, loomed big and large into my consciousness. 'Girlfriend' is a bit too strong a word, of course. She was my regular lay, that was all, and maybe it was because I was feeling a tiny bit randy that I thought of her. She hadn't bothered with me while I was in prison. Well, she couldn't get her fill of me, could she? Although she did write a couple of pretty disgusting letters during the first couple of months of my incarceration; disgusting because I personally can't think of anything more degrading than a woman who is downright vulgar. Well, not only was old Heather vulgar, she was positively pornographic. Mind you, those two letters came in pretty handy. I used to sort of rent them out, let the morons read them and have their fantasies, in return for goodies for myself. One bloke, a bloody Welshman as you might have expected, kept on at me for her address so he could write to her direct. Promised me just about the earth in prison terms. I was tempted to let him have it, I must confess, but then decided against it. After all, the Brazier-Youngs might be useful to me if I ever got out, and I didn't want to burn all my bridges. So I told Taffy that, alas, Heather had recently broken her neck in a riding accident.

'You mean she's dead?' Taffy asked.

'Yeah, Taffy. Dead and buried,' I told him thinking that would be an end to things.

Not on your life. Taffy now became my most regular customer for the letters. Seems he got some particular thrill out of reading dirt written by a corpse. Well, not written by a corpse, but you know what I mean. Anyway, whenever I wanted anything, a wave of those letters under Taffy's nose and whatever I needed was mine so, between you and me, I was stoned just about every night. I could easily have got any drugs but I figure the hard stuff is just for dickheads. Besides, once you go *that* far, you're in *their* clutches and I certainly wasn't going to let that happen.

Anyway, I decided I'd give Heather a tinkle. Just for a laugh. And maybe for something else.

'Is Miss Heather there, please?' I asked. That's what you had to say. 'Miss' Heather. Just so the servants knew their place, I suppose.

'May I say who's calling?'

'Eh, yes well, just say it's an old friend.'

'One moment, please.'

As I waited for Miss to come to the phone, a funny idea raced through my mind. You remember I told you what I'd told Taffy: that Heather had broken her stupid neck in a riding accident? Well, I sort of wondered if it might not be quite interesting to make that happen. I wasn't seriously thinking of killing Heather: it just seemed as if making her break her silly neck wasn't actually killing her. It was almost as if it was simply giving myself something to do. A little mild entertainment.

'Hello?'

'Heather?'

'Who is this?'

'Me.'

'And who's me?'

'Marcus.'

I heard Heather give a sort of a gasp. A strangled kind of sound like the wind had really been knocked out of her sails. 'Marcus! Where are you? I mean – '

'I'm out. Didn't you know? It's been big in all the rags.'

'No. No I didn't. We only got back from France yesterday. You're out!'

'Yep.'

'How did you manage that?'

'Long story. I'll tell you about it when you've a night to spare.'

She gave one of her dirty giggles. 'I bet.' *She* hadn't changed. I could almost hear her panting down the line.

'Thanks for your letters,' I said.

'Oh. Yes. I'm sorry, Marcus. I just couldn't think of anything to – '

'Hey, that's okay.'

'And my parents were – '

'Heather, I understand.' I paused to give her a chance to realise how really understanding I was. 'So, what have you been up to?'

'Oh, you know. This and that.'

'Like?'

'Well, I'm – ' She stopped suddenly and started to laugh again, that awful neighing noise which used to get on my nerves. Still did, as I listened to it whinnying through the phone. 'I'm engaged,' she told me finally.

'You? Engaged?' I don't know why I was surprised, but I couldn't see old Heather as a housewife no matter how hard I tried. 'Who's the lucky guy?' I asked, thinking it must be some right chinless moron to get himself tied down to someone like Heather Brazier-Young.

'You wouldn't know him.'

'Would I want to?'

'Probably not. He's terribly boring,' Heather told me, starting to neigh again.

'Rich, I suppose?'

'Terrifically.'

'Good steady job?'

'A banker. Like Daddy.'

'Ah. Very appropriate. Good in bed?' I asked.

Heather made a groaning noise.

'Oh, like that, eh? Still, you can't have everything.'

'That's what you think. He's away most of the time. Big in Europe, you see.'

'Poor bastard.'

'Well, thank you, Marcus,' Heather said but giggled anyway.

'When's the big day?'

'Oh, God. Eight weeks' time.'

'Nice. Do I get an invitation?'

'To the wedding?'

'I didn't think I'd need an invitation for anything else.'

'Still the same old cocky Marcus, I see.'

'Well?'

I could just imagine Heather's slow mind trying to figure out how to see me without landing herself in the shit. 'Let me think,' she said, almost to herself. 'What about next Thursday?'

'That far off?'

'Have to be. Mummy and Daddy leave then for Brussels and Geoff won't be here until the Saturday.'

'Geoff? That his name? Fucking Geoffrey?'

'He's very nice really.'

'And very boring,' I reminded her.

'Boring but nice. Trainable,' she told me, and gave a terrific hoot.

'I was thinking more in terms of tomorrow.'

'No chance.'

'For me?'

'Not even for you, Marcus.'

Well, I wasn't about to get to the stage where I had to make appointments for a screw. 'I'll think about it and give you a ring,' I told her.

But by now she'd had a chance to remember how good I was in bed, and she was getting a bit hot. 'Oh, do *please* make it Thursday, Marcus. You won't regret it.'

'Might be busy Thursday. Got my life to sort out. Got to start all over again. You know, "pick myself up, brush myself down" – and all that sort of thing.' There was silence on the phone. 'Heather?'

'I'm thinking.'

'Painful.'

'Listen. Maybe I could see you tomorrow.'

'Don't do me any favours, Heather.'

'I didn't mean it like that. It would have to be in the afternoon.'

'I can drive up. I've still got my car.'

'No. No. I've got a place in London. Just a little place. I'll come down.'

'Fine. Where is this little place?'

She told me. A flat just off Sloane Street. Very handy, I thought, and just the sort of area where Heather would feel at home.

'What time?' I asked.

'Three?'

'Look forward to it.'

'So do I, Marcus.'

'I bet you do.'

And that was that. I now knew I still had Heather more or less where I wanted her, and after a quick session in her flat tomorrow afternoon she'd be putty in my hands. Why I thought this was important, I don't know. It just *seemed* important at the time so maybe my intuition was in good working order.

Just to fill myself in, I asked Ma about the Brazier-Youngs when she got home. They'd been really close friends of Ma before I got sentenced. But now she winced when I mentioned their name. 'I haven't seen them since – since, you know,' she told me, looking hurt.

'Dumped us, did they?' I asked.

'I think they were just embarrassed, dear,' Ma said, always ready to make an excuse for someone when it suited her.

'Why the hell should *they* be embarrassed?' I demanded, knowing full well why but getting angry nonetheless.

'Oh, darling, you know what people are like.'

'I'm beginning to, anyhow.'

And that was certainly true. One thing about prison is that you meet just about every make and shape of human being, and because you really do have to look out for yourself, look out for your back more like, you soon start to get the knack of analysing people, of being able to tell more or less at a glance what way such and such a person will react to such and such a situation. The quiet ones you have to watch out for since when they explode all hell is likely to break loose, but the noisy bastards, the braggarts, you can forget since usually they're all mouth and no balls, as we say in polite prison parlance. And even inside there's a sort of hierarchy: the upper class who think they're the bees knees; the middle class who tend to be the ones with a bit of brains; and the working class, the ones who get manipulated left, right and centre.

'Anyway,' Ma was saying, 'It doesn't really matter, does it?'

'What doesn't?'

'That they've decided to ignore us.'

'It doesn't matter, no, Ma. But it's a bloody cheek,' I told her, nearly putting it a good deal stronger than that. 'Who else has vanished?'

Ma took to titivating herself unnecessarily in the mirror: a sure sign that she was getting nervy.

'Ma?'

'Oh, just a few others.'

'Like?'

'It doesn't matter, dear.'

'It matters to me,' I told her, and I could see that it mattered to Ma, too, only she didn't want to admit it. Then, eventually, she told me and I realised for the first time, I think, what poor old Ma had been through. Not only the Brazier-Youngs had shunned her, but she'd been booted out of the bridge club – well, frozen out if you know what I mean – and even her supposed best friend in Scotland, Sue Fortune, had gone all snooty and abandoned contact, although what any of them had to be so damn superior about I really don't know. In fact, when it came down to it, Ma had been well and truly ostracised and I can tell you I know that must really have hurt her. It made me feel quite warm towards old Harry, even if his motives were somewhat base. Something made me say, 'We'll show them, Ma.' I didn't know what I meant by that exactly, but Ma answered, 'Of course we will, darling,' and that started me thinking. It also made me put my arms around her and give her a big hug, a sort of comforting gesture with an intrinsic apology, if you know what I mean. 'It's been tough, hasn't it?' I whispered to her.

'Not really, dear. Unpleasant. Disappointing.'

'I'm really sorry, Ma.'

'Shush, dear. It's all behind us now, isn't it?'

'Yeah. I guess it is.' I held her away from me. 'Fresh start and all that, eh?' I smiled.

Ma smiled back. 'Yes, dear. A fresh start.'

Well, I thought, a *new* start, if not a fresh one.

FOUR

I brought Ma her breakfast in bed the next morning: orange juice, coffee and a couple of slices of thin toast. I'd done this quite often before going to prison and it was nice to be able to do it again: sort of getting back into the pattern of things. Civilised.

As usual, Ma looked terrific even at that time of the morning. I don't know how she did it. She can't have moved an inch while she was asleep since that expensive hair-do of hers didn't shift a hair, and even without her make-up her skin was smooth and white and practically unwrinkled. I say practically because there were a couple of hangy bits under her chin but that was only to be expected.

I brought my own mug of coffee with me, too, and sat on the edge of her bed. When I'd been very young and Dad was away, I used to creep right into bed with Ma, and we'd have a cuddle and a whisper. She used to blink her eyelashes against my cheek and we'd pretend they were butterflies. Crazy when you think of it. But even if I was still tiny we couldn't have done that now, I suppose. Poor Ma would have been had for corruption of a minor or abuse or something like that. Kids today don't know what they're missing really, do they? Got to grow up too quickly. That's half the trouble, I'm sure. No childhood at all. Thinking about sex and stuff by the time they're nine or even less.

'This *is* nice,' Ma said, stretching and sitting up to take her tray.

'Just like old times,' I told her.

'Yes. Yes, it is, isn't it?' she asked, and looked quite sad.

'So,' I said cheerfully. 'What have you got planned for today?'

'Not a thing. I'm going to be totally lazy.'

'Good, 'bout time you indulged yourself, Ma.'

'And you?'

'Me?'

'What are your plans?'

'Ah. Well, nothing much.'

'Maybe we could watch the tennis together?'

'This afternoon?'

'Yes.'

'Ah, well, actually, I was going to take myself out for a little drive this afternoon to tell you the truth.'

'Oh. I see,' Ma said and sounded disappointed.

'Not for long. Maybe an hour or two.'

'I see,' Ma said she saw again.

'Like, it's Sunday and there won't be too many people about. I want to sort of ease myself back into – '

'I understand, darling. It can't be easy for you.'

'To be honest, Ma, it's not,' I lied. No harm in gathering an extra little bit of sympathy, was there? 'I'm actually finding it much harder than I thought. Guilt, I suppose,' I explained and nearly burst a gut trying not to laugh and keeping a sad and serious face.

I thought the German Requiem was appropriate, so I had that playing as I got ready to go and meet Heather, and during the Dies Ire I had a really good look at myself. Not bad. Not bad at all, I can tell you. My little holiday behind bars hadn't done me the slightest harm, physically at least. Maybe I'd lost a little weight, but that suited me.

I dressed carefully. That is to say I put on the clothes I knew Heather liked to see me in. Even though she put on all the airs and graces her wretched family expected her to, she really enjoyed a bit of rough. She'd have shacked up with every bricklayer in London if she thought she'd get away with it. So jeans, a denim shirt and my leather jacket were donned. I tousled my hair a bit, and I decided not to shave. When Ma saw me she said, 'Well, I certainly hope you don't meet anyone we know, dear. You look like a labourer!'

I wasn't sure whether she was joking or not, so I just said, 'Stuff them. If they don't like us as we are, Ma, stuff them.'

Then I found out she wasn't jesting. 'But we do have standards, dear.'

That was Ma all over. I swear to God if we were ever reduced to living in Cardboard City she'd still be talking about standards whatever they are. 'It's unlikely I will meet anyone,' I told her.

'Thank God for that,' she announced emphatically.

'See you later,' I said, and kissed her on the cheek.

'You haven't even shaved, Marcus,' she said horrified and even recoiling a little.

'Ma, I'm not even going to get out of the damn car,' I lied.

'Well, just make sure you don't.'

I waited until Ma had settled herself in front of the television for an afternoon of Wimbledon. I had to smile at the way she did things. Even though she couldn't actually be there she wasn't about to miss out on anything. She had her little plate of smoked salmon sandwiches and her bowl of strawberries and cream at the ready, not to mention her half bottle of Moët et Chandon. *She* wasn't about to let *her* standards slip even if no one was there to witness them being upheld.

Not so Heather. Mind you, her standards were about as high as any other tart's. She opened the door for me and within seconds was panting like a bitch in heat, climbing all over me. I don't suppose we did more than exchange a couple of hellos until after we'd had sex which, as usual, she enjoyed a lot more than I did. To me it was just a relief; to her it was a very different kettle of fish. A necessity, I suppose. Anyway, it appeared I hadn't lost my touch.

'God, Marcus, you're terrific.'

'Yeah, I know. They all tell me that.'

'Bastard. How on earth did you manage in – ' She couldn't bring herself to say prison.

'In prison?' I said for her. 'No bother, really.'

'You didn't – ' Again she left her question unfinished.

'Didn't what?' I asked, knowing full well what she meant but deciding to have a bit of a laugh with myself.

'You know.'

'Sorry. Haven't a clue what you're on about,' I said, and swung off the bed.

'I've read things,' Heather said, trying to make her readings sound significant.

'So've I. Dickens, Chaucer – '

'In the papers.'

'Believe everything you read in the papers?' I started to get dressed, sitting on a chair to pull on my socks. Then I looked up at her. 'Oh, you mean did I have it off with some of the other inmates?' I made the question sound nice and casual, giving her a little bit of a problem since by not making a big deal out of it she was left wondering, or maybe even believing, that I *had* dabbled in the naughty. Which, needless to say, I hadn't. Actually, there's far less of that going on than we're led to believe. Oh, sure, you get the odd rape and even the odd affair between a couple who have a long stretch in front of them, but so what?

'Well, did you?' Heather wanted to know again.

'You don't want to know,' I told her, zipping the fly on my jeans.

Oh, but Heather wanted to know all right. And if I'd told her yes, she'd have wanted all the details, too. So just to take the wind out of her sails I told her, 'Sorry. No. I didn't.'

'Oh. Good,' she said, but sounded disappointed.

'I just thought of you and choked my chicken.'

'You *what*?' Heather asked and hooted with laughter.

'Thought of you and choked my chicken. "Wanked" to you common folk.'

'God, Marcus, what a horrible way to put it.'

I shrugged. 'Better than "tossing off". More imaginative, I think. "Choking your chicken". Quite like the expression myself.'

Probably all this talk about masturbation had got her going again because Heather started lolling about naked on the bed, trying to make herself sexually appealing. Some chance she had of that. 'You don't have to go yet,' she informed.

''Fraid I do.'

'Not just yet.'

''Fraid so.'

'This minute?'

'This very minute.'

'Oh, shit!' She rolled off the bed and came at me. 'God, Marcus, I could eat you.'

'You just did. Go home now, like a good girl, and have a meal on dear Geoff.'

'Be like chewing mutton after beef.'

'Whatever.'

'When will I see you again?'

'Dunno, really. Give me a ring. I'm going to be quite busy for a while, though, so you mightn't catch me.'

'Busy? Doing what?' Heather was all ears again, wondering, I suppose, if I was about to plan another little escapade. Maybe she wouldn't have been quite so eager if she could have read my thoughts which were that *she* was about the only one I could have cheerfully strangled – at the moment anyway. Not seriously. Well, I don't know. I really think I could have killed her and felt not even a whiff of remorse. But she wouldn't have been worth all the bother.

'Well, got to get myself sorted out, don't I?' You know, mundane things like a job.'

'Oh, yes, I suppose so,' Heather supposed in that bewildered voice of someone who'd never had to hold down a job in her life.

'Maybe your Daddy could give me one?' I asked.

Heather giggled. 'I hardly think so.'

'No. I suppose not.'

And as I drove home I gave the business about getting a job some serious thought. I *would* have to do something. Not that I needed the money or anything; just to hold on to my sanity. Maybe the publishers I'd worked for before would give me my old job back. I'd been damn good at it, so it was worth a try. Definitely worth a try. And there wasn't really much else I *could* do. My record would certainly not be viewed as an asset in most places, and physical labour wasn't my cup of tea. Ma wouldn't have let me do anything too demeaning anyway, and, being a good boy, I had to consider my mother's feelings, didn't I?

Anyway, the result of my meditations was that the following Tuesday I trotted along to see if I could get my old job back, and my presence caused a little consternation. Not, however, as much as you might have suspected, since the turnover in staff in publishing is about the same as in a burger bar, and there were plenty of new faces who hadn't a clue who I was. Not then. Mind you, just about the first person I saw was good old Camp Carl, still there, still doing the same boring job. He let a little shriek out of him. 'Marcus!' he yelped, and I thought for a minute he was going to kiss me.

'Hi, Carl. How's things?'

'Ugh. Awful. Nothing's been the same since you left, dear boy.'

'Thanks, Carl.'

'I mean it, Marcus.' He leaned towards me confidentially. 'All tarts and chinless shits now. Not so much Sloane Rangers now, dear heart, as bloody Range Rovers. And camp! Why, Marcus, I sometimes think *I'm* the most normal thing here.'

I had to laugh. 'You always were, Carl.'

Carl gave me a grateful look. 'It *really* is good to see you again,' he said, and I was quite moved because I knew he meant it.

'Is she in?'

'The Dragoness? Oh, yes,' Carl told me and then gave me a quizzical look. 'Why?'

'Thought I might try and get my old job back.'

Carl sucked in his breath.

'No chance, eh?'

'Oh, no. That's not – I was thinking of *you*, my dear. I mean, wouldn't it be . . . well . . . difficult?'

'Life's difficult, Carl. Life's difficult.'

Carl laughed. 'Tell me about it.' The phone rang. 'Go on up, and good luck,' he told me and went to answer the phone, but as I moved off he called after me. 'Be sure and let me know how you get on,' he said.

'Yeah.'

'Be sure you do.'

'I will. I will.'

I'm not a great one for gay people. I'm not homophobic or anything but they do usually set my teeth on edge, and I've never found the need to be fashionable and say things like 'some of my best friends are queer'. But Camp Carl was different. I really did like him a lot and not just because he had come to every single day of the trial and had always been there in the gallery ready to give me one of his camp, encouraging little waves. And another thing. I had never heard Carl say anything really bad about anyone, although he knew some of his fellow workers were forever slagging him off. He was about the only intrinsically nice person I'd ever known. Bless him.

Well, there's no point in giving you a detailed account of my chat with the Dragoness. She put on her favourite 'of course I *do* understand' voices but was adamant that she didn't want any ex-cons besmirching her wonderful establishment.

'The bitch!' was Carl's assessment of her when I told him as I made my way out.

'Ach, it doesn't matter, Carl.'

'But what will you do now?'

I shrugged. 'Dunno. Keep looking, I suppose.'

'I suppose you've tried Nick?'

'Nick who?'

'Nick Putty, of course.'

'Well, no. No, I haven't,' I told him. Nick hadn't even entered my head, to tell the truth. I'd worked with him a lot before I'd gone down. Been mates, really. But he resigned before things had come to a head and I suppose I just thought he'd given up publishing as a career.

'Well, why don't you, for heaven's sake?'

'I didn't think he was still – '

'Oh, Nick is quite the bees knees now, ducky. Senior fiction editor at Bogets. Not very high class, I know, but they *sell*, dear. They sell and that's what it's all about these days.'

Carl had certainly brightened my day. 'Yeah,' I decided. 'I'll go see him. You're a jewel, Carl.'

'Indeed I am. A fake pearl, though.'

'Don't you believe it,' I said, and before I knew what I was doing I'd given him a wee kiss on the cheek.

Carl went all misty. 'You keep in touch with me, hear?'

'I will.'

'Promise?'

'I promise,' I said, and it was one promise I meant to keep.

When I left Carl I fully intended to go straight to Bogets and talk to Nick Putty. In fact, I set out boldly in that direction. But, as luck would have it, that meant walking up Regent Street and that, of course, meant I had to pass pretty close to the Carlos Pizzeria where Karen had worked. I shouldn't have, I know, but some little imp got the better of me and I decided a small snack in familiar surroundings was just what I needed to fortify my soul before probably getting another rejection – if the Pizzeria was still there, of course.

Well, it was as it happens, although it had changed hands. The outside had been painted somewhat garishly, and inside all the tables were gone and those wretched benches like cow stalls had been inserted. There was a jukebox, would you believe, and 'Volare' was being sung by some dreadful off-key quasi tenor as I went in. For some reason I felt quite angry that they'd changed everything. I felt they should have consulted me before they did anything to this little shrine of mine. I slid onto one of the benches and before I even had a chance to look at what was on offer, this fat blonde tart was hovering over me saying, 'Yes, dear?' which really got my back up.

I gave her a cold stare but she couldn't take the hint. 'Want some time, do you, love?'

'A coffee. Black,' I said. 'And I'm not your love.'

She was so thick my words of admonishment didn't penetrate her skull. 'Anything to eat, dear?'

'No. Nothing at all, in fact,' I said and got up, stalking out, leaving the stupid cow standing there with her gob open.

When I got outside I found myself shaking. Stupid, I know, but I was furious. I hate this fucking familiarity that everyone thinks is so 'with it'. No respect for anyone, and that's half the trouble with the world, if you ask me.

But I cooled off in a bit and called a taxi to take me to Bogets. I even let the driver call me 'mate' without blowing a fuse, which was pretty good of me, I thought.

Nick, naturally, was surprised but really pleased to see me. 'You look pretty good,' he told me.

'For someone who's been locked up, you mean?'

Nick has a toothy grin. 'Something like that. How are you?'

'Not too bad. Not too bad at all.'

'Hmm. I should have kept in touch. Sorry.'

'No problem, Nick. Must have been a bit of a shock for you.'

Nick grinned again. 'To put it mildly.'

'Yeah.'

'Grab a seat. Coffee?'

'No thanks.'

Nick walked round behind his desk and sat down. He made a steeple out of his fingers and supported his chin on that. He looked exactly the same as the last time I'd seen him, which was comforting. 'So,' he said. 'What can I do for you?'

'I thought you might give me a job.'

'Ah,' Nick sighed.

'I've just been round to see if I could get my old job back but – '

'No luck? Not exactly surprising.'

'No.'

Nick took to staring hard at me for a while. He mightn't have changed in looks but his manner had changed. I suppose the power of his new position had got to him like it does to everyone – power, I mean. He made little sucking noises through his teeth. 'Let's see,' he said finally, and reached for the phone. He spoke to someone called Miriam. 'Miriam. Nick here. That junior editor's position been filled yet?'

Apparently not.

'I might just be able to get it for you,' Nick told me.

'I'd really appreciate it, Nick.'

'But don't count on it. I can only recommend you. After that, it's up to the – '

'I understand.' And now that the reason for my visit had been dealt with I think Nick started to get embarrassed. 'Well, I better leave you to it,' I said, to save him. 'You're a busy man now, I see.'

'Right.'

'How's Kate, by the way?' I asked, just to be polite.

'Fine. Fine. I'll tell her you were asking.'

'Yeah. Do that.'

'Okay. Give me a ring – let's see – day after tomorrow, and I should have some news for you, one way or the other.'

Another push-off, I thought, but I smiled pleasantly nonetheless and said, 'That's great, Nick. Thanks.'

'I'll do what I can, Marcus.'

'Oh, I know you will.'

Ma was at a bit of a loose end now that Wimbledon was over. It wasn't something she had got used to yet, even after three years, and she became a bit morose. And Harry was away at some conference in Brussels, doing his bit for what was left of the Empire, I imagine.

'You all right, Ma?' I asked.

It was Thursday evening and we'd just finished supper. I was washing and Ma was drying. That was another change in Ma's life. No little ethnic person coming in every day, just Mrs Bruton once a week now to give the place a good going over every Monday. I think Ma was scared of having a daily, scared the skivvy might just say something or give her a look if Ma gave out to her. Ma could just about tolerate such impertinence from one of her ex-cronies, but to have to put up with it from some working-class member of a minority group would be more than she could stand.

'Yes, dear. I'm fine.'

'You're not really, are you?'

'Yes, dear. Of course I am,' Ma told me firmly so I decided to let the matter rest.

I wasn't feeling too great myself to tell the truth. I'd rung Nick only to be told he was in a meeting. So I left a message asking him to ring me back. He hadn't rung back, which didn't altogether surprise me, but it did cheese me off. 'When does Harry get back?' I asked.

'Late this evening, I think. Or tomorrow morning.'
'Ah.'
'Why?'
'Just wondering.' I let the water out of the sink and ran a cloth round the edges. 'He's all right, Harry,' I told Ma.
'He's been very kind.'
'Yeah. I know. Ma – why don't you marry him?'
'I – '
'I mean, he's asked you often enough, hasn't he?'
'Yes, but – '
'Well, then, you should marry him and start having a good time again.'
'You wouldn't mind, darling?'
'Me? Mind? If you married Harry? Hell no, Ma. I'd be delighted. Really I would.' I tried to sound genuinely enthusiastic.
'We have been talking about it – quite seriously – for a while.'
'Well, if you want my advice, you should take the plunge.'
Ma sighed. 'It's not quite that simple, dear,' she said and gave me a tiny glance from the corner of her eye, not intending me to notice it.
So that was it. Me. And then it dawned on me. The tabloids would have a field day if they found out the mother of a jailbird had married one of the country's top lawyers. I could almost see the headlines screaming at us: MOTHER OF ACCUSED MURDERER MARRIES LAWYER WHO GOT HIM RELEASED, or some crap like that.
'It's me, isn't it,' I said. 'What I did.'
Ma turned her back on me and started folding up the cloth and hanging it over the rail that ran the length of the Aga. 'No,' she said finally.
'Don't fib to me, Ma.'
'Well, *part* of it, maybe.'
'I'm really sorry, Ma,' I told her, and I think I meant it.
'There are other things as well, dear.'
'Like?'
But Ma said she didn't want to discuss it, which meant she couldn't think of any other things. 'Have you told Harry why you won't – ?' I began, and Ma was in like a flash.
'Of course, I have.'
'And what does he say?'
'He – he says – look, darling, Harry just wants to marry me. He says he doesn't care about – he says – oh, just let's leave it, may we?'

All of which made me feel really terrific, of course. And maybe Baby Jesus felt He'd given me enough hassle for one day because the phone rang, and it was Nick Putty saying he was desperately sorry he hadn't got back to me earlier but his meeting just went on and on.

'That's okay, Nick. I understand.'

'Bet you thought I was fobbing you off?'

'Of course not,' I lied. Then I laughed. 'Well, yes, as a matter of fact I did.'

Nick laughed too. 'Not surprised. Anyway, when can you start?'

'You mean you've got me a job?' I could hardly believe it.

'Yep.'

'Jeez, Nick, you're an angel.'

'Oh, sure. When can you start?'

'Doing what, Nick?'

'Assistant editor – sort of glorified title for what you were doing before,' Nick told me, and then he gave a snigger. 'In the crime section,' he added.

I don't know whether it was nerves or the relief in knowing I'd got a job or the fact that it really was quite funny under the circumstances, but I just about rolled on the floor laughing.

'I thought you'd like that,' Nick commented when I'd calmed down. '*Now* will you tell me when you can start?'

'What about next Monday?'

'Fine. Welcome to Bogets.'

I must have looked a bit weird when I put the phone down because Ma asked, 'What's happened, dear?' in a whispered tone as if she was expecting the worst.

I put my arms about her and waltzed her about the room. 'I've got me a job, that's what, Ma.'

'Oh, darling, that's wonderful news.'

'You can say that again.'

Later that night, after Ma had gone to bed and I was alone in my room, I made a decision. I decided that as soon as I was settled into my new job I was going to get a place of my own. I told myself that this would be only fair on Ma, give her some space, let her get on with her life without having to worry about me too much, give herself and Harry a chance to sort things out. That's what I told myself. But you can lie to yourself just as easily as to someone else. The truth, I knew, was a bit different.

FIVE

I drove Ma to Mass on Sunday morning. Brompton Oratory. It wasn't that she had taken to religion while I was away or anything like that. She just liked to go sometimes – mostly, I confess, in times of stress or when she wanted to put in a special plea for something, or just to say thank you for something that had happened and in which she felt God might have taken a hand. Actually, I quite enjoy the occasional Mass myself. I can't say I pray or anything. I just sort of chat with the Big Unknown, and that can be very satisfying as long as you can overcome, or block out entirely, the crap the priest says in his sermon. I always think funeral services are a killer – the way the priest says just about everything the mourners *don't* want to hear. And have you noticed there's a special tone adopted for funeral services, a pious, unctuous, condescending tone that really gets on my wick.

'I enjoyed that,' Ma told me as I drove her home, which might seem an odd way to express one's feelings for Mass but which to me seemed eminently sensible.

'Good. So did I,' I told her. 'What about I take you out for lunch?'

Ma looked as if she was about to demur. 'Somewhere nice and quiet,' I pressed. 'Somewhere on the river.'

Maybe Ma had been fortified by her contact with the Almighty, or maybe she finally was getting back to her old self. Whatever the reason, she said, 'I think that's a wonderful idea,' and I purposely didn't remind her that Harry was supposed to be coming round for a light lunch – Ma's terminology for salad and cold meat, which I could well do without, thank you very much.

When we got back from Henley Harry was on the doorstep looking none too pleased. Ma spotted him as we drove up and she slapped both hands to her cheeks and said, 'Oh, my God. I forgot all about Harry.'

'Do him good.'

'You should have reminded me, dear,' Ma said but with a bit of a gin-and-tonic giggle in her voice.

'He never entered my head,' I lied. 'Besides, it was nice to have you all to myself for a while.'

'I'll have to fix the poor man something.'

'Give him a cat-food sandwich.'

Ma let her giggle loose. 'Darling!'

So, while Ma and Harry settled things between them (no big deal since Harry was never much good in any argument with Ma) I went up to my room and lay on my bed to have a little think.

Mahler always helps me think. I know it's a bit naff but, nevertheless, his Fifth Symphony is just about the best bit of music I've ever come across. Especially the Fourth Movement, the Adagietto. I know it's been over-played a bit since it was used in the film *Death in Venice* (the best thing Dirk Bogarde ever did, if you want my opinion) but it still moves me nearly to tears, if you can imagine such a thing. So that's what I played as I had my think. And I had plenty to think about. Naturally enough, I suppose, I gave a long time to thinking about what Birt was up to, when I was going to see him again and all that. This made me think about Kranze, and I made a tentative note in my mind that I would have to pay him a little surprise visit. Maybe that very evening. And thinking of Kranze made me think about Karen – and Sharon and Darren. It was the strangest thing: lying there, calm and cool, I could think about all three of them as if they had never been real people. A bit like reminiscing about some film I'd seen. Celluloid characters. I honestly felt nothing. Well, no remorse or guilt, anyway. It was as if everything that had happened before my conviction was some sort of weird fiction, something that never happened except in a kind of dream. I couldn't even get the sequence of events correct. It was, in short, a jumble. All I did know was that everything I had done had been highly pleasurable, to me at any rate.

So, it was in a pleasurable frame of mind that I told Ma and Harry that I was nipping out for a while, and drove to Cricklewood to visit Kranze. And as I drove it struck me that maybe Kranze had moved, and I gave out to myself for not bothering to check up first. Sloppy. Something I would not have done three years ago. I was always so meticulous. Noted for it, in fact. Ah, well, as long as I recognised the fact, I could always redeem myself, couldn't I?

I needn't have worried though: Kranze still lived in the same house in Cricklewood. I knew that even before his Brünnhilde of a wife opened the door. I could, in a sense, *smell* him, or at least experience the odd atmosphere his presence created.

'Good evening, Mrs Kranze – Mrs Zanker,' I corrected myself.

Mrs Zanker peered at me.

'Is Helmut in?' I asked, deciding to be familiar.

Mrs Zanker never budged. Not a flicker. And I began to wonder if she'd gone deaf since I'd last seen her. I raised my voice, 'Is

Helmut in?'

'Who are you?' Mrs Zanker demanded, and then, from inside, Kranze's voice called, 'Who is it?'

I leaned sideways and called over Brünnhilde's teutonic shoulder. 'It's me, Helmut. Your old pal, Marcus.'

Mrs Zanker gave a twitch like she was having a spasm.

'Marcus?' Kranze's voice said. 'Marcus Walwyn?'

'One and the same.'

'Come in, come in.'

So in I went, past Mrs Zanker, and up the stairs to Kranze's room. Halfway up those stairs I began to regret having come at all. The terrible power of the man started to overwhelm me, just as it had the very first time we'd met. No, that's not right. Not his power – that was something I could cope with. It was his menace that unnerved me, for Helmut Kranze was a man who gave the impression of always being on the point of doing something evil, which was all the more surprising as he was such a small, fat little fart who, at first glance, you'd think wouldn't say boo to a goose.

However, I wasn't going to let him see my feelings, so I bounced into his room, beaming, looking for all the world like a man without a care in the world.

Kranze was sitting in his armchair. 'Marcus,' he said quietly to himself, almost as if he was puzzling out who exactly I was. 'Marcus Walwyn,' he said, his voice getting a little louder. 'Well, well, well!'

'Oh, very well, thanks.'

'I knew, of course, that you were out.'

'Of course.'

'How are you?'

'Couldn't be better.'

Despite the warmth of the evening Kranze's room felt cold, but that could have been my imagination. I gave a sudden, involuntary shiver.

'Was it dreadful?' Kranze asked dispassionately.

'Dreadful? Prison? Naw. Okay, really.'

Kranze nodded.

'But you should know,' I pointed out, reminding him that Birt had sent him down for a rather longer period than mine.

Kranze nodded again, and a nasty little glint came into his pale, washed-out eyes. 'You soon forget,' he told me.

And that was undoubtedly true. In fact, it is one of the most amazing features of prison. No matter how long you've been inside, the moment you get out, the moment those prison doors close behind you and you can breathe fresh, undisinfected air again, you have the greatest difficulty in recalling just what it was like inside. Maybe that's why so many people re-offend. The overwhelming joy of being out seems to obliterate everything about prison life and it's almost as if you never were behind bars at all.

'Yes,' I agreed. 'So, tell me: ever get that book of yours published?'

Kranze shook his head slowly. 'I withdrew it.'

'Oh?'

'It didn't seem right – to go ahead – without you,' he said enigmatically.

I made a face. 'Don't follow the logic of that,' I told him.

'Not logic, Marcus. Nothing to do with logic. A question of appropriateness.'

'Oh,' I said as if I understood.

'Do you see?'

'Yeah. Anyway,' I went on, determined not to get hauled into one of his debates, 'maybe we can do something about it now that I'm out. Got me a job in another publishers. Start tomorrow, in fact.'

'Ah.' Kranze heaved himself out of his chair and waddled to the window, staring out. It was all I could do not to burst out laughing: there was a huge gaping hole in one of Kranze's socks and, somehow, this diffused, for the moment, any sense of fear I had of him. And then, just when I was feeling relaxed, Kranze swung round and demanded, 'Why have you come here, Marcus?' making the question an accusation.

I was pleased with how cool I kept. 'Just thought I'd come and see you. No reason.'

'No reason?'

'Just – you know.'

'And the police?'

That floored me. 'What police?'

'The police sitting in the car across the street.'

I was out of my chair and across to the window in a flash. 'Where?'

'The blue car. The Peugeot.'

I peered out. Sure enough there was a blue Peugeot with two men sitting in it. 'They're police?'

'Don't try playing the innocent, Marcus. It doesn't suit you.'

'I swear to God I'd no idea – '

Kranze held up a pudgy little hand to stop me. Then, suddenly and without warning, he started to laugh. 'I believe you, Marcus. Really I do. Actually, they've been here on and off since the day you were released.'

'You mean they've been waiting for me to come and see you?'

'I should imagine that's their ploy.' He took me by the arm and led me back to my chair. 'Don't fret, Marcus. We fooled them once, we can always do it again, eh?' he said, and started chuckling away to himself.

When he was seated again, his hands folded primly on his lap like an old maid, he asked, 'Seen much of our good Inspector Birt?'

I felt my cheeks going red. 'He came to see me in prison.'

'Ah. How kind. But since you've been out?'

I shook my head. 'Naw. Haven't seen sight of him.'

Kranze didn't believe me, I could tell. 'Strange,' he muttered.

'Why strange?'

'I know Birt. Oh, I *know* Birt.'

'Yeah, maybe you do, but that's no reason why he should contact me now.'

Kranze gave a menacing little snort. 'You don't believe for one minute that Birt is going to let the matter rest, do you?'

'But it's over. I've been inside and now I'm out. It's over.'

'Birt isn't interested in *you*,' Kranze told me, making me feel like some turd to be flushed out of the way. 'It's *me* Birt wants. Always *me*,' he repeated, and there was real venom in his thick voice.

'I don't see why he – '

'Because he *knows*, that's why. That's what's eating his heart out. He *knows* but he can't do anything about it. Yet.'

'Knows what, for God's sake?'

'Knows that *I* killed that stupid little girl. Not you. *Me*.'

I suppose I should have been shocked or something but, funnily enough, all I felt was – God, I can't explain it. It was a mixture of things. I sort of admired Kranze for the way he could come out with his confession without flinching and without showing the slightest emotion other than anger at Birt. But I also realised that I truly hated the fat little man. That I had hated him all the time I was in prison but, for some strange reason, had never admitted it to myself. 'So you *did* kill Karen?' I heard myself ask, and there wasn't a tremor in my voice.

'Of course,' Kranze snapped, as though such a question was an impertinence.

'And you let me get convicted for – '

Kranze interrupted by slapping his knee with a great whack. 'You were convicted for killing the other two. The other girl and the boy. Convicted because of your own stupidity. No one was convicted of killing that Karen girl. I was careful. I *knew* what I was doing,' Kranze said, verbally patting himself on the back.

Mind you, what he said was true enough: I'd never been brought to trial for killing Karen.

'– and Birt knows that,' Kranze was saying almost as if he was talking to himself. 'He'll keep on and on and on until – ' Suddenly he stopped as if realising he was rambling. He smiled at me, a thin smile. 'Never mind, Marcus.'

Never mind! Oh, sure, you fat-arsed bloody little Kraut. Never mind! I could really feel the loathing boiling up in me, so I pretended to get a sudden itch in my ankle and bent down to scratch it, hiding my face in case my detestation of Kranze showed. When I straightened up I was calm again, calm enough to make the decision that I was definitely going to help Birt nail this shithead anyway.

'But there's no way Birt can prove anything now, is there? Against you, I mean.'

Kranze just stared at me as if he was trying to read my mind.

'You're in the clear,' I told him. 'You've done the perfect murder, really,' I added.

Kranze still continued to stare, saying nothing.

I looked at my watch. 'Well, better make a move,' I said, and stood up.

'Marcus?'

'Hmm?'

'You wouldn't *help* Birt, would you?'

I acted astounded. 'Help Birt? To do what?'

Kranze shook his head. 'Never mind.'

'No, tell me. Help Birt to do what?'

Kranze's eyes bored into me.

'You mean help Birt to get you for Karen's death?'

Kranze's head nodded slowly.

'Don't be stupid. How could I? Like I said, he can't prove a thing; and like you said, he already knows you did it, so what could I add to that?'

'He might – ' Kranze began but stopped again.

Suddenly it dawned on me that Kranze was genuinely scared to death of Birt. 'Might nothing,' I said, opening the door, hardly able to wait getting out of that room. 'Anyway, no matter what he *might* try, he won't get any help from me.'

'Thank you, Marcus.'

I gave him a sunny smile. 'No problem,' I assured him and made to go out. Then I remembered something. 'By the way – '

Kranze looked up – a wee bit anxiously, I thought.

'The dedication in your book. That was something I always meant to ask you about.'

For a brief instant Kranze looked alarmed, and I made a careful note of this reaction. I seemed to have struck a chord, as they say, and the music was sweet to my ears.

'That chap you dedicated it to – what was his name? Speed. John Speed. Who's he when he's at home?' I asked trying to sound as if it was a matter of little import.

'Why?' Kranze asked, still looking uneasy.

'Just wondered.'

'Someone I know.'

'I gathered that much,' I remarked sarcastically. 'You'd hardly dedicate your work to someone you didn't know.'

'Just someone.'

'Okay. Okay. You don't have to tell me. I didn't mean to be nosey,' I said, but of course his refusal to give me a clear answer made me all the more interested in this John Speed. 'See you,' I said, feeling quite cocky.

Outside, I could feel Kranze watching me from the window but I didn't bother to look up. He wasn't the only one watching me. The two plods in the Peugeot were gaping at me too, although, of course, they were busy pretending not to. I really longed to go up to them and pose so they could have a proper gawp, but resisted. I barely even glanced at them. I had a feeling one of them was taking photos of me, but why I had that feeling I've no idea. As far as I was concerned they could take as many bloody snaps as they wanted.

The house was dead quiet when I got home, so quiet I thought maybe Harry had taken Ma out somewhere. I went and had a drink of milk in the kitchen, drinking from the carton which is vulgar, I know, but I couldn't be bothered getting a glass. I gave the dregs to Pissquick. He got all excited until he discovered there was only about enough for one little lap. He gave me a filthy look which made me laugh. 'Life's a bitch, ain't it?' I asked him, and when he continued to stare at me I gave him a bit of a lecture on how lucky he was to get anything what with all those people starving to death in Bosnia or wherever it was. I don't think the selfish brute was in any way impressed. Then Ma called, 'Marcus!' and I nearly jumped out of my skin.

'You just about gave me a heart attack,' I told her when I went into her room.

'I'm sorry, dear.'

'I thought you'd gone out with Harry. When you called you frightened me to death.'

'Oh, I didn't mean – '

'Just joking, Ma,' I said, and kissed the top of her head. She'd been reading a gardening magazine, which was sort of odd since the flat didn't have a garden, and I started flicking through it, waiting for her to say something. When she didn't, I asked, 'Why the gardening mag?'

Ma got a bit flustered.

'You're up to something, Ma,' I told her.

Ma giggled like a schoolgirl so I knew I was right. She was up to something.

'Come on, tell me.'

'You won't get upset?'

I threw the magazine on the bed and gave her a long look, loading my voice with reasonableness. 'How can I answer that when I don't know what it is you're plotting?' I asked, and added a smile just to put her at her ease.

'It's just – ' Ma began and then got all coy.

'Just what?'

Ma took a deep breath. 'Just that Harry and I – we've been looking – you know . . .' She stopped again.

I didn't say anything. Just waited, making a long-suffering grimace and adding a wee sigh.

'Looking at a house,' Ma said finally. It took a few seconds for the ramifications to set in, and I suppose my expression must have been fairly dour since Ma started getting upset. 'We were going to tell you, darling. I mean, I *was* going to discuss it all with you, but – '

'Ma, would you ever stop nattering and just tell me what – '

'Harry and I have decided to get married,' Ma blurted.

'That's terrific,' I told her. 'I'm really pleased, Ma,' I added and gave her another little kiss, this time on the hand.

'Are you really, darling?'

'Of course I am. Been trying to get you two married off for years, haven't I?'

'I didn't know if you were being serious or whether – '

'I'm really delighted, Ma. Best decision you ever made – apart from having me, of course.'

Ma was clearly very relieved. I suppose she expected all sorts of opposition from me although I haven't a clue why that should have been. Then it struck me: looking at a house. They were planning a move which could cause me a problem or two. I know I'd been planning to get a place of my own but I have to admit now that those plans were more or less a pipedream. 'And this house?' I asked. 'You're planning to move?'

'Well, I wanted to talk to you about that.'

'I'm all ears.'

'Well, Harry wants to keep his flat here in London – just for when he has to stay over late.'

I nodded.

'And there's this very pretty Queen Anne house that we've been viewing. It really is pretty, darling. Near Bath. You'd really love it.'

'Bath?'

'*Near* Bath,' Ma corrected. 'Not *in* Bath. Near it.'

'I can't live in or even near Bath, Ma. I mean, now that I've got this job and all – ' Then I noticed the look in Ma's eyes. She was all embarrassed. So, it hadn't been their plan for me to live with them at all. I decided to be my usual generous self. 'Besides, when you're married you won't want me in the way, will you? Tell you what,' I went on quickly as Ma tried to interrupt. 'Why don't I get a flat of my own, here in London. Do me good to stand on my own two feet for a while.'

Ma gave me a huge, maternal smile. 'You're so thoughtful, darling,' she told me. 'What Harry suggested was that you have this place.'

Good old Harry. For a split second I actually liked him. 'This place. Ma? God, that would be terrific.'

'And you can come over and see us at weekends – whenever you wanted, really.'

'Yeah,' I agreed although visiting them near Bath whenever I wanted was the last thing on my mind.

'It's such a sensible idea, don't you think, dear? It would save you so much disruption. And I'll only be taking a few bits and pieces, so the place would be fully furnished.'

'Yeah,' I agreed, not paying full attention to what she was saying.

'And of course I'll come and visit you when I'm in London,' Ma went on, enjoying herself now and determined to play housey-housey or something like that.

'Great.'

Ma gave me a look. 'You are happy about the arrangement, darling?'

I came back to earth. ''Course, I am. I told you, Ma. I'm really delighted for you both. So, when's the big day?'

'We thought, maybe, late next month, if that's all right with you?'

'Ma, for heaven's sake, it's your wedding. Not mine. Anything you want is fine by me,' I told her, wishing they'd organised things for a bit sooner. The sooner the better as far as I was concerned.

I felt like doing handstands when I got back to my room. Everything was falling nicely into place, I thought. And then I stood stock still as the idea lodged in my brain. Why had I thought that? Everything was falling nicely into place. Strange. Very strange, because I really had no conception of what it meant. No conception of what was falling into place or where, even, that place was. It was as if, at that precise moment, I knew I was going to do something momentous and that my being alone in this house was significant.

S I X

It was Nick Putty himself who brought up the subject, throwing it at me almost as if he was trying to catch me off balance, which surprised me because Nick wasn't really that sort of person. Unless he'd changed more than I suspected, of course. He breezed in ostensibly to ask how I was settling in: something I was doing very nicely, thank you very much.

Bogets was one of those old-fashioned type of publishers insofar as it hadn't gone in for flashy modern offices and instead did all its editorial work from a fairly small Victorian building near Soho that probably was splendid at one time but had run to seed somewhat. This meant that instead of those dreaded open-plan offices where if one person gets the flu everyone gets it, there were loads and loads of small rooms leading off gloomy corridors. This in turn meant that most people had their own little office which suited me down to the ground, being a person who likes his privacy, as you've probably guessed. The office I was given was right at the top of the building in what I imagine had once been the servants' quarters but it had been modernised to a degree. That is to say, the tiny window in the wall had been blocked up and an enormous skylight put into the ceiling. In fact, the ceiling was almost one big skylight, giving the room a studio effect which was very jolly, I thought.

Needless to say, the first thing I did was post a No Smoking sign on the door, just to stamp my authority on my territory, if nothing else. I also bought my own private coffee-maker and three mugs: my own black one with a Gothic M on it, and a couple of rather more plain ones for the use of anyone who happened to come in. It was one of these I gave to Nick.

'Didn't take you long to make yourself comfortable,' he said.

'You don't mind, I hope?' I asked, deciding a bit of humility might not go astray.

'Mind? This is your domain now.'

I gave Nick a grateful grin. 'Yes. Thanks. That's what I thought.'

'Got to keep the workers happy.'

'Indeed, yes.'

Of course, Nick could remember the way I used to keep my office when we both worked for the Dragoness, so he'd have guessed I would add a few frills, as it were, and not treat my office as a mere somewhere to work. I've always been like that: turning anywhere I had to spend some time into as comfortable a place as possible. I did it in boarding-school (when I was a senior and had my own room), and I did it in prison. In fact, my cell was something to behold. Nothing like those grim squares the public are told about in case they think the Prison Service is going soft. Of course I'm talking about *proper* prisons, ones filled with long-term prisoners, not your poxy little remand centres or places for shoplifters and muggers. In high-security prisons you get all sorts of privileges and you don't have to earn them either. The governor and screws know that most of the inmates won't see daylight for fuck knows how long and that those inmates have nothing to lose; so, to keep everyone happy, restrictions are down to a minimum. Shit, some of the lifers had cells more like Savoy penthouses: curtains, rugs, duvets, and just about every kind of electrical equipment you can imagine. We used to sit there hooting like demented owls when we watched that TV programme, *The Governor*. Screws included. Never seen anything like it in all our lives. If you really want to know, the true objective has nothing to do with the garbage that you see on television: it's nothing to do with rehabilitation, bugger all to do with re-establishing some godforsaken work ethic. It's simply to prevent riots, pure and simple. Keep the cons happy and prevent them rioting, which might cost the establishment a fortune in repairs – and lose the governor his cushy job, of course.

'Good,' Nick said and nodded approvingly. And then, as if it were a mere aside, 'Tell me, Marcus, you remember that book, the one that – how can I put it – ' he smiled briefly, '– the one that featured large in your trial?'

'*A Letter from Chile*?' I asked, innocently enough, but feeling a bit of a shiver nonetheless.

'Yes,' Nick said, sustaining the word a bit as though musing. 'Yes, that's the one.'

'What of it?'

'Exactly. What became of it?'

'Can't say,' I said, which wasn't altogether true.

'Never did get published, did it?'

'No idea,' I lied.

'Maybe – when you've time – you might look into it.'

I knew full well, that Nick had already looked into it and knew, too, that it hadn't been published, which was why I didn't mind lying to him. 'If you want,' I told him.

'Just when you've time.'

'Right.'

'Good. Well, thanks for the coffee. Better than the stuff I've got,' he told me. 'I'll be down again.'

'Up again,' I corrected him. 'I'm in the garret.'

I had one of those swivel chairs and I twirled myself round and round after Nick had gone. It seemed an appropriate enough action since there were things whirling round in my head too. Resurrect the book Kranze had written. Chance for me to get close to Kranze again. That would suit Birt. Suit me too. What *was* Birt up to? Why hadn't I heard from him? That final thought was still in my brain when the phone went. I brought the chair to a halt and grabbed the phone. 'Marcus Walwyn,' I said.

'Ah, Marcus.' It was Inspector Birt.

'Oh, you. I was just thinking about you.'

'Indeed?'

'Unfortunately.'

Birt gave a cackle.

'How did you know I was here?'

Birt put on a pompous voice. 'I'm a detective, Marcus.'

'Oh, that's right. I forgot,' I said sarcastically.

That must have hit a bull's-eye since Birt sounded pretty terse when he answered. 'Well, don't forget. I want to see you.'

'I'm busy.'

'I don't mean now. When you finish work.'

Just to aggravate him, I said, 'Hang on a tick 'til I take a look,' and pretended to be reading my diary. I could almost hear Birt seething. 'How about – ' I began.

'This evening,' Birt interrupted. 'Seven o'clock sharp.'

'No can do,' I told him. 'Sorry. I can see you for half an hour between five thirty and six – or it will have to wait until later in the week.' I wasn't going to let *him* dictate to me.

Grudgingly he agreed. 'Very well. Five thirty. Where?'

'You say. Somewhere near here, though.'

'You know the McDonalds in – '

'Hang on. Hang on. You don't expect *me* to meet you in a bloody McDonalds, do you? Christ, think about my image. Tell you what. Fortnum's. Downstairs. You can buy me some decent tea.'

I thought Birt was about to explode but, 'Very well,' he said, and hung up sharpish.

There's something about Fortnum's that makes me feel good, even if it isn't what it used to be. Ever since they started letting the riff-raff in and welcoming the working classes. You can easily spot those who don't belong – they always refer to the place as Fortnum and Mason's, which only upstarts and people who have no right to be in there call it. It's Fortnum's and that's it. And at least they still retain waitresses in the tea-room. Like my late father used to say, 'Waitresses for tea, waiters for lunch and dinner,' and he had a point.

I gave the waitress a lingering smile and quietly asked for a nice corner table if she had one available please, allowing my tone to hint at secret matters of state to be discussed. And she fell for it. With a sort of miaow she led the way to the far corner of the room and asked me sweetly, 'Will this be all right, sir?'

'This will be fine,' I told her, and sent her off feeling chuffed with her efficient good deed when I told her I'd order as soon as my guest arrived.

I think Inspector Birt had made an effort. At least, his tie was straight and his hair was freshly combed. He'd gone to seed a bit since I first knew him but he still sported those flash suits of his, though I suspect that was just to get up his superintendent's nose. I was really quite surprised at the way he managed to fit in to the surroundings, being altogether pretty suave and nonchalant as he came across to the table.

'Evening,' I said.

He gave a wee snort. 'Evening all,' he replied and grinned sheepishly when I groaned. 'Have you ordered?'

'I waited for you,' I told him.

Birt glanced around him to try and flag down a passing waitress but with no success. He started getting testy. 'Hate these places,' he remarked.

'It's a question of knowing how,' I told him, and discreetly raised a finger when I spotted my waitress already coming towards us.

'Yes, gentlemen,' she said before I had time even to lower my finger.

'See?' I said to Birt.

He gave me a scowl. 'Just a pot of tea,' he said.

'I think I'll have – let me see. A pot of Darjeeling, some sandwiches and bring a selection of cakes, would you?'

'Any particular sandwiches, sir?'

'Whatever's handy – except egg.'

'Very good, sir.'

Birt waited until she was gone before moaning, 'Might as well have ordered a three-course meal,' he said.

'Can't. Not here, chum. Besides, it's your treat so I thought I might as well enjoy myself.' I glared at some American woman at the next table who was about to light a cigarette.

'Oh,' she said. 'Am I not allowed?'

'I guess you're *allowed*,' I told her, and when she started to flick her lighter again I added, 'but it's pretty ignorant, don't you think, just when other people are about to eat?'

Birt looked as if he wanted to crawl under the table. 'Marcus,' he hissed.

'Well, I mean,' I said. 'What do you expect? I don't want to be gulping mouthfuls of someone else's refuse every time I take a bite.'

By this time the woman was the colour of beetroot. But she didn't light up which was the whole object of the exercise. She gathered up her tatty shopping and left in what Ma would have called high dudgeon.

'Right,' I said, feeling pleased as punch. 'What's so urgent?'

Birt waited until the waitress had placed the tea, sandwiches and cakes in front of us. Waited until she had withdrawn in fact. 'Been a busy little man, haven't you?' he asked.

I shrugged. 'Not particularly.'

'Been getting around.'

'You mean the job?' I asked innocently.

'I mean last night.'

'Oh. That.'

'Yes. That.'

'I saw your goons there. Been following me, have they?' I asked, making it sound as if I couldn't have cared less.

'No, as a matter of fact, they haven't.'

'Ah. Just happened to be sitting there enjoying the evening sunshine?'

'No.'

'What then?'

Birt reached out to take one of the sandwiches I had ordered. I had this sudden urge to slap his hand in the way Ma used to slap mine when I was tiny and went for my favourite cake without offering the plate to the visitors first. Maybe Birt suspected what was in my mind – he was a detective! 'May I?' he asked.

'But of course. You're paying, aren't you?' I let him munch on it for a while and then asked again: 'What were the goons up to?'

'Watching Kranze, as a matter of fact. Well, his house.'

'Any particular reason?'

'In case anyone interesting turned up,' Birt said. Then he smiled. 'Someone interesting did. You.'

'And you've got pictures to prove it,' I told him just to ensure he was aware that I wasn't quite as dense as he might have wanted to believe.

'And I have the pictures to prove it,' he agreed. He eyed my little cakes so I took the one I wanted before he grabbed it, a cream-and-strawberry confection. Birt gave me a baleful look and I grinned mischievously back at him. He selected an eclair and cut it into little pieces, putting one slice into his mouth and washing it down with some tea. You can tell a lot about a person from the way they eat. Ma says the working class *always* have to wash their food down. Something to do with not having been taught how to chew their intake properly.

'Everything all right, sir?' the waitress asked, looking straight at me and ignoring Birt.

'Everything is just fine, thank you.'

'More tea?'

I raised my eyebrows questioningly at Birt.

Birt shook his head, waiting until the waitress had withdrawn before saying, 'Not at these prices.'

'Only money. By the way, what am I supposed to call you? Inspector or Birt, or are we chums now and I can call you Maurice?'

'Whatever.'

I decided to call him Maurice. It seemed quite ridiculous not to be on semi familiar terms with someone who was taking me to tea. Besides, if we were going to be working together, which I still presumed we were, I wasn't about to be second fiddle and give him a title while he called me by my Christian name. Yes, I would call him Maurice to his face, but I'd think of him as Birt, I decided.

Birt had finished his eclair and took the last sandwich, making my stomach heave a bit at the thought of cucumber and cress following chocolate and cream down his gullet. 'You shouldn't do that, you know – take the last sandwich. Always leave a sandwich, Maurice.'

'I've got to pay for it.'

'That's not the point. You don't want the staff thinking you're starving, do you?'

Birt grunted and stuffed the tiny sandwich into his mouth. 'Don't care what they think.'

'Oh dear,' I sighed. 'Remind me to lend you Ma's book on etiquette.'

Birt slurped his tea again, and then pushed the cup away from him in a businesslike gesture. 'So, what did Kranze have to say?'

'Not a lot.'

'What?'

'Oh, we chatted about old times. You know, who'd been killed recently, who might be next on the list – that sort of thing. Good, cheerful stuff.'

'I don't find that funny, Marcus,' Birt told me.

'No, well, you wouldn't.' I hadn't actually meant it to be funny. I'd really just been trying to rile him. 'Oh, and he told me he did kill Karen,' I added almost as if it was an afterthought of no consequence.

Birt stiffened. 'He told you *that*?'

I nodded. 'Yep. Won't help you any. My word against his.'

'The bastard,' Birt said to himself. 'How did *you* feel about that?'

The funny thing was I had felt nothing. I shrugged again. 'Dunno. Nothing, really.'

'I thought you loved Karen. You always maintained you did.'

'That was then. Now – well, it's different, isn't it?' I emptied my teapot, getting about half a cup. 'Besides, he'd have said he did it to save me, wouldn't he? To stop Karen identifying me.'

'Oh, he stopped her all right,' Birt said angrily. He started opening and closing his fingers and every time he formed a fist he bounced them off the table.

'You really do hate Kranze, don't you?' I asked.

'Yes. I really do hate him,' Birt admitted with a venom I hadn't heard come from him before.

'That's why he's so clever.'

Birt looked at me quizzically.

'Not my place to tell you your job, Maurice, but when you become, let's say, too passionate, you miss the little things that could help you. And Kranze knows that.'

'And you're an expert at being dispassionate?' he asked me, meaning to be sarcastic.

'Yes. As a matter of fact I am.'

Birt stared at me, and then started to nod when he realised that what I had said was true. I don't know if you're born passionless or whether it's something you acquire, but I think I've always been phlegmatic. And although Fortnum's was an odd enough setting to think about it, I couldn't help recalling how calm, how disinterested almost, I'd been when I'd killed Sharon and Darren. As I saw it, Sharon was something for me to practise on, and Darren had been in the way, simple as that. So why make a big deal out of it?

'– say anything else?' Birt was asking.

'Sorry?'

'Did Kranze say anything else?' he demanded testily.

'This and that.'

'What?'

'Oh, nothing of real interest. Just chat,' I said and let Birt wallow in his disappointment for a while. 'One interesting thing, though – ' I began.

Birt pounced on it. 'What?'

'Well, maybe it's nothing,' I said and paused again.

'What?' Birt had to restrain himself from shouting.

I was enjoying myself. 'I don't want to get your hopes up.'

Birt looked as if he was about to lean over and throttle me.

'He got a bit upset when I asked him who John Speed was. Very upset, in fact.'

'John Speed?'

Nice. I thought Birt might have forgotten about him. 'I thought you were a detective. John Speed. The bloke Kranze dedicated his book to.'

'I know that,' Birt snapped, deflating me a whit. 'I was just trying to think how he might fit in.'

'Oh. So you know who this Speed character is, do you?'

It was quite touching the way Birt reddened when he shook his head. 'No,' he admitted. 'There's no trace of a John Speed anywhere. None connected to Kranze, in any case.'

'Oh, dear. That's a shame.' I gave an enormous sigh. 'I suppose I'll have to find out who he is.'

'You could do that?'

'Oh, I think so.'

'Well, do it then,' Birt snapped.

'Is that an order?' I asked making my tone ensure that Birt knew I wasn't about to act as one of his fucking minions.

'It's a request,' Birt told me.

'I'll see what I can do then. Won't be for a while, though. Got other things to attend to first,' I told him, making those other things sound a bit sinister just to upset him.

'Like what?'

'Well, for one thing, Ma's getting married again. Harry Rutherford. You might remember him?' I asked with a wee smirk since it was Harry who got me out.

Birt frowned. 'I remember him.'

'Well, they're getting married. Going to live in – near – Bath, which will be nice,' I said hoping Birt would fall into my little trap.

He did. 'You're going to live in Bath?' he asked, sounding both irked and disappointed.

'*Near* Bath. No. No, I'm not. Taking over Ma's house in Chelsea, actually.'

Birt relaxed. 'I see.'

'Be living all on my owny-o.'

'I see,' Birt repeated, only half listening to what I was saying.

'No one to know what I'm getting up to. No one to pry,' I added to bring him back to earth. I really did enjoy taunting poor old Maurice.

'I'll be watching you,' he said, sounding surly.

'Be my guest.'

'Don't try playing games with me, Marcus.'

'Wouldn't dream of it, Maurice,' I said, being cheeky.

Birt didn't like that. 'I'll have you inside again as sure as – '

'You see? There you go again, Losing your calm over nothing,' I told him with a huge, disarming grin, but at that moment I couldn't decide who I detested more, Kranze or Birt.

'I'm just warning you.'

'No need to. I meant that you would be able to confer with me in the comfort of my home without having Ma – or Harry for that matter – wanting to know what's going on,' I lied.

Birt eyed me for a few moments, trying to decide if I was having him on again, I suppose. But the fool must have believed me. 'I see,' he said and made the two words sound apologetic.

'We're partners, aren't we?' I went on. 'Partners in crime.' I liked the sound of that. 'I mean, what you're plotting *is* a crime, isn't it? Trying to fit Kranze up? What do they call it? Perverting the course of justice or something.'

Birt just stared coldly at me.

'Not that you'd look at it that way.'

'No, I wouldn't.'

'Probably see it as encouraging justice.'

Birt clearly didn't want any more of this. 'You finished?'

'Thank you. I enjoyed the tea very much,' I said, purposely misconstruing his question. I raised my head and mouthed 'Bill please' to our waitress, making a little writing gesture at the same time.

'My friend is treating me,' I said, when she handed the bill to me.

She looked really surprised. 'Oh,' she said and handed Birt the slip.

'I know,' I told her. 'Life is full of little surprises.'

Of course, Birt didn't leave a tip so I slipped a couple of quid under my plate just to be sure the waitress knew who had given it to her. Always keep in with waitresses is my advice.

Outside Birt looked much more his old self, blending into the curious world of anonymity quite nicely. 'We'll be in touch,' he said.

'I look forward to that.'

'Meanwhile – '

'I know, I know. See if I can find out who Speed is. Right?'

Birt nodded. 'Please,' he said, which must have hurt him.

SEVEN

I'd guessed that preparations for the wedding were going to cause considerable disruption but I didn't expect them to start quite so soon or to be quite so invasive. The comings and goings to the house were something which had to be seen to be believed since Ma was one of those people who expected the tradesmen to come to her. Quite right, too. By tradesmen I mean, of course, all those leeches who make a fortune out of a lady's big day: caterers, florists, dressmakers and all the other parasites who believe in making a fast buck while the going is good and the customer is in the right frame of mind.

'Hope you've got a deep pocket,' I mentioned to Harry, knowing full well that he had.

'Your mother's enjoying herself,' he answered, as if that was all that mattered. 'Money isn't everything, Marcus,' he added, making me flinch at his clichéd smugness just when I was thinking that he really was a generous old sod at heart.

''Course it isn't – when you've got it, Harry. That's the trick, isn't it? Be well loaded and then you can tell everyone else what a curse money is, right?'

I admit that I'd never had to worry about the filthy lucre (what dimwit called it *that*, I wonder?) but I didn't go around pontificating about how evil it was. I've yet to hear anyone on the dole telling me how dreadful money was and how it ruined their lives. Not that Harry or Ma would have met anyone on the dole. I doubt if Ma even knew what the dole was. And, to be truthful, I didn't know all that much about it until I went inside and learned all about Giros and how whole families have to live on them. I worked it out that the average family of four got enough dole money in a month to cover Ma's expenditure on one Saturday shopping expedition to Fortnum's and Harrods. Crazy. But at least Ma had the right idea: if you've got it, spend it.

Anyway, back to the wedding preparations. A small wedding perforce since most of Ma's so-called pals had deserted her, as I explained, and most of the guests would be Harry's chums. They planned about thirty guests, which suited me: crowds I can do without, thank you. The ceremony in a registry office – something that Ma wasn't crazy about since she had the idea that registry office weddings were for pop stars, drug addicts and the working classes who couldn't afford a *proper* wedding – followed by the reception in Byrons, a classy little restaurant which Harry took over for the day. And then it was off on the honeymoon: three days in Paris, a week in Florence, and two weeks 'in the sunshine' was as much as Harry would reveal, getting all coy and wanting to 'surprise my bride'. As it happens, it turned out to be Mustique, where one of Harry's clients had a shack.

Ma was like a giggly little girl, which got a bit embarrassing at times, but it was nice to see her so happy. 'It's nice to see you so happy, Ma,' I told her.

'I *am* happy, darling.'

'Yes, I know. That's why I said it's nice to see you so happy.'

We laughed at that, and then Ma got serious. 'You don't *mind*, do you, darling?'

'Sure I do. I mind most dreadfully,' I told her. 'Don't be daft, Ma. I've told you a hundred times I'm delighted. Should have done it years ago.'

'And you'll be all right, won't you?' Ma wanted to know, meaning, I suspect, I wasn't about to bump anyone else off. She looked on murder as a possibly recurring disease, a bit like malaria or something.

'I'll be all right.'

'Oh, good,' Ma said, brightening as if I'd handed her a doctor's certificate to say I was not totally immune. 'And you do *promise* to come and stay as often as possible?'

'Just you try and stop me.'

Ma reached out and took my hand. 'You don't think your father would mind, do you?'

'Your getting married? Hell, no, Ma. He'd be delighted, like I am.'

'You really think so?'

'I'm certain.'

That cheered Ma up and she started telling me all about the outfit she'd ordered. I listened without hearing too much: creamcoloured silk two-pieces by some designer favoured by the Princess of Wales are not what I'd call the most fascinating of subjects. 'You'll look terrific in anything, Ma. An old tweed coat and wellies and you'd still knock them all into a cocked hat.'

Ma hugged me.

Fortunately I had my new job to take me out of the house and away from all the camp florists and hairdressers who seemed to be invading the house. Besides, like I told you, I'd made my office more than just a place to work and I really enjoyed going there, shutting the door, and having my own little private world. In my old office I used to have this pretty exotic plant, a sort of trailing orchid the name of which escapes me. And when I rang up Camp Carl to tell him about my new situation, what did he do? You've guessed it: sent me another of those plants, which was really sweet of him, I thought. He sent a card, too, wishing me luck and happiness. That meant I had to ring him again to thank him. I know I should have written (Ma was very insistent on that: always *write*, darling. Only slovens and the uneducated use the phone to thank people for gifts and favours) but I wanted to talk to him about something else: kill a couple of tits with the one stone.

'Hi, Carl.'

'Marcus! How are you, dear boy?'

'Thanks a bunch for the plant.'

'Ah, you got it.'

'Sure did. It was very thoughtful of you, Carl.'

Carl tittered. 'I'd only do it for you, you know.'

'That makes it even more precious,' I told him, and I could just about hear him swoon.

'Make sure you deadhead the flowers as they fade,' he warned.

'I'll do that. Listen, Carl, you remember that Kranze book, *A Letter from Chile*?'

'Do I ever.'

'What happened about that? I mean, I know it wasn't published but can you tell me why? Was it Kranze's decision – '

'Kranze's.'

'You're sure?'

'Certain.'

'Any reason he gave?'

Carl went spectacularly silent on the other end of the phone. I thought for a minute we had been cut off.

'Carl? Carl?'

'I'm here, Marcus.'

'Oh, sorry, I thought we'd been cut off.'

'No. Can I ask you why you want to know all this, Marcus?'

'Sure. Nick Putty was asking about it, that's all. Could be he's thinking of publishing it.'

'I see. Well, the official reason was that Kranze felt it would be wrong to have it brought out after – well, after – you know, the publicity it got at the trial and all. Mind you, the Dragoness was dead keen to exploit all that and was furious with Kranze.'

'I can imagine. And the *unofficial* reason?'

'I shouldn't be telling you this,' Carl told me.

'But you're going to.'

'Kranze wrote a letter – '

'Which you just happened to see,' I said, knowing Carl's appetite for prying.

'Which I just happened to see.'

'And?'

'He said he didn't want the book published *yet*,' Carl told me, making the statement sound significant.

'So?'

'He said the day would come when he *would* want it published, and that the day would be when the *right* editor came along.'

'I see.'

I've no idea why but something about Carl's information struck me as being particularly sinister. I could feel my palms go all sweaty, and yet the rest of my body was icy cold, like the blood had been syphoned out of me temporarily. In my mind's eye I could see Kranze composing that letter, and I couldn't help wondering if the devious bastard wasn't somehow planning to set someone else up, just as he had me. Now, this you will find hard to believe, but I swear it's true: I felt suddenly jealous, jealous that anyone else would have access to the book. I know that makes no sense whatever, but it's absolutely true.

'Marcus?' Carl was asking.

'Yep?'

'You're not – you're not going to get – get involved again, are you, dear heart?'

''Course not,' I assured him with a bit of a tut.

Carl sighed with relief. 'Oh, good. He's a very evil person, Marcus.'

'Tell me about it. Don't worry your pretty old head, Carl.'

'Not so much of the old, if you don't mind. But I do worry about it, Marcus. I have this feeling sometimes – '

'Your overactive libido,' I told him, making the joke to try and get him away from the subject because I knew just what he was on about. Every time I thought about Kranze or his book I had feelings, feelings of something approaching terror, but it was a glorious terror, a genuine buzz I think the teenagers call it. 'Well, I better get some work done,' I said to Carl before he could reply. 'You and me will have to get together for a drink or even a meal some time.'

That perked him up. 'That would be lovely.'

'I'll ring you.'

'Make sure you do.'

'It's a promise.'

I put down the phone and had myself a muse. Something struck me. Maybe, just maybe, although it was a bit far-fetched, but maybe Kranze had meant he was going to wait for *me* to come out and then edit his book. But he couldn't have meant that, could he? By all the law of averages he'd have been six foot underground if I'd served my full sentence and he certainly couldn't have guessed I'd get out early on appeal. Yet, the thought persisted. Somehow I felt I was irrevocably linked to that book. There was only one way to find out.

I trotted along to Nick Putty's office, nearly choking on his wretched cigarette smoke. He smoked Camels, which was even worse, since they stank of what comes out of the rear end of that inane-looking dromedary. I picked up the packet from his desk. 'There are quicker ways,' I told Nick.

He gave me the look of someone who's heard that before. 'Don't *you* start, Marcus. I've enough to put up with from Kate.'

'You should listen to her.'

'Is that what you came in for?'

I grinned. 'No, but good advice is never wasted.'

'If taken.'

'If taken. I've found out about Kranze's book. It hasn't been published, but there's a chance it could be.'

Nick was instantly all ears, and he could barely contain his excitement as I gave him *my* version of the details, ending by saying I'd give it a go if he wanted me to.

'You think you can persuade him?'

I gave a small grimace. 'I can but try.'

Nick had a think. Then: 'Do you mind pursuing this, Marcus?'

I made light of it. ''Course not.'

'You're sure? I don't want you to – '

'I don't mind,' I told him firmly, certainly not wanting him to have a change of heart. I wasn't having anyone else muscle in on my territory. 'You don't really think it's going to make me go on another little spree, do you?'

Nick smiled, but his voice was pretty serious. 'It had crossed my mind.'

'Well, you can forget that. I'm not a total fool, you know, Nick.'

'It's not a question of foolishness.' He went to light another cigarette but changed his mind when he spotted me automatically backing away. 'The fact that it happened once doesn't preclude it happening again,' he said which didn't make much sense to me – grammatically, that is.

Anyway, I wasn't in the humour for a lecture, certainly not from Nick posing as an amateur psychiatrist. 'Do you want me to look into it or not?'

'Only if you feel comfortable with it.'

'I feel really cosy with it.'

That made Nick grin. 'Go ahead then.'

'Thank you.'

I didn't phone Kranze to tell him I was coming. Something to do with that good old element of surprise, I suppose. Shake the bastard. Catch him on the hop and all that. I needed him hopping to try and find out about John Speed, anyway.

Henry Kelly was blathering away about special concessions for listeners to Classic FM as I drove towards Cricklewood. He kept on and on until I felt like shouting at the radio to make him stop. As if to really aggravate me he then went on about Henry's bloody highflier – some horse he was tipping to win the 3.30 at York. It used to be Wogan that drove me mad, now it was Kelly. Why is it the Irish can be so fucking irritating? Charm, my arse. Finally, he condescended to play some music: Smetana, which was better than listening to his voice, but not that much better. Music for the multitudes, I suppose. Something not too difficult so that they could feel they were inhaling culture without any pain.

It had nothing to do with Mr Smetana that I started thinking about that phrase from Kranze's book again: 'From the moment I could first think reasonably I knew I would kill somebody.' And I began to wonder – just in passing, mind – if there was, in truth, any foundation for Nick Putty's concern. Would I be seduced again and perhaps have just one more go? I didn't know. But I did know that the possibility of that happening didn't faze me in the least, and for some inexplicable reason I started thinking about the waitress who had served Birt and me in Fortnum's. It was very strange. There was no build-up to it, but suddenly I could *feel* her going limp in my arms, slipping to the floor just like Sharon had done, and lying there, quite still and unmoving. But I soon came back to earth when I had to swerve to avoid hitting a transit van. The driver gave me the finger, so I mouthed 'Up yours, mate,' in return, feeling better for it.

Oddly, and fairly disturbingly, Kranze didn't seem in the least surprised to see me. It was almost as though he'd been expecting me, expecting me on that particular morning and at that precise time.

'Marcus,' he greeted me, with a nod, economically using the same nod to indicate the chair he wanted me to sit in. We sat in silence for a few moments. Then, 'So,' Kranze said. It wasn't a question. I didn't know how to reply, so I kept quiet for the moment. There was another longish silence, and it was getting to the stage when it seemed we were having a minor battle of wills to see who would stay quiet the longest. I wasn't having that.

'Yes. So,' I said to break the deadlock, not having a clue what I meant.

'It's the book again, isn't it?' Kranze asked.

That made me jump. 'Well, yes, as a matter of fact.'

Kranze wriggled his fat bottom more comfortably into the cushions of his chair. 'Tell me,' he ordered.

'Quite simple, really. The new publishing house I'm with wants to – is quite interested in – publishing it.'

'I see,' Kranze said, and then incongruously closed his eyes. Keeping them shut, he asked, 'Would you be editing it?'

'Probably.'

Kranze shook his head. 'Only probably?'

'You could make it part of the deal. Tell them you'll only let them have it if I edit it.'

Kranze snapped open his eyes. They were suddenly very bright.

I decided to have a bit of fun. 'I'm not all that sure that I *want* to be involved, though,' I told him and watched with glee as his eyes clouded over again, taking on their usual watery look. Clearly *that* possibility had never entered his calculations. One up for Marcus Walwyn, I thought. 'There'd be conditions,' I added, and as soon as I'd said it my mind started racing as it tried to think up some conditions.

'Ah,' Kranze said, and gave me a wispy smile. 'Conditions. And what would they be, pray?'

To give myself time, and, if you really want to know, to avoid Kranze's gaze, I got up and went to the window. I turned my back on it, keeping the light behind me.

'I'm waiting,' Kranze said.

I decided to jump in at the deep end. 'To begin with, I'd want to know everything,' I said. 'Everything there is to know. Including who that chap you dedicated the book to is.'

I could see Kranze's body give a little twitch and then freeze. 'He has nothing to do – '

'It's one of the conditions,' I said, keeping my voice nicely modulated and reasonable.

'Why?'

'Insight,' I said off the top of my head.

That seemed to throw Kranze. 'Insight? Into?'

'You. The author,' I said. 'We,' I went on rather grandly, 'like to know as much as we can about the author. The author is very important to us. The more we can understand him, the better the job we can do on his work,' I said, which was just about the biggest load of crap ever to have passed my lips. In my experience, publishers don't give two proverbial hoots about the author. It's the 'product' that's important, and that's precisely the way they view any author's work. A product. And as long as that product is commercially viable – another of their well-loved phrases – they'll fall all over the author, or pretend to.

But I must have sounded reasonably sincere because Kranze turned his head and gazed in my direction. 'You mean that?'

'Of course,' I lied, most convincingly. 'It's like a family,' I went on, getting a bit carried away. 'The publisher, the editor, the author.'

Kranze took to nodding as if he quite liked the idea of happy families. I hadn't the heart to tell him he'd be the brat who got sent to bed without his supper every so often. 'Very well,' he said finally. 'Come and sit down.'

Obediently I went and sat down.

'There's no such person as John Speed,' Kranze began and I felt a terrible sinking feeling. 'What I mean is, there is a *person* but his name isn't John Speed.' I bucked up. 'John, yes. Speed, no,' Kranze explained.

'John what then?' I asked.

Kranze hesitated.

'John what?' I insisted.

Kranze kept staring at me, trying, I suspect, to see if his gaze could make me back down and not pursue the subject. I felt myself in the driving seat, though, and as sure as hell wasn't going to pass that advantage across.

'Fifteen years is a long time,' Kranze announced after a while.

'No doubt,' I said. 'John what?'

'That's what I had to serve. Fifteen years. All because of Birt.'

'All because you killed a couple of old women and got caught,' I corrected him.

He wasn't exactly chuffed with that. 'Birt,' he repeated. 'All because of Birt.'

'Yeah, yeah,' I mocked, getting really cocky now.

'Fifteen long, long years.'

'You'll have me in tears soon,' I said, and then realised that what Kranze was trying to do was to ensure I really was on his side. I changed my tack sharpish. 'Look, I know what it must have been like. I did three myself, for Christ's sake. But you've had your own back on Birt, haven't you? Killing Karen and getting away with it?'

Suddenly Kranze whacked his fist down on the small table beside his chair, frightening the shit out of me. 'It's not enough,' he said in a kind of scream. 'Not nearly enough,' he repeated quietly.

'Okay. I understand that,' I told him.

'Nobody can understand it,' Kranze told me.
'Okay, I *don't* understand it, but can we get back to – '
'John was inside with me.'
'Ah. I see.'
'He was a kind young man.'
'I'm sure,' I said, getting the drift of where this was leading, and getting a bit nauseated into the bargain. 'But his name wasn't Speed, you said.'
'No. Farrell. John Farrell.'
'Farrell?' That came as a bit of a shock. 'Why did you call him Speed, for heaven's sake?'
'Because,' Kranze began, and then gave a small, choking laugh, 'because he liked it.'
'Oh, a junkie, eh?' I asked, knowing I was being cruel.
'It was our little joke, you see.'
'Very romantic,' I said, and was pleased to see Kranze give a little squirm.

I didn't really want to hear any of the gory details. The vision of Kranze and this Farrell creep having it off together made me just about want to vomit. I mean, even a tart would have to be hard pressed before doing anything with Kranze unless, of course, she was into some really weird sort of sexual perversions. 'So, where is he now?' I asked. 'This John Farrell?'

Kranze gave me a mournful look. 'I've no idea.'
'Oh, didn't last, then?'
'John got out well before I did.'
'And didn't bother keeping in touch?'
Kranze shook his head.

It was quite extraordinary. Kranze looked genuinely hurt and saddened. I'd never seen this side of him before and it was truly incongruous to witness. Indeed, he looked so miserable I kindly refrained from rubbing it in. 'That's love for you,' I did say, just as one little needle. After all, God knows how long it would be before I had this sort of advantage over Kranze again. But he didn't take offence. He just nodded his great bald head as though all I'd done was speak the truth.

There seemed little point in staying there any longer. Kranze had withdrawn in a right blue mood and, anyway, there weren't any more conditions I wanted to lay down. I didn't even confirm whether or not we were going to publish his damn book, but that didn't bother me. It gave me the excuse for a return visit without raising his suspicions.

There didn't seem any point, either, in going back to the office, so I headed for home. Taking the odd half-day off was one of the perks I'd decided to bestow on myself. I could always tell Nick I'd had to spend the entire day making Kranze see my point of view, and he'd never be any the wiser.

On the way, I thought about this John Farrell character. I didn't really want to tell Birt about him yet. Ideally, I wanted to find him myself and have a nice little homely chat with him. Keeping him up my sleeve (and in my pocket for that matter) would, I felt, be most beneficial. I didn't realise then just how beneficial. But finding the shit was going to be a serious problem. Impossible, I decided, until I remembered Stuart Bean, the Blow Job Queen, who'd been in prison with me and got out just about the same time as I did, a few days earlier to be precise. *He* wouldn't be hard to locate, that was for sure, and if anyone could help me find Farrell, he could. That cheered me up.

'Hiya, Ma.'

'Marcus! You're home very early.'

'Yeah. Been doing some research. Got finished nice and quick so I thought I'd come home just to be with you,' I said.

Ma didn't believe that, of course. 'I'm sure you did, dear,' she said with a tut.

'Well, only a short while to go now and you'll be abandoning me. Got to see as much of you as I can now. Might forget what you look like.'

Ma enjoyed that, and we had a nice little laugh about it. Life was looking up for me. Everything in the garden, as they say, was rosy. That's what went through my mind that afternoon, anyway.

EIGHT

It was a good feeling to have an objective again, a bit like when I had to plot and plan to rid myself of Darren, making my mind tick over clearly and precisely. One mistake I did make, though, was to imagine Stuart Bean would be a doddle to find. Just because he had been such a notorious queen in prison I somehow figured – wrongly – that he would be equally infamous in the great wide world outside, and that every Tom, Dick and Harry would at least know *of* him, if not availing themselves of his particular services. The trouble was that I kept thinking of him as this thick-set, incongruous perverted faggot, forgetting that he was, in fact, a pretty vicious thug who'd done quite a stretch for armed robbery. Talk about your split personality! Still, it was a challenge, and I knew that if anyone could help me locate John Farrell it was the Blow Job Queen. And why should that be? I'll tell you. You'll have heard of the Old Boy network, I'm sure. Well, your Etons and Harrows have nothing on your Brixtons and Strangeways. It's all based on a sort of need-to-know criterion. Men whose lives are dominated by crime, and I mean *serious* crime, like to be able to put their hand on the right person for the right job, and where better to find such a confederate than from the ranks of ex-cons. With very few exceptions, if you're done for, let's say petty theft, the chances are you can be persuaded to do the same crime again if the rewards are satisfactory. Likewise, if you've killed someone or done an armed robbery, you don't really worry all that much about morality and you'll certainly have another go if only to try and prove you can do it and get away with it. Funny thing is that it doesn't really matter if you *don't* get away with it: next time you will and so on. Anyway, since that Farrell character had been banged up in the same nick as Kranze, chances were he'd done something pretty serious, and if that was the case he'd have gone down in somebody's notebook as a possible recruit were his particular talents required. I was hoping that his name had been entered in Stuart Bean's little filofax. The first thing I had to do was to find out more about John Farrell to make Bean's job that much easier.

'Well,' I told Nick Putty, 'he's not all that interested, but I *think* I could persuade him.'

Nick sucked air through his teeth.

I knew what *that* meant. 'No, don't worry, Nick. It's not a question of money.'

Nick exhaled gratefully.

'He doesn't need the money. It's – well, I know it sounds a bit naff, but I think he's just afraid of letting go of his book, if you know what I mean.'

Nick looked blank.

'It's like giving up a baby for adoption. He doesn't want to lose it.'

'He won't be losing it,' Nick pointed out, still baffled, thinking, I suppose, that Kranze must be even weirder than he thought.

'I know that. You know that. But Kranze doesn't. I mean, he'll never write another book, I shouldn't think. This is a one-off. *His* one-off, and he sort of feels if he hands it over for publication it won't be *his* any more.'

'Oh, for God's sake, Marcus – ' Nick began.

'He'll have to *share* it,' I explained, making the explanation sound ever so reasonable. Nick started shaking his head and I suddenly got worried he might be thinking Kranze and his book weren't worth all the trouble that seemed to be looming. I jumped in quickly. 'Look, why don't you leave it with me. Let me work on him for a while. Another visit could clinch it. I can be very persuasive, you know.'

Nick gave me a mocking look. 'Don't I know it.'

'Well, then. It'll be worth it, I'm sure. Best-seller, movie, TV, all that shit,' I said. Nothing like money as a carrot.

'You really think it's that good?'

'Better.'

Nick sighed. 'All right. I'll leave it to you.'

'You won't be sorry.'

Nick grunted. 'If I am, you will be, too,' he told me ominously.

I grinned at him. 'I'll go and see him again first thing tomorrow.'

I didn't go to see Kranze first thing. I had a couple of other things I wanted to do first. I'd had a long think during the night about how to go about finding Stuart Bean, and was getting pretty frustrated when suddenly it dawned on me. I was just about to fall asleep, sort of dozing in that comfortable period just before unconsciousness takes over when it struck me and I sat up with a start as if I'd had an electric charge sent through me. It was so simple I had to laugh.

I got up early the next morning, and went downstairs on tiptoe so as not to wake Ma. I used the phone in the kitchen. My call was answered with a growling sound.

'Wakey, wakey,' I said cheerfully. 'I thought you lot were always on duty.'

'What time is it,' Birt asked.

'Just after seven. Time you were up.'

Birt groaned again.

'I need to meet you – urgently.'

That made Birt sit up. 'Something's happened?'

'No, I just want the pleasure of your charming company. Of course something's happened. Or will happen if you can find out something for me.'

'What?'

'Not on the phone,' I said, sounding mysterious.

'For Christ's sake, Marcus. No one can hear us.'

'That's not the point,' I said fatuously. 'We've got to discuss it.'

'Discuss what?'

'I'll tell you when I see you. Half nine – okay?'

Birt sighed. 'Where? Not bloody Fort – '

'That's a good idea,' I interrupted quickly, trying to keep the jollity out of my voice. 'See you there at nine thirty, same place as before,' and hung up.

I went back upstairs and took a nice, long, leisurely bath. Then I shaved and dressed carefully. It was after eight when I'd done all that so I trotted downstairs and made up a breakfast tray for Ma.

'Good morning, darling,' Ma said, purring. Then she saw the tray. 'Oh, you are so kind.'

'Milk of human kindness. That's me. Overflowing with the stuff,' I said and set the tray on her lap. 'Mind, don't spill your juice.'

'I'm going to miss this,' Ma said and sounded as if she meant it.

'I'm sure Harry will do the business.'

'It won't be the same.'

'Be better.'

'No, it won't.'

I leaned down and kissed the top of her head. 'Have to go,' I told her. 'Busy day today.'

'Marcus?'

'I do love you, you know.'

I gave her a huge smile. 'I know that, Ma. And I love you.' I made for the door, then turned. 'You in or out this evening?' I asked.

Ma rubbed her brow. 'In, I think.'

'Right.'

'Why?'

'No reason.'

'Oh.'

''Bye.'

I was halfway down the stairs when Ma called me back. 'I'm sorry, darling. I quite forgot. Harry's sister is coming down from Chester and we're all going out for dinner.'

That was a surprise. 'I didn't know Harry had a sister.'

'Oh, yes. Two, in fact. Grace who lives in Chester, and Julie – Julie Farrar, she is – who lives in Rome.'

'Well, well. Any brothers?'

Ma shook her head. 'Just the two sisters.'

'Well, have a nice time.'

'I'll try.'

''Bye again.'

''Bye, darling.'

I got to Fortnum's before Birt and chose the same table we'd used on our previous visit. There weren't too many customers at that time of day, just a few cobblers and shirtmakers from Jermyn Street trying to look affluent by reading the *Financial Times,* slurping coffee before trying to flog their overpriced gear to the morons who are willing to pay those prices.

'Good morning, sir. Nice to see you again.'

I looked up, and there she was. The same waitress, looking really nice and fresh after what must have been a good night's sleep. I guessed she must have been in her late twenties or maybe even early thirties, but still very appetising for all that. 'Well, hello,' I said with one of my special smiles. 'I'm surprised you remember me.'

She didn't answer that, just simpered a bit.

'Just coffee for me, please. Oh, and that man who was with me the last time, he'll be along too.'

She gave a little frown. Clearly she didn't recall Birt, which was quite interesting. 'You wish to wait for him?'

'Heck, no,' I said with another smile, and this time got a very pretty smile back.

I was on my second cup when Birt came in. 'This better be good,' he said by way of greeting.

I held up my coffee cup. 'It's excellent, as usual,' I said. 'You want some, or are you a tea person?' I asked as the waitress came to the table.

'Coffee,' Birt said.

'Another coffee, please,' I told the waitress.

Birt scowled at my manners. 'So?'

'Let's get your coffee first, then we'll talk,' I said, determined to keep hold of the whip hand.

I let Birt take a few sips of his coffee before leaning forward conspiratorially. 'I went to see Kranze again,' I told him in a low, secretive voice.

'I know,' Birt said, which momentarily took the wind out of my sails. Birt had a grin. 'Didn't spot the boys this time, then?' He gave a chuckle.

'No, as a matter of fact, I didn't. They must be improving.'

Birt ignored that. 'And?'

'We had quite an interesting little chat.'

'Did you find out anything. About Speed?'

I made a grimace of frustration. 'Well, no, I didn't as it happens,' I lied.

'Shit.'

'I did try, but – well, I've been thinking. There *might* be another way.'

Birt straightened his back and raised his eyebrows.

'I'll need your help. That's what I want to talk about.'

'Go on,' Birt said, sounding suspicious all of a sudden.

'You'll have to give me your word that you'll let *me* handle it.'

'Can't do that till I know what it is you want to handle.'

I leaned back in my chair and gave him a disappointed stare.

Birt waited a bit, and then demanded, 'Well?'

'Sorry.'

'You have to tell me what you're up to first.'

'No can do, I'm afraid. Your word first, then the information.'

'All right, all right,' Birt said, but I knew he didn't really mean it. Not that that mattered as far as I could see. 'You ever hear of someone called Stuart Bean?' I asked.

This clearly wasn't what Birt had been expecting. He gave me a curious look. 'Bean. Stuart Bean,' he said aloud but mostly to himself. 'It rings a bell.'

'Ding dong. Think,' I told him.

Birt thought but didn't get anywhere. He shook his head. 'No.'

'Armed robbery? Securicor? Ten years back?'

A little light glinted in Birt's eyes. 'Stuart Bean,' he said triumphantly.

'Well done,' I told him. 'Dry rot hasn't set in completely then.'

'What about Bean?'

I leaned forward again. 'I want an address on him.'

Immediately Birt froze. 'Why? What's Bean got to do with any of this?'

I leaned back. 'I'm not sure. No, I *am* sure. He's got nothing whatever to do with it except . . . Well, Bean was inside with me, right?'

Birt just blinked.

And then it occurred to me that I was about to put my two big feet right in it. I'd forgotten, you see, that I wasn't supposed to know anything about Speed alias Farrell or vice versa, so I couldn't have known he'd been in prison with Kranze. And if I didn't know that, why, then, would I want Stuart Bean to help me find him? How would Beany know him?

I poured another cup of coffee to give myself time to regroup my thoughts. 'As I was saying,' I went on as the muddle began to unravel itself in my brain. 'Bean was inside with me. Now, Bean knows just about everyone who's ever set foot inside. He'd know Kranze, I'm sure of it. And if he knows Kranze he might, just *might*, mind, know something about Speed.'

Birt didn't look very convinced.

'Yeah, I know it's a long shot, but it's better than nothing, isn't it?'

Birt, I hoped, was willing to grasp at anything. 'A very long shot,' he said, but didn't sound too despondent. 'What do you want me to do, though?'

'Simple. All I want is for you to get me an address on Bean. I'll go and see him. See what I can glean.'

'Glean,' Birt repeated with a bit of a smirk.

'Find out,' I explained.

'I know what it means,' Birt snapped huffily.

'Can you do it? Get an address on Bean. You must have one in the records.'

'Only if – '

I knew what Birt was going to say, so I interrupted him. 'He'll be on the computers somewhere.'

Birt nodded slowly.

'So you'll get it for me?'

Birt continued to nod.

I beamed at him. 'Good.'

'And supposing Bean *doesn't* know anything about Speed?'

I shrugged. 'We're back to square one, but no worse off than we are now,' I said logically.

'And if he does know, why should he tell you?'

I gave him another expansive smile. 'Because I'm part of the clan. One of the boys. An ex-con. Better still, I'm one who beat the system and got out on appeal making you lot look like right halfwits,' I said, enjoying the wince Birt gave. 'I'll think up some reason why I want to know, don't worry. It's my guess Kranze won't have won any prizes in the prison popularity contest, so my reasons can be along the lines that he owes me something – or *for* something.'

Birt went into a pensive mood which didn't thrill me.

'Trust me, Maurice,' I told him.

Birt looked hard at me. 'Don't seem to have any alternative, do I?' he said finally, and I could feel my breath easing itself out of my lungs.

'There you go,' I said cheerfully. 'Now, got to love you and leave you. Some of us have to work for a living.' I stood up. 'And thanks for the coffee,' I added. 'Don't forget the tip this time.'

I smiled at the waitress as I left.

So, with that under way, it was time for another visit to Kranze. I nipped into the office first, though, just to let people see I was still alive, and left a message for Nick with his secretary saying I was off to try and get 'that book' signed up.

Kranze was in a testy mood. He looked as if he hadn't been sleeping all that well. His watery eyes were quite red, giving him an extra demoniac appearance. 'You look tired,' I told him.

He just ignored that.

'Not pleased to see me?'

'That depends.'

'Everything depends,' I informed him. 'Anyway, the good news is that Bogets are interested in publishing your book and they've agreed that I'll edit it.'

I was surprised that Kranze wasn't a bit more enthusiastic. 'I see,' was all he said.

'I thought you'd be pleased.'

'I am pleased.'

'Well, show it, for God's sake.'

Kranze showed his pleasure by grunting.

'Means you'll have to put up with publicity and stuff, but you won't mind that.'

Instantly Kranze became alarmed. 'Publicity?' he asked.

'Yeah, you know. Public like to know bits about the author.'

Kranze – well, he cringed. 'No. Oh, no. I won't have that. Forget the book. Forget – '

Shit! I thought. 'Okay, okay,' I went on hurriedly. 'You can be the mysterious author if you want. The book's good enough to sell itself anyway,' I added as a nice little sop. 'Besides, think how pleased your mate will be. Speed. Farrell. Whatever his name is.' Kranze's agitation subsided, which was a relief I can tell you. 'Might even make him get in touch with you again,' I said, pushing it a bit, I know.

'You think?' Kranze asked, sounding ridiculously childlike and naïve.

'Why not? Hell, if someone did *me* the honour of dedicating such a good book to me I'd certainly want to thank them in person.'

It worked. I could have kissed Kranze with delight. 'All right,' he said, in a dreamy sort of way, as though he was already imagining what his reunion with Farrell might be like.

Fine. I decided I could now push a wee bit harder. 'You miss him, don't you?'

'I was very fond of him,' Kranze said, still not quite back to earth.

'What was he in for anyway, poor sod?'

Kranze suddenly became alert, eyeing me.

'Drugs, was it?' I hazarded.

Kranze sighed and nodded.

'Thought so. Doesn't do a damn bit of good locking addicts up. Stupid. Really stupid,' I said, getting myself nicely on Farrell's side. 'Talk about your enlightened society, eh?' I let Kranze think about our enlightened society for a while. Then I asked, sounding as casual and chatty as I could, 'From London, was he?'

'Glasgow.'

'Glasgow!' That wasn't all that promising. Fucking Glasgow. 'Never been there,' I confessed, trying to stay calm. 'You?'

'Just once. After I came out. Tried to – ' Kranze stopped abruptly and stood up. He stretched and shook himself like a horse: from the neck down.

'Tried to find John, eh?'

But I could see Kranze wasn't saying anything more of interest. He was his old, objectionable self again. All he wanted now was to be rid of me for the time being. 'I've said you can publish my book,' he said coldly.

I stood up. 'Yeah. That's great. Really great.'

'You know the way out,' Kranze said.

'Oh. Yes. Sure.'

I've been kicked out of places with more grace, I must say.

NINE

Glasgow! How the hell was I supposed to get up to that dump and talk to Farrell, even supposing Bean knew his address? Some explaining that would take. I couldn't really say I was going up there for a holiday, or even a weekend break, since no one in their right mind would go to fucking Glasgow unless they were dragged there. Oh, well, something would turn up, I decided as I drove back from Kranze's. It was just eleven thirty. Time, I thought, for a coffee before returning to the office.

'Again?' my waitress said with a smile.

'"Fraid so.'

'Is it lunch or – '

'No. Just coffee again, please,' I told her. It hadn't gone unnoticed by me that she'd stopped calling me 'sir', which could have been construed as being overly familiar; but under the circumstances I let it go.

'Nothing at all to eat?'

I gave her tits a good hard stare, then looked up into her eyes. 'No, nothing,' I said, and was amused at the way she blushed. Mind you, from her accent I gathered there was a touch of the Irish in her, so she was probably a Catholic and you know what Irish Catholic women are like when it comes to the erogenous parts of their bodies. 'By the way, do you have a name?' I asked.

'I do.'

'And?'

'Miranda.'

For some reason that came as a bit of a shock. She didn't *look* like a Miranda, if you know what I mean. Mirandas in my book are slim and tall and willowy, and not too bright. *This* Miranda was just about the opposite. Oh, she was tall enough, but she was what Ma would call a *big* girl, stressing the big, which conjured up visions of the Miranda that stood beside me, pad in hand: strapping, buxom and decidedly nubile.

'Nice,' I told her. 'I'm Marcus,' I added and got the strangest feeling of *déjà vu*. It was such a strong sensation that I literally had to blink and look up at Miranda again to make sure it was happening *now*. It was only as she walked away that I remembered my introduction to Karen had been just about the same – only then, too, that I noticed what a nice pair of buttocks Miranda possessed, like a gorgeous double mandolin. And soft. Not like Heather's leathery arse caused by all that bouncing up and down in the saddle, enjoying the feel of some sweaty beast between her legs, no doubt. But Miranda – couldn't see her on a horse; she had that reclining look about her – languidly and voluptuously lying on a chaise longue while Rubens or Manet painted her. Definitely a lady for the notebook when Ma got married and moved to near Bath and I had the place to myself.

When I'd finished my coffee and was getting the bill, I smiled at Miranda: 'Can I ask you something?'

She didn't look up from her pad. 'Ask away.'
'You married?'
'Yes.'
'Oh.'
'Why?'
'Just wondered.'
'You?'
'Me? Married? Naw.'

She gave me a faint, encouraging smile and handed me my bill. As she did so I noticed no sign of a wedding ring. I caught hold of her fingers as I took the bill and stared at those fingers. 'No ring,' I pointed out.

She pulled her hand away. 'So?'

'Nothing. Just wondered. A bit odd not having a ring, that's all.'

She bridled. 'Nothing odd about it whatsoever. Your bill, sir,' she said in an exaggerated way.

'Gee, thanks. See you again.'

Miranda looked for a moment as if she was going to remain defiant, but under my warm and tender gaze she softened. She gave one of those coy little sideways glances which the Princess of Wales has perfected, and then said, 'I hope so.'

Well, I was pleased as punch to know that I hadn't lost my touch. The thought of not being able to pull a bird and being condemned to shagging the likes of Heather Brazier-Young *ad infinitum* made me shudder, I can tell you. But it was quite curious, I thought, as I made my way to Bogets, quite, quite curious that I was suddenly interested in another waitress although what it could possibly be about this particular species that I found so attractive eluded me. I was still wondering about that, wondering in a vague sort of way if Miranda might end up like Sharon (but really in a very vague way, just a passing thought) when Nick stopped me in the corridor, standing bang in front of me to get my attention.

'Well? Any luck?' he demanded.

He'd caught me on the hop. 'Yep – I think so. He needs a day or two to think about it, though,' I lied. 'I told him he could have two days and no more.'

'Right,' Nick said, and then breezed off, probably for one of his expensive expense-account lunches.

I wasn't sure why I'd lied to Nick. There hadn't been any real need for it. It was a sort of automatic reflex action. And I must say that every time I *have* lied on instinct, it has been proved the right thing to do. For me, anyway. It's as if I have some little, mischievous god of lies watching over me, giving me the go-ahead when he deems it beneficial. Sweet thought, that.

I found it difficult to settle down to any work that afternoon, and there was quite a pile of it I should have been doing even though my expeditions to Kranze had been sanctioned by the Man on High. Quite a pile of crap, though. Unsolicited garbage. I really don't know why so many people think they can write a book. And, laugh, you can always tell which well-known author has just had a new book published – we get an avalanche of manuscripts *à la* that particular writer. Jilly Cooper's a great one for stirring up trouble, as far as I'm concerned. I swear to God, just let her even hint that she's writing another bonking saga on, say, big-game hunters, and I can absolutely guarantee you every bored little spinster and housewife in the country will be getting out their portable Coronas and the sparks will be flying off it before you can say 'erection'. Not only the women, of course. There's plenty of male aspiring novelists – wankers, mostly, who wouldn't know a split infinitive if it leapt off the page and spat at them. Men, actually, are even worse: their manuscripts are filled with their macho erotic fantasies, and boy, what erotic fantasies some of these dirty little men have.

But there wasn't even any of that for me to go through that afternoon. Just a real load of bland, unoriginal rubbish with titles like, *And Now for the Fun*, *Rage in Heaven* (which I'm sure had been used before – it sounded like a Wilbur Smith title anyway) and *A Medal for Fanny*, which at least gave me a bit of a laugh. I gave them all a glance and then marked them all to be returned with what we call a Courtesy Note: telling the author to fuck off and take his shit with him but in the nicest possible way and in the best possible taste as the late Kenny Everett used to put it. I missed Camp Carl just now. Jesus! We used to have some laughs at what idiots sent in thinking it was literature. He could be very shrewd in his judgements, could Carl. Shrewd and wickedly cruel but in a really hilarious way. Not that he'd anything to do with that side of publishing. He was, in fact, just a glorified postman, but he'd been with the company so long it really couldn't have functioned without him. I swung back in my chair and began to wonder if I couldn't seduce him away and get him the same job in Bogets. Unlikely, alas: unlikely that he'd move, I mean. He'd been there so long he knew all the tricks of the place and was probably the most secure person in the whole fickle world of publishing.

I got up and took a good look at the plant he'd given me, just to make sure there wasn't any deadheading to be done, and that made me think about Ma's obsession with withered flowers. She couldn't stand them, became really jittery if any flower in the house even bowed its tired little head. 'They're like old love affairs,' she'd say and I'm not altogether sure I know what she meant.

'Sorry, Marcus, but – '

'Shit!' I exploded, and rounded on Sally Greenworthy who had put her head round the door without even having the manners to knock. 'Can't you bloody knock?' I asked angrily. Immediately, of course, I regretted being so brusque as the stupid little tart wilted and looked as though she was about to burst into uncontrollable tears. 'Sorry, Sally,' I apologised. Then gave her a nice disarming grin. 'I could have been up to anything,' I told her. 'Having it off with Carmen,' I added, knowing that the likelihood of me or anyone else having it off with the ugly midget who ran the publicity department was about as likely as Saddam Hussein winning the Nobel Peace Prize.

'I'm sorry, Marcus.'

I beamed at her. 'Don't worry,' I told her. Then, assuming a very severe attitude and wagging a finger at her, I added, 'Do it once more and I'll have to give you a spanking,' and got a bit of a fright when her eyes told me the idea of that didn't altogether turn her off. 'What was it?' I asked hastily.

'Oh, there's a man at reception asking to see you.'

'Does he have a name?'

'Birt. Mr Birt.'

That was a bit of a shock. I hadn't expected Birt to call at my office, but at least he'd had the discretion to introduce himself as *Mister* Birt. 'Oh, yes,' I said casually. 'I'm expecting him. Send him up, will you?'

While I waited for Birt I settled myself in my chair and opened one of the wretched manuscripts, spreading the pages across my desk to give the appearance of dedicated industriousness. I held my head in one hand and kept a felt marker pen poised in the other.

Sally Greenworthy knocked, and waited until I said, 'Come,' imperiously. 'Mr Birt, sir,' Sally said, sort of mocking me over Birt's shoulder. 'Thank you, Miss Greenworthy,' I said. I could play-act too.

Birt took his time looking about the office, waiting, I think, for Sally to make herself scarce.

'Impressed?' I asked when she shut the door behind her.

'Very,' Birt admitted.

'Some of us make it, some of us don't,' I told him, and swung in my chair, twiddling the pen in my fingers, watching Birt as he took a little stroll about the room, noting every detail, I should imagine. 'I wasn't expecting you to come here.'

'I was just passing.'

'Oh, sure.'

Birt grinned wickedly.

'Sit down, will you? You make me nervous hovering about like that.'

'That's a turn-up. Me making you nervous,' Birt said, but he sat down nonetheless.

'So, to what do I owe the pleasure?' I wanted to know.

'You've been to see Kranze again,' Birt told me, admonishing me, I think.

'Oh, come on, Maurice. I've got to see him. The company want to publish his book. I've got the job of trying to persuade him to come to us. That's all. Nothing to do with you.'

Birt nodded as if he already knew what I'd just told him.

'I told you,' I went on. 'If he tells me anything I think you should know, I'll let you know – okay?'

'As long as you remember so to do.'

'So to do?' I repeated, having a small laugh.

Birt looked embarrassed. 'You know what I mean.'

'I know what you mean. Is that all you came here for?'

'No. You said you wanted an address on Stuart Bean.'

I suddenly felt the muscles in my stomach tighten and for some reason my fingers seemed to freeze and the pen slipped to the floor. I bent down to pick it up, using this action to hide my excitement when I asked, 'Get it, did you?'

'I got *an* address.'

I came up from under my desk. 'Meaning?'

'I don't know if it's his current address. It's the only one we have. His mother's actually. Always lived with his mother,' Birt told me, narrowing his eyes. 'Why is it I'm always suspicious of men who live with their mothers?'

I knew he was having a dig at me. 'Something to do with your nasty mind, perhaps?' I suggested blandly. I wasn't about to let him rile me.

'I suppose,' Birt agreed. 'Usually *is* something odd about them, though.'

I fluttered my eyelids at him. 'How interesting.'

Birt reached into his top pocket and took out a folded slip of paper. He placed it on the desk and then flicked it towards me like he was playing subbuteo, if anyone can remember that for an innocent game. There was an odd, impish look in his eyes which I couldn't quite understand. Not until I read the address on the paper. I felt the whole room start to buzz. I felt my old heart start to buzz too, but I did my best to conceal it. Stuart Bean's address was identical to Karen's except for the number of the flat, and if that wasn't a coincidence I don't know what is.

'Blimey!' I heard myself say, Freudianly slipping into the parlance of south-east London.

'I thought that might make you sit up,' Birt remarked.

'You sure this is right?' I asked and my voice was hoarse. I cleared my throat. 'You sure – there isn't some sort of cock-up?'

'That's the address we have on him,' Birt confirmed adamantly.

I shook my head in disbelief.

'Fate,' Birt pointed out. 'Coming to pay its respects.'

'Small world, eh?' was all I could contribute.

Birt stood up. I stood up.

'Let me know if you speak to him.'

I nodded.

'Immediately.'

'Yes.'

When Birt left the room I literally collapsed into my chair. I certainly hadn't expected anything like this. Then I heard myself laughing. There really was a funny side to it, wasn't there? Depending on your sense of humour, I suppose, but it surely began to amuse me. There was an odd kind of justice in it, too – somewhere. Kranze had killed Karen in the lift at this address, and now I was going to have to revisit it to talk to the man who could help me find the man who might, just might, give old Kranze his comeuppance.

Ma was a bit put out when I told her I wouldn't be staying in that evening. 'Oh, darling. I *so* wanted you here.'

'Sorry, Ma.'

'Harry's got this miserable trial he has to prepare for and I'll be all on my own.'

'Got to see this guy tonight, Ma.'

'Couldn't you see him tomorrow? Who is he, anyway, that he's *so* important, dear?'

'He's a really important author, Ma. I mean *really* important. If I can get him to let us publish his next book, it'll be a mega feather in my cap.'

Ma put on her schoolgirl, wheedly voice. 'But why tonight? A few hours – '

'He goes back to South Africa first thing in the morning.'

'What a shame,' Ma said, and I knew my lies had worked.

'I know, Ma. Always the way, isn't it? Tell you what. You have a nice hot bath and get all tucked up and when I get home I'll come in and we can have a good old natter. I won't be *that* late, I shouldn't think.'

Ma cheered up. 'I suppose I honestly could do with an early night,' she said, fingering her cheeks to check on lines.

'Do you the world of good,' I assured her. 'Want me to nip up and run the bath for you now?'

'Oh no, dear. You run along. The sooner you go, the sooner you'll be back, won't you?'

'Very sound logic, Ma.' I kissed her and hurried out before she could get moody again, or start to think it very odd that I was going to see this hot-shot Boer writer dressed so casually in jeans and my faithful old leather jacket. It would have been lunacy to wear anything more dressy where I was going.

Now, I honestly cannot find the words to describe the feeling I got when I drove down the Old Kent Road and turned into Hatfield Close. I was both calm and ajitter. I was cool and sweating. My skin felt icy cold but I knew it was burning. I parked the car in exactly the same place as I had parked it years ago when I'd first followed Karen home and from where I'd seen her as she necked with that common Darren. Amazingly, nothing had changed. The grotty block of flats still rose high and grey. Perhaps it was a bit seedier now, or maybe it was the intense warmth of the heatwave we were suffering that gave the impression the concrete was melting. The forecourt still had those huge, conical concrete containers, and they were still devoid of the promised flowers, although scutch grass seemed to be thriving in the cracked paving stones. The grass was patchy, burned and brown. It was littered with old food wrappers and cans, and with the residents of the flats who found even this wasteland less stifling than their homes. Small children in swimsuits and white bonnets ate dirt (and dog shit, probably). Fat women, their breasts heaving and sweating and straining to pop out of the thin cotton dresses that restrained them, sat crosslegged on the ground with what looked like dishcloths wrapped around their heads, fanning themselves like courtiers with newspapers. Bare-torsoed men, cooking to a turn, lounged in makeshift deckchairs, dozing, newspapers spread across their faces. Directly under the flats, sensibly in what shade there was, small groups of teenagers hobnobbed, playing music as loudly as they could from ghetto-blasters, swilling lager from cans and passing joints from hand to hand.

I got out of the car and the heat hit me like a club. I took off my jacket and slung it into the boot, locking it away. Then, as nonchalantly as I could manage, I strolled across to the flats, checking where I put my feet.

The lift, of course, wasn't working, so I had to climb the stairs to the third floor: two floors up was where Karen had lived, and I said a little prayer to myself that her mother wouldn't come huffing down the stairs. She didn't, and I was outside the door I needed without meeting anyone. I pressed the bell but couldn't hear it ringing so I hammered on the door for good measure. Nothing. I hammered again and the door opened an inch. 'Is Stuart in by any chance?' I asked.

The door didn't budge and then, just as I was about to repeat my question it was thrown open, and there stood the Blow Job Queen in person. 'Well, blow me down,' he said, which struck me as a slightly unfortunate turn of phrase that almost had me sniggering. 'If it isn't his Lordship in person.'

I suppose I better explain that. It was my accent and, I think, the fact that I used joined-up writing and could use words of more than two syllables that had made the other cons give me that nickname. At first it hadn't entered my head how lucky I was – that they just gave me the nickname and let it go at that. Normally, anyone who spoke with anything but a barely understandable dialect was considered a poof and suffered considerably as a consequence. But, as you might expect, my exploits had been greatly exaggerated by the gutter press. I was a psycho. I was an animal. I was evil. I was lethal scum ready to strike again. I think that last one was a local Northern rag trying to compete with the sleaze merchants in Wapping. So, no matter how much the other cons might have disapproved of the fact that I killed a girl and a young man, engaged 'and with their whole lives ahead of them' (and all the rest: 'Fun-loving Sharon', 'Caring Sharon', 'Looking-forward-to-the-Future Darren', 'Just-about-to-Buy-his-First-Bloody-House Darren') – something, I must tell you, that should have had me labelled a beast if the strict con code had been adhered to, with all the intimidation, threats and bullying that goes with such an indictment – the inmates must have believed some of the things written about me, deciding I just might be a psycho, albeit a friendly enough one on the outside, and decided, too, that self-preservation was a better idea than incurring my presumably horrendous wrath. So they left me alone, most of them, anyway. And those that did communicate were pally enough since I was useful to them. I read their letters and wrote their replies, although what those slags they wrote to thought of some of my more lurid and flowery prose I cannot imagine. Probably put it down to the effect incarceration was having on their loved ones. Oh, and most importantly, I didn't smoke, which meant I could always have a ready supply of tobacco if they happened to run out.

'It's me all right,' I said, trying to look bashful.

'Come in, for fuck's sake,' Stuart said, clearly not having improved his choice of vocabulary.

Despite his obnoxious sexual preferences, there was nothing effeminate about Beany. Had he so been, it would really have been grotesque. I told you he was a vicious thug, didn't I? Well, that's exactly what he looked like. He was simian to a high degree, one of those ghastly hirsute creatures with thick strands of hair bushing up from every conceivable part of his body. He wore natty shorts now and a pair of trainers – nothing else – and an image of the Yeti floated into my mind.

'Thanks.'

'How the fuck are you?' he asked, slapping me on the back with a paw the size of a chopping board.

I made an iffy gesture. 'Not bad. Not bad. And you?'

'Only fucking brilliant.'

'Good. Good.'

He steered me into the sitting-room, an oblong room filled with what I suppose were some of the spoils of the various robberies he had been involved in. He all but forced me into an enormous armchair covered in an incongruously old-fashioned chintzy material, all rosebuds and peonies.

'Settle your arse there,' he ordered. 'Mum, bring us a couple of lagers, will you, like a pet,' he bellowed.

Mum, a surprisingly tall and gaunt woman to be the mother of this squat little ape, obediently shuffled in with a couple of Budweisers (the fashion drink of the working classes, as we call it) and handed me a can.

I thought Stuart was about to explode. He went bright red and snorted fire. 'Mum, bring his Lordship a glass, for fuck's sake.'

'No, really – this will be fine,' I protested, holding up the can with all the delicacy I would Venetian glass.

That threw Mum completely. She dithered, clearly unaccustomed to ever hearing her little precious contradicted. She switched her gaze from her son to me and then back to Stuart again, finally deciding that what he said would be obeyed. 'Bring him a *glass*, Mum,' Stuart insisted, and both Mum and me agreed tacitly that further protest would be unwise. 'And bring some of those fancy crisps I got, too,' Stuart called after the retreating figure. 'On a fucking plate,' he added, and gave me the sort of martyred look which both apologised for his Mum's lack of etiquette and made me aware of how trying it could be to live with a recalcitrant parent. Then he settled himself in the chair opposite, the twin of the one he'd pushed me into, which just about swallowed him. He put his feet up on one of those pouffes that used to be popular souvenirs with tourists passing through the Suez canal: different-coloured leather patches with a red, possibly sunburnt, camel as the centrepiece. He passed the time until Mum returned with a glass and the crisps by shaking his head in wonderment. 'Never expected to see you again, mate,' he said, tilting back his neckless head and taking a huge swig from his can.

I half-filled my glass (after wiping the rim as surreptitiously as I could) and raised it to him. 'Cheers,' I toasted.

'Yeah, cheers, mate.'

I had a peep about the room over the top of my glass. It would never have made *Homes and Gardens*, I can tell you, but some tacky furniture emporium must have been rubbing its hands with glee when Stuart Bean and his Mum went shopping. The eyecatcher was an enormous bunch of artificial flowers in a nightmarish-coloured vase: poppies in colours God never intended, green delphiniums, would you believe, and puce foliage. Stuart saw me eyeing it and must have mistaken my melancholic gaze for one of admiration. 'Made them myself,' he announced proudly.

'*Really?*' I asked.

'Yeah,' Stuart admitted again, and then, as though he felt I might think he was boasting, he added, 'Easy when you know how.'

I gave him a smile. 'Same with everything, isn't it? Easy when you know how.'

Stuart decided to give this his unswerving deliberation. 'You're right,' he concluded. 'So, then, what brings you here to see your old mate?' he wanted to know.

I put my half empty glass on the floor and leaned forward, resting my elbows on my knees. 'Need your help, Stuart,' I told him, and I could see that pleased him.

'Ask away,' he said.

'I need to find someone.'

Stuart waited.

'Ever hear of someone called John Farrell? A Scot. Glasgow. Probably a junkie. Did time.'

I decided to stop there, not wanting to overload Stuart's limited brain capacity.

'Not with us,' Stuart said.

'Oh no. I'm not sure when exactly he got out, but it could have been maybe five or six years ago.'

Stuart sucked in his breath. 'Don't know of him off-hand,' he confessed, and my heart sank. 'I'll find him for you, though,' he added, and my spirits rose. 'If he's still alive and kicking, that is,' he concluded.

Stupidly, I hadn't thought of that: that Farrell could be dead, probably *was* dead if he'd followed the usual path of addicts.

'How soon do you need to know?'

'Soon as possible.'

'Owes you, does he?'

'No, no. Nothing like that.'

Stuart's eyes questioned me further.

'He might just know something I need to know.'

'Oh. Right. Leave it with me.' And then, as if we'd never had the discussion, 'What you been up to, anyway?'

I made a resigned expression. 'Working, would you believe.'

Stuart guffawed. 'Oh, I'd believe it all right.'

'And you?'

Stuart gave me a wicked grin. 'Yeah, I've been working too,' he said and gave a casual glance towards the TV and stereo equipment in the corner that must have been worth a few grand at least.

I laughed, just to please him. Then I swallowed the last of the lager, just to be polite, and stood up. 'Must make a move, I'm afraid. Got a heavy date,' I lied.

Stuart didn't stand up. He'd a good view of my crotch from where he was and he eyed it with considerable longing. 'Pity,' he said, looking up hopefully.

'You haven't changed,' I told him, glad that I'd been able to keep the nausea out of my voice.

'Nah,' he said. 'Too old to change now even if I wanted to, which I don't. Why the fuck should I, anyway?'

'You shouldn't,' I told him. 'You wouldn't be you if you did,' I added, knowing he'd find this appropriately profound and maybe get his mind and his fucking eyes off my privates.

I don't know what it did to his mind, but he stopped staring at my fly and stood up. He walked me to the door, throwing one huge, tattooed arm about my shoulder. He opened the door for me. 'How will I let you know if I find – '

'Oh, shit, I forgot. Got a pen or something?'

'Mum, bring us a pen and a bit of paper, will you?' Stuart shouted, and sure enough, Mum came lumbering down the passageway with a pen and a bit of paper. Stuart gave his Mum a slobbery kiss by way of reward. 'Great, my Mum is,' he confided to me.

'I can see that. Must be nice for her having you about the place,' I said, and Christ alone knows how I kept a straight face as I wrote down my home phone number for him. 'If my mother answers be careful, will you. Just say Stuart rang and I'll understand. I'll nip down here and see you again, okay?'

Stuart nodded and started reading my number aloud, actually getting it right.

'That's it,' I told him. 'Nice to see you again, Beany,' I said, and that brought an enormous grin to his face.

'Haven't been called that in a while.'

'No?'

'The shits round here wouldn't dare,' he confided ominously.

'They know better, eh?'

'Yep.'

'Know who's boss?'

'You said it.'

Clever of him to notice. 'Say goodbye to your Mum for me, will you?'

'He says goodbye, Mum,' Stuart bellowed, and a grunt came back like an echo. 'She says goodbye,' Stuart told me although how he interpreted that from the noise was beyond me. 'You take care now, hear?'

'And you.'

I was glad to be out of the flat, away from Stuart and his looks of longing. A few kids had gathered round my car, and a couple of them made cheeky remarks about the BMW and me. I really would have liked to give them a clip round the ear but didn't feel in the mood for starting a riot. I thought I'd put Stuart's bragging to the test. 'You got something to say, say it to my mate Stuart,' I told them.

The little shits eyed each other, then one of them asked, 'Stuart Bean?'

I nodded. 'Stuart Bean.'

'He your mate?'

'He's my mate.'

And then they were gone, haring across the forecourt as if the devil himself was after them. Good for Stuart, I thought, and then wondered how long it would be before he sucked those kids into his net, if you'll pardon the expression. Dirty pervert.

TEN

There was nothing to do now but wait. Wait for Beany to see if he could locate Farrell. Wait to see if Farrell could tell me anything useful about Kranze if he ever *was* located, located alive, that is. Wait before making any final decisions as to which way *I* was going to jump, before deciding how best *I* was going to come out of all this. One thing was certain: I wasn't going to be the meat in any sandwich, and no matter how things turned out I was going to come up smelling of roses – Enid Harkness, preferably.

I had a few things to keep myself occupied, though. I had Kranze's book, *A Letter from Chile*. I had Heather Brazier-Young who had to be kept sweet and on the right side just in case, but that was an easy enough task: a satiated libido worked wonders for Heather. And I had Miranda to ponder on. She was beginning to loom large in my thinking, but more about that later.

Looking back on it now, I don't know why I was so surprised that I found Kranze's book only a fraction as interesting as I had done three and a half years ago. Don't get me wrong. It was still a very good book indeed, but it didn't appear to have the same hold over me as it once did. Not to begin with at any rate. I imagine it was a bit like seeing some film and being overwhelmed by it and then seeing it again a few years later and wondering what all the fuss was about. I remember that happened to me with *The Red Shoes* with Moira Shearer and Marius Goring – at least I think it was Marius Goring. When I first saw it I was captivated and absolutely entranced. I used to imagine myself going on some radio programme in which the rich and famous are interviewed and asked what their favourite films, plays and music are. I'd always come up with the German Requiem by Brahms for music, *La Cage aux Folles* as the play, and *The Red Shoes* as my film. The interviewer, a smooth customer, would always arch his eyebrows and say, '*The Red Shoes*, Marcus? That's *most* interesting.' Then I saw it years later and found it really very tacky; totally baffled as to what I'd liked about it to begin with.

Anyway, it was getting on for the end of July and I hadn't heard anything, but my work on the book was nearly complete, just another couple of chapters to edit and I'd be ready for a showdown with Kranze. I call it a showdown since in my experience most authors are such pompous arseholes they can't stand having even one word of their bloody *oeuvre* altered, and tend to raise hell if you criticise so much as a colon. I was anticipating some such ruckus with Kranze, quite looking forward to it actually, since by now I didn't give a shit if the damn book was published or not. It had simply become a means of my keeping tabs on Kranze and was fulfilling that purpose quite adequately.

Like I said, it was getting on for the end of July, a Friday, coming up to lunchtime, coming up to the weekend, too, so I was feeling somewhat blasé about work as one does when everything is conspiring to put you off it. I had come to the end of Chapter Eleven. I had planned to stop there, and maybe I should have stuck to my guns. But I didn't. I made the mistake of taking a peep at the opening sentence of Chapter Twelve. 'The desire to kill is no different from any other emotion. One indulges if one enjoys it. And if one does enjoy it, killing can so very easily become a habit.'

On first reading, the sentence struck me as just another of Kranze's quirky little observations. Then I read it again. This time it filled me with unease. I read it a third time and felt an extraordinarily warm sensation, as if, almost, what I had read had been a deep and sincere comfort to me rather than something which was pretty terrifying when you think about it. I leaned back in my executive chair, took a couple of spins, and then halted myself and stared at the typed pages scattered on my desk. It struck me forcibly as very strange that, although I must have read that sentence many times before when I first got the manuscript all those years earlier, it had made no significant impression on me. I wondered if maybe that was because at the time I hadn't actually killed anyone myself so the question of habit didn't enter into the equation. But now, with two killings to my credit . . . Suddenly I started to shake uncontrollably. I lurched to my feet and nearly toppled as if I was about to faint. I leaned back against the wall and gazed up through the huge skylight. A white cloud presaging small relief from the searing heat eased its way across my vision. I could *feel* Sharon ease herself out of my arms and slide to the floor. I could *feel* the old Sierra judder and thump as I drove it back and forth over the prostrate Darren and his precious Kawasaki. I could also feel a sensation within me which, to this day, I cannot explain. It was almost an urge, although that word is somewhat too strong. Maybe a desire would be more applicable, although that, too – I suppose to be honest it was an uncomplicated wish to kill again. Nothing crazed. No great fieriness in my eyes. No Jekyll and Hyde crap. Just a warm and pleasant longing.

I moved slowly back to my desk and shoved Kranze's manuscript into its file. I put the file in my desk drawer and locked it away, thinking, 'Out of sight, out of mind'. And, silly me, I thought it had worked.

BOOK TWO

ELEVEN

Ma's wedding was quite a sad little affair, really. Oh, outwardly it was as jolly as the next one, all kisses and smiles and lots of luvvie, luvvie crap. But I could tell Ma was suffering inside. Once or twice I caught her gazing about the reception and could see she was really hurt that so few of her so-called chums were there. I know she sent out about forty invitations (I know because, like a fool, I volunteered to write the envelopes). I know, too, that only fifteen bothered to reply, and only eight of those accepted. Bastards. I felt quite bad that I was the reason for her being ostracised. I knew there was nothing I could do about it, but I felt bad nonetheless. Okay, Harry's friends and relations were very nice to her, and I'm sure they meant it when they said they were absolutely thrilled that Harry had finally taken unto himself a wife. But that wasn't much comfort to poor old Ma.

    I did my best to make it a memorable day for her, though. 'Ma, you look positively stunning,' I told her as she came into the sitting-room all togged out and ready to go. And that was nothing but the truth. She *did* look positively stunning, and I was immensely proud of her.

    Ma gave me a wan little smile. 'Thank you, darling.'

    'No. Really. I'm not just saying that. I've never seen you look so terrific.'

    Ma gave me another smile.

    'Come on, Ma. Cheer up,' I urged her, giving her a peck on the cheek and being careful not to damage her make-up. 'You're getting *married*, for heaven's sake,' I reminded her.

    But again all Ma could muster was a slip of a smile. 'Yes, dear,' she said.

    'You're not having second thoughts, are you?'

    'Oh, no,' Ma said quickly, but her tone didn't altogether convince me.

    'You sure, Ma?'

    She reached out and touched my cheek. 'I'm sure, darling. It's just – oh, nothing. I'm being silly.'

    'Come on, Ma. Tell me. What's bothering you?'

    It was then she told me how hurt she was at being rejected by her friends, and I felt really awful. Especially when tears welled up in her eyes. 'Now look what you've made me do,' she said, and went to the mirror to examine her mascara. Luckily, though, she'd had the foresight to apply some of that new stuff which is, apparently, tear-resistant so no damage was done. She turned from the mirror, smiling.

'That's better,' I told her. 'You don't need them, Ma.'

Ma stuck her chin out. 'You're quite right, Marcus. I don't bloody need them, do I?'

I had to laugh. It was the first time I'd ever heard Ma use any sort of swear word, if you can call 'bloody' a swear word. Ma started laughing too, and before we knew it we were really laughing our heads off, even a wee bit hysterical.

When we'd calmed down Ma got serious again. 'You *will* be all right, won't you, dear?'

'Ma, I'll be fine. Don't worry about me. Really. I'll be perfectly all right,' I assured her. I looked at my watch. We'd plenty of time. 'Tell you what. You and me, we're going to have a drink, and we're going to have that special bottle. Just the two of us,' I said.

'Oh, darling – ' Ma started to protest.

'He'd have wanted it,' I said and went off to get the bottle. The special bottle. A bottle of vintage champagne that my Dad had bought and put to one side to be drunk only when I graduated from university. Then he'd hanged himself and I'd never gone to university so the bottle had remained unopened.

'You don't think he'd mind, do you, Marcus?' Ma asked anxiously as I handed her a glass.

'He'd want us to drink it,' I assured her.

'No, dear. I meant – he wouldn't mind me marrying Harry, would he?'

Dad would probably have been spinning in his grave since he'd always regarded Harry as boring and something of a closet lecher. I suspect he'd have thought Harry the least likely person to be suited to Ma's needs, but I couldn't very well say that, could I? 'He'd be over the moon,' I told her. 'You know he always thought very highly of Harry. I bet if he'd had the chance he'd have selected Harry for you himself,' I went on, lying through my teeth. 'Besides, I know he wouldn't have wanted you to spend the rest of your life all alone.'

'But I wasn't alone, darling. I had you.'

'You know what I mean, Ma.'

Ma knew what I meant all right. She brightened a bit and gave me a healthier-looking smile. 'You're right, of course,' she told me, and

I think I was right also in suspecting that it had just dawned on her that marrying Harry was probably going to get more approval from my deceased Dad than just screwing with him whenever the urge came upon her.

'I know I'm right,' I said. 'Now,' I added, raising my glass. 'Here's to the best Ma anyone ever had. To her health and happiness.'

Ma took a sip. 'I do love you *so* much, Marcus.'

'I know, Ma. I know. And you know I love you, don't you?'

'Yes, darling.'

It went on in that vein for a while, getting even more maudlin as the champagne did its work. Luckily, the car arrived to take us to the registry office before we both got completely sozzled.

As we went into the hall I made one of those casual remarks that really mean nothing but which seem to lead to some enormity. 'I suppose I'll have to get one of those awful answering-machines now.'

Ma slapped her hands to her cheeks. 'Oh, darling, I forgot to tell you,' she said. 'Someone rang for you the other night.'

Immediately I felt a little buzz. 'Who?' I asked as nonchalantly as I could.

'I'm so *sorry*, Marcus. I can't – I can't remember.'

I was furious. 'It doesn't matter, Ma. Probably not important anyway.'

'I think it might have been,' Ma said. 'I mean, I remember he stressed – he – it was a man, I do know that much – he said something about my making sure you got the message.'

God, Ma could be so bloody irritating. 'What message, Ma?'

'That he had rung. "You will be sure to tell Marcus I rang." That's what he said, I think.'

'You think.'

The chauffeur rang the front door bell again.

I was seething by now and having the devil of a job not exploding. Some do that would have been if I'd strangled my Ma just as she was on her way to get married. That really *would* have given the tabloids a field day. But I controlled myself admirably. 'He'll call again if it's that important,' I told Ma.

'It might have been one of your authors, darling,' Ma said, determined to blame herself. 'Maybe that famous one you told me about.'

'I doubt it, Ma,' I said. Then, 'Would you recognise the name if I said it?'

By the look on Ma's face I gathered that this was most unlikely. 'I might, darling,' she told me, though.

It was worth a shot. 'Stuart, maybe?'

Ma gave a little whoop. 'Oh, Marcus, *yes*. I'm sure it was Stuart. Yes, it *was* Stuart. I remember thinking it was a curious name for someone with such a common accent.'

That figured. Ma's mind would work in that convoluted way. 'Sort of London?'

'Definitely cockney, dear,' Ma told me and then gave me that look which asked what the hell I was doing with Cockneys ringing me up.

'Yes. You're right. It is an author. Not a very good one, I'm afraid, but then you don't have to be a very good writer to sell these days.'

'Oh, Marcus, you are *so* clever,' Ma informed me.

I hadn't a clue how she came to that conclusion as a result of our conversation, but I agreed with her nevertheless. And I don't have to tell you what occupied *my* mind as the Registrar did his party piece and made my lovely Ma the first Mrs Rutherford.

I couldn't wait for the festivities to come to a close. Luckily Harry had foreseen the problems his relatives and friends might create when presented with the opportunity to guzzle free booze, and had arranged to get away at a reasonable hour, ostensibly to catch the flight to Paris. As soon as we saw Harry and Ma off I too made a dash for it. I couldn't very well go to bloody Cockneyland all togged out the way I was, so I had to go home first and change.

It was really quite eerie in the house with Ma gone. I know she'd only *just* gone. I know that she hadn't even been home all that much either. But the fact that she had gone for good was different: it was as if she'd taken not only her body and possessions with her but her spirit also, if that makes any sense. All that was left was the scent of her: Joy by Patou at a hundred and forty quid or so for enough to barely drown a fly. I had the damnedest feeling: I actually missed her!

I went to my room and changed. Pissquick (who was a lodger until they came back from their honeymoon) tried to pull rank and had the audacity to come into my room. 'Piss off, Pissquick,' I told him. He gave me one of his cheeky 'stuff you, mate!' looks, turned tail and padded out of the room. 'No dinner for you, chum,' I shouted after him. 'No goddam Choosey tonight.' Mind you, that damn feline probably wouldn't have thanked me for any ordinary cat-food. Ma had totally spoiled him, getting him slivers of smoked salmon from Harrods, and even cooking chunks of lamb's liver for him, stinking the place out. Well, I told myself, checking my hair and grimacing to make sure I hadn't got any caviar stuck between my teeth, by the time they were back from Mustique, Pissquick would have his bags packed and be only too willing to emigrate to near Bath. See if he wasn't.

I didn't dare drive to the Old Kent Road. Way over the limit I was, and all I needed was to lose my licence. I took the Underground to New Cross Gate. The rush-hour was over and there weren't that many people on the train, just some very tired-looking middle-aged men who'd probably done an hour's overtime so they could sneak out and get themselves a pint while their nagging wives weren't watching, and a few fat women with shopping in plastic carrier bags from Woolworths and the like. I sort of dozed off: probably the drink making me sleepy. I remember I came to and got the fright of my life. For a split second I thought Karen was sitting opposite me. I blinked and then saw that the seat was empty. Then I remembered that I'd taken this route the very first time I'd followed Karen home. I pressed my eyelids hard together and sat up sharply, making the old West Indian chap opposite me give me a bleary look. I gave him a nice haughty stare, an imperious stare, you might say, and he looked away quick enough. I wasn't in any humour to have the guy try and get cheeky with me. Not by a long chalk. Not that I'm a racist or anything. I just happen to think immigrants don't show enough gratitude for us letting them come and take over the way they have.

When I left the Underground and started to make my way down the Old Kent Road something else happened which reminded me of Karen. When I'd first seen Karen and Sharon walking down that road there'd been a couple of winos sitting outside the Tube – well, a few hundred yards down from the Tube entrance, actually. And there were a couple of old winos there again that evening, and once again one of them offered me his bottle which, I suppose, was quite a generous gesture seeing as how it must have been quite hard for him to come by. 'Vintage or non-vintage?' I enquired.

He gaped at me.

I looked at the bottle. 'Oh,' I said. '*Sherry*. Only *before* I eat, thanks,' I told him and walked on.

'Fuck you,' he called after me.

'Fuck yourself, chum,' I called back, and had to laugh as he fell flat on his stupid drunken face when he attempted to get up and chase me.

I was still chuckling as I made my way up the stinking stairs to Stuart Bean's flat.

Stuart himself opened the door. 'Ah, got my message then?'
'Only this morning. Ma forgot to tell me.'
'Typical.'
'Sorry?'
'Mums. Never tell us anything until it's too late.'
'Oh.'

He pointed to the sitting-room and went off into the kitchen by himself. He came back with two cans of that awful Budweiser. 'Mum's out at her Bingo,' he explained, but he didn't explain why I had to have a can this time and not a glass. Mind you, I wasn't about to demand any explanation. He seemed to be in a surly sort of mood and I knew he could be pretty unpredictable when churlish. I noticed there had been some garish additions to his flower arrangement.

'New flowers, eh?' I said cheerily. 'Nice.'
That bucked him up. 'Like 'em? Good, eh?'
'Great.'
'Make you some if you want.'
'Wow. That would be terrific. Thanks.'
'No bother, pal.'

The thought of having to live with any of Stuart's horticultural monstrosities put the fear of God into me, but I was, apparently, his pal, which was a good thing. 'Got some news for me, have you?'

Stuart decided to play act. He tapped the side of his nose and made a face suggesting that he had gigantic news for me. 'Have I got news for you,' he said.

'Have you?'
'I have. I sure fucking have.'

I waited. Stuart took a couple of swigs of lager. I waited some more.

'Aaah,' Stuart noised and then belched most vulgarly. That done, he burst out laughing. 'Arabs do that, you know. Belch when they've enjoyed their drink.'

I was on the point of correcting him, of pointing out that Arabs allegedly belch when they've enjoyed their *food* although I've never heard this particular rumour substantiated, but I thought better of it. 'Come on, Stuart. Tell me,' I said, playing a meek David to his towering Goliath. I knew this was what he wanted. Always liked to dominate, did Stuart, stupid little gobshite that he was.

'I've found your John Farrell,' he said finally and triumphantly.
'You haven't?' I asked, filling the room with sheer amazement at his genius.

'I fucking have.'

'Jesus, Stuart, you really are the greatest.'

He swelled. 'Wasn't easy.'

'I bet it wasn't.'

'But I did it.'

I shook my head in wonderment.

'That's the good news.'

I didn't like the sound of that. 'Oh?'

'He's a fucking mess.'

'You've seen him?'

Stuart nodded.

'You went to Glasgow?' I was beginning to be impressed with the Apeman's assiduousness.

'He's here. Here in London. But, like I said, he's a fucking mess.'

Mess, fucking or not, I could sort out later. It was spectacularly good news that Farrell was in London. 'Where can I see him?'

Stuart gave an evil cackle. 'That's all you will be able to fucking do, see him.' For a horrible moment I thought Bean was telling me Farrell was dead. But, 'Can't get a proper word out of him,' Stuart told me.

I gave a deep sigh of relief. 'I thought for a moment you were going to tell me he was dead.'

'Bugger might as well be.'

'What ails him?'

'Huh?'

'What's the matter with him?'

'Up to his fucking eyeballs in dope, isn't he.'

'That bad?'

'Worse.'

Again I took to waiting.

'In a squat. Bayswater. Back of Bayswater. So full of holes he's like a fucking sieve.'

'But he *can* talk. I mean, if I can get him to talk he *can* talk?'

Stuart shrugged. 'S'pose so.'

He got up out of his chair and took a road map from behind a china Clydesdale on the windowsill. 'I've marked the street. Number twenty-two. You'll find it easy.'

'That's very efficient of you, Stuart,' I told him, and I meant it. 'Thanks a bunch. I owe you.'

'That's right, pal. You owe me. And don't forget it.'

I wasn't likely to. 'I won't.'

'Might just need you for something,' he told me and I had a feeling he was already planning some little caper with a role for me to play. Not that I'd the slightest intention of being in debt to the cretin. 'Anytime, anything,' I told him. I finished my lager. Time for a hasty exit, as they say. I stood up.

Stuart followed me to the door. 'You drive, don't you?' he asked.

'Yeah, I drive.'

'Fast?'

'If I have to,' I answered. 'If I'd you after me I'd drive like a bat out of hell probably.'

Stuart enjoyed that. He squeezed my arm, almost dislocating my elbow. 'I'll bear that in mind.'

'Do that. One good turn deserves another, I say,' I replied. I held up the cheap little road map. 'And thanks again for this.'

'No problem.' He opened the door.

'Can I ask you something?'

Stuart looked at me.

'How come you never asked why I wanted to find Farrell?'

'None of my business,' Stuart said with studied simplicity.

I nodded, and gave him a friendly little tap on the shoulder.

'Just like if I ask you to do something for me I'd expect you to do it with no questions asked.'

'Sure. Sure,' I told him hurriedly. 'Well, thanks again.'

Stuart waited until I was outside on the concrete runway that linked the flats before saying, 'Did I tell you that fucker Birt was round here the other day?' He asked the question so casually I knew it was calculated and that he'd been waiting for just the right time to ask it.

I stopped dead in my tracks. 'Birt? Inspector Birt? What did he want?' I was irked that my voice sounded so hoarse.

Beany was enjoying himself. 'Wanted to know why you'd been here.'

'Shit!'

Stuart let me stew for a while, his face mock serious although there was a light in his eye that warned me he wasn't too far off having one of his psychotic turns, would have one and probably gut me if I said the wrong thing.

'What did you tell him?'

'That you'd asked me if I could find someone.'

This was where I had to tread carefully. One hint of an accusation or any slur on Beany's warped, criminal integrity and I could find myself having a free flight from the balcony. 'Typical,' I snorted. 'Never can leave a man alone, can they?' I said and then, with an expansive smile I added, 'Good thing is that with you I don't have to worry that they got what they came for.'

And, boy, was I pleased to see that smug, self-congratulatory expression smear itself across Beany's unshaven face. 'Led Birt and his pal a bit of a merry fucking dance,' he told me proudly.

'I bet you did.'

'Told them you'd asked me to find this guy I'd never heard of.'

That was a relief. All I needed was for Stuart to mention the name Farrell and Birt would have discovered *my* little secret. But I needed this confirmed. 'He must have asked you *who* I was looking for, nosey bastard,' I suggested.

''Course he fucking did.'

'How did you get out of that one, Stuart?'

'Easy. Just told him since I didn't know the guy in the first place I'd forgotten his name. The name you gave me like.'

I bathed him in an admiring gaze. 'Brilliant,' I said. 'Bloody brilliant.'

'Wasn't going to tell those shits anything, was I?'

'Hell, I wouldn't think you would. Not you, Beany. Others would, fucking grasses. But not you, mate. See you.'

'Yeah. You'll see me,' Stuart told me. 'Bet your life on it.'

I can tell you one thing: no way was I ever going to bet anything, let alone my life, on anything the Blow Job Queen offered odds on.

By the time I got home I was really dead beat. All I wanted was a nice long, hot bath, a Jack Daniels, a joint, and my bed. Perchance to dream, but that would be okay.

What wasn't okay was to find Inspector Birt on my doorstep. Well, not literally on my doorstep; he was sitting in his car waiting for me. And, to add insult to injury, he had that thick bullock Sergeant Wilson with him. 'Got your minder in tow then?' I asked.

Birt gave me what looked like a wink and Wilson glowered.

I unlocked the door. 'You'd be safer without him, I'd have thought,' I said, opening the door. 'You want to come in, I take it?'

Birt inclined his head.

'Well, tell Dumbo to wipe his flat feet.'

Whether it was because the Sergeant took umbrage at my attitude or whether he and Birt had agreed it between them previously, I don't know, but Wilson didn't come in. He waited until his boss and myself were in the hall and then spun on his heel and stalked off back to the car. 'Temperamental sod, isn't he?' I asked Birt with a grin.

'Sensitive,' Birt said, returning about half my grin.

'Yeah. Sensitive as a lavatory seat. Kitchen,' I said as Birt made to turn into the sitting-room. 'I suppose you want coffee?'

'It would be nice.'

''Specially when you don't have to pay for it, eh?'

'Certainly makes a change.'

I fixed a couple of mugs of coffee and put them on the kitchen table. Birt eyed his mournfully. I looked at it. 'Oh, yeah, you take milk, don't you.' I went to the fridge and had myself a little giggle when I sniffed the milk and found it had gone sour. 'Sorry. Milk's off,' I told Birt, and poured the rancid liquid into Pissquick's bowl, knowing he'd be livid when he went to taste it. 'Can you drink it black?'

'I'll manage.'

'Let me know when you're coming next time and I'll have fresh milk in.'

Birt just nodded at that.

'Like a biccie? Got some Jaffa Cakes somewhere, I think.'

Birt seemed to have other things on his mind. He ignored my generous offer, but I put the packet of biscuits on the table anyway. Just because he was an ill-mannered git didn't mean I had to be inhospitable.

'So?' I asked. 'What's on your mind, Maurice?'

Birt decided to play it cool, as the expression goes. He shrugged and placed his hands, palm upwards, on the table in a sort of pleading gesture. 'Just wondered if you had any news for me,' he said.

Okay. I'd be cool too. 'Not a lot really.'

'Been to see – what was his name?'

Very cunning. 'Stuart Bean? Yeah. I've been to see him.'

'And?'

'Useless. He'd never heard of John Speed. A right dead end that turned out to be.'

Birt eyed me for quite a while, and must have decided I was telling the truth. He nodded. 'Ah, well.'

'Pity, really. I had high hopes for Beany being able to help. Still, you can't win 'em all, can you?'

'No,' Birt agreed with some emphasis.

'I'll just have to work on Kranze a bit harder.'

Birt gave a little sniff as though he didn't hold out much hope of my having success in that area.

'Don't underestimate me, Maurice,' I said cheerfully.

Birt went very serious when he replied, 'That's one thing I would never do, Marcus. Underestimate you.'

I decided to ignore the menace. 'Good,' I said. 'And I won't underestimate you either, Maurice. Okay?'

Birt finished his coffee and stood up.

'That all?' I asked.

'That's it,' he replied.

'Bit of a waste of your time then, wasn't it?'

He gave me another of his penetrating stares. 'Talking to you is never a waste of time, Marcus.'

'Oh, good. I'm glad you feel that way. You know I get a deep thrill out of your visits.'

'You wouldn't be foolish enough to withhold anything from me, would you, Marcus?' Birt asked over his shoulder as I followed him to the door.

'Why would I do that?' I countered, and then to divert him, I asked, 'Tell me, Dumbo out there – is he in on it?'

Birt swung round and gave a fair impression of being surprised. 'In on what?'

I shook my head at him. 'Oh, that's how we play it, is it? Okay. Mum's the word and all that shit.'

Birt wasn't happy. 'All I want is to get Kranze for young Karen's murder.'

'Of course,' I agreed sarcastically. 'No question of you trying to fit him up for anything else, eh?'

'Of course not,' Birt told me adamantly.

'No, of course not,' I responded and gave a hoot.

Even Birt couldn't keep up his deceit. 'Mind you – if it so happened that . . .' he left the sentence unfinished. 'Good night, Marcus.'

'I had hoped it would be,' I said and shut the door behind him.

From force of habit I tidied up the kitchen, washing the mugs and putting the biscuits back in the cupboard. Pissquick joined me as soon as he heard the cupboard door shut. I've no idea where he'd been: he always did a bunk when there were strangers in the house. Probably his guilty conscience playing up. He took a sniff at the sour milk in his bowl and gave me a dirty look. 'What you expect, Pissquick? Bloody cream? Those days are gone, mate. Anyway, think of all the cats starving in Ethiopia and Bosnia and think yourself lucky to get anything,' I told him, switched out the light and left him in the dark to meditate on the plight of the starving felines.

Birt's visit had got me somewhat jittery so I decided to have a little joint before I ran my bath. I don't actually smoke hash a lot. I'm certainly not addicted or anything like that. I just find that the occasional joint relaxes me, and I can't see any harm in it. Personally, I'd make it legal but I don't suppose the powers-that-be would pay much attention to my way of thinking. I rolled it carefully since I only had a dribble of tobacco.

I lay on my bed, naked, with the ashtray balanced on my navel, inhaling and letting the dope circulate at will. Well, things were going okay, I thought. Stuart had done his job. Birt was in the dark. Kranze could be approached without him getting suspicious. All that was left for my immediate attention was Farrell, and I'd deal with that tomorrow. Mind you, if what Beany had said was true about Farrell being a total junkied mess, things could be difficult, but that was a bridge to cross when the time came. No point in giving up if there was just a chance the problem could be surmounted. Slowly an idea began to take shape. True, it was a confused, vague idea, something about maybe offering to put Farrell up for a while. Something to do with my feeling desperately sorry for a fellow ex-con who'd fallen on hard times. Something to do with getting the junkied shit to trust me, confide in me. Nothing definite. Nothing I could think about with total lucidity just then.

I finished my joint and put the ashtray on the table beside my bed. I felt really good about everything. I took a long luxurious stretch, enjoying the sensation of hearing the odd joint crack. I knew I should get myself up and take my bath but I simply couldn't be bothered. I just lay there and let the sandman come and get me. And I didn't, in fact, dream. Not that I know of, anyway.

TWELVE

I detest those answering-machine contraptions. I detest them so much I won't even speak to them, getting my own back on the bastards who install them by making them wonder who the hell it was who called. But I regret to say, with Ma off honeymooning and moving to near Bath when she returned, I decided I'd have to get one of the damn things though only because I wanted to be on the safe side and not miss any calls which might be important. I know that's the excuse everyone gives for having them and I'm sorry I can't come up with something more original.

So, early on Saturday morning I took myself off to BT and bought one. I spent the rest of the morning installing it, which might seem an inordinately long time to take over shoving a couple of connections into sockets, but I had to make sure I gave the right impression with the message I left the caller. I certainly wanted to avoid those grim witty ones which some people think are such terrific fun, and I didn't want to be too impersonal either. I tried a whole load of things but they all sounded pretty damn horrendous. In the end I left the one BT had already recorded: 'I'm sorry there's no one here to take your call at the moment. Please leave your message after the tone.' That'll have to do, I thought.

I'd just left the phone when it rang, and up came Mr BT with his announcement. Whoever had called paused for a moment and then hung up without speaking. That was a right bummer. Some sod getting their own back on me apparently. Before I could dial 1471 to find out who it was, the phone rang again. I waited anxiously for Mr BT to do his bit. Then, 'Marcus? Marcus?'

I recognised the voice all right. I picked up the phone. 'Yeah, Heather. What's up?'

'Oh, it *is* you.'

'No, it's Doctor bloody Doolittle. Who'd you expect?'

'I mean the machine. I didn't know you had – '

'Just put it in ten minutes ago.'

'I thought you hated them.'

'I do. So, what's the matter?'

'Nothing. Don't be so unpleasant, Marcus.'

'Unpleasant? Me? Never! You rang and I'm simply enquiring *why* you rang. What's unpleasant about that?'

'Your tone.'

'Oh, my *tone*.' This wasn't getting us very far. 'Sorry. You just caught me on the hop. Let's start again. Hello, Heather, my little darling. What can I possibly do for you?'

Heather whinnied like a foal. 'I just rang up to see how you were managing without your mother, that's all.'

Like hell that was all. I hadn't seen her for about a fortnight and, knowing Heather, her sexual longings had reached snapping point. 'Oh, is that all? I'm managing fine. Goodbye.'

I didn't hang up, of course, but I got some amusement out of the panic in Heather's voice. 'Marcus, Marcus don't hang up.'

'I'm still here.'

'I also wanted to know when I'm going to see you.'

'You mean you're dying for a screw and you thought it might be diplomatic to introduce any such query by enquiring after my well-being.'

Heather giggled again. 'Something like that. So, when?'

To tell the truth I felt like having sex myself. I looked at my watch. 'In ten minutes?' I asked.

'Oh *yes*,' Heather agreed. 'I'll be waiting.'

'No, you won't. *I'll* be waiting. You can come round here for a change.'

'I'm on my way.'

We used Ma's bed. For some reason the thought of having Heather's scent in my bed nauseated me. I lay on my back and let Heather gnaw away at me to her heart's content, having a little snigger to myself each time I gave a bit of a heave and all but choked her.

Heather suited me. She was truly basic about sex. It was sex, just sex and none of your romantic crap. There was one small problem: the cow was practically insatiable and could have it umpteen times in one session. I couldn't. Well, maybe I could, but I didn't want it more than once. Not with Heather, anyway. So, after I'd screwed her and shut my ears as best I could to her animal gruntings, I rolled off her and sat on the edge of the bed.

'Oh, don't get up yet,' she said in an absurd dreamy sort of voice which she probably thought was seductive.

'Got to. Got things to do.'

'What things?'

'Things. Besides – to tell the truth, I feel guilty having it off with you now that you're engaged,' I lied magnificently.

I must have sounded convincing. 'Do you really, Marcus?' Heather asked, sitting up and propping herself on one elbow.

'Of course I do. Just think, if you were engaged to me and someone else was knocking you off, how do you think I'd feel?'

'But – '

'So I have to have some feeling for poor old Geoff or whatever-hisnameis, don't I?' I headed for the shower.

'He's away, Marcus.'

'That's not the point.'

I left the bathroom door open as I took my shower. 'He won't *know*,' Heather called.

'*I* know,' I called back, feeling very self-righteous all of a sudden.

She was still sprawled on the bed when I came back into the bedroom.

'Up,' I said, and gave her leathery arse a healthy whack.

'Ouch,' Heather said, but she got up just the same. And blow me down with a hurricane if, while she was still dressing, she didn't start trying to arrange another session. 'Tomorrow?' she asked hopefully.

'No chance. I told you. I've got things to do.'

'You're seeing someone else, aren't you?'

'Yep.'

'Bastard!'

'Yep.'

'Who is she?'

I gave her a lewd grin.

She got quite ratty. 'Tell me, Marcus, who is this bitch?'

'No one you'd know. And it's a fella, actually. Business, Heather. Business. We're not all motivated by just sex, you know.'

The relief on her face was quite touching to behold. 'Phew!' she said.

'In fact, he *might* be coming to stay for a while.'

Heather's eyes lit up.

'Forget it, Heather.'

'I just thought – '

'Yeah, I know what you just thought, but threesomes you can forget as far as I'm concerned.'

'Spoilsport.'

'Have a word with darling Geoffrey. Maybe he's into that sort of crap. You never know. He might just surprise me.'

'Oh, he surprised me all right,' Heather told me. She held up her little finger and wiggled it about. Then she guffawed.

'You can't have everything in this life, my girl.'

'Oh yes I can,' she said and made a lunge for me.

I sidestepped her. 'Piss off Heather. Jesus! Aren't you ever satisfied?'

She shook her head. 'No,' she said frankly.

It was nearly five by the time I got rid of her. She had to have a drink, she said, so I got her one. She had to fix her face, she said, but there was nothing I could do about that: plastic surgery is not one of my strong points. Both of these were ploys to stay with me and maybe seduce me again. In the end I had to get quite rude with her. Not that it mattered. Heather was so thick-skinned it was all but impossible to insult her.

Anyway, she left when I promised I'd phone her the next day, and that I'd let her meet my friend if he came to stay. Some treat in store for old John Farrell, eh?

Abercrombie Terrace was at the back of Bayswater, deceptively pretty with its trees and handsome houses. Dusk helped, of course, because in the dim light you couldn't really see how shabby those houses actually were. You couldn't see the blankets used as curtains or the peeling paintwork. The street reeked of curry and cabbage – at least I think it was cabbage.

I found number twenty-two no bother. Here there weren't even blankets; the windows had been covered in chipboard on the top two floors and with corrugated iron on the lower ones and the basement. The front door, painted Pakistani blue, was well locked, probably barred as well if I knew anything about squatters. I gave it a couple of hefty bangs with my fist. The noise echoed inside the house but that was all that happened. I gave another couple of thumps. Above me a window opened and a head stuck out. I didn't know if it belonged to a long-haired male or a short-haired female. Even after it spoke I didn't know. 'What you want?'

'Looking for John,' I said.

'John who?'

'John Farrell.'

'No one here called that.'

'Pity,' I shouted up. 'Got some stuff for him,' I added, turned on my heel and started to walk away.

'Hang on, hang on,' the head called after me and vanished. It didn't take too long before it was back again. 'Who're you?'

'Never you fucking mind who I am. Does he want the stuff or not?'

'Hang on.'

I was right: there were bars across the door and I could hear them now being removed. Then the door opened. 'You're to come in,' the head said, and showed its body. A flat-chested girl in her late teens, I reckoned.

Christ, it was a dump. I mean, a real dump. There was dog shit all over the place. Old cans, cartons, papers everywhere. A wheelless pram had to be clambered over to get up the stairs. The stairwell had been half painted as though someone had started out with the best intentions in the world and then given up in despair. 'Enjoy life's little luxuries, do you then?' I asked.

DEALING WITH KRANZE 119

Flatchest didn't answer me. Maybe she didn't hear me.

'No comment, eh? Best approach,' I told her.

She ignored me again, but she did open a door on the second landing. Just opened it without a word and continued walking up the next flight of stairs, leaving me to my own devices, I guess.

I peered into the room. It was huge and high and almost bare. There was a small lamp burning in one corner with enough wires coming out of it (across the room and out the window) to suggest it could probably have lit up Blackpool at a push. The mantelpiece had been ripped away from the fireplace, and there was the remnants of a fire in the grate with a blackened saucepan standing nearby. Somewhat over the top home-cooking, I thought. None of your Delia Smith's Summer Puddings here, I shouldn't think. In one corner there was a mattress and on it someone was lying. I say 'lying' since the figure was recumbent, but it was jumping about to such a degree that the peaceful impression the word 'lying' gives is quite misleading.

I moved over to the mattress quietly, almost on tiptoe. I didn't want the turd lying there to take fright and maybe have a go at me with some infected needle. I crouched down. 'John,' I said, assuming a gentle, caring tone. 'John, it's me, Marcus,' I said, taking it for granted he was so delirious he wouldn't have a clue if he'd ever come across a Marcus in his life.

He stopped shaking and stared up at me with huge, haunted eyes. Jesus, I don't think I've ever seen anyone quite so emaciated in my life. Not in the flesh at least. It would have taken Saint Geldof more than a Live Aid to get this ray of sunshine back to anything like normal. I must say, though, that I did feel a small pang of regret. I could see he must have been quite a handsome young chap at one time. My knees began to hurt so I twisted round and sat on the mattress. Farrell gave a start and panic was written all over his face. 'Hey, hey,' I said consolingly. 'Don't panic, pal. I'm only here to help.'

Now don't ask me why but I took hold of one of his hands and stroked it, and I was genuinely moved at the gratitude that shone in his eyes.

'That's better,' I told him. Something told *me* I was going to have to play this a different way than the way I had planned. 'Like I said, I'm only here to help,' I repeated. I wasn't going to get far in these sordid surroundings so I decided to take the plunge. 'Can you walk?' I asked.

Farrell nodded.

'Okay. Come on. Up you get. I'm getting you out of here to start with.'

You'd have thought *that* would have scared the living daylights out of him, wouldn't you. But not a bit of it, and I have to admit I was really proud of myself, proud at my prowess in convincing Farrell that I was all light and sweetness, with only his bloody interest at heart. Okay, I *did* feel sorry for him, but not *that* sorry. I helped him to his feet. 'Don't worry, pal,' I confided. 'I'll look after you,' I assured him, and thought one good thing was that if I wanted to get rid of him for any reason, an overdose would be simple to arrange and arouse no suspicion whatsoever. 'Just put your arm round my shoulder. That's it. Now, off we go.'

I'd parked my BMW at the entrance to the terrace, not wanting to take any chances of having it scratched by some demented yob. I carted Farrell along, and then settled him in the front passenger seat – a mistake, as I discovered as soon as I got in beside him: he stank to high heaven although I hadn't noticed it with the stench of the squat being even more overwhelming. I lowered all four electric windows. 'Nothing like some fresh air to clear the head,' I told him, just in case he took umbrage. Not that he was capable of taking umbrage, or anything else for that matter. He had reached a sort of zombie stage which was just as well since Christ alone knows what I would have done if he'd started acting up, getting violent or frenetic or something.

We got back to the house without incident, thank God. In fact, Farrell hardly moved a muscle all the way. I think he was sleeping but he could have passed out. One way or another, he was quiet as a lamb, which was fine. I put the car in the garage, and opened the connecting door to the house before rousing him. Just as well I did since he started flailing about as soon as he came to, shouting at me, cursing someone else he thought he could see in the garage. It was quite difficult restraining him since there was surprising strength in those skinny limbs of his. But drugs do that to you, don't they? That's what I've heard anyway. Give you strength way beyond your normal capacity. But restrain him I did, and calm him down, and manage to get him into the house.

My first thought was to get the stinking sod into a bath, batter him over the head if needs be just so long as I could clean him up a bit and stifle the smell. Easier said than done, of course. I think he'd forgotten what a bath was for, because he started to panic again when I sat him on the bathroom stool and ran the water. 'It's okay,' I had to keep telling him over and over. When the bath was full I emptied about half a bottle of Dettol into it, caring not one bloody whit if it burned his balls off, and a good dollop of some cheap, overpowering aftershave some prat had given me God alone knows how many Christmases ago. Then I helped him strip off.

Luckily I'd had the foresight to bring a binbag up to the bathroom with me and I was able to put each article of clothing directly into it, smothering the smell, smothering any fucking creepy crawlies that might have been courting in the material. I really gagged when it came to his feet, though. I swear by all that's holy he can't have had those trainers off in months. His feet were quite literally stuck inside them, and it took some heaving and puffing and twisting to get them out. Instantly I wished I'd left them in. His feet were all sores and blisters and the cotton from his socks had eaten into the flesh. Right, I thought. 'You stay there,' I told him, and off I went downstairs to get a plastic basin from the kitchen.

When I got back upstairs he was lolling about, swaying to and fro on the stool, singing a stupid little ditty to himself. 'Okay, Pavarotti,' I said. 'Put your feet in that.'

Farrell obediently put his stinking feet in the basin, looking a little puzzled. I soon knocked the puzzlement of his face, though, when I poured a full bottle of TCP in on top of his feet.

At first he seemed to just wonder where the pain was coming from. Then he realised the pain was actually hurting him. Then it dawned on him that the pain hurting him was in his feet, and he gave a sort of howl and tried to curl up his knees, removing his feet from the stinging liquid.

'Oh no you don't,' I told him, and pushed his knees straight.

He gave me a bewildered look.

'It's just so we get any germs killed off,' I explained, suddenly thinking those fetid socks were going to have to come off too. Well, he could bloody well do that himself.

To give him his due, Farrell *did* get the socks off himself, taking half the skin off his feet with them 'tis true, but what's half a pound of skin between pals? And he certainly looked a lot better after his bath. Looked semi-human anyway.

'Feeling better?' I asked.

He gave me a toothy smile and I was amazed at how clean and bright and white his teeth were. Maybe he'd been chewing on bones or something. 'Yeah. Much. Thanks,' he said. A man of few words, clearly.

'Good. Now it's bed for you, my lad.'

While he was having his bath I'd dragged Ma's mattress off her bed and manoeuvred it into my room. I put it on the floor so that it was in the furthest corner from the door, and just in case Farrell felt like going walkies during the night he'd have to get past my bed first.

I lent him a pair of my boxer-shorts (gave them to him, really, since I'd no intention of donning them again after they'd been in contact with his deranged testicles) and a T-shirt. He was appropriately grateful. 'Thanks,' he said and put them on. He then said something which I couldn't understand. I'd forgotten, of course, that the git was a bloody Glaswegian, hadn't I, and I don't believe anyone understands the Glaswegians except maybe fellow Glaswegians. But I didn't want to get into any sort of interpreting act at that time of night. 'Look, we'll talk in the morning – okay?'

He seemed agreeable enough to that. 'Aye.'

'Bed then,' I ordered and pointed to the mattress.

Farrell crawled in and lay back with a grateful sigh.

'Okay?'

'Fine.'

And, would you believe it, he went to sleep like a babe in arms and was snoring his wee Scots head off in two seconds flat.

There was one discovery I was pleased about: Farrell wasn't as full of holes as a fucking sieve as Stuart Bean had maintained. In fact he hadn't a hole in him apart from the normal orifices. So maybe he wasn't needling it after all. Maybe it was just tablets and the like. That would certainly make things easier from my point of view. His speed habit I knew about from Kranze and he hadn't, as far as I could see, been injecting that. He could have been snorting it, of course, but his snout seemed okay. So he was probably just swallowing it, and I could handle that. All in all, the next day looked like being interesting to say the least.

THIRTEEN

And it certainly turned out to be.

I didn't get to sleep until pretty late. Would you, with a snoring druggy on the floor by your bed? A bloody Glaswegian druggy to boot. I think I dozed off about four in the morning and didn't wake up until after nine. Woke up is putting it mildly. I shot up in my bed hearing what sounded like a steel band rehearsing in the kitchen. Clearly Farrell had managed to slip past without waking me. I leapt out of bed and ran to the kitchen, overlooking the fact that I hadn't a stitch on.

Ma had been very fond of her copper pots and she'd hung them in a neat row from a beam in the kitchen. I was fond of them, too, and since I knew Ma couldn't really do much more than boil an egg I'd persuaded her to leave them behind – just in case I decided to do a course in cordon bleu cooking, I said. Well, John Farrell, bright-eyed and bushy-tailed, was standing underneath the pots hammering out something like the Anvil Chorus from *Il Trovatore* with a wooden spoon. I was so relieved I saw the comical side of it. 'Some bloody alarm clock you are,' I told him, taking a towel from the drying rail and wrapping it round my waist.

'Oh, sorry, pal,' Farrell said. 'Don't know why I – they just looked like they were there for the hitting. Made some porridge,' he told me.

'Porridge?' I couldn't believe it – not just the fact that he'd made it but that Ma had the stuff in the house at all. Far too common and working class for Ma, I would have thought. Unless she'd had an aberration of some kind.

'Yeah. Like porridge, don't you?'

'Can't say I've ever had it.'

'Never had porridge? You haven't lived, pal.'

It was remarkable what a bath and a good night's sleep had done for John Farrell. Certainly he was a bit twitchy and jumpy, but apart from that you'd never have guessed he was an addict. Mind you, I wasn't going to let myself be lulled into any false sense of security with him. I'd known enough junkies in prison to be well aware of their nasty little traits. No, I was going to keep a close eye on John Farrell; and perhaps while I was thinking this, I *did* overdo the staring.

This made Farrell stare back, and maybe he was seeing me for the first time. 'Did you tell me last night that I knew you?' he asked suddenly.

'Yeah.'

'I don't – '

'I lied,' I admitted.

Surprisingly, this confession didn't faze him one whit. I thought for a moment he hadn't heard me, being so engrossed in the complicated culinary art of slopping water in on top of oats. But, as I was to learn, this was just his way. He took a long time thinking about what was said, but whether this was because he was a methodical soul or just thick, I still don't know.

'Any salt?' he asked. Not the question I was expecting.

'Yep. In the cupboard over your head.'

He took out the salt-cellar and poured enough of the stuff into the pot to compete with the North Sea. Then he stirred the mess with a spoon. 'Why?' he wanted to know now.

'Why what?'

'Why'd you lie?'

'Well, it was only half a lie. I hadn't met you but I had heard about you.'

'Oh,' he said and set his mind in motion to have a think about that. 'From who?' he asked eventually.

I didn't really want to get into that conversation just yet, not when faced with the prospect of having to down the mess of pottage he was creating. Besides, I wanted to have his full attention, whatever that might turn out to be, when I broached the subject of Kranze. 'I'll tell you all about it after you've eaten.'

That appeared to be a plan he could live with. 'Okay, pal,' he said, turning his head and giving me an understanding smile.

There was, however, something about the smile that prompted me to ask, 'You all right?'

That didn't take much thinking about, apparently. 'Never better,' he answered immediately.

I couldn't know for certain, naturally, but I sensed that he had told me the absolute truth: he had truthfully never been better. And that touched me. It also explained why he could so calmly accept the fact that he was with someone he didn't know, in a house he didn't know. And being streetwise, as I presumed he would have to be, he would have known you get nothing for nothing in this beautiful world, yet whatever payment I might be thinking of exacting didn't seem to cause him any concern. I suppose when you've been abused and used all your life you simply go with the flow: take what's given to you and make the payments without complaint. And I realised then that I could have this geek eating out of my hand in no time at all. 'What was that?' I asked as I heard his voice penetrate my thoughts.

'Your name. What's your name?'

'Oh. Marcus. Marcus Walwyn.'

'I'm John Farrell,' he told me, forgetting I must have already known that. He left the spoon balanced on the edge of the pot and came across to the table. Then he shook hands with me in a very dignified way. 'Nice to meet you,' he said.

I really wanted to laugh, but I didn't. 'Nice to meet you, too,' I told him, which was almost the truth. It wasn't nice but it was, I hoped, going to be useful.

Anyway, he served up the porridge and started wolfing it down. I tasted a little and nearly puked. I began to understand why the Scots have the highest rate of heart disease in Europe. Christ, it was no wonder they all ate chips and pies if this was what was supposed to be their national diet.

When Farrell had scraped his plate clean he eyed mine dolefully. 'Not like it?' he asked, but there was no disappointment or rebuke in his voice.

'I don't actually eat breakfast,' I told him. 'But the bit I tasted was pretty good.'

'You mind?' he asked, and before I could answer, before, in fact, I had fathomed what he was on about, he had reached over, taken my plate and was consuming my leftovers with gusto, looking up from time to time to bathe me in a well-fed smile.

Surprisingly, Pissquick put in an appearance, scouting the table, giving Farrell (and myself for that matter) a wide berth but keeping his eyes on us. Farrell spotted him between shovels and gave him a good hard stare. Whether he was sizing up Pissquick as a potential main course or whether it was because he'd never seen quite such an exotic Persian I know not. Mind you, Farrell's eyes were pretty peculiar also, so they made quite a pair ogling each other. And I suppose it said something for Farrell's generosity because instead of eating all the porridge he kept a little and scraped that into Pissquick's bowl. That suited me, I can tell you. If it had nearly poisoned me it might just finish the job on Pissquick. Alas, the wretched cat had more sense than to attempt to even taste it. One sniff was enough, and then, tail held high in lofty arrogance, he stalked off whence he had come.

While Farrell washed up and tidied up the mess he had made, I fixed us both some coffee. I'd forgotten to get milk, of course, but I reckoned that Farrell wouldn't mind. He'd accept anything gratefully. And even if he didn't, that was his tough shit.

We sat at the table in silence drinking our coffee, me wondering what would be the best way to bring up the subject of Kranze, and he – well, who knows what was going on in his pickled mind. I'd lent him some clothes – jeans, an old top I no longer wore, and some socks. He had a mild attack of coughing and spilt some coffee on the top. His reaction was astonishing. It was the closest thing to panic I'd ever seen. Like I was God and he'd committed a whopping mortal sin right before my eyes. 'Oh, I'm sorry, pal. I'm sorry,' he all but whimpered, trying to wipe away the stain with his sleeve. 'I'm sorry, I'm sorry,' he went on and on, almost in tears.

'Shit, don't worry,' I told him.

But no, 'I'm sorry, I'm sorry.'

I could see these apologies taking up the rest of the morning so, in a fit of desperation, I said, 'Take the damn thing off.'

He took it off and handed it to me. With considerable aplomb I ripped the stupid top to shreds. 'I've got a hundred of those,' I told him with some exaggeration.

Now the tears really did well up in his eyes. For one horrible moment I thought he was going to use my shoulder to cry on. 'I'll get you another one,' I said, and dashed upstairs. Luckily, when I came back down, he seemed to have recovered his composure. He accepted the Adidas sweatshirt and pulled it on, stroking it like he might have stroked Pissquick if the cat wasn't such a hostile brute. But I noticed he took inordinate care when drinking his coffee again, holding one hand under his chin to catch any drips. Couldn't see myself taking this one to the Savoy.

'You don't have a fag, do you?' Farrell asked while I was recalling the fact that I'd taken Karen to the Savoy, remembering how thrilled she'd been to be mixing with the nobs as she put it.

'Eh? No. No. 'Fraid not. I don't smoke.'

'No bother,' he told me although I could see it was very much a bother.

Then, out of the blue, a little incident came to mind. More than a little incident, really. A flaming row I'd had with Ma. One of her more obnoxious friends had been to visit and had left her trademark of ashes and cigarette butts in almost every room in the house – the old house in Balham, that is, not this one. Ma's excuse for letting the old bag contaminate our house was what infuriated me. 'But I couldn't very well ask her not to, darling. She was a guest.'

I exploded. 'For Christ's sake, Ma. It's *our* house, not hers. She should have some respect for the way we live.'

'But, darling – '

'If she wants to choke her stupid self to death that's her look-out but she's no right coming in here and leaving her cancerous germs behind her.'

'It was only a few cigarettes, dear,' Ma said defensively.

'A few packets more like.'

'Oh, no,' Ma insisted. 'I can tell you *exactly* how many she smoked,' she went on with a note of triumph and went to her desk. From one of the drawers she pulled out a pack of Marlboro. 'She opened this packet when she arrived,' Ma informed me and then started to count the remaining cigarettes. 'And there's twelve left.'

'Eight fucking cigarettes – '

'Marcus please don't swear. It's – '

Anyway, the upshot of it was that Ma stormed off, taking the offending cigarettes with her.

Months later I'd come across the packet tucked into a fancy old tea-caddy Ma kept because she liked the pictures on it. I counted the cigarettes. There were only ten, so Ma had either lied to me or she was having the odd puff herself on the sly.

Anyway, I wondered if she had left the caddy behind her and if the fags might still be in it. 'Hang on a tick,' I told Farrell. 'You might be in luck.'

His luck *was* in. I found the caddy under the stairs and the dry, crispy Marlboros were still there. 'Here you go,' I told Farrell, tossing the packet onto the table. 'Don't know what they'll taste like,' I admitted, opening the kitchen window. 'Been here donkey's years,' I concluded, getting a box of Swan Vestas from the drawer and tossing those onto the table too.

'Cheers, pal,' Farrell said as happily as if I'd told him he'd won the bloody Lottery.

I let him suck away on his cigarette for a while: four draws and it seemed to be finished. He economically lit another one from the first before stubbing it out, giving me a shy grin into the bargain. I shook my head at him just to underline my disapproval, and maybe it was to sidestep any recrimination I might have had in mind that he asked, 'Why'd you bring me here?'

I cleared my throat. I furrowed my brow. 'I want to talk to you, John,' I said seriously.

That clearly surprised him. It made him give me a coy and disbelieving look, too, since it was obviously not the usual reason given him when some strange man took him home for the night. I generously decided to overlook the implications of his gaze. And then, when it dawned on him that I might, genuinely, just want to talk to him about something, Farrell asked, ''Bout what?'

It's not like me to dodge the issue but for once I felt it was the sagacious thing to do. For a while at any rate. A circuitous route towards hitting him with the name of Kranze (or Zanker as he would certainly have known him) seemed to be in order. I decided to take a chance and be reasonable. 'First things first,' I said. 'Let me tell you a bit about myself to begin with.'

And I told him bits about myself, bits that would be of interest to him and hopefully useful to me. I told him I'd been inside for murder and it was wonderful to behold how all the old prison training made him respond to that snippet of news with an admiring look. I told him how I had got out on appeal, hinting that the clout I had was so terrific that I'd been able to get a shyster to fiddle things for me. Farrell's admiration grew apace. And when I felt he was sufficiently in awe of me I confided that the only reason I'd been sent down in the first place was because some bastard had grassed on me. Not strictly true, of course, but I didn't want to confuse the poor idiot by involving his brain in the ramifications of what had actually happened. His reaction to that was just what I'd hoped for. Quite venomous. 'Bastard,' he said, and those Pissquick eyes of his gleamed with a lust for revenge. Revenge on my behalf, which was touching. 'Know who he was?'

'Oh, yes. I know him.' I decided to take the plunge. 'So do you as a matter of fact.'

'Me?' he asked, suddenly alarmed, perhaps thinking that I was going to accuse him of being involved in the grassery, if that's what you call it.

I gave him a reassuring smile, nodded, 'He did the dirty on you too, I think.'

He was obviously getting very confused. And he started to get jumpy again which worried me. 'It's all right,' I told him, reaching out and giving his arm a little pat. 'Calm down,' I added. 'There's nothing for you to worry about.' I said a few more comforting words as well, but I don't remember what they were. I was only playing for time anyway. I knew that once I mentioned Zanker's name I would be fully committed and I wasn't sure yet if such a commitment with Jumpy John Farrell involved was the greatest idea in the world. But, there you go, chances have to be taken and I realised that it was now or never as they say. 'Name Zanker mean anything to you?' I asked, not looking directly at him but watching him out of the corner of my eye.

I don't rightly know what reaction I expected, but it sure as hell wasn't the one I got. I know it's a really naff expression but I honestly have to say that the full gamut of emotions slithered across John Farrell's haggard face. But as they did, he sat dead still. Not a muscle moved. Then his lips started to shudder and little flecks of spittle oozed out at the edges of his mouth. Then he jumped to his feet sending his chair clattering across the kitchen. He stared down at me with such hatred in his eyes I wondered if he was seeing me as the devil incarnate. 'Zanker,' he hissed, literally spitting the name.

'Know him, eh?'

Farrell didn't answer. He turned away from me and walked to the sink, staring out of the small window over it. And as he stared he kept thumping the sink with both fists.

'Take it easy,' I told him. 'They cost good money, sinks do,' I added, hoping a little levity might calm the situation. 'Come back and sit down,' I then said, allowing a sterner note to come into my voice.

Obediently Farrell gathered up his chair, placed it back at the table, and sat down. He was breathing as if he'd just run a marathon.

'I take it you *do* know him?' I asked.

Farrell didn't seem capable of talking for the moment. But he nodded, and I was surprised just how much detestation he could get into a nod.

'Pal of yours?' Well, if looks could kill I was a goner there and then, but at least Farrell started breathing normally again. I pretended to be baffled. 'Look, John boy, tell me if I've got this wrong but I've been told you and Zanker were, well – you know – pretty close when you were both inside.'

That certainly did the trick. It opened the proverbial floodgates and the whole tirade was landed in my lap. And it was exactly what I had longed to hear. I won't bore you with the sordid details, but in a nutshell it transpired that while Kranze might have had dubiously genuine feelings of fondness for Farrell, Farrell loathed Zanker, loathed him with a passion. Why? Well, according to St John, Kranze had taken his pleasure, if you get my drift, by supplying Farrell with the drugs he so desperately needed. It was, in truth, a classic prison situation. A question of supply and demand. A question of supply *on* demand as far as these two lovebirds were concerned. Alas for Farrell, his need for drugs was greater than any macho feeling he had to protect his arsehole. And so, over the years, Kranze had degraded the poor weak moron, probably blissfully unaware of the hatred that was building up inside him. Jesus, I couldn't wait for the two of them to meet!

There was a strange silence in the kitchen when Farrell had completed his pathetic little tale; strange because I could feel that he was waiting for me to tell him not to worry, that everything would be taken care of, that I didn't blame him, that we were both in the same boat in a manner of speaking. So, it was strange because that silence was filled with a pleading anticipation, although I couldn't honestly understand why Farrell appeared to need my – well, my approbation so badly. I gave it to him anyway. 'Hey,' I said, giving him another friendly pat, on the shoulder this time. 'I understand,' I assured him. 'I know just what fucking Zanker is like. I know how he uses people.'

Farrell gave me a look of undying gratitude.

'That's why I went to a lot of trouble to find you.'

That woke him up.

'I want you to help me get my own back on Zanker. Just the two of us. We could do it, you know.'

But such was the power Kranze still seemed to hold over Farrell he looked dubious. So then I had to go into further details. Tell him about Kranze's book for one thing. Tell him how I could visit him at any time without suspicion. Tell him Kranze actually had the nerve to think I'd forgiven him. I really laid it on thick. And, as a final twist, I said, 'You know he dedicated his book to you, don't you? To John Speed, actually. Taking the piss out of you right up to the end,' I made sure to mention, just in case he decided to get flattered by the dedication and feel that, maybe, Kranze wasn't such a shit after all.

But I needn't have worried. Farrell wasn't, it became clear, the forgiving kind, not when it came to buggery anyway. 'How?' he asked.

'How can we get our own back? That what you mean?'

Farrell nodded.

'Ah. Well. That's something you and I will have to work out, isn't it?'

For the first time John Farrell gave me a smile that was genuinely sincere, not one of those alternative smiles that he had learned to switch on and off as the occasion demanded. It told me we had a deal.

'Right,' I said, getting businesslike. 'Now, you've got to be straight with me. What do you need?'

Farrell gawped at me before shrugging his shoulders and asking, 'Need?'

'What are you on?'

'Oh,' he answered, and produced one of his 'I'm not all bad, you know', phoney smiles. 'Anything.'

'You mean everything?'

I'd insulted him, apparently. 'No,' he denied. 'Not everything. Don't touch heroin no more. Just stuff, you know.'

'I don't. That's why I'm asking.' I was pleased heroin wasn't going to be a problem. It might have been tricky getting that, but most other stuff I knew I could pick up, and I wanted Farrell dependent on something until I was finished with him.

All of a sudden he became shy. 'Well, jellies,' he said. 'Vallies – '
'Hang on. Jellies?'
'Temazepam – you know, tranquillisers.'
'And Vallies are valium, right?'
'Yeah.'
So far so good. 'What else?'
'Speed.'
'Of course. Speed,' I said. 'Could you manage on just jellies and vallies, though?' I asked, slipping with alacrity into the terminology.
'Could manage on just jellies. Maybe with a wee bit of hash too,' he told me.
'Okay. Tell you what we'll do. You can stay here until we decide what to do and I'll get you enough hash and jellies to satisfy your craving. But – ' I paused here before issuing my warning just to make sure it penetrated a brain already cluttered with the prospect of free drugs, '– but I don't want you going on any binges, right? I'll only give you enough to keep you happy, not so much that you're out of your tiny mind morning noon and night. Agreed?'

By this stage Farrell would have agreed to anything, so as a sign of good faith I went upstairs and cut enough for three joints off my stash of red seal cannabis. I gave it to Farrell along with a packet of cigarette papers, and leaned back to watch him skin up, just in case the bastard front-loaded it. Just as well I'd found the Marlboro, I thought, and made a mental note to buy another pack in case I needed a joint later in private.

In fact, he made a good job of rolling the joint. He offered it to me first, but with a wave of my hand I let him have the first few draws. Immediately the last of his jitters vanished. He passed it to me. The thought of hygiene did cross my mind but I knew this was an important little ceremony for Farrell. It was, if you like, a bonding. One shared joints with mates, with those one can trust, and I certainly wanted Farrell to trust me or I'd never get anywhere.

No doubt you must be thinking I had taken leave of my senses having John Farrell to stay, especially since I'd have to leave him at home alone when I went to work. The thought did cross my mind. But chances had to be taken, and anyway, I had concluded that Farrell wasn't all that untrustworthy. I reckoned as long as he had enough of his jellies and hash he'd behave himself and not steal from me or wreck the place. And that's exactly how it turned out. He behaved himself admirably. He cleaned the house. He mastered the art of heating pre-cooked meals. He just about fawned on me, bless him. For a week we lived as happily and as amicably as any odd couple can, and a week is a long time not only in politics. Alas, all good things have to come to an end. Terminally, for some of the unlucky ones.

FOURTEEN

On 1 September I completed my editing of *A Letter from Chile*. With some satisfaction, I might add. Not that I was particularly proud of the job I'd done – it was excellent, but that was only to be expected. My satisfaction derived from the awareness that I could now well and truly don my Machiavellian hat and start my manoeuvres rolling, if you can say that. I had devised my strategy without any help from Farrell, who was so chuffed to be living in the lap of relative luxury with the majority of his needs supplied that he seemed to have forgotten why he was there in the first place. A short, sharp shock was what he needed, obviously. A little bringing down to earth. But not just yet. First I had to orchestrate proceedings. I had to get Kranze in the right frame of mind. I had to feed titbits to Birt. I had to get all of them slightly on tenterhooks, keyed up, their minds prepared to accept some things at face value. Their mutual dislike of each other would certainly help there. In fact, when I thought about it, I was mildly astonished to discover that *modus operandi* was based on nothing less than pure and simple hatred. And hatred is a grand thing to have on your side. Makes people genuinely blind. Which is why I'm lucky. Sure, there have been moments when I've hated Birt and Kranze, but I know I can switch it off and control it.

'I'm going to see our friend tomorrow,' I announced to Farrell when I got home in the evening, and when I saw him stiffen I added, 'By myself,' and he relaxed. 'You don't have to be afraid of him, you know,' I said. 'Not any more,' I added, making it sound all buddy-buddy.

'Not afraid of him,' Farrell protested, albeit half-heartedly.

''Course not.'

'I'm not.'

'That's what I said – 'course you're not.'

I was, though. Scared out of my knickers of Kranze and I think that's what gave me the edge. Self-preservation: nothing like it to make one careful.

'And once I've seen him, you and me, we're going to have to sit down and have a wee talk.'

Farrell nodded.

I wanted him to answer me properly. 'All right?'

'Yes.'

Good. Psychologically that was important, or so I told myself.

'I hope you're properly appreciative of the fact that I've sacrificed my Saturday off to come and see you,' I told Kranze.

He peered at me balefully. 'Most kind. Most kind,' he muttered with undisguised sarcasm.

We spent until lunchtime going through the manuscript, me explaining the changes I'd made, him bitching or agreeing but, in fact, *always* agreeing in the end. I was knackered when we'd finished. I leaned back in the chair and rubbed my eyes while Kranze wandered over to a cabinet in the corner and returned with two tiny glasses of sloe gin. 'Wow, really pushed the boat out, haven't you?' I said. 'Cheers,' I added before he could come back with any sardonic retort. I swallowed the drink in one gulp and felt it ease through my body. 'Good, that,' I told him, and held out my glass. Reluctantly, as if I was asking for his life's blood, Kranze pottered about giving me a refill. 'You really mean that – that killing can become a habit?'

Kranze left me at the table and walked across to his armchair. 'Yes,' he said quietly as he lowered himself. 'Yes,' he repeated, more emphatically, when he was seated.

'Interesting theory,' I said. I took a sip of sloe gin. 'If it *is* only a *theory*, of course.'

Kranze didn't answer. He looked very gloomy, as though something was preying on his mind, so I decided to have a bit of fun.

'I agree with you, of course, that it's very pleasurable. Killing. Very pleasurable indeed. I remember the pleasure I got from it anyway. I – '

Suddenly Kranze hurled his glass into the fireplace, smashing it to smithereens. I was sorely tempted to follow suit and shout *dos vedanya!* or whatever it is the Russians say, but figured that might be going too far.

'What's up, doc?' I asked instead. But Kranze ignored me, possibly because he wasn't in any condition to respond. His hands were shaking. His face had an odd bluish tinge to it. He was having trouble breathing. Oh, Christ, I thought. The shit's going to die of a heart attack with me in the room. Fuck that for a lark. I went over to him and loosened his collar. I put a cushion behind his thick, bristly neck. I was petrified I was going to have to give him the kiss of life but he could keel over and die before I did that, I can honestly say. But it didn't come to that. Slowly he recovered, recovered enough to point to the mantelpiece, to the container of pills that stood there. I gave them to him, and he popped a couple into his mouth.

'Okay?' I asked.

He nodded, and gesticulated to give him a minute.

I gave him five. 'Frightened the shit out of me, you did,' I told him. 'Can't have you kicking the bucket on me now.'

'I get them from time to time.'

'Yeah, well, send me a postcard the next time you're going to have one and I'll stay well away.' And then I had an impish thought. 'Unless you're *planning* to drop dead with me here and have me blamed. That wouldn't be it by any chance?'

Even Kranze had to try and laugh at that. 'It is appealing,' he managed to say.

'Oh, very. You sure you're all right?'

He nodded.

'Right enough to stand some good news?'

Kranze got a suspicious tinge in his eye, but he nodded anyway.

'I think I might know where your pal John Speed is.'

Now, whether it was the effects of the sloe gin, which I doubt, or whether it was the attack he'd just suffered that was to blame, I don't know, but suddenly I saw a side of Kranze that absolutely dumbfounded me. And it was pretty grotesque, I can tell you. There he was, this small, fat, murderous brute on his knees before me, all but slavering, as he mouthed over and over again, 'Where? Where? Where?' Gone to pieces he had, and I was none too happy about it. I made to stand up but he grabbed me by the knees in a fair imitation of Will Carling. 'Tell me, Marcus. Please tell me.'

I sat back down with a thud. Jesus! 'I don't *know*,' I all but shouted at him. 'I said I *might* know, that's all. For Christ's sake, Kranze, will you get up off your knees and stop acting like a moron!'

It must only then have dawned on him that he was acting a bit strange. He released my legs and stood up. He brushed himself down. He ran a hand over the top of his head as though smoothing his long-since dearly departed hair. 'I'm sorry, Marcus.'

So was I. 'That's okay,' I told him.

'You really think you might know?'

'Might,' I stressed.

'Where?'

'I don't *know* exactly where. Listen, leave it with me. When – if – I do find out for certain I'll let you know.'

'You promise?'

'Cross my heart,' I said, not adding 'and hope to die' since that could prove apposite with Kranze involved.

'How soon – '

'In a day or so. A week at most.'

Well, Kranze was primed, I told myself as I drove back from Cricklewood. A gay little Vivaldi number shared my mood. Next on the list was Birt: appropriately the Vivaldi ended and a particularly pedantic Orff composition trounced the airwaves. But Birt would be tricky. He was a shrewd enough old bod for all his seeming haphazardness and benign façade. He was well capable of lulling one into a false sense of security, making one less fastidious about details than one should be. Still, I was confident I could handle him. And that was why I resolved to have him round to see me again. Mentally I chose which carrots I was going to dangle on the end of the string, if you get my meaning, and, as if by magic, a fault developed in the Orff CD and they had to substitute it with Wagner. Much better. Much more apt now that I was feeling victoriously cheerful again.

Of course Farrell was all agog to know what had taken place between Kranze and me. He'd heated up some Marks and Spencer chicken Kiev although how he guessed I'd be ravenous at three in the afternoon was beyond me. Maybe I was letting him get to know me too well.

'Problems,' I told him.

He stopped dishing up the chicken and stared at me.

'Nothing too serious, I don't think, but a problem nevertheless. Thanks,' I said and took a sniff at the food. It didn't smell too bad. I tasted it. Didn't taste too bad either. A bit cardboardy, I suppose, but what could you expect?

'What problems?'

I wasn't sure how to put it. I gave a little laugh before saying, 'Well, I think the old bastard is still in love with you,' and when Farrell made a move which suggested he might be about to hurl his meal across the room I grabbed his arm and added, 'He's just fucking crazy, that's all,' which, of course, might or might not have been true. Depends how you define crazy.

'He just fucking used me,' Farrell insisted on telling me.

'Yeah, well, we all get used from time to time.'

'I never even took drugs till I went inside and got mixed up with him.'

Now, that was a revelation. 'You mean Kranze – Zanker – got you started on drugs?'

Farrell nodded sorrowfully. 'Got me hooked and then wouldn't give me any if I didn't – you know.'

'Life's a bitch,' I told him. 'But don't worry. Every dog has his day, and it'll be yours before you know it.'

'You mean that?'

'Oh, boy, do I mean it!'

'Jesus, Marcus, you're the greatest,' Farrell informed me and for one horrible moment I thought he was going to embrace me. 'You're the only one who understands.'

Well, it wasn't a question of understanding. Not as far as I was concerned. To tell the truth, rape has always struck me as being a somewhat overrated misdemeanour. I mean, I ask you, how threatening can some looney with a six-inch penis be for God's sake? Much worse, *I* would have thought, would be to be disfigured, have your face all carved up. Okay, if I was into that sort of thing, I suppose the sight of my *twelve* inches might cause some mild alarm, but when it was over it'd be over with no visible signs to have to live with. And as for all that psychological damage the quacks go on about. Come off it! But that's half the trouble with the world. All the whingeing and moaning that goes on instead of simply getting on with the business of living.

'Sure I understand,' I told Farrell, sounding nice and sympathetic. 'It must have been terrible for you.'

I shouldn't have said that. It gave Farrell the opportunity he'd been waiting for to 'unload' himself, to pour out his stupid little heart, and, boy, did he go to town. He dumped everything in my lap: his miserable childhood, his bullying stepfather, his loneliness on the streets of Glasgow, Manchester, Leeds and London, and then, as an appropriate climax, the fat lady really started to sing. I got the full bit about the loss of his manhood at the hands of Kranze. I didn't really listen all that closely, though, because something was nagging me: Kranze had told me Farrell was in prison for selling drugs, yet Farrell had told me that Kranze had started him off on drugs.

I waited until he had finished his heart-rending confessions, and then said, 'Mind if I ask you something? What were you sent down for in any case?'

Farrell shut his mouth, and gave me a shifty look.

'I mean, I don't *care* why you were locked up. Just curious. You don't have to tell me if you don't want to.'

Farrell kept looking at me.

'Zanker told me you were in for dealing drugs,' I told him, just to see if that would goad him into an answer.

'Nothing to do with drugs,' Farrell said angrily. 'Told you, I never touched drugs till fucking Zanker got me into them.'

'Oh, yeah, so you did.'

There was another unpregnant pause and I was beginning to think that Farrell had wandered off into one of his dazes when, out of the blue, he asked, 'You ever been starving?'

'Peckish sometimes,' I admitted. 'Can't say I've ever been close to actually starving though.' I wondered up what sordid back alley I was about to be led. 'Why?' I asked.

'I have,' Farrell said. 'Been really starving.'

I still couldn't fathom why this lack of nutrition was being brought up, but I decided I better play along. I shook my head as though it was the most awful bit of news I'd had in a long time. 'That's terrible.'

'Makes you do anything. Makes you do things you'd never think of doing if you'd got a full belly.'

Delicately put. 'I'm sure it does.'

'Makes you really humiliate yourself.'

Wow, a four-syllable word from the Scots git. Christ alone knows where he'd culled that one from. Probably from another mad social worker doing her bit again. 'Makes you lose your dignity,' Farrell added. Definitely social-worker jargon, this. I'd heard them in prison – social workers, I mean. They have a few stock phrases they love to trot out. The word 'dignity' is hot favourite since it covers a multitude of sins. 'The most important thing,' they tell you as you come close to finishing your prison sentence, 'is for you to regain your dignity.' Which is a laugh when you think that the most important thing to most prisoners on the point of release is the possibility of a good shag and a pint of Tennents. But, 'Yeah, I can see how it would,' I lied to Farrell since I couldn't see any such thing. You've got to have some dignity before you can lose it, and Farrell, in my book, had as much dignity as a pile of dog shit.

'Makes you dirty,' Farrell now said with a shudder, as though lice were holding a barn dance on his skin.

I was getting bored. 'So does coal-mining,' I reminded him, and stood up as if to terminate his recollections.

And then, in a flurry of words, he confessed to me why he'd been sent down. I still don't know why he'd felt it necessary to make such a song and dance about it. Happens every day of the week. Quite simply, he'd been starving and he'd gone with this old pervert he'd met somewhere in Soho. After they'd done 'the business', as he coyly put it, a Hugh Granter in the back of the homo's car, there'd been a tiff about the payment agreed, and Farrell had knifed his client. Not killed him, mind, just stuck the knife in his guts and given it a bit of a twist. I didn't even bother to enquire as to why Farrell was carrying a knife in the first place because what he was telling me was music to my ears. Suddenly he was a blood-brother, so to speak.

'Should have got yourself paid *before* delivering the goods,' I told him.

'I know that now.'

'Good. There you go – you've learned something.' There was something *I* wanted to learn. 'Tell me, how did you feel after you'd done it? Knifed the bastard?'

Farrell shrugged. 'Felt nothing,' he told me.

Just what I wanted to hear. 'Nothing? Nothing at all?'

'Can't remember feeling anything.'

'Bet you were scared gutless,' I suggested.

Farrell bridled. 'No I fucking wasn't,' he shouted a bit too aggressively for my liking. 'Shit deserved it.'

'I'm not arguing that. But you must have felt *something*.'

'No.'

So now I had to ask, 'Do it again would you?'

'If I had to.'

Bless his little cotton socks – my little cotton socks to be exact. I'd found out what I needed to know so I made light of it. 'Have to keep an eye on you then, won't I?' I said, wandering across the kitchen and, for some reason, letting my eyes rest on the neat row of kitchen knives.

Poor old Farrell sounded horrified when he answered, 'Christ, Marcus, I'd never do anything to you.'

I swung round and faced him. 'Glad to hear it,' I told him with a grin.

'You're the only one who – ' he began, but I cut him short. I wasn't in the mood for hearing what a wonderful chap I was. 'Do anything for you, I would,' Farrell promised me.

I could hardly contain my pleasure. 'I'll remember that,' I said, and went over to him and tousled his hair in a very friendly way.

'Anything. Just you ask me and I'll do it.'

'I'll remember that,' I said again. I fully intended to.

Things were going swimmingly.

That evening Ma phoned me from Italy. She was having a whale of a time. Or so she said. Having taken the big step and married Harry, Ma wouldn't have been beyond telling the odd fib if things weren't working out as planned; she'd do that just to prove she hadn't made a ghastly mistake.

But all I could do was take her at her word. 'That's great, Ma. You go for it, hear? Let your hair down and show 'em.'

Ma tittered down the phone.

'Is Harry behaving himself?' I asked.

'Harry's just wonderful.'

'Oh, Mr Wonderful is he now?'

Ma tittered again. 'He's terribly sweet,' she said.

Yuk.

'And how are things with you, darling?'

'Fine. Fine. Got a friend staying, actually. Keeping me company.'

'Oh, anyone I know?'

'No. Someone from work,' I lied. 'Lease ran out on his flat so I'm letting him stay while he looks for another.'

'Oh, you *are* kind, dear.' Then, typical Ma, she decided to tell me she didn't like that answering-machine. 'Sounds just like an office,' she told me.

'Yeah, I know, Ma. But you've abandoned me so I have to have some way of getting my messages,' I said. 'I did tell you I was getting – '

'Oh, I *didn't* abandon you, darling,' Ma said, sounding quite upset.

'A joke, Ma. A joke.'

'Oh, Marcus, before I forget, I – '

At that point the line went dead. Well, not dead exactly. There was a fierce crackling. Then voices from all over Europe, it seemed, commandeered our line: a bit as though purgatory had had a phone installed and all those waiting for a reprieve were on the line to God trying to be heard. Then, finally, it really went dead. Total silence, and I hung up.

'My mother,' I explained to Farrell who was slouched in front of the TV, not looking all that relaxed, though. Time for his fix, obviously.

I was most benevolent. I gave him three temazepams a day – three an evening to be more precise. That was his ration and I made him stick to it, and by now he was getting his highs off just that small amount. I'd sort of weaned him, if you like. It was important that I made him cut down because I wanted him to get really hyper when the time came for him to perform. I'd read up on these jellies and discovered that, mixed with alcohol, they could make you really aggressive, give a sense of invulnerability, make you do just about anything. And that was exactly what I was aiming for.

I'd no trouble getting the little green capsules, of course. I think I told you my Dad was a gynaecologist before he took up swinging by his neck as a hobby, so I knew a good few medical types. I trotted round to each of them in turn, giving them this spiel about not being able to sleep, about finding it very difficult to de-institutionalise myself, about needing something to calm me down so I could cope. They were all kindness itself, scribbling the required prescriptions. They weren't after all, to know what I was really up to. Temazepam, in case you don't know, is just a kind of sleeping pill, and very good at its job if you take the prescribed dosage. It's only when you shovel them down that the fun and games begin. So, all my doc friends came to my rescue, and all of them gave me the same stalwart advice: 'You take care of yourself, now, Marcus, and if you feel you need any more help please don't hesitate to call me again.' I took them at their word, naturally.

So, I gave Farrell his three jellies and watched him wash them down with some Coca-Cola. He'd have preferred a thing called Irn Bru (made from girders, apparently) but I hadn't been able to find that. So it was Coca-Cola.

I watched the jellies take effect. Much better than watching some so-called classic TV programmes on Channel 4. It was really quite fascinating. After about twenty minutes he started to mellow. The little twitches stopped. His eyes took on a benign sheen, and he smiled at me constantly. But it was one of those Bombay smiles I told you about, quickly erased but almost instantly replaced by another equally phoney one. After another twenty minutes he wanted to talk although why he should want to do this when his voice was all slurred, as if his tongue had suddenly swollen, was beyond me. Not that he talked any sense. Not that the stupid git *ever* talked sense, come to that. But with his jellies circulating, his talk became even more incoherent and vague. Still, I wasn't about to try and stop him. Despite his ramblings, a few interesting little titbits came to light and I was able to store these away in my mind for future reference. One thing was abundantly clear: I had become something of a hero to his addled way of thinking. I had taken him in. I had tried to help him. I had saved him. He didn't know how on earth he was going to repay me. Well, he needn't have worried about that. I knew exactly how he was going to refund my deposit, but extracting that payment was going to be tricky and require all my guile. It would be imperative, I knew, that Farrell make *himself* believe that everything he did was off his own bat, and that everything he did was by way of rewarding yours truly for my kindness.

I was still watching him and listening to his protestations of affection and gratitude when the phone rang again. I assumed it was Ma calling back: she wouldn't have taken kindly to being cut off by some wop exchange just before she forgot something. I picked up the phone before Mr BT had finished the message. 'Ma?'

'Hardly,' Birt said.

'Oh. It's you.'

'It's me.'

I sighed audibly. 'What is it now?'

'Just – is everything all right?'

'Yeah. Why?'

'You sound – funny.'

'Well, laugh then,' I answered flippantly, but I rebuked myself nonetheless for obviously allowing some untoward tone creep into my voice, even though I wasn't aware I had done so. But something warned me that an explanation was required, and I said, 'Well, actually, I've got some pretty exciting news.'

In my mind's eye I could just about see Birt stiffen with excitement and interest. I needed some time since I hadn't actually thought up what news, exciting or otherwise, I was going to give him. So I dallied a while, letting the sod stew. When I'd made up my mind I just blurted it out, being a great believer that the best decisions are made on the spur of the moment, letting instinct be the guide. And when I eventually heard Birt ask, 'And what might that be, Marcus?' I answered immediately, 'I've found Mr Speed for you.'

There was another silence for a while, and then Birt asked, 'Where is he?'

'Safe,' I said cryptically.

Birt got hugely agitated. 'Where is he, Marcus?'

I cleared my throat. 'I'm not *exactly* sure of his location at this very minute,' which was true enough since Farrell had followed me out of the sitting-room when I went to answer the phone. 'But I'm expecting a call soon to tell me – '

'Has he said anything?'

'I haven't spoken to him, Maurice,' I lied. 'I've just located him. I can't do everything in a jiffy, you know.' I gave another cough although I haven't a clue why. 'Like I say, I'm expecting a call and then I hope to go and meet him. As soon as I do that, I'll be in touch. Okay?'

I hung up before Birt could say any more. Then, systematically, I switched off the electricity at the mains, made sure the doors and windows were locked, and went in search of Farrell. It was still just light enough to make my way about.

He was lying sprawled on his mattress at the foot of my bed looking happy enough. I thought about telling him about Birt but decided against it. No point in frightening the idiot and depriving him of a night's sleep.

'You listening?' I asked.

He gazed up at me.

'There's no electricity. I've switched it off,' I told him which was stupid of me. I should just have said there was a power cut.

Instantly bewildered, Farrell asked, 'Why'd you do that?'

I wasn't about to give the true explanation: that, if I knew Birt, he'd have a car outside within minutes and a couple of goons waiting to see where I went to meet up with John Speed. I figured if the house was in total darkness by the time the car did get to Chelsea they'd reckon that they'd missed me, that I'd already taken off. 'Economising,' I told Farrell.

'Oh,' was all he had to contribute.

'Get your clothes off and go to bed,' I told him.

Obediently he stripped off, tossed his clothes on the floor and got in under the duvet. I should have told him to wash his stinking feet.

FIFTEEN

Kranze had the cunning knack of getting power over people by making them believe *they* held the whiphand. He had certainly operated in this manner as far as Farrell was concerned, if I could believe what Jelly John had told me, and that wasn't anything to bet the mortgage on. But *if* what he said was to be believed Kranze had played the role of whimpering slave, telling Farrell he couldn't live without him, how he worshipped the ground he walked on, how he, Farrell, was the only reason Kranze was able to survive the rigours of prison life. And if you give credence to that you must really believe in the fairies.

With me Kranze had used an altogether different method. He had, the crafty sod, allowed me to manage all the affairs relating to his book. He pleaded an unaccustomed ignorance of matters literary, begging me to deal with his contract, his advance, indeed with everything pertaining to publication, ending that particular phone conversation with the statement, 'I trust you, Marcus,' but managing to imbue it with some sort of threat.

So, I had arranged his contract – a pretty good one for a first-time author, although I did make sure he didn't hold on to any film or TV rights, which is where the real lolly is. Well, I wouldn't want him getting too uppity, would I? And I didn't overdo the advance either. A few thousand only, just enough for Frau Zanker to have a bit of a spree in Asda, put a couple of Bratwurst on the table. Maybe some Pumpernickel.

Anyway, two days after I'd given Birt the news that I'd located Farrell (or Speed, as he still knew him) the proofs of Kranze's book arrived on my desk, and the very same afternoon Jim Callaghan brought me the design for the cover. Very arty, was our Jim. A real Versace kid. 'What d'you think?' he asked, but clearly not giving a damn what I thought.

I gave the cover a cursory glance. 'It'll do, I suppose,' I told him, not giving him the chance to get too big-headed. Actually, it was very good. Nicely spooky. What they call in the trade an 'eye-catcher', something to stand out on the shelves of Smith's and Waterstone's.

'I'll go ahead along those lines then, shall I?'

'Yes,' I instructed him.

He shoved a piece of paper under my nose. 'That's the blurb,' he said, obviously deflated by my offhand manner.

I took my time reading the blurb, and I had a job not laughing. It was the usual publisher's balderdash telling the unsuspecting reader what a thrill they were in for. 'A chilling insight into the mind of a murderer' was one phrase which struck me. 'Who wrote this?' I asked.

'Hmm?' muttered Jim, his mind elsewhere. 'Oh, Judy, I think. Judy Diamond.'

'Tell her she's a gem,' I said, honestly not intending the pun.

'You like it, I take it.'

'A humdinger,' I agreed, determined to show much more enthusiasm for this than I had over his bloody cover design.

When he'd left my office, I called Judy. 'Hey there, Judy. Ever think of taking up writing fiction yourself?'

'I'm sorry?'

'The blurb for the Kranze book. Best bit of make-believe I ever came across,' I told her, keeping my voice serious. We'd been engaged in a sort of half-hearted rivalry for some time now, though for some reason she always seemed to get the better of me.

'Well, Marcus, if you made a bit more of an effort and actually came into the office occasionally, you could have written the blurb yourself. It is supposed to be your book, after all,' she replied casually and hung up.

Cheek! I would obviously have to try a bit harder if I was going to catch her out.

All of which activity naturally enough brought my mind round to concentrating on Kranze himself. What I needed to know, needed to know very badly indeed, was what the hell Kranze was playing at. All that bullshit about him having a deep and sincere affection for Farrell was nothing but poppycock since, as I well knew, Kranze was incapable of even a modicum of affection, deep, sincere or otherwise. And as for that absurd charade he had pulled on me, trying to convince *me* of his passion for the unfortunate Farrell – well, that hardly bore thinking about unless it was for the plot of some utterly fantastical farce. So? *Why* was he so desperate to meet Farrell again? Why make such a dramatic gesture as to dedicate his book to him? It was, as my mate the King of Siam was wont to say, a puzzlement. A puzzle I better solve without too much delay. I could easily understand him buggering the mindless Farrell, but not out of any sense of sexual gratification. That didn't fit. In fact, it was and had always been my contention that Kranze was just about asexual, maybe even using sex as a vehicle to express his loathing for sex, if you can follow my drift. No, if he buggered Farrell it would be simply to humiliate another human being, if that's not giving Farrell too much credit. Or maybe to get a hold over him so he could use him for something else. But what the blazes was that something else?

I stood up and took a little turn round the office, switching on the coffee-maker as I passed it. The only conclusion I could come to was that Farrell/Speed either had something Kranze wanted, or knew something Kranze was afraid of sharing. Yet both these premises struck me as being unlikely. I poured myself a mug of coffee, and sipped it for a while. In either case it would have meant, in effect, that Farrell had a hold over Kranze and there was no way that situation would have been allowed to raise its ugly head. Not by our lovely Kranzipoo. I slumped back into my chair. Unless, unless . . .

Slowly I put my mug on the desk and gazed at the photo of Kranze that was to be used on the back cover of his book, and gradually something began to simmer in my consciousness. It wasn't so much that *I* was staring at the photo, but that the picture was staring at me, those cold, infernal eyes penetrating right to my soul. I felt my lips widen into a great broad smile. That was it! Of course that was it, and suddenly I was laughing my head off. It was *me* Kranze was after. Sweet and innocent little me. And he was planning to use Farrell to kill *me*. God, I loved it. I really loved it.

Then, of course, the fallacy of this came home to roost. It *couldn't* be me. Kranze had dedicated his book and organised his control over Speed *before* he even knew me. Shit! So it must be Birt who was – that would fit. And then I thought: but it doesn't have to be Birt. It could have started out as a way of Kranze getting his revenge on Birt but there was nothing to stop him switching targets, was there? True, Birt was the more likely, the more obvious, but with Kranze the obvious was seldom what he had in mind. So it could be me the bastard was after. And the more I thought about it the more this theory struck me as just what Kranze would do. That would explain why he admitted to me that he had killed Karen even though I already knew this to be the case. He admitted it thinking that maybe I would tell Birt and then. . . . It was certainly convoluted. Then, just as Birt thought he had me as a witness or whatever, Kranze would call in Farrell to dispose of yours truly and leave Birt with egg on his face. Again. That was surely the way Kranze's devious mind would work. I started to laugh again, admittedly not with such vigour as I had the first time. I was disposable, was I? Well, we'd soon see about that. I resolved there and then that I had to get things moving to a canter. And the first thing to do was to get Birt and Farrell together. I immediately phoned Birt and arranged for him to drop in and see me at home that evening.

An almighty thunderstorm broke out just as I walked from the Underground to my house, making me scurry, something I hated doing. Ma always maintained that people who do so are either very working class, hurrying so as not to be late for their menial toils, or criminals in a rush to get away from the scene of their crime. All a bit facile, I agree, but that was Ma for you. There is, though, something very undignified about the way people try to dodge the rain.

I ducked into a shop doorway, just to gaze skywards to see if any sort of let-up was in the offing. It did look a bit brighter away to the north so I decided to wait and give that blue patch a chance to filter across the sky. I wondered if it wasn't somehow symbolic the way I had hurried through the rain, because I had thought on the tube that maybe I'd rushed things a bit, getting onto Birt so quickly. After all, there was still quite a lot of work to be done on Farrell and I hadn't exactly given myself much time in which to do it. Even less time if I waited for the rain to stop.

I was soaked to the skin when I got home, and I could cheerfully have throttled Farrell when he stuck his head out of the kitchen and asked in that moronic way of his, 'Is it raining then?'

'No. Been swimming,' I told him, and went upstairs to change.

I showered quickly and slipped into my jeans and a top. I was sitting on the bed trying to get my damn feet into a pair of socks when Farrell appeared in the door. 'Made dinner,' he announced. At least, I thought, he'd learned to call our evening meal 'dinner' and not 'tea' as he used to. 'Oh? What? Porridge?'

'No.' he answered seriously. 'Done eggs.'

'I see,' I said, and felt my stomach give a little heave.

'And rice.'

'Oh.'

'And sardines and bacon and mushrooms and some of those green and red things.'

'Got carried away, did you?'

'It's nice.'

'I'm sure.'

And to tell the truth it wasn't at all bad. He'd hard-boiled the eggs and chopped them. Chopped the rest of the ingredients also and added them to the rice, making, although he wasn't aware of it, a kind of monstrous risotto. This concoction, with brown wholemeal bread and butter and a glass of Chardonnay, made a tasty enough repast. 'My compliments to the chef,' I said.

'That's me.'

'That's you. My compliments to you.'

He collected the dishes and looked as if he was about to set about washing them. 'Leave them John,' I said. 'We have to talk.'

'I can wash and talk.'

'Leave them,' I ordered. 'Come and sit down,' I said. 'Like a good chap,' I added when I saw him getting that nervous look in his eyes. Time enough for him to get nervous.

He took his time about getting seated, sort of circling the table like a hound trying to make up its mind where to settle. Normally this would have agitated me no end, but I was too busy racking my brains trying to think exactly what I was going to say to him. However, I was ready when he finally came to rest on his perch.

'Tell me,' I asked, 'You ever hear of a policeman called Birt? Inspector Birt? Inspector Maurice Birt?'

Farrell screwed up his face and gave my question his most serious consideration. Then he shook his head.

'You sure?'

'Don't *think* I have. Who is he?'

'Zanker never mention him to you?'

'Zanker? Maybe. Seems like I've heard the name. Maybe.'

'Okay. Listen. Inspector Birt is the guy who put your friend Zanker away,' I began.

'He's no fucking friend – '

'It's a manner of speaking,' I interrupted him, not wanting to allow him to sidetrack himself with irrelevancies. 'Anyway, this chap Birt wants to try and nail Zanker for something else.'

Farrell brightened perceptibly. 'For what?' he asked with something akin to glee in his voice.

I had no intention of going into all the ramifications of Karen's death. Not at this point in time, certainly. Besides, if I knew Farrell, he would get nothing but confused, and I needed him to be as clear-headed as it was at all possible for him to be. 'I'll tell you all about that later. The main point is Birt is very keen to know who the John Speed who Zanker dedicated his book to is,' I said, wincing at the horrendously improper grammatical construction of my sentence.

Farrell gave a little jerk. 'Why?'

'Because he thinks this Speed character might know something.'

'Don't know nothing,' Farrell said quickly.

'*I* know you don't. But Birt doesn't. He doesn't even know your real name is Farrell.'

Farrell sucked in his breath. 'He'll find out,' he said like a person who has unqualified faith in the ability of the police to find out anything they want.

'No he won't,' I assured him. 'There's only three people who know that you and Speed are one and the same – Zanker, you and me. Zanker won't say anything. You can bet your knickers on that. Nor will I. So if you don't, Birt will never find out.'

That, fortunately, seemed to register as sense in Farrell's brain, and he nodded, and mouthed a noise that I interpreted as positive. But I wanted to make certain Farrell understood the importance of secrecy.

'It's up to you and me to keep Birt in the dark. We don't want any shit copper muscling in and spoiling *our* plans for dealing with Kranze – Zanker – do we?'

Of course Farrell wasn't aware that we had any plans, but I was sure that wouldn't enter his calculations. It didn't. 'Shit, no,' he agreed.

Now *I* nodded. 'Quite.'

'It's you and me, isn't it, Marcus?'

'Certainly it is. You and me.'

I paused so that he could enjoy the smile he bestowed on me, a huge, caressing smile as though we'd slit our wrists and become blood-brothers or something. And now that this much had sunk into his skull I could proceed to the next step. 'Now, I've told Birt that I know where Speed is,' I said cautiously.

'You mean me?'

'Yeah. I mean you, but he doesn't know you're Farrell, does he?'

Farrell gawped at me. 'Why?'

'Why what?'

'Why'd you tell him you knew where I was?'

'Because I need Birt to think I'm on *his* side. That's why. Need him to think I'm doing everything in my power to help him.'

'But you're not?'

Get the boy a Victoria Cross for intelligence. 'Of course I'm not. Like I said, John. It's you and me. Only you and me. But Birt could bugger everything up if he gets even an inkling that something's going on behind his back.'

Farrell was silent for a while. I thought for a bit that he'd gone into some sort of petrified trance, but he'd been thinking, it turned out, so no wonder there was a look of strain on his face. 'I get it,' he said eventually.

I breathed a sigh. 'There you go,' I said.

'Clever. Very clever,' he told me.

What did the sod expect. 'Thanks,' I said.

There was another short silence. And then I got something of a shock. Farrell *had* been thinking, thinking more deeply than I had given him credit for. 'So why are you telling me all this?' he wanted to know.

I honestly hadn't considered the possibility that he might want a reason. But since he did want one, I decided to give it to him straight from the hip. 'Because Inspector Birt is coming round here later this evening.'

It took a while for this to register. Farrell looked at me bleakly. He shifted uneasily on his chair. He started drumming the table with his nailbitten fingers. I knew the signs. They were a prelude to a sort of seizure, not in the medical sense but the sort of fit that came when he was about to panic. There was one sure way to control it, however, 'What you and me need is a joint,' I told him, and as if by magic he started to relax. Even the thought of a whiff of cannabis was enough to calm the jittery bugger down. So before he could start thanking me for my generosity I nipped upstairs and got a five-skinner from the little stock of ready-rolled joints I kept. I lit it coming down the stairs, taking a few decent draws for myself. I surely needed them. Just two hours and Birt would be here, and, boy, did I still have work to do. 'Here you go,' I said and passed the joint to Farrell.

Indulgently I allowed him two draws before proceeding with his education. 'Feeling better?' I enquired eventually.

He nodded. 'Thanks.'

'Good. Now, like I was saying, Birt is coming here this evening but there's nothing for you to worry about – if you do exactly as I tell you, that is.'

Farrell nodded again. He even looked eager to please. He passed me the joint but I passed it back immediately, not, mind you, out of generosity but because he had slobbered all over the tip and soggy joints are not my cup of tea. 'No, you finish it.'

'Thanks.'

'Okay. Right. Now, when Birt arrives I want you upstairs.'

'Upstairs,' Farrell repeated, as if imprinting this instruction on his mind.

'And you only come down when I call you.'

'Come down when you call me.'

'And *when* you come down I don't want you to say anything. Understand? Not a single word. Let me do all the talking.'

'You'll do the talking.'

'In fact, the best thing would be for you to act stupid,' I told Farrell and had to control myself and keep a straight face. *Act* stupid indeed.

'How?'

'Just – shit, I dunno – just mope, I suppose.'

'No, I mean why.'

'Ah.' One of his little peculiarities shared, I understand, by a fair number of his Scots brethren. 'How' could also mean 'why' and it was left to the listener to decide which was being used when. 'Because I don't want him questioning you, that's why – how. I'll have given him a line by the time you do come down, and I don't want you screwing everything up.'

Farrell approved of this. 'Okay, Marcus.'

'And for Christ's sake don't forget your name is Speed. Not Farrell. Speed. Will you remember that?'

'I will,' Farrell assured me with vigour.

'You're sure? It's really important.'

'I'm sure.'

'Excellent. You could earn yourself an extra jelly baby if you perform with alacrity,' I told him and instantly regretted it.

'With what?' Farrell wanted to know, fearing, I suppose, alacrity might be something like a trapeze.

'Perform well,' I simplified with a sigh.

'Oh.'

I watched him suck the last dregs of cannabis from the joint and stub it out. 'Better get rid of this,' he told me.

'Good idea,' I confirmed. 'You can do the washing up now, too, if you want,' I added, not wanting to deprive him of his little pleasures.

'Okay,' Farrell agreed willingly.

'I need to think,' I said.

Farrell nodded. 'Sure you do. I can see that. Got to get everything in order, don't you?'

'That's right. You're sure you understand everything now?'

'Yeah. I understand, Marcus,' Farrell answered and although I didn't really want to hear him repeat everything I'd told him, I hadn't the heart to stop him as he set off on the perilous journey of trying to remember all that I'd said. 'Be upstairs when Birt comes. Don't come down till you call me. I'm not Farrell, I'm Speed. And say nothing.'

'Perfect. Ten out of ten.'

He gave me a wily grin. 'You forgot something.'

That put the wind up me. 'What?'

'Act stupid,' Farrell said in triumph. 'I've got to act stupid.'

'Christ! You're right,' I said as though stunned by his remarkable sapience.

'See? I do remember.'
'Glad you do,' I told him. 'Very glad you do.'
And there endeth the first lesson.

Birt arrived at twenty-five past eight. I ushered him in and immediately created an aura of mystery, putting my finger to my lips in a gesture of keeping silence. As we passed the stairs I purposely gazed up, listened, and then all but crept into the kitchen with Birt toddling along behind. I shut the door. 'Sorry about that,' I said quietly, but didn't explain.

'What's going on, Marcus?' Birt demanded.

'Keep your voice down, will you?' I hissed.

'What's going on?' Birt tried again, this time whispering.

'I've got Speed upstairs and I don't want him frightened off, that's what's going on.'

Birt gaped at me. 'You've got Speed – ' he began, but decided to sit down instead of finishing his question.

I finished it for him. 'Upstairs,' I said.

Birt shook his head. 'How did – '

'Never mind the hows,' I interrupted. 'The fact is he's here and I've been trying to question him.'

Birt got disgruntled. 'You should have left that to me.'

'That's just where you're wrong, Maurice. You'll get nothing out of him. He's a mess. Almost a bloody zombie. But he knows something. I'm sure of it. There's something in there amid all that junk that –'

It was Birt's turn to interrupt. 'Hold on a tick,' he told me, and I could see he was clearing that particular little part of his brain set aside for the reception and retention of important information.

'I need more time to work on him,' I continued, however. 'He's just starting to trust me.'

'Huh,' Birt grunted.

'He is, really he is. I'm his pal. His mate. He *needs* someone he can trust and that's little me.'

'He must be a mess,' Birt scoffed.

I ignored that.

Birt thought for a while. 'I want to see him,' he said finally.

'Of course you do. No problem. I'll call him down in a minute. But listen, Maurice, you've got to handle this baby with the old velvet gloves. You scare him off and we lose everything. Hell, we're working together, aren't we? I know what I'm doing.'

Birt gave me a wary look.

'I needn't have told you he was here at all if I was up to something,' I pointed out.

'You're always up to something, Marcus,' Birt said, but I could tell he was convinced I was right, which was all I cared about. He could insult me as much as he wanted as long as he went along with my plans. 'And you think he really does know something about Kranze?'

Very seriously I answered, 'I'm convinced of it. You've only got to mention Kranze's name – Zanker's name, he knows him as Zanker, don't forget – and you'll see the reaction. And I can tell you this,' I added, just to whet Birt's appetite further, 'it's something pretty damn important.'

'I still want to meet him,' Birt insisted.

'Like I said, no problem. But just be – well, be delicate if you can possibly manage it.'

'Delicate,' Birt scoffed.

'You know what I mean. Oh, and by the way, no way must he know who you are. Not a Mr Plod anyway. He'd be out the door and gone before we could say, "Evening all".'

'So who am I?'

'A very dear and well-beloved friend,' I told him with a smirk. 'That's what you are, in fact, isn't it?'

Birt ignored my jibe. 'Get him down,' he said, and took a seat by the kitchen table, while I took just about the deepest breath I'd ever taken and called Farrell down.

'John,' I began. 'This is an old pal of mine, Maurice. Maurice, this is John Speed.'

Well, talk about overacting! Farrell put his face close to Birt's and peered intently into his eyes for a while. Then he looked up at me questioningly. Then he pulled out a chair and gaped at that. Finally he sat down, folded his arms on the table and put his head down on them. Birt looked at me. I shrugged as if to say 'I told you so'.

Birt cleared his throat. 'John, I hear from Marcus that we know someone in common.'

Farrell never budged. I signalled to Birt to play it cool. A waste of time.

'Helmut Zanker,' Birt said bluntly.

Farrell sat up as if someone had stung him with a cattleprod. He jolted upright and a most curious mien came into his eyes. *I* knew it was that old look of hatred but it was fighting a valiant battle with the glazed, soporific tinge that the cannabis had induced so it came out as a mixture of cunning and fear. It was, in effect, perfect.

I strolled over to him and put a consoling hand on his shoulder. 'Nothing to worry about, John,' I said, and shook my head in disgust at Birt.

But Farrell was rehearsing for his own particular audition with RADA. He shrugged my hand away angrily. He glared at Birt. He mumbled incoherently. 'Not telling anything,' was all that could be deciphered.

'That's *okay*, John,' I assured him. 'You don't have to tell anyone anything,' I added pointedly, hoping against hope that the moron would shut up now. But he didn't. Not quite.

'Want to go now,' he said, and without leave he shambled out of the kitchen, and seconds later the door of my bedroom slammed shut.

'Satisfied?' I demanded of Birt. 'Just about ruined all the effort I've made to get him to talk.'

To his credit (and my relief, I might add) Birt seemed appropriately contrite. 'I didn't think that —'

'That's the trouble with you people. You don't bloody think, I *warned* you to be careful, but no, in you go with your two big feet and frighten the shit out of the poor chap.' I was really enjoying myself.

'I'm sorry, Marcus . . .'

Even better, that was. 'No point in being sorry *now*,' I told him. Then I heard a thud from upstairs and had the dreadful feeling that Farrell was about to descend on us again, maybe thinking Birt had gone and his acting days were over.

'Look,' I told Birt in haste. 'You'd better go. I'll have to try and get Speed back on an even keel. As soon as I know anything – *anything* – I'll give you a shout.'

Birt nodded his enforced satisfaction with this and stood up.

'Christ alone knows when that will be after what you've done,' I said, giving myself leeway and guiding him to the door.

'I see what you mean,' Birt conceded.

'Sorry?'

'His reaction to the name of Zanker.'

'Oh, that. Yeah, well, I'm used to it. That's why I'm certain he *does* know something that will be useful to us.'

'And you've no idea *what* that might be?'

'Not a clue. When I know, you'll know. Okay?' I opened the door and peered out and across the road. Wilson, the reject from *Junior Mastermind*, was sitting in the car, smoking. I blew him a kiss.

Birt stopped on the edge of the pavement and turned. He gave me a hard stare.

I smiled beatifically. 'Problem?'

Slowly Birt shook his head. 'Not yet.'

'Jolly good. Tell Einstein to drive carefully,' I concluded, and shut the door. I leaned against it until I heard the car start and drive away. Then I let out one of those footballer's whoops and dashed up to check on Farrell. He was sitting on his mattress looking pretty disconsolate, the contents of his ashtray scattered on the floor.

'Dropped it,' he said. 'Sorry.'

I'd have forgiven him just about anything. 'You were brilliant,' I told him.

'I was? Didn't do anything.'

'That's what I mean.'

I kept my promise and gave him an extra jelly, for which he was duly grateful. I allowed him to take his little wander down the Yellow Brick Road without interference. And then, feeling mischievous, I asked him, 'Ready to meet Zanker, are you?' But he didn't hear me. Ah, well. Not to worry. Tomorrow was another day, and a pretty hectic day it promised to be.

SIXTEEN

And sure enough the hecticity was intense, although none of it was of my own making.

To begin with the proofs for *A Letter from Chile* needed looked at, and no sooner had I sat down at my desk when Nick Putty was in my office asking when I could have them checked. 'Day or two?' I suggested.

'Today,' Nick said.

I shrugged. 'Right.' If that was what he wanted that's what he'd get. 'What's the rush?'

'A lot of interest from across the pond,' he told me, evidently very chuffed.

'Oh. Yeah. Well. You might have expected that. Nobody like the Yanks for a bit of the serial killer, is there? 'Specially one whose Daddy was a good old Nazi. Give the TV psychiatrists a field day, that will.'

'Probably,' Nick agreed. 'Incidentally – ' Suddenly he looked embarrassed. 'There's something I've been meaning to ask you, Marcus.'

I raised my eyebrows.

'You wouldn't think of – it hasn't ever crossed your mind that – given any thought, I wonder, to writing a book of your own? You know, how the *Chile* book influenced you, how you came to be under the spell of Kranze, all that sort of – '

'Crap,' I interrupted swiftly.

'Oh.'

'You *are* joking, aren't you, Nick?'

He gave me a shy smile and almost blushed. 'I wasn't actually.'

'Well, the answer is no.' I put the back of my hand to my forehead and cried dramatically, 'No, no, a thousand times, no.' I took my hand down and grinned at him. 'The answer is no.'

'I gathered that.'

'Tell you what: if I ever find myself in the nick again with loads of time on my hands – *then* I'll write you one. Okay? Just for you, Nick, dear.'

He gave me an evil leer. 'Might just be worth fitting you up for something. Have to have a chat with some of my CID friends.'

'Always suspected you mixed in the wrong circles, Nick. Should elevate your sights a bit now – now that you're *somebody* in the publishing world.'

Of course, when he'd gone, I started to think that maybe I *should* set down my side of the tale. It'd be a gas, wouldn't it? I could have one hell of a time implicating all sorts of people who had nothing to do with it. Cause utter mayhem. Cause suicides by the dozen, every respectably high building in London a diving-board. But I knew I'd never really get round to doing it. Too much effort and, besides, I certainly didn't have the time even to contemplate such an undertaking right now.

I skipped lunch, settling for coffee and a diet of *A Letter from Chile*. And by five o'clock I'd been through the proofs and made only a few necessary notations – typesetter's errors, mostly.

I personally took the corrected proofs to Nick, and placed them on his desk with a mocking bow. 'As ordered,' I told him.

'Thanks, Marcus. Given any more thought – '

'Not a moment's. 'Night, Nick,' I said and breezed off.

It had been my intention to get home as quickly as possible since

I needed another session with Farrell. He'd acquitted himself admirably once, but that certainly was no guarantee he'd do so a second time. Especially when this time it would be Kranze he was facing. But, as you'll have gathered, I'm sometimes a creature of impulse, and it was definitely impulse that made me sidestep the Underground and head for Fortnum's. A cup of decent coffee, maybe a scone, and a little ogle at Miranda struck me as being just what I needed. The coffee and the scone to revive me, a study of Miranda to see if she fitted my needs. I wanted, you see, to make sure there wasn't a budding Amazon under that black frock and frilly apron. I required a fragile flower for . . . I don't know if I've mentioned that when I disposed of Sharon it was as a sort of practice run, to see if I *could* actually kill someone. Well, that *was* my reason for killing the silly girl. And it had been running through my head that maybe Farrell might appreciate just such a rehearsal, might benefit from it considerably. But since he wasn't the strongest of giants, no Atlas he, I'd been wondering if maybe simpering Miranda wouldn't be just the ticket. I must stress these were just vague conjectures. Yet, time was pressing on and I'd have to make up my mind about a lot of things soon.

So, I need hardly tell you that I was rightly cheesed off to find that Miranda wasn't working that day. 'Miranda? Oh she's off on Thursdays,' I was told by the toothy old biddy who had taken her station.

'Oh.'

'Friend of hers, are you?'

Nosey cow. 'Yeah,' I drawled.

'Nice girl.'

'Smashing.' I stood up. 'Changed my mind,' I said.

'Just in for a little chat with Miranda, were we?' Nosey asked, tapping her nose with her pencil.

I gave her a grin. 'Something like that.'

'Nice girl,' she told me again.

'Smashing,' I repeated so as not to confuse her.

'Message,' Farrell said by way of welcoming me home.

Probably I'd been overzealous with my praise for his culinary efforts or possibly his mother's ante-natal demands had included too many herbs in her haggis but, whatever the reason, Farrell had taken to cooking in a big way. And now he stood in the kitchen doorway all tarted up in a red-and-white striped apron which Ma had favoured, his hair tied up in a dishcloth. He wielded a carving fork and created an aspect that would have caused even the most hardened burglar to flee for his life. I shook my head in bemused awe as I waited for him to kindly deliver the message. When he didn't, I asked, 'Well?' and when that just made him gape, I added, 'The message?'

'Oh,' he said, stabbing the fork in the direction of the hall table. 'On the phone.'

'Thanks.'

There were, in fact, two messages. The first from Heather, a sing-song, 'Marcus? Marcus? Marcus? Are you there? Marcus? Marcus? Marcus? You're not. Alas and alack. Do call me. I pine for thee.' Well, she could pine a bit longer. I was, in a manner of speaking, in training, preparing for a major event, a sort of murderous Olympics, and I couldn't allow anything as boring as sex with Heather to sap my energy, or my concentration for that matter.

The second message, however, was quite a different story. It was extraordinarily chilling in its simplicity: 'Marcus. Stuart. Payment is due. We need to meet. Soon.'

'– got capers,' Farrell was saying.

'What?' I demanded, rounding on him.

'You haven't got any capers,' he complained.

'So?'

'Delia Smith says – '

'Fuck Delia Smith,' I said ungraciously, meaning no offence to the Queen of Fennel, The Lady of Shallots.

'Sorry,' Farrell apologised and looked truly abject.

'No, I'm sorry, John,' I said. 'It's just – ' I gestured towards the phone, 'just got other things on my mind.'

Which was true enough. I hadn't really expected Stuart Bean to exact payment quite so quickly for finding Farrell. Don't tell me he was going to jeopardise everything by trying to involve me in some scatterbrained plan he'd devised.

'No problem,' Farrell told me.

I followed him into the kitchen. 'Smells good,' I said with a sniff. 'Getting to be quite the domesticated type, aren't you?'

'Like cooking,' Farrell said, skirting an explanation of what domesticated might mean. He raised the lid of one of the pots he had bubbling on the stove, and peered into it, wrinkling his nose like an hyena seeking a cadaver. "Be ready in about half an hour.'

I looked at my watch. 'You couldn't, I suppose, delay it a bit?' I asked, wondering if Farrell would fly into a sort of Marco Pierre White rage.

But he took my request as just another test of his culinary prowess, and beamed at me. 'No problem,' he answered to this also. 'I'll just turn down the gas and let it simmer.'

'Great. I have to nip out for a while, see? That message – ' I nodded towards the phone. 'Urgent.'

'Okay,' Farrell told me agreeably.

'Might be more than half an hour, though.'

Farrell shrugged.

'Might be as much as two hours.'

Farrell shrugged again.

'Give you the chance to make a pudding,' I suggested.

'Done that,' was Farrell's answer. 'In the fridge.'

'Oh. We have been busy.'

Farrell had nothing to say to that. Something had caught his eye in the cookery book, and he lowered his head to peer more closely at it.

I left him and Delia to swap notes.

'Got my message then?' Stuart Bean asked.

It was quite a different Stuart Bean now. A serious, menacing thug of a Stuart Bean. A Stuart Bean you didn't cross. A Stuart Bean you agreed with.

'Yep.'

We sat in his gaudy sitting-room, Stuart looking like a midget Kray, me wondering what the hell was coming next. As it turned out, coming next was Mum, shuffling into the room in a pair of well-worn slippers and carrying a tray with tea. In silence she placed the tray next to Stuart, and retreated. She stumbled as she did so, and Stuart was out of his chair and by her side in a flash, putting a hairy arm about her. 'I told you to change those fucking slippers, Mum,' he said. 'I've told her a hundred times to change those slippers,' he told me after he'd seen Mum safely back to whatever cage he kept her in and returned to the sitting-room. 'It's not that she hasn't got other slippers, mind. Got six pairs. In boxes. Still in boxes,' he explained in case, I suppose, he thought I might be thinking times were hard or something.

'They get attached to things,' I said. 'I know my Ma does.'

Stuart agreed with me, nodding, and pouring out two cups of tea. He put milk and sugar in both without asking, and I certainly wasn't about to be the one who told him I took neither. He watched me take a tentative, obliging sip. 'All right?'

'Perfect,' I lied.

'Like the cups?'

'Really pretty,' I said. They were horrendous: Woolworths pottery circa 1991. Crimson shrub roses on a beige background.

'Made Mum break out the best china for you,' Stuart told me.

'I can see that. You shouldn't have gone to all the bother, though.'

'No bother at all,' Stuart said expansively.

I didn't dare suggest that maybe the next time he get Mum to wipe the dust out of them first: it floated on the tea like a tidal scum. 'So. What's so urgent?' I asked.

Stuart put his cup and saucer carefully back on the tray. Then he pursed his lips and folded his hands, staring at me. I got the impression he was trying to make some final decision about me. When he'd satisfied himself, he said simply, 'Need you to drive a car for me.'

I pretended to see nothing untoward about this. 'Sure. Fine. When?'

'The twenty-ninth.'

'Of this month?'

Stuart nodded, still watching me like the proverbial hawk.

'Should be okay.'

'It *has* to be okay.'

I changed my attitude rapidly. 'It'll be okay.'

'Good.'

I took another sip of the putrid tea. Maybe subconsciously I was thinking suicide was a better alternative to getting involved with matey across the room. 'Do I get told any more?'

Stuart leered at me. 'It's a job,' he said bluntly.

'I gathered that.'

'Doesn't bother you?'

I shrugged. 'Why should it? A job's a job – right?'

I'd said just the right thing, apparently. Stuart Bean gave me a huge smile. 'Always knew I could trust you, pal. Always knew I could trust you.'

Nice that he always knew he could trust me twice. 'Well, you helped me when I needed help, didn't you? Got to repay good deeds and all that,' I said. 'So what sort of job is it?' I asked, trying not to sound too inquisitive.

'A robbery.'

'Oh, a heist,' I said, quite liking the sound of that word. Rather more sophisticated than just plain robbery.

'A robbery,' Stuart repeated, so maybe there's a subtle difference between the two.

'And I drive the getaway car?' More melodramatic terminology.

'Yes,' Stuart agreed, still eyeing me carefully.

'Fine. Always wanted to drive a getaway car,' I lied.

I desperately wanted to know what or whom precisely Beany was planning to rob, and although I guessed I shouldn't I was on the point of asking him when he beat my question to it with another. 'What sort you want?'

'Sorry?'

'What make of car?'

'Oh.' I was a bit flummoxed. 'Dunno really. What would you suggest?'

'You drive a BMW, right?'

'That's right.'

'Get you one of those then.'

'Fine.' Then I decided maybe I was being a bit too lackadaisical. 'I'd like it for a day or two before the job – just to get used to it, like. To see if it's got any quirks.'

Stuart approved. 'I'll arrange it. More tea?'

I shook my head. I'd survived half a cup of the scummy brew and wasn't about to push my luck. 'No, one cup's just fine. I can't drink too much tea,' I explained as a small scowl appeared on Stuart's face.

'You should have said. You could have had something else.'

'No. Really. I just can't overdo it, that's all. Your Mum makes a really good cup of tea.'

'The best.'

'Definitely the best.'

My refusal to have my cup replenished appeared to bring matters to a close. Stuart stood up. Oddly enough, he seemed to have grown in stature, but I suppose fear of someone makes you think that. 'Thank your mum for me,' I told him.

'Marcus says thanks, Mum,' Stuart roared, keeping his eyes fixed on mine all the while, without even a glimmer of a smile.

Mum grunted from the back of the flat.

'She says it's a pleasure,' Stuart interpreted.

We reached the door, and Stuart gripped me by the arm: one of his trademarks. 'Don't forget, Marcus. The twenty-ninth.'

'I won't forget,' I answered truthfully.

'I'll be in touch before that, of course, but keep that day free.'

'The whole day?'

'The whole day.'
'Anything you say.'

As I drove home my mind was working overtime. The twenty-ninth. Three weeks from now. And although it was fairly ludicrous at the time, I began to try and figure out how I could turn this famous heist (as I still preferred to think of it) to *my* advantage. There had to be a way. There's always a way for everything if you can just come up with it, as the actress said to the bishop.

I parked the car outside my house and just sat there in it for a while. Something giddy by Sarasate was on the radio, not fitting my mood, so I tuned from Classic FM to Radio 3: one of Berlioz's more dreamy creations but better than Sarasate by a long chalk. I could, of course, earn myself Brownie points by tipping off Birt about Stuart's proposed caper, but who needed Brownie points, for God's sake. Besides, Beany was sure to find out and I didn't want that psycho on my tail for the rest of my living days – days that would be pretty well numbered if I knew Beany Boy. And then I thought, hang on – supposing, just supposing I *did* tip off Birt and then, with his knowledge, go ahead with the driving job, that would give me a really airtight alibi, wouldn't it? An alibi for what, you ask. Well, an alibi for what I was most sincerely hoping to get Farrell to do for me, that's what.

And as I sat there, Berlioz giving way to the cello solo in Brahms' piano concerto no. 2, everything began to slot nicely into place. Or almost. It meant I only had three weeks to get everything organised and that was going to take some doing. But I was up to it, wasn't I? Damn right I was.

SEVENTEEN

And as if to underline the confidence I had in my ability to organise everything within that short space of time, I cut it down even further, taking two days off, putting Beany and Kranze, Birt and Farrell out of my mind. Or intending to. And I succeeded pretty well, helped by the fact that Ma arrived home, bronzed and beautiful, and looking better than I'd seen her for years, better than all those dolly birds put together at any rate. Even Harry had a spring to his step, and Ma had worked wonders on him, too, getting him out of his fuddy-duddy Savile Row suits and into Armani two-pieces. 'Well, all I can say Harry, is, that you must be doing something right. I've never seen Ma look so well.'

Harry accepted my compliment with an inclination of his head.

'And you're looking pretty damn good yourself, into the bargain.'

They'd stopped off on their way back to near Bath, just staying the one night, dear, so that Ma could pick up a few things. So that was my weekend and my two days off taken care of, but I was grateful for the diversion. 'I'm sure Harry has things he wants to see to,' I said. 'And he won't want to go traipsing round the shops with you, Ma. I'll come with you,' I volunteered as a dutiful son should.

That hit the jackpot. Harry gave me a genuinely grateful smile, even though he knew it would probably cost him in the end, one way or another; and Ma was ecstatic, tears of joy welling up in her eyes as she babbled on about it being just like old times. 'And we can have lunch in Fortnum's,' she concluded.

'That's a great idea,' I told her as though I hadn't thought of it myself. I'd actually been going to suggest we stop for coffee, to catch my second wind, at about eleven, but lunch suited me fine. 'And maybe we could take John? He could help carry the bags.'

Ma looked momentarily doubtful. She wasn't at all happy about poor John Farrell, I'm afraid. Luckily they'd phoned from the airport and we had time to drag her mattress from my room and set it back on her bed. What she'd have done if she'd known Farrell had been kipping on it, God alone knows. At a guess, I'd say the Savoy would have had two more guests. But she didn't know that. What she did know was that John Farrell was far from the sort of person she wanted her beloved son to be mixing with. 'He's so *strange*, darling,' she told me later, when Harry had gone to get the overnight necessities from the Jag, and Farrell had retreated to my room to take his daily quota of jellified manna.

'He's got problems, Ma.' I said. 'Needs help,' I added.

'He gives me the willies,' Ma said with a little shudder.

'He's okay, really,' I assured her.

Then, being very casual about it, Ma asked, 'What on earth does he do in publishing?' Which wasn't precisely what she meant. Well, only partly. What she really wanted to know was what on earth I was doing associating with such a common type, a common Scots type to boot. A common Scots type who bit his nails, which was the final straw.

'I didn't meet him at work, Ma,' I said, trying to look suitably shamefaced. 'I only told you that because I didn't want you to worry. He was inside with me.'

Ma looked appalled. 'He's been in prison?' she asked with a tiny squeak in her voice.

''Fraid so.'

'Oh, *darling*,' Ma said, the term of endearment miraculously transformed into one of reproach.

'So have I, in case you've forgotten, Ma. Been in prison.'

'Oh, I know, dear. But that's different,' Ma told me, utilising that peculiar logic of hers which dictated what had befallen her only son was quite different to what befell common Scots types who bite their nails.

However, I knew how to settle this matter. 'He was really good to me in prison, Ma. He knew the ropes and he looked after me,' I lied, and as a clincher I added, 'I'd probably have had my face slashed or been raped if it hadn't been for John.'

Instantly the moronic Farrell became a knight in shining armour, a guardian angel, the protector and mentor of her darling little boy, albeit a working-class protector in the mould of the old retainer who was allowed gratitude but definitely not allowed to sit at the same table as his betters, if you know what I mean. 'Oh, I didn't know,' Ma admitted.

'How could you, Ma?'

'You should have told me.'

'No point in worrying you. Anyway, I'm putting all that behind me.'

'Of course, you are, dear,' Ma said and patted my hand. 'And it really is very sweet of you to take John under your wing and repay his kindness to you,' she conceded.

'Fair's fair,' I said. 'Anyway, all I'm doing is giving him a roof over his head for a few weeks. Just until he gets back on his feet. It's a lot harder for him, you know.'

'I suppose it must be,' Ma said; everything was harder for the working classes in Ma's book but only because silly politicians had tried to educate them, and had given them ideas above their station without the brains to cope with tribulations in the way the upper classes could.

'He doesn't have a Ma like I do,' I said, and off I went into a long and tragic fairytale about the woes that had fallen upon John Farrell: the bullying, drunken stepfather who whipped the child unmercifully; the mother who had chosen this brute before her child and cast him out (in the dead of winter, of course, snow on the ground, blizzards, high winds, and so forth); the poor wee mite having to fend for himself on the cold and cruel streets, living off scraps that even the dogs turned up their noses at . . . I really laid it on thick. By the time I'd finished, Farrell had stepped right from the pages of Dickens. Interestingly, although she listened intently and was clearly upset by John Boy's saga, Ma didn't seem to care all that much. All she could think of was what a truly wonderfully kind and generous and Christian son she had produced, a veritable saint, which suited me just fine. 'Darling,' she told me, 'You're a saint.'

Ma's shopping spree turned out to be quite an experience. I'd tarted Farrell up, allowing him the use of some of my better clothes (for Ma's sake) and even getting him into a pair of my Bally slip-ons and out of those stinking Adidas trainers to which his feet had become moulded. When I'd finished he looked quite presentable. Even Ma was impressed. 'He *can* look human,' she whispered to me on the way out to the car.

'He *is* human, Ma.'

Ma gave me a look which said she wasn't altogether convinced about that.

'Really he is,' I insisted, but smiling.

Alas, it would take more than even my word to convince Ma a Scot could belong to the human race. But she was, in the end, grateful to have him along since he turned out to be a willing and able porter, humping her purchases from shop to shop, and even trotting back to the carpark to unload when his burden became too much, returning to be reloaded. Farrell was gobsmacked at the way Ma spent money, spent her gold credit card, anyway. He'd never seen anything like it, obviously, but then he'd never bumped into anyone like my Ma, had he?

Ma must have suspected that near Bath was going to come under siege in the near future and that rations would be short. She had a field day in her favourite department store, with a brace of assistants tending to her needs. Of course, not everything went smoothly. Because she was buying so much the little Arab manager put in a simpering appearance in the food hall, asking if Madam was being properly tended. A definite mistake. Ma rounded on him and demanded to know what was the big idea of lowering the tone of the place by making customers take tickets and stand in line at the cheese counter. It wasn't Asda he was running, she hoped he knew.

Taken aback, and hopefully chastened, he began to create explanations, but Ma wasn't having any of that. Bad enough that he had come in from the Gobi or wherever and taken over, but to try and impose bazaar traditions was more than she could tolerate. She swept him and his explanations aside with a caustic, 'Jermyn Street, I think, Marcus,' and off we went.

'You're incorrigible, Ma.'

'*I'm* not about to lie down under any *Arab*,' she informed me which I thought was a particularly unfortunate turn of phrase for Ma to use.

'He does own the place, Ma.'

'More's the pity. Far too many of these wretched Tuaregs moving in and buying Britain up if you ask me.'

Fortunately, the Tuaregs didn't seem to have moved into Jermyn Street. Not that you would notice, anyway. In Floris Ma was welcomed with open arms by a nice English youth who spoke properly and served her with panache. She bought enough eau de cologne to sink a battleship, and some shaving cream in a tube and aftershave for Harry. For me she got a box of my favourite soap, and was, I think, about to buy the same for Farrell until she took a look at him and asked the assistant if he had anything *stronger*, something in the carbolic line, I imagine she meant. In the end she settled for a box of lavender-scented soap, and since I knew lavender was always associated with embalming in Ma's mind, the choice was pretty symbolic.

Farrell was overcome. 'Thanks very much, Mrs Walwyn,' he said, all but kow-towing.

Ma dismissed his gratitude with a small wave. 'You've been very kind to Marcus,' she said, luckily not noticing the bewilderment that swept over Farrell's face, and added, 'and very helpful to me.'

'No problem,' Farrell told her, which made Ma wince. She glared at him.

'Lunch, I think,' she said sharply.

'I thought you'd never suggest it, Ma,' I said.

Immediately we got into Fortnum's I spotted Miranda. Luckily she was serving someone else and didn't see us come in. I steered Ma, with Farrell in tow, towards a table well away from Miranda's station, and sat down with my back to the rest of the room. I had to be careful now. I didn't want Ma noticing anything, not even so much as a glance passing between us. I *did* want Farrell to notice Miranda, however, so I made sure he had the seat that would give him the full view of the restaurant. He was in a sort of dazed seventh heaven. I suppose the closest he'd come to being in a restaurant was the Salvation Army mess hall. I just hoped his manners wouldn't be too awful, and that if he did have soup he wouldn't slurp it the way he tended to at home. He studied the menu with care, running his finger down the starters, main courses and sweets – an appalling *faux pas* as far as Ma was concerned, an affectation: puddings were puddings, sweets were things you bought in a sweet shop – all under the watchful eye of Ma.

'Decided, darling?' she asked me eventually. I chose a crab salad. 'And John?' Ma wanted to know.

'Seen anything you like, John?' I asked.

He leaned across to me, shoving the menu under my nose. 'I'll have that,' he said.

'I don't think so, John,' I said. 'Steak tartare wouldn't be exactly your cup of tea.'

'I like steak.'

'This isn't exactly steak. Not like you know it, anyway.'

'It says steak,' Farrell insisted.

'Yes. I *know* it *says* steak but –'

'If you'll excuse me,' Ma interrupted. 'I'll just go and freshen up while John makes up his mind.' She stood up. '*Do* help him, dear,' she pleaded.

I helped him. After a lot of explanation, and more toing and froing, I got him to accept that raw mince wasn't going to be to his liking, and managed to make him choose lamb cutlets, which I thought were a safe enough bet.

So now, with Ma in the powder-room, I had a chance to get Farrell interested in Miranda. Not in any sexual way, I hasten to add. I'd probed him a bit on that subject and he seemed unnaturally disinterested in women except in a fanatical way. Sure, he'd have lewd thoughts about them but when it came to the nitty-gritty something seemed to have happened to Farrell's animal urges. Maybe the drugs he was into had botched them up, or maybe he'd never had any such urges – how was I to know? In any case his interest in the fairer sex was pretty academic: they were a species that inhabited his planet and why they were there or for what reason they differed from men seemed to interest him not one whit. I honestly don't think it ever crossed his mind that there was gratification to be had by lying down with woman sapiens. If it did, he never showed any signs of wanting to do anything about it.

I turned my head a bit and took a surreptitious glance over my shoulder. Miranda was well and truly occupied. Good. I leaned across the table to Farrell. 'Don't look now,' I said, so immediately the idiot became alert and started looking about him which was what I'd wanted, 'but you see that waitress over there in the corner? Behind me. Over near the door at the cash desk?'

Farrell peered in more or less the right direction.

'The one with the reddish hair, tied back?' I elaborated.

'Oh, yeah. I see her.'

'I want you to take a really good look at her,' I instructed.

Farrell took what, for him, was a really good look at her.

If he'd been anyone else I'd have supposed he was undressing her in his mind, but being Farrell it wouldn't have surprised me if he was allowing his imagination to rig her out in something Mother bloody Teresa might choose to wear.

When I decided even Farrell must have registered her impression, I said, 'I want you to remember her.'

Farrell nodded obligingly. 'Why?'

'She's a close friend of Zanker,' I lied, giving him something really fantastic to chew on. And, you know, he suddenly showed a spark of interest. More than that. The now-familiar look of intense hatred came into his eyes, and I thought I might as well stoke it a little. 'She could be a threat to us,' I told him conspiratorially.

And bless his cotton socks, Farrell switched his gaze to my face, his eyes softening for a moment, and he said, 'She won't be, Marcus. I promise.'

I could have hugged him. 'What makes you say that?' I asked.

''Cause.'

''Cause how?'

''Cause I won't let her.'

'Not much you or I can do about it,' I said, shaking my head and looking fairly cheesed off.

'We'll think of something, Marcus,' Farrell told me.

Well, the likelihood of Farrell thinking of anything was pretty slim. Not that I expected him to. I already knew precisely what was in store for the unsuspecting Miranda and *that* was all that mattered.

'I hope we do,' I said earnestly. 'I really hope we do.'

Then, to my utter surprise, Farrell indicated that I should watch what I was saying. He widened his eyes and froze, and there was Ma, back at the table, having powdered whatever she had gone to powder. I could hardly contain my delight that Farrell was, finally, getting into the swing of things.

The next morning, Sunday, I saw Ma and Harry off. Early, because Harry wanted to avoid what Ma called the 'tenement gypsies' – folk who took their holidays in caravans and caused havoc on the roads. 'Why they can't simply use hotels like everyone else, I really cannot understand,' Ma liked to say.

'Cost, Ma,' I'd tried to explain.

But Ma dismissed this triviality. 'If they can't *afford* holidays they shouldn't take them,' was how she saw it.

Anyway, off they went about eight o'clock. Ma had only said two things as she kissed me goodbye. One was that she regretted we hadn't been able to go to Mass together just once more, as if one of us was heading for the gallows; and the other was that she hoped I wasn't going to allow John to hang around much longer. She didn't say 'hang around', of course. Such a crude expression wouldn't have found breathing-room in Ma's mind. What she actually said was, 'I do hope that man will go and leave you in peace soon, darling. You've done quite enough for him already and his type will only abuse your generosity if you let him.'

'Don't you worry, Ma,' I said. 'He'll be going soon.'

'And then you'll come to us and stay for a couple of days, won't you, dear?'

'Sure I will, Ma.'

And as though to guarantee Farrell's departure with the utmost speed, she asked, 'When can we say? Next weekend?'

I shook my head. 'I wouldn't bank on it being that soon, Ma. All I can promise is that he'll be gone for good by the end of the month.'

'Not until – '

'Maybe before. I'll let you know,' I said, avoiding Harry's eyes since I felt he had given me a curious look when I'd said Farrell would be gone *for good*, but I could have imagined it.

I helped Ma into the car and shut the door. She lowered her window and pouted her lips for another farewell kiss. And I gave her one just to keep her happy. 'You two be good now,' I said, and waved like crazy as the car purred off down the road.

I was halfway up the stairs to wake Farrell when I changed my mind. I needed some time to myself and with him safely tucked up in an old sleeping-bag I'd found I figured now was my chance. I came back down the stairs and padded into the kitchen. And, yes, you're right, bloody Pissquick was there looking up at me in the best approximation he could muster to an obscene gesture. 'Shit,

Pissquick,' I said. 'You were supposed to be on your way to near Bath by now.'

I swear to God that cat knew he'd pulled a fast one, keeping a deathly silence so we wouldn't remember to pack him. 'Well, don't count your chickens,' I warned him. Not that he *wanted* to stay with me. I knew damn well he didn't. It was simply to spite me that the wretched animal had stayed mum and kept out of sight. 'I can always pack you in an airtight box and post you to near Bath, you know. One false move, mate,' I warned, and left him to ruminate on that.

I had plenty of other more important things to occupy my mind. And the most important of these was to get Farrell and Kranze face to face.

I made myself another mug of coffee. Waiting for the percolator to do the business, I gave the meeting some thought. The actual *meeting* was dead easy to arrange: simply take Farrell along there. However, I would have to make sure Farrell both understood and carried out my instructions to a tee and that, as the manic depressive from Elsinor said, was the rub. It depended, of course, on who could wield the more explicit power over Farrell: Kranze or me. I knew full well that Farrell would do just about anything for *me* when he was with me, but if I left him alone with Kranze God alone knew what might happen. And I needed him to have some time alone with Kranze. And then I needed to get Farrell to tell me exactly what Kranze said to him in private. And I needed to get Farrell into such a frame of mind that he would agree to fall in with any request Kranze might make, agree with it convincingly. It certainly was a challenge. I took the calendar off the wall and looked at the dates. Today was the third and I had until the twenty-ninth. I decided it would take me a couple of days to work on Farrell so I tentatively pencilled in Wednesday the sixth as the fateful day of reckoning between Kranze and Farrell. With that decision made, I felt as though a great weight had been lifted from my shoulders. I stretched. And just to underline my well-being I also pencilled in 'Visit Ma' in the little space set aside for Saturday the thirtieth. Nothing like being confident.

I then began to make notes in the other daily spaces: when I wanted Birt over again; when – well, when Farrell and Miranda should bump into each other with tragic consequences; when Kranze and Farrell would have their final, momentous get-together; when Farrell would depart this life and head for the great opium den in the sky. If everything went as simply as writing it down did, then everything would be fine. One slip-up, though, one tiny cog out of kilter, and everything would come crashing down about my ears. I put the calendar back on the wall. Like a warrior about to enter the fray I needed to cleanse my spirit. My groin, actually. Heather wouldn't be in London on a Sunday, I didn't think, but maybe I could persuade her to make a little trip to see the man who so adored her. Worth a try, anyway.

EIGHTEEN

Heather did make the short journey from Bray to London. Although she *said* it was only to see me it turned out later that she was leaving at seven the next morning on a flight to Brussels to be with her beloved fiancé, the unexciting Geoffrey. So, it suited her better to go from her flat in London to the airport rather than come all the way down first thing in the morning. I suppose it was because she was going to have to spend the next six weeks with Geoff that she was so rampant, chewing me raw and hopping up and down on me as if I was a bloody pogo-stick or something. I'm not sure if she'd have been all that enthusiastic or energetic if she could have read my mind. It would have given me the greatest pleasure to use Heather for my experiment instead of the unwitting, witless Miranda. As she humped away I closed my eyes and saw her face twisted in surprise and disbelief as she was killed. I opened my eyes and her face was twisted, all right, her eyes with that fixed glare she had when riding hard towards a double oxer as she approached orgasm. She looked absolutely idiotic and I couldn't help but laugh. Of course, with my laughter my penis collapsed (probably in a fit of giggles) and poor old Heather was left stranded, up the pole, you might say. But I couldn't use Heather for any experiment. Too close to home. Too many connections between me and her. So, sorry about this, Miranda, 'tis you, my sweet.

I spent all afternoon and most of the evening with Heather, and she thought this was terrific, that I'd developed a new lust for her. The only reason I did stay was because I just wasn't in the mood for Farrell, and, besides, I knew that if I stayed away for a while without letting him know he would worry, and when he worried the relief he felt when I brushed his anxieties away made him just that little bit more amenable.

He greeted me with collie eyes, standing by the kitchen table with the meal he had prepared for me, now cold and congealed and looking pretty damn unappetising. 'You didn't come home,' he told me.

'Fancy you noticing that.'

'I was worried.'

'No need to be, chum.'

'But I was.'

'Can't help you there.' I was being purposely brusque. Putting him in his place, in a manner of speaking.

'I cooked you a meal.'

'So I see. Thanks.'

'I wanted to please you.'

'I said thanks. What d'you want me to do? Get down on my knees and – '

I stopped there. Farrell adopted his hangdog look which I knew could lead to tears and I wasn't in the mood for any lachrymose lamenti. 'Okay. I'm sorry. I should have let you know but I was busy, right?'

Farrell shrugged and started clearing the table.

I gave him a hand. 'I was organising things,' I went on. 'Getting everything ready. This is going to be a very important week for us, you know.'

Farrell didn't know, of course, but the fact that I now told him it was cheered him up no end. 'It is?' he asked.

'Yep.'

'Tell me what we're doing,' he begged.

I felt pretty bad about wiping the smile off his inane face, but that's life. 'Tuesday you're going to meet Zanker,' I said.

I suppose the Nippons had the same look on their faces when Harry S. dropped the bomb on them. I don't know if our Japanese brethren *can* go white but Farrell certainly did. It was interesting to see the blood actually *drain* from his face, starting from about his temples and working down. He gripped the side of the sink but that didn't quite stop him giving a stagger. 'Twas time to ooze concern and fraternity.

'Hey,' I said, reaching out and taking his hand. 'You don't have to worry about a thing. Believe me. I'll tell you exactly what to say and what to do, and I won't leave you alone with Zanker for a second.'

That calmed him. 'You promise?'

'That I won't leave you alone with him? Sure, I promise. You have my word.' Farrell let go of the sink, but kept a grip on my hand. I let him hang onto it. 'Unless I have to go for a pee or something,' I added with a smile. Farrell smiled back. 'Come on,' I said. 'Let's you and me open a bottle of wine and sit down. You choose one.'

That was a big deal as far as Farrell was concerned. He knew I was pretty *au fait* with wine and he knew sod-all, so to be told he could choose what we were about to drink was a bit like telling him he could select the Queen Mum's bonnet for Ascot. What he didn't realise was that it didn't matter one hoot what he chose since all the wine I had in stock was more than palatable.

'Good choice,' I told him admiringly as he handed me a bottle of Pouilly-Fuissé.

'Good, eh?'

'Very good. Glasses?'

He got the glasses.

I uncorked the bottle and gave him the cork to sniff after I'd sniffed it myself. Then I poured the wine, settling myself comfortably in my chair, knowing this could be quite a long session. Probably a four-jelly session, in fact, but he'd have to wait for them for a while.

To be fair (to Farrell, that is), I have to admit that I may have been overdoing his stupidity a bit, and I'll confess now, *mea culpa, mea culpa, mea maxima culpa* and all that jazz, that he was actually quite bright when you could get through to him. He *sounded* stupid, but that was because he had no vocabulary whatsoever, I suppose because no one had ever bothered speaking *to* him in his miserable life so he'd never had to practise the art of communicating. It's my guess people spoke *at* him, and that's a very different matter. Speaking, for Farrell, was a bit like someone who'd paddled all their life going in at the deep end for the first time. And, of course, the drugs didn't help. They did give him a sort of bravado confidence and if he'd had the words I'm sure he could have carried on some reasonable and maybe even witty repartee. But words he didn't have, and I noticed that as soon as I used a word outside his ken he got all embarrassed and ashamed, and that got his back up, and down came the shutters.

So now, sitting there in the kitchen, swigging the wine, I knew I had to proceed with extreme care. Although, as you'll have gathered,

Farrell just about worshipped me, and was nicely impressionable and easily led, his mental state had improved by leaps and bounds since he'd been staying with me, and his pride was returning, and it would be fatal for me to dent that blossoming dignity.

I was quietly mulling over what to say to him, and how exactly to phrase it, when he said, 'I'm sorry, Marcus.'

'For what?' I asked, genuinely surprised.

'For thinking you'd land me in it with Zanker.'

'Hey, that's okay. Natural you might think that. I mean, you've been dumped on most of your life, haven't you?'

'Not by you.'

'No. Well. It's different with me. We're pals, right?'

His eyes got all dewy. 'Know something? You're the only real pal I've ever had.'

He must have told me that a dozen times already. I felt a spot of embarrassment was called for. 'Hey, come on,' I began.

'No, I mean it, Marcus.'

I already knew he meant it. 'Well, it's my good fortune then,' I told him. I raised my glass. 'Cheers.'

'Cheers, pal,' Farrell said, and I felt I could now go ahead with the business in hand.

'Right,' I began, putting my glass on the table and twisting it round and round, gazing into the wine as though for inspiration. Then I looked him straight in the eye. 'You know what I think, John? I think Zanker is out to get me and he's going to try and use you to do that.' It took a few seconds for the enormity of my conjecture to register in Farrell's brain. When it did, he looked at me and opened his mouth to reply. Immediately I interrupted. 'And when he's got you to do whatever it is he *wants* you to do, he's going to shit on you, too.' Letting that sink in, I refilled both our glasses.

I wondered if I'd overloaded his mind because he lowered his head and shook it as though trying to rattle the information into some semblance of logic. Then he looked up at me again. He nodded slowly. 'Yeah, he'd do that, too,' he said.

'If he could,' I pointed out.

'If he could.'

'But we won't let him. We're one step ahead of the old bastard because we *know* what he's up to. Right?'

Farrell beamed at me. 'Right.'

'And that's why Tuesday's going to be so important, John. An awful lot – everything, really – is going to depend on how you handle things. Think you can handle it, pal?'

He wasn't sure. But he was a brave little soldier, the sucker who carried the banner in front of the troops, a glory kid ready to obey his orders regardless of the cost to himself. 'You tell me what to do, Marcus,' he told me quietly but with unaccustomed eagerness, 'and I'll do it.'

That merited another drink, I felt. I got another bottle of Pouilly (Fumé, this time) and opened it. I stood behind him as I filled his glass. 'I don't want you to get involved if you don't want to, you know,' I told him.

'Just tell me what you want me to do, Marcus.'

I sat down. 'Well, John, part of the trouble is that you'll have to play most of it by ear. I don't know, yet, what *exactly* Zanker is up to. And we can't just ask him what he's playing at, can we?' I asked with a breezy laugh.

Happily, Farrell laughed also. 'No. S'pose not.'

'So we're going to have to be very subtle – canny – and try and find out. I mean, *you'll* have to try and find out.'

Farrell looked at me steadily and for one awful moment I thought he'd sussed the fact that I was using him. 'How do I do that?' he asked, and I breathed easily again.

'Well, he's going to give you a whole line of shit. I do know that. He'll pretend *he's* your friend and that *I'm* using you.'

'He better fucking – '

'Let him, John. Let him say what he wants. And – now this is *really* important – I want you to pretend to agree with him.'

Farrell considered this. Then he brightened. 'I get it. You want me to sort of put one over on him?'

'Exactly. But, listen, John. We both know Zanker's no fool so I don't want you agreeing with him immediately. You know what I mean, sort of take your time. Look doubtful. Say, no, Marcus has been really good to you, that sort of – '

'You have been.'

'Okay. Yes. Thanks. Maybe I have. Okay, I have been terrific to you, but we don't want Zanker knowing that. So you go slowly, slowly. Let him think he's convincing you that I'm up to no good. If you're too quick to agree with him he'll know you and me have got something up our sleeve.'

By now Farrell was getting quite excited. 'Yes. Yes. Yes,' he said, mostly to himself. And then he looked puzzled. 'But he won't try any of that if you're there with me,' he pointed out. I told you he wasn't *that* stupid.

'Oh, shit,' I said, feigning annoyance. 'You're right, of course. I never thought of that.'

I folded my arms on the table and buried my head in them, purposely adopting one of Farrell's favourite positions. I waited. Would he or wouldn't he? He would, God love him. 'Listen, Marcus – remember you said something about going for a pee?'

I raised my head, and adopted a bewildered look.

'When I asked you not to leave me alone with Zanker?'

I continued to look puzzled.

'And you said you wouldn't unless you had to go for a piss or something – remember?'

I pretended to recall. 'Oh, yes,' I said in a disinterested sort of way, which was difficult since my heart was going hell for leather, waiting for Farrell to say what I wanted him to say.

'Well, why don't you do that? Go for a piss. Or say you've got to get something out of the car? Get out of the house for a while.' He was getting there, the little ray of sunshine.

'And leave you alone with him after I promised I wouldn't?' I asked, acting shocked that he would even suggest such a thing. 'No way, John. A promise is a promise.'

Farrell stretched across the table and took my hand, which was a cute variation on the theme, and gave me a look as though a halo had sprouted from my head. It was really strange. In the twinkling of an eye, for some inexplicable reason, Farrell had, as it were, grown up. He was taking control of things. *He* was going to tell *me* what to do. 'I'll be okay,' he told me, squeezing my hand. 'I can handle Zanker. Just you give me some time with him alone.'

It was time to be doubtful. 'Oh, I don't know, John. He's a dangerous – '

'I *want* you to do it, Marcus.'

'Well, if you *want* me to – '

'I do.'

Better and better. And then it struck me that maybe Farrell was planning something rather more than letting Zanker try and turn him against me. Maybe he was plotting something, shall we say, terminal for Kranze, and I certainly didn't want that, not yet. 'John, you're not thinking of – not planning – '

Farrell's newly gifted authority was still functioning, apparently. 'To do him in?' he asked.

'Something like that.'

Farrell smiled at me. 'No.'

But I wasn't entirely convinced. 'You're sure?'

Farrell nodded. 'I'm sure. Not unless you want me to.'

I don't think I've ever been overcome with such a sense of joy as I was at that minute. Rashly, I stood up and gave Farrell a huge, tight hug. 'God, John Farrell, you're the best pal anyone could have,' I told him, but came back to earth with a bump when he looked up and asked, 'You want me to do him in?'

'No I don't,' I said emphatically.

'Okay, okay,' Farrell said as though he'd been having a little joke at my expense. 'I won't.'

And that was that. We didn't mention Kranze again that evening. We finished the wine. We became esoteric and discussed friendship, fast food, fashion, would you believe. He had his jellies and I had a joint. We went to our separate beds. We dreamed. I did, anyway.

I hadn't intended to talk to Farrell about Kranze until Monday, so I was ahead of schedule. Thus, on that Monday morning I got up and dressed feeling pretty good about everything even though there was still a lot that had to be done.

I left a note for Farrell telling him not to go out, just in case our conversation of the previous evening had gone to his head and he felt he could take on the world.

'You're looking very chipper,' one of the girls at the front desk commented. The ugly one. The one who was so starved of attention that she compensated by being unwelcomely familiar.

'Chipper?'

'Yes, you know – '

I waited.

She got flustered under my gaze.

Still I waited.

She reddened.

I gave her a glare and walked down the corridor. That'd teach the silly bitch to use words she didn't really know the meaning of.

The pile of manuscripts that had been dumped on my desk made my heart sink, but seeing them reminded me of Camp Carl and I decided to give him a ring. To cheer myself up before tackling the trash hopeful authors thought was *Gone with the bloody Wind*.

'Hiya, Carl, my love.'

'Marcus!'

'None other.'

'How are you?'

'Terrific. And you?'

'Lousy.'

'No romance in your life, eh?'

'Bugger the romance, dear heart.'

'Oh. I get it. None of the other either.'

'Nothing worth talking about.'

'Life really is a bitch, ain't it?'

'Tell me about it. So, what can I do for you?'

'Nothing. Not a thing. I just needed cheering up and you've done that already.'

'Well, I'm glad I'm useful for something.'

I laughed. 'Jesus, I can tell you another thing, Carl. I really miss having you drop in for our little chats.'

'Ditto, ducky. God, the boring shits we have here now. Accountants, most of them, it seems to me. No *imagination*. Dullsville.'

'You should try moving over here.'

'Too old to shift now, deary. Anyway, I've decided to retire gracefully at the end of the year.'

'You? Retire?'

'Yes. Before senile decay sets in. Or dry rot. Whatever. Anyway, I want to travel.'

'Ah, the fleshpots of the world.'

'That's it.'

'Take me with you?'

'Any time, dear heart. Any time.'

We chatted on for a while, promising to meet up soon for a drink. I felt much better when I finally settled down to work. And luck was with me. The first manuscript I tackled wasn't half bad, if you like quasi adventure tales set in enlightened Africa. With apartheid gone, the tinted folk were coming into their own. They were suddenly the goodies, and here they were, led by one Umzomo Pekwangi, battling to save a game park from being taken over by some American conglomerate who wanted to use it for nefarious reasons too numerous to mention. Lucky, I thought, for Mr Pekwangi that it wasn't the Japs who'd had their eye on it or he'd have had the veldt pockmarked with bunkers. Anyway, it was, as I said, a pretty good read, and the morning passed quickly enough even if, by lunchtime, I was pretty much brain dead. A headache seemed in order.

'If anyone's looking for me I'll be at home,' I told the ugly receptionist, just to show her I held no grudges.

But I didn't go home. I went instead to see Inspector Birt.

Birt didn't keep me waiting long. I'd barely planted my backside on the bench by the front desk when he popped his head through a door and beckoned me to follow him. 'This is a surprise,' he told me.

'Life's full of 'em,' I answered, and entered the interview-room, although I just about felt like doing an about-turn and marching out of the station again when I saw Sergeant Wilson already ensconced by the table. 'Does he have to be here?'

'Eh, it would be better.'

'You think I might compromise you or something?'

Birt didn't answer that so I knew I was right and that made me smile.

'What you mean is that you want a witness to anything I say, right?' I asked.

'Covering my back.'

I tapped my nose. 'Wise.'

'I know.'

I sat down.

'So. I'm all ears,' Birt said.

I decided to play it casually. 'Just a couple of things. First, I thought you better know I'm taking Speed to see Kranze tomorrow so I'd appreciate it if Genius there could park his car where Kranze can't see it. I mean, I presume you're still watching Kranze's house for whatever reason?'

Birt nodded slowly. 'From time to time.'

'Well, try and make tomorrow morning one of the times you're *not* watching it, will you?'

'Very well,' Birt agreed, to Wilson's chagrin.

'Does he *really* have to be here?' I now asked, not so much because I cared. I simply felt like getting up Wilson's nose.

Birt got testy. 'Yes.'

I shrugged. 'Means I have to use words of less than three syllables, I suppose.'

'Listen you – ' Wilson began, half rising, but sitting down again when Birt placed a restraining hand on his arm.

'Sit, boy,' I said, like I might to a Dobermann, and added a really cheeky grin for good measure.

'You said there were a couple of things,' Birt reminded me.

I took my time about answering, giving Wilson another fierce glare. Then I said, 'I might have some info for you on a robbery.'

'Into a bit of housebreaking now, are we?' Wilson asked with a smirk.

'See?' I asked. 'Told you. The man's a no-no.' I stood up. 'Sorry I bothered you.'

Birt was one of those passive creatures, probably the sort who prided himself in never losing his cool. But he lost it now in a big way. He slammed his fist on the table. 'Will you two stop it?' he shouted. 'You, sit down,' he ordered me, 'And you, keep it shut till I ask you something,' he told Wilson.

I sat down. Wilson shut it.

'Now – what were you saying?'

'Before I was interrupted by – ' I stopped when it looked as if Birt was going to take a swipe at me. I gave him a grin and ducked. Then I held up my hands by way of surrender. 'I was saying I might have some information for you about a robbery.'

'Go on,' Birt said.

'That's it. Nothing's been planned yet as far as I know. But I think it'll be big.'

'And how come you know about it?' Birt wanted to know.

I gave a hoot. 'Because I've been asked to be the driver.'

That took the wind out of Wilson's sails, I can tell you. Ever since Birt had rebuked him he'd been sitting there all hunched up but with a sneering, sceptical look on his fat face. But now he straightened. His eyes took on that shifty aspect much favoured by Hollywood FBI agents in old movies.

'Who asked you?' Birt asked quietly.

'Ah, now that – that's a horse of a different colour. I'll tell you *that* when I know a bit more about the affair myself. Anyway, if you really are as good as you pretend to be, all you have to do is put two and two together and not get five like Genius there would.'

Birt understood. He nodded. 'I see.'

'Better explain to Bozo, then. He hasn't a clue.'

Birt ignored that. 'This robbery – when is it supposed to happen?'

I made a grimace. 'Not sure,' I lied.

'You must have *some* idea,' was Wilson's conclusion.

I simply pretended I hadn't heard. I said to Birt, 'I'll let you know as soon as *I* know. Okay?'

Birt nodded. 'Just make sure you do,' he warned.

'Don't you trust me, then?'

Wilson reverted to type and gave a bray like a jackass.

'It'll be a bad day for you when I don't,' Birt said.

'God, Inspector Birt, you're a difficult man to please,' I said, purposely refraining from calling him by his Christian name, although I was tempted to do so just to see Neanderthal Man's reaction to *that*.

'On the contrary,' Birt said.

'Could have fooled me.'

'Yes. Well. Just as long as *you* don't try and fool *me*,' Birt told me.

I looked at my watch. 'Jeez, is that the time?' I said, acting astonished. 'I'll have to get my running-shoes on.' I stood up. 'See you later, then,' I said to Birt. He nodded, watching me closely. 'And take care of Vera Lynn there, won't you?' I added as a parting shot, and scuttled out just in case Wilson put his glare into action and strangled me.

Everything was proceeding nicely apace. I felt pretty damn good when I came out of the police station. Cleansed almost. I wanted to celebrate. I phoned Farrell and told him not to cook anything, told him we were dining out. 'Eating out,' I said when I heard his mind fumbling with what I actually said.

'Oh.'

'You haven't started cooking anything?'

'Just about to.'

'Well, forget it.'

'I know. I heard you. We're eating out.'

Which we did. Just locally. A small, family-run Italian place where I'd discovered the canneloni was out of this world.

'Had a good day then?' Farrell enquired when we'd just about finished and I was scraping up the last of my zabaglione.

'I had a *very* good day, thank you.'

'So did I,' Farrell informed me.

'Oh? What did you get up to, then?'

'Nothing.'

There was no answer to that. I just hoped and prayed that I'd be able to say the same thing this time tomorrow, but I wasn't all that confident.

Before I went to bed I decided to call Kranze to let him know he'd have visitors the next day.

'What do you mean – visitors?' he hissed when I told him.

'What do you think I mean – little green men from Mars?' I shot back. 'I'm bringing your druggy friend Farrell round in the morning.'

There was silence on the line.

'You still there?' I asked impatiently.

'Do you really mean it, Marcus? You're not just winding me up?' came back a hoarse whisper.

'Yes, I mean it. Tomorrow morning.' And I hung up before I had second thoughts.

And I slept badly, which was irksome. I kept tossing and turning, thinking of just about everything that could go wrong when Farrell and Kranze came face to face. Everything depended on Farrell doing his bit, and that, I knew, was really hoping for miracles.

NINETEEN

But miracles wouldn't be miracles if they didn't come as something of a surprise. And although there was no indication whatever that anything untoward was to take place when Farrell and I set out to visit Kranze the next morning, I can truthfully say unto you that a miracle *did* take place later, or something close enough to one as to make no difference.

True, we had a bit of an argument before we left the house: Farrell wanted to look his best, and it took me a while to convince him that this wasn't the way to play things. He needed to look like little boy lost; look as if he'd been plucked from the streets and not as if he'd been staying with me; look vulnerable. After a couple of joints he saw my point of view and entered into the spirit of things, donning his own original dirty clobber which, as fortune would have it, I'd put in a binbag in the garage and forgotten to leave out for the garbage collectors. Clothes might not maketh the man but they sure as hell can detract from him. Farrell looked for all the world as if he'd spent the last few weeks kipping in cardboard city, and he stank a treat.

I opened all the windows and the sunroof as I drove towards Cricklewood. 'Feel okay?'

Farrell nodded. 'Feel fine.'

'Good. Now, I don't want to keep on at you, but you will remember to – '

'I'll remember,' Farrell interrupted, in such a way as to tell me he was actually remembering at that moment, rehearsing, going through every detail in his mind. Then, maybe for my benefit or maybe just for his own, he launched into a litany of all the things he had to recall. 'I haven't been staying with you. I don't know who you are except your name. I know nothing about you. You only picked me up this morning. Met you twice before but we didn't talk much.'

'Very good,' I said.

Farrell frowned as though my comment had seriously damaged his concentration, and he added a little cluck of annoyance.

'Oops. Sorry,' I apologised.

He gathered his thoughts together again, laboriously as a shelf-stacker in a supermarket, and continued. 'If he mentions that policeman, Inspector Birt, I've not to let on I know who he's talking about. I've got to make him think I'm not scared of him – '

'Heh-em,' I interrupted. 'Not quite, John.'

'Oh. Right,' Farrell acceded, nodding vigorously. 'I've got to let him think I'm willing to fall in with any plan he has even pretending that I *am* scared of him.'

'Exactly. Well done.'

He gave me a sideways glance. 'That's it.'

'Except that you have to try and prod him if he doesn't tell you what he's up to by himself.'

'Oh, yes.'

'Good,' I said, and patted his knee.

'I *am* scared of him, though,' Farrell now confessed.

'Don't blame you, mate. So am I, if you want the truth. But he won't do anything to you. Not with me around. I can promise you that,' I assured him. 'He's not one for taking any chances.'

Farrell withdrew into silence for a while. Then: 'It'll be okay. I'll be fine,' he announced, and it really sounded as if he had convinced himself of this.

'I *know* you will, John.' I didn't, but there was no harm in hoping.

Mrs Zanker opened the door. Maybe Helmut had warned her that this was a state visit of some importance, or maybe we'd just caught her on a good day. Whatever the reason, she actually had her hair done: two long grey braids, twisted with agonising rigour over the top of her head and affixed there with what looked like barbed-wire clips. She ignored me completely and concentrated her beady gaze on Farrell. And as she gazed she kept us waiting on the doorstep, almost as if she'd forgotten we wanted to get in. At last, however, she came to her senses and stood aside. 'Come in,' she said in her guttural tone, and this was definitely one greedy spider talking to two flies.

'The parlour?' I quipped.

'Upstairs,' Mrs Zanker said.

Joke wasted. 'Thanks. Come on, John.'

You know how most nationalities have their own national aroma? Indians, curry; Irish, cabbage; Turks, coffee? Well, I figure the Germans have theirs also, if the Zanker household was anything to go by. Every time I'd called to see Kranze there was the same smell: Bratwurst and sauerkraut. Maybe that's all they lived on. Anyway, as Farrell and I made our way up the stairs I sniffed the air and raised my eyes to heaven. 'Stinks,' I said. Farrell nodded. 'Really stinks,' I added, knowing that even this mildly insulting remark would help to lower the degree of anxiety Farrell was feeling. For some mad reason, if you can associate a bad pong with the enemy they don't seem to be all that dangerous.

'He had the same stink in his cell,' Farrell informed me.

'Really? That's interesting. I thought it was a kitchen smell. Maybe it's his special Teutonic body odour.'

Farrell nodded and even gave a small smile.

But the smile had gone when we reached the door of Kranze's study. 'Don't *worry*,' I told him. 'Just remember what you have to do and say and everything will work a treat.'

I knocked on the door. The moment Kranze's voice told us to come in I had to grab Farrell. The effect of that voice clearly unnerved him. Christ, I thought, if that's how he reacts to the mere sound of Kranze's voice, what the hell is he going to be like when he meets him? I gave Farrell's arm an encouraging squeeze, and opened the door.

There's only one way to describe the atmosphere that ensued: electric. It crackled. I let John go in ahead of me since I wanted a full view of Kranze's reaction. He was, as usual, sitting in that over-stuffed armchair of his, looking for all the world like some dwarf Germanic Borgia, if you could have such a thing. For what seemed an age under the circumstances he didn't say a word, so neither did we, needless to say. He just fixed his watery eyes on John, ignoring me totally, and stared at him without blinking. I can only presume that Farrell was staring him back: I couldn't actually see since I was behind him, close enough behind him to feel it when he started to get those little imperceptible shakes that led to greater things. I didn't want him collapsing on me, thank you very much, so I broke the silence. 'This staring going to go on much longer?' I asked.

Still ignoring me, Kranze said, 'John,' and gave a small nod.

Farrell nodded back.

'Can we come in now?' I wanted to know.

'Come and sit down, John,' Kranze said.

I gave Farrell a nudge and got him mobile again. 'What about me? Do I get to sit down?'

Kranze gave me a testy look but pointed to a chair. Not the one I usually sat in, the twin of his own at the other side of the fireplace, but a straight-backed, uncomfortable, cane-seated contraption set back from the main scene, in the wings as it were. Still, this happened to suit me since it gave me a good look at both of them without intruding, a sort of Polonius without the arras, although there was an added advantage: Farrell could, if he so desired, glance up and see me, and I could, if *I* so desired, encourage or dissuade him.

'How are you, John?' Kranze asked.

And this was when Glasgow's answer to Gielgud began his Oscar-winning performance. 'Not too good,' he answered in an appropriately hangdog way.

'Ah,' Kranze sighed which could have meant any number of things. That he was sorry to hear it, which was unlikely. That he was delighted to hear it, which was probably closer to the mark. Or maybe it was just a sigh of satisfaction since Farrell's misery would leave him nicely vulnerable to any Kranzean ploy.

'And you?' Farrell asked unexpectedly. At least, *I* hadn't expected him to ask it.

'I survive,' Kranze told him.

Farrell took a long look about the room, taking his time about it, screwing up his face and studying some items which particularly interested him. 'Doing okay by the looks of it,' he said approvingly.

'I survive,' Kranze repeated, using his eyes to bore into Farrell's skull.

Not for much longer, mate, I thought to myself, and then just about shat myself when Kranze rounded on me, and demanded, 'What did you say, Marcus?'

'Me? Nothing. Never said a word.'

Only very slowly did Kranze release me from his gaze and return his attention to Farrell, who had taken to having another look at the room, even leaning to one side to see what was concealed by Kranze's chair.

Farrell gave a little snort. 'Better than sleeping rough, though, isn't it?' he asked. 'On the streets,' he added.

'Is that what you're doing?' Kranze asked, and I froze. As far as I could remember I'd told Kranze I'd found Farrell in a squat and I knew even this tiny slip, the minute difference between sleeping on the streets and in a squat, would make Kranze suspicious. And, as though to confirm my anxiety, Kranze asked again, 'Is that what you're doing, John? Sleeping on the streets?'

Farrell lowered his head. 'No,' he said, and left it at that, left Kranze a bit nonplussed into the bargain which gave me a thrill.

'Are you eating?' Kranze then asked.

It was all wrong. Kranze, I was certain, couldn't give a shit where Farrell was sleeping or whether he was eating or not. *These* weren't questions he wanted answered. What he wanted to know – I suddenly stopped wondering what Kranze wanted to know when Farrell answered, 'Sure I'm eating. Have lunch at Fortnum's, don't I?'

Well, I nearly fell off my chair. The fact that he'd actually remembered the name of Fortnum's was surprise enough, but to toss out the fact that he'd eaten there with such sarcastic aplomb just about floored me. Farrell was enjoying himself! A good time, I felt, to leave them alone. 'Oh, shit,' I said.

Immediately Kranze twisted his head in my direction, his eyes demanding an explanation. So, I gave him one. 'I left the proofs – the corrected ones – of your book in the car.' I stood up. 'Won't be a tick,' I announced. 'Just get them,' I concluded and got out of the room as fast as I could without seeming to be in any hurry.

I'd had the foresight to park the car round the corner so Kranze couldn't see it from his window, see me sitting there twiddling my thumbs. I had to be careful, though: stay away too long and Kranze would certainly know I was up to something; go back too soon and Farrell wouldn't have had a chance to find out what I hoped he'd find out, what I desperately needed to know. Henry Kelly was in one of his Poulenc moods (a bit esoteric for him) so I listened to that for a while. Some flute concerto, played by that bloke from Northern Ireland on the golden flute he keeps bragging about. I say I listened to it but that's not really true: I heard it but I wasn't listening to it. I was far too concerned about what was going on in that room at the top of the stairs. It came the time to find out. I made my way slowly back to the house and I can honestly say I have never been quite so apprehensive in my life. Nor had I ever witnessed anything like the scene that greeted me when I went into Kranze's study – without knocking, just to see if I might catch him on the hop. Let me describe it to you so you'll understand why I felt something very akin to panic sweep over me.

Farrell was seated, his head in his hands. Kranze was standing over him. I would have said 'towering over him', but it's a mite difficult for a midget to tower. Neither of them gave any sign that they noticed my arrival. I stood and watched, fascinated, in the way, I think, that I'd be fascinated if I ever went to one of those good old American executions. What was really weird was that although Kranze was saying nothing he *seemed* to be speaking, and Farrell, incredibly, *seemed* to be hearing. For, as Kranze stood there motionless, Farrell went to pieces. He started shaking worse than I'd ever seen him shake. He began muttering incoherently to himself, muttering wildly. And when he took his hands from his face I saw his eyes were red-raw and the tears were streaming down his cheeks. So, I thought, Kranze, the bastard, has broken him. The game's up. Time to steal away and lick my wounds. And then Kranze turned his head and looked at me. And it was also time for me to be appalled. 'What – ' I began, about to try and bluff my way out of whatever cesspool Farrell had landed me in. The reason, however, that I stopped after just that one single word was I flicked my eyes from Kranze to Farrell, and, through his tears, through his shaking and his agony, John the Jelly Farrell bestowed on me quite the most enormous wink before starting to sob again and shudder as though all his bodily control had gone haywire. It was all I could do not to burst out laughing, I can tell you. I recovered. I coughed. I started again. 'What the hell's going on?' I demanded. 'You all right, John?' I asked.

Kranze answered. 'John is fine,' he told me.

'Oh, yeah, he really looks on top of the world.'

I made to move across the room to Farrell but Kranze stopped me by holding up a pudgy little hand. 'I wouldn't,' he said.

'Oh, wouldn't you?' I retorted. 'I go out for a couple of minutes and come back and find that poor sod in a state of jitters like you've been giving him the third degree or something.'

'We were recalling – '

'I bet you were,' I interrupted.

'We have shared – ' Kranze started.

And then, without warning Farrell was on his feet, screaming at the two of us. I can't remember *what* he screamed but it sure as hell wasn't a bunch of compliments. And the next thing he was out of the room, tumbling down the stairs and out of the house. Automatically both Kranze and I went to the window and there was Farrell running up the road, waving his arms like a lunatic, and disappearing round the corner. Round the corner where I'd parked my car, I was pleased to note.

'I'm going after him,' I announced.

And to my surprise, quite calmly and coldly, Kranze answered, 'Yes, do that.' And then, almost as an afterthought, he added, 'Are those my proofs?'

'Yeah. Catch,' I said and tossed them to him. Without further ado, I skedaddled but not before hearing Kranze's voice follow me down the stairs.

'I'll phone you,' he said.

I didn't answer.

Mrs Zanker was at the foot of the stairs, looking very stern and clearly concerned about what was going on. She gave me a couple of high-pitched barks like a cheetah calling its cubs to gorge after a kill, and tried to block my way. But I gave her an unceremonious shove and left the house. I knew Kranze was at his window watching me so I sauntered nonchalantly down the road, without a care in the world, and certainly not in the least concerned as to where Mr Farrell had hightailed it to. That was the impression I *hoped* I was giving. Inside was a different story: I was dreading coming to the corner and finding Farrell *not* there. It also crossed my mind that maybe Kranze *had* persuaded Farrell to shift allegiances, although when I recalled Farrell's wink I felt encouraged. Still, maybe *that* was meant to mislead me too. That's the trouble with being slightly devious yourself: you start to think everyone else is being the same.

A furniture removal van came trundling down the road, giving me an excuse to stop and look left and right before crossing over. It also gave me the chance to take a surreptitious peep back towards the house and, sure enough, I could just make Kranze out, standing by the window, those ghastly net curtains slightly parted. Why did I get the feeling he didn't give a damn whether I found Farrell or not? I don't know, but it sure as hell worried me.

But then I saw Farrell waiting for me at the car, leaning his buttocks against the boot, looking pretty smug and pleased with himself. 'Did all right, didn't I, pal?' he asked.

I still wasn't sure, so there was perhaps a smidgen too much seriousness in my voice when I asked, 'You want the truth?'

Farrell looked worried suddenly. 'Yeah,' he said hesitantly.

Wisdom dictated that I shouldn't let Farrell see that I had any doubts, so I beamed at him. 'You were only fucking terrific,' I told him.

He blushed with pleasure. 'Just get me out of here.'

'Yes, sir,' I said, and gave a salute.

Needless to say I was dying to know what had gone on between Kranze and Farrell while I'd been out of the room but I didn't ask yet. *That* information would require my full attention and concentration (not only because of the content but because I was sure I would be able to tell from Farrell's demeanour whose side the sod actually was on) and I couldn't give it either as I dodged through the traffic, making my way back to civilisation. I decided instead to keep buttering up Farrell, keep him in a good mood. 'You really had me convinced,' I told him.

A compliment indeed. 'Did I?'

'Sure did. And then when you winked – shit, I nearly pissed myself.'

Farrell cackled.

'Tell me, how did you get your eyes all red like that?'

'Old trick. Used to do it inside to get off work. Salt. Just rub a bit of salt in them. They come up red and runny like you've got an infection.'

I just glanced at him and smiled.

'They come up a treat,' he told me.

'Sure do. That was very clever of you, John.'

I thought that I should really go back to the office and finish reading the exploits of Mr Pekwangi and his henchmen, but I also thought there was no way I was going to do that until I'd debriefed Farrell, in a manner of speaking. Umzomo and his safari park could wait until the morrow; Farrell couldn't. A further thought: 'Where did you get the salt?'

'Brought it with me,' Farrell said, and to prove he was telling the truth he turned the pocket of his jacket inside out and let the remainder of the salt spill out.

I was genuinely surprised that he had thought to do such a thing. 'You amaze me sometimes, John,' I said.

'Got to be prepared.'

'Yes, but – '

'I know him – Zanker.'

'Yes, but – '

'Had to be sure I didn't mess things up for you,' he told me, and there was such a depth of shy sincerity in his voice that much of my anxiety about his possible double-dealing evaporated. 'Thanks,' I said simply.

I felt I should give him something for his dedication to duty, above and beyond the call, actually. Give him a real treat. A buzz the likes of which he'd never had. But not yet. Not until I'd learned in detail what Kranze had said. I wanted nothing to distract Farrell, nothing extraneous to enter and clutter his brain, so I didn't even mention the possibility of a reward in case it got him thinking along different lines.

And, as though he read my thoughts, Farrell asked, 'You want me to tell you what Zanker said when you were down at the car?'

'Sure I want you to tell me. But not just yet.'

Farrell said, 'Oh,' in a disappointed way.

'When we get home,' I added hastily. 'It's really important that I *listen* to you properly, John. I mean – '

'I understand,' he said, and lapsed into a hardy silence. I hoped he was remembering everything Kranze had told him, but he could have been thinking anything, or not thinking at all.

'Tell you what,' I said cheerfully. 'We'll go home. You tell me what went on. And then we'll have a bit of a celebration. How's that sound?'

'Sounds okay.'

'That's what we'll do then.' Which just shows you I can change my mind and adapt.

And that was how it was. We got home and I made some coffee. We sat at the kitchen table. I said, 'Ready?'

Farrell nodded.

'Okay, shoot,' I said, and started to watch him like the proverbial hawk.

He began with a statement. 'He's mad, you know,' he told me, tapping the side of his head. 'Really mad.'

I nodded. I knew that.

'He hates you. Really hates you.'

I nodded again. I'd guessed that. 'Did he say why?'

'What he said was he'd taught you everything and you were going to use it against him,' Farrell told me ponderously. 'What'd he mean by that?'

'Tell you later. Go on. What else did he say?'

'He – no,' Farrell started to rub his head like he was sorting out some sort of jumble. 'The *first* thing he said was to ask me, very sly like, how I knew you and how long I'd known you.'

That figured. 'And you told him – what?'

'Like we agreed. That I'd only just met you when you picked me up at the squat.'

'Good,' I said approvingly.

'He didn't believe me, though.'

Not so good.

'It was like he *knew* we'd known each other a while.'

'Why d'you say that?'

'Well – other questions he asked.'

'Like?' I prompted.

'Like – well, like he sort of said things like, "Been looking after you, has he", and, "I suppose you've met his great friend Inspector Birt", and stuff like that.'

Yes, I thought, that would be exactly how Kranze would do it. He'd pretend he knew what was going on just to find out *if* anything was going on. Try and lull Farrell into believing – .

'I fixed it though,' Farrell was saying.

I raised my eyebrows.

'Sure did,' he added, and then gave me a wicked grin. 'Told him I wouldn't have any ponce like you looking after me.'

'Thanks a bunch.'

'Told him I'd never heard of any Inspector Birt. Said "Bird" on purpose instead of Birt.'

And there I was thinking *I* was the devious one.

'That was when he told me you were out to get him. To use everything he'd taught you against him.'

Farrell stopped talking for a while, probably waiting to see if I'd tell him now what Kranze meant by that. I didn't though. I used the time to top up our coffee mugs. I put the percolator back on its stand, and sat down again. 'Then what?'

Farrell thought for a moment, trying, I imagine, to make a real effort to get things in sequence. 'Then he started talking about what had gone on between us in prison. I mean, how *he'd* looked after me.'

'Got you the drugs and stuff?'

'Yeah. And how . . . how . . . we'd been special to each other.'

'Huh.'

'Gave me a load of crap about how he still thought of me as special.'

I made no comment.

'How he still wanted to see to it I was okay.'

'Nice.'

'Kept going to the window to see if you were coming back, like he'd something important he wanted to say before you did get back, but like he had to get the time of saying it right.'

That was pretty observant of Farrell, I thought. And I was sure he was right.

'Kept plugging on about how much he thought of me. Being really nice. Saying we all need someone special in our lives.' Farrell was reeling off a sort of litany of quotes now. 'Saying I was more of a son to him than his real son.'

'Fucks his real son, too, does he?' I couldn't resist asking. 'Sorry. Go on.'

'That's when I started to do my crying. Like I've seen people do that. Cry when someone's being nice to them. So I put my head in my hands and used the salt and let on I was really touched by what he was telling me.'

'He must have liked that,' I observed.

'He thought it was for real, anyway.'

'So did I,' I said. 'So did I. You were terrific.'

'Then he spotted you coming back and had to rush things,' Farrell said. He looked me straight in the eye. 'He came back from the window and stood over me. He said he needed me to help him stop you doing something awful to him.'

I was forced into giving a sneer. I gave a snort, too, for good measure. 'And what did you say to that?' I asked.

'Nothing. Didn't have time. You came back.'

Although I was fairly certain by this time that Farrell was on my side I needed a crumb of reassurance. I asked, 'What would you have said if I hadn't come back?'

Very seriously Farrell told me, 'I'd have said yes. That I'd help him.'

I felt the muscles tighten in my stomach. I was confused. In truth, I was a bit scared. Could I really have misjudged Farrell? No, I couldn't, it transpired. 'That's what we agreed, wasn't it?' Farrell added, and I found myself breathing easily again. Breathing easily but getting angry with myself. I was getting lax. I was letting things slip through my mind without giving them the attention they merited.

I heard myself ask, 'But would you have meant it, John?'

And that was the precise point when everything gathered itself together and fell back into place. 'Would I fuck!' Farrell exploded. '*You're* my pal, ain't you?' he asked, and I swear a couple of genuine tears welled up in his healing eyes.

I smiled at him benignly. 'Yes, John. I'm your pal,' I confirmed.

Well, there was no point in disillusioning the poor laddie at this stage, was there?

TWENTY

So, come the following Friday, there I was, ensconced in my office, finishing off my reading of Mr Umzomo Pekwangi's exploits. The writing wasn't exactly brilliant, but it was a good enough read and it would sell, which was the important thing as far as the hedonists down the corridor were concerned. I gave it my imprimatur and marked it for Nick Putty's personal attention. Then I pushed it aside and selected another manuscript, *The Wind That Flickered the Candles*. Holy God! I sighed the sigh of the despairing. I wondered blasphemously if the title referred to a Reverend Mother's fart. Probably not even anything as interesting as that.

Then, as luck would have it, the phone rang. Kranze. Kranze again, I might point out. He'd been trying to get to me both at the office and at home since Farrell scarpered from his house, but I'd pointedly ignored his calls. Let the bastard stew, I'd thought.

'Marcus?'

'Oh, it's you.'

'I've been trying to reach you.'

'I've been busy.' Curt, I think, is the appropriate word for the way I dealt with this call.

'Did you catch him?' Kranze asked.

'Catch who?'

'John.'

'No, I didn't catch him, as you put it. I didn't want to catch him. I couldn't care less if I never saw the horrible little shithead again in my life, if you really want to know.'

That, you'll appreciate, took the wind out of Kranze's sails. He was silent on the other end of the phone. Stunned, I hoped.

'I only brought him along because you said you wanted to meet him again. Any chasing to be done, you do it,' I said.

'I wouldn't know where to look,' Kranze told me.

'Same places I did. Every sewer between here and Marble Arch.' I nearly added that this would make him feel at home but I didn't want to push it.

'Has he gone back to that squat you found him in?'

'How should I know? Probably. Or some other one.'

'Where was it, Marcus?'

'The squat?'

'Yes.'

'Dunno. I mean, up Bayswater way but I can't remember the

exact address.'

'Could you find it again?'

'Possibly, if I was so inclined.'

'Would you do it for me, Marcus?' Kranze asked, a subtle – well, not all that subtle – change coming into his tone. His wheedly, pleading voice, and I enjoyed a little, silent snigger to myself at the irony of it all: Kranze begging me to find the chap he hoped would help him dispose of me.

'No chance,' I told him. 'I'm up to my eyes in work.'

'It's very important to me, Marcus.'

No kidding, I thought to myself. 'Yeah, well, it's about the most *un*important thing to me,' I said. 'Do your own dirty work for a change,' I added, deciding to be cocky.

'All I ask is that you find the address and let me have it,' Kranze said, sounding ever so reasonable now. 'You don't have to meet or speak to him again.'

I decided I'd had a good run for my money. 'Well, it so happens I do have to go and see another author out that way in the next day or two. I'll see what I can do.'

'I won't forget this, Marcus.'

'I won't *let* you forget it,' I told him. 'And I'm not promising anything. I'm not going to go traipsing all over Bayswater when he mightn't even be there.'

'All I ask is that you try.'

'Okay. I'll try.'

'Thank you, Marcus.'

'Yeah,' I said, and hung up.

Funny, I seemed to be ending all my telephone conversations on that begrudging affirmative recently. Birt had phoned the same evening that Farrell and I had been to see Kranze wanting to know if anything 'interesting', as he put it, had happened.

'Not sure yet,' I told him.

'Sorry?'

'I haven't discussed it with Speed.'

'But you were there.'

'Not all the time – didn't the Mongol tell you that?'

'No.'

'Well, he should have. Spank his botty. I left them alone together on the pretext of getting something from my car. Didn't spot your wagon anywhere,' I commented, meaning it to be a compliment and a small pat on the back.

Birt gave a little chortle. 'Clearly he didn't position himself to spot you, either.'

'You get what you pay for,' I told him. 'Employ the dregs and you end up with sediment all over your face.'

'Couldn't you tell anything from Speed's reactions?'

'Reactions? Speed? You're joking, aren't you? It'd take a bomb up his backside to make him twitch.'

'But you are going to quiz him?'

'Eventually. When the time's right. A kid-glove job is our friend Speed.'

'You'll let me know the result?'

'Of course.'

'Marcus.' He said my name threateningly.

'What?' I asked lightly.

'You will let me know the result.'

'Yeah.'

And Ma phoned the same evening, rattling on about the charm and joy of living her idyllic life near Bath. Suddenly everything in her range had become sweet, and dazzling, and radiant, and super. 'Sounds like you've found Utopia, Ma.'

'Oh, darling, that's *exactly* what it's like.'

'And Harry's behaving himself?'

'Harry's wonderful.'

'Sure, but is he behaving himself?'

'Yes, dear. Of course he is.'

'No of course about it, Ma. These old lechers know a trick or two. Keep a sharp eye on that one if I was you.'

Ma gave one of her Tinkerbell giggles. 'Well, he did have a trick or two up his sleeve,' she admitted.

'It's not what's up his sleeve that bothers me, Ma.'

Ma laughed again. She wasn't opposed to a bit of vulgarity now and again as long as she shared it with the right person. Me, in particular. 'You will be down to see us soon, won't you, dear?'

'Oh, sure. As soon as I get a free weekend – a *long* weekend. I'll hitch up the nag and be down.'

'That would be lovely.'

'For me, too, Ma.'

'And – darling?'

'Yes, Ma?' I asked with a load of resignation in my voice since I guessed what was coming.

'You will be nice to Harry, won't you?'

'Yeah,' I said.

And on Thursday Stuart Bean checked in. 'You okay?' he wanted to know, but it wasn't my health he was concerned with.

'Sure am.'

'Good. Don't forget, it's the – '

'Twenty-ninth,' I said for him.

'That's it. So long as you don't forget.'

'Not likely to, am I?'

'Just be ready.'

'I'll be ready,' I assured him. 'Got me a car yet?'

'Not yet. Too early.'

'Oh.'

'Got lots to organise before we come down to that.'

'Oh.'

'You're sure you're okay about this?'

'Sure I'm sure.'

'Wouldn't want you trying to pull out at the last minute, fucking us all up.'

'Relax, Stuart. I said I was okay, didn't I?'

'Just so long as I can count on you.'

I didn't answer that.

'Can I?'

'Can you what?'

'Count on you?'

And that's when I answered 'Yeah,' yet again.

However, I digress, as they say. When I'd finished talking to Kranze I made a solid effort to concentrate on *The Wind That Flickered the Candles*, but failed. Edwina Hopkins, the author of the rubbish, clearly fancied herself as a kind of Maeve Binchy of the North. But if you don't have the Irish gab you can't emulate old Maeve, and Stockport, where Edwina abided, has a paucity of Celts and blarney. The only redeeming feature about the work was that it was simply so terrible I didn't have to waste time on it, which was just as well as I had a number of other rather more pressing things on my mind.

Jermyn Street was rush-hour busy: all the chinless wonders hastening back to their Rovers and Volvos which would take them home to their nagging wives, and shop-girls, thick with now jaded make-up (presumably an obligatory requirement for the selling of overpriced shirts and shoes) scurrying for the Underground but knowing their place and walking close to the gutter, allowing the toffs (as they no doubt thought of them) the privilege of the pavement.

I pretended to study some ghastly snakeskin shoes in the window of a shop that conveniently reflected the staff entrance to Fortnum's. Who in the name of God, I wondered, would want some venomous serpent wrapped about their feet? 'Spivs,' Ma would have said firmly, but I wasn't sure that spivs existed as a species any more. Pimps, I would have suggested, although they'd have needed a pretty large stable of whores to be able to afford the slip-ons I was looking at. Maybe that's what Oxfam should do: instead of begging for the odd quid to help some natives help themselves, maybe they should ask the pimps to donate their old shoes. Even second-hand they'd be worth a bob or two if their original cost price was anything to go by.

And then I spotted her coming out. She looked different out of her uniform, looked what she was, really: dowdy, uninteresting, plain. Still, I wasn't contemplating bedding her so it didn't matter, and I doubted if Farrell would even notice what she looked like.

She stood outside Fortnum's and glanced at her watch, and then took to looking up and down the street. Waiting for someone. That was fine. I hoped. Casually I crossed the road and made my way towards her. When I was within feet of her I gave a puzzled frown, looked at her, then looked away. She recognised me, all right, and saw my confused look also. When I came alongside, she said, 'Hello.'

I stopped and gave her a good, hard stare. 'I'm sorry. I don't seem to – ' I said a bit haughtily but not overdoing it. Giving her the impression that I was a nice young man who didn't speak to unknown women.

'I'm sorry,' she said. 'I thought – ' She got very embarrassed and blushed prettily.

'Of course,' I exclaimed. 'You're – ' I gave a quick glance at Fortnum's. 'Now I remember. I'm sorry. You look different out of your little white apron.'

She simpered. 'Yes.'

'Are you going or coming? From work?'

'Oh, going. I mean, I've finished for the day.'

I decided to take the plunge. 'How about us going for a drink. Let this mob go home first.'

The poor girl was torn asunder. I could see she hadn't had an offer like this for a while. 'I'd love to but – '

'Ah,' I interrupted. 'The good old but. I understand. I shouldn't have asked.'

'Oh, no,' she protested quickly. 'It's just that I'm waiting for a friend.'

'Lucky him.'

'It's a her, actually.'

'Ah. She work in here, too?'

'Charlotte? Oh, no. She's a psychiatric nurse, in fact.'

I made an appropriate face to indicate I didn't think a whole lot of psychiatric nurses.

'She's very nice. Very funny,' Miranda explained.

'Oh, they're a hilarious bunch, psychiatric nurses. Laugh a minute, they give you.'

'No, really.'

'I believe you. Going somewhere nice, the two of you, are you?'

'Not really,' she said, and then gave a smile. 'The dentist, in fact.'

'The dentist? At this hour? Talk about being gluttons for punishment.'

'Charlotte has a – well, she's got a special appointment.'

Didn't speak well for Charlotte, did it? Probably getting her buck teeth fixed at night so no one could see her. But I was glad I was able to extricate myself with dignity. 'Maybe another evening?'

She looked at me quizzically.

'Maybe another evening we could have a drink?'

'I'd like that.'

'Good. Well – ' I began, and began to move off too, but she stopped me by asking, 'When?'

That put me on the spot. I didn't yet know when I'd need her, when Farrell would be ready. 'Maybe one day next week?'

'Fine.'

'I'll either come in during the day and tell you exactly when, or I might just surprise you and be waiting out here.'

'Not Thursday, though. I don't work Thursdays.'

I very nearly slipped up and told her I already knew that. 'Okay, not Thursday. See you,' I said, and toddled off with a wave. Then I turned and came back. 'Better warn your friend Charlotte that it was a dentist who invented the electric chair,' I said, and this time I did leave her, smiling to myself at the astonished look on her face.

One day next week. I'd certainly have to get a move on. And as though to underline this I broke into a little trot.

And it could have been to prepare myself for that week ahead, or maybe I had some subconscious premonition of all that was about to befall me: whatever the reason, I went to Mass on Sunday. I tried to get Farrell to come, too, seeing as he was probably going to need

God's forgiveness more than me. But he rejected the suggestion, which somewhat surprised me, he being a good Scottish Catholic lad. In fact it struck me from his reaction that he was just about as afraid of God as he was of Kranze, and that was some fear, I can tell you. He got positively shirty with me, telling me I could pray as much as I wanted but to leave him out of it.

Well, I didn't actually pray, as I think I've already told you. I just sat in my pew and let the celebrant (a visiting Benedictine by the cut of him) get on with it. I bowed my head and had a right good think for myself. And I'd plenty to think about.

'I did your praying for you,' I told Farrell when I got home, got home about one since I went to a pub first, feeling parched and arid and in no way spiritually uplifted.

'I've done food,' Farrell told me.

'Lunch,' I corrected him.

'Whatever,' he said.

'Well, that's fine. I've taken care of our souls and you're taking care of our bodies.'

He gave me a baleful look. 'You ready to eat?'

'Starving.'

Well, it seemed, Farrell had partaken of his own little ceremony in the kitchen. I'd had beef Wellington and beef Stroganoff. Now it was time to chew on beef Crucified. Done, as they say, to a frazzle. I wouldn't have minded but it was an entire fillet that I'd been saving in the freezer for some special occasion: the sort of joint that pays but a fleeting visit to the oven. In Farrell's hands it had certainly overstayed its welcome. It had shrivelled. The inside which, to my taste, should have been pink and tender as a baby's bottom, was leathery as a jockey's arse, and the outside had burned itself to a crust that would have broken the teeth of a Rottweiler. I shoved the few slices of meat he gave me about my plate for a while, beef curling. 'Taking no chances that mad cow disease will survive your cooking, I see?'

Farrell frowned.

'The meat. A wee bit overdone, wouldn't you say?'

Farrell put on a pouty look, and I suspected he was setting off on one of his sulking sessions. I didn't say anything else for the moment. I certainly didn't want to antagonise him. I really needed to talk to him seriously, and he wouldn't even listen to me if I got his back up. So, I just sat there watching him. I watched as he tried to cut his meat. I watched as he tried tearing his meat. I watched as he tried chewing his meat, having taken a piece in his fingers and ripped a sliver off with his teeth. It turned out that I'd reacted in precisely the right way. Slowly Farrell allowed a sheepish grin to spread across his face as it became clear even to him that his fangs weren't about to make any indentation on the beef. 'Bit tough, eh?' he asked after a while.

'A bit,' I agreed.

'Must have read the book wrong.'

'Could happen to a saint.'

'Sorry.'

'No problem,' I told him cheerily. 'Bet anything you like that when J.C. Himself turned the water into wine it came out like real plonk,' I added, but when I saw that was wasted on Farrell I went on, 'Why don't you clear up this lot and I'll nip out and get us a Chinky?'

'Sorry, Marcus,' Farrell said again.

'Don't worry about it.'

Spare ribs and prawn chow-mein aren't exactly your standard British Sunday lunch, you'll agree, but that was what we tucked into, and with Farrell suitably chastened and in a receptive mood, I relaxed and gorged myself. 'Wow,' or something similar I said when I'd finished, leaning back and patting my well-filled belly. 'That was okay.'

'Great,' Farrell agreed.

We tidied up together, Farrell washing our two plates while I put all the foil cartons into the bin and wiped down the table. And as Farrell was just putting the dried plates into the cupboard, bending down, I said, almost casually, 'We're going to have to do something about Zanker, you know.'

Farrell stayed bent double for a second. Then he straightened and shut the cupboard door. 'I know,' he said, turning and facing me.

'Don't see what we *can* do though,' I said solemnly.

'Got to think of something.'

I now said, 'I know,' handing Farrell the initiative, and switching on the percolator.

'And soon,' Farrell went on, which surprised me.

'Why d'you say that, John?'

Farrell didn't know why he said that. ''Cause,' he said, and then stopped.

I pressed him. 'Must be *some* reason why you think we have to act soon.'

'Dunno,' Farrell confessed, and I thought that was that. But then he screwed up his face which meant he was thinking. 'Must be something he said,' he informed me finally.

I waited.

'Maybe not. Just something – ' Farrell stopped again and, to give him time to gather his thoughts, I took a couple of mugs from the rack and filled them with coffee, adding sugar and milk to his.

'A feeling I got,' Farrell decided after we had sat down at the table.

'What sort of feeling?' I ventured.

'A feeling *he* wasn't going to waste any time getting back at *you*.'

'Figures.'

'I think he wants you dead, Marcus.'

I gave a snort. 'You can bet your life he does. Kranze – Zanker – doesn't do things by half.'

'I think,' Farrell went on, doing a lot of thinking, 'I think he's going to try and get me to do it.'

'Probably,' I agreed, keeping my responses short so that Farrell could follow his own train of thought which, I hoped, was chugging along nicely on the right track.

'And if I did that then he'd want me dead, too, so I couldn't say anything to anyone.'

'That's a safe enough bet, I'd say.'

Farrell's brain stopped to refuel. He started to stir his coffee, round and round, staring at it as though mesmerised by the tiny circles he was making in the mug, maybe seeing something in them that was invisible to other mortals. To me, anyway. Then he put his spoon on the table, and started nodding to himself. He was coming to a decision, and when he reached it he looked up at me with a glaze in his eyes I'd never seen before. 'Only one way to be sure,' he said.

Innocently I enquired, 'What way?'

'We've got to kill him.'

I pretended to be shocked. 'Us kill *him*?' I said with an appropriate gasp.

Farrell just stared at me.

I then pretended to agree with the motion. 'I suppose it *is* the only way.'

Still Farrell just stared at me.

I now pretended to pooh-pooh the concept. 'It'd never work,

John. No way would we get away with it.'

It was, in truth, getting unnerving the way Farrell just stared and stared, just like he was waiting for me to raise all the possible objections to his suggestion while knowing that these same objections would, in the end, have to be overruled. So, I played along. 'Look, John, there's no way I could get involved in killing Zanker. Firstly – you know Birt? – well, he'd be on to me like a shot. Jesus Christ, he knows all about me and why I hate that Kranze bastard. I'd be the prime suspect. He'd have me arrested quicker than you could say – shit, I don't know – quicker than you could say Marcus,' I concluded feebly.

'Doesn't know me, though, does he?' Farrell asked, and I could have hugged him.

'Of course he knows you. Met you here, didn't he?'

Farrell shook his head. 'Uh-huh. He met John Speed here. Not John Farrell,' he said quietly, looking as proud as punch.

Of course, I had to protest, but not too much, even easing my way into my protestations. 'I don't see how that – '

'No need for you to be involved,' Farrell told me.

I acted bewildered, as though I didn't get the drift of what he was telling me. 'I don't – ' I began as if about to confess my lack of comprehension. Then, very slowly, I aped a slow dawning of awareness. 'You mean – ' I said and stopped again. 'Oh, no! Definitely not, John. No bloody way. There's no way on earth I'd let you get – '

'It's the only way,' Farrell told me.

I decided a little false levity was in order. 'Come off it, John. *You* couldn't kill Kranze,' I said and infused my statement with a small but kindly laugh.

'Could if you told me how to do it,' Farrell informed me.

'It's not that simple, John.' I took hold of one of his hands in a close and friendly way. 'Look, it's really nice of you to volunteer and all that, and I agree absolutely that it probably would be the answer to our problem, but – well, it's one thing *talking* about killing someone but it's something else actually doing it. Believe me, I know.'

Farrell put his other hand over mine. Getting really cosy, we were now. Then he started to squeeze my fingers in a grip so tight I thought I was in serious danger of being permanently crippled.

'I hate the bastard too, you know,' Farrell told me quietly in a whisper filled with venom.

'Yeah. I know you do, John. I understand that. I mean, what he did to you was – well, it was really awful. But just because you hate him with a passion doesn't mean you'd be able to kill him.'

'I could.'

'You *say* you could. And I'm sure you mean it. And maybe you would have, well, the *will* to do it. But there's more to it than that. There's a question of technique.'

He looked at me, puzzled.

'Of knowing *how* to do it,' I explained.

'You could tell me that.'

I sighed. 'Of course I could *tell* you that, but it still isn't the same thing. Dead easy to sit here and have me say to you, do this and that. Come to actually doing it, though, and it's totally different. I'll tell you a secret. Before I killed Darren I had to have myself a little practice on someone. That's why I killed Sharon. Just to see if I *could* do it. No other reason.'

I suppose, ludicrously, I was hoping that Farrell would say something like, 'Well, let's nip out and find someone for me to practise on', but he didn't, of course. He let go of my hand and started running his fingers through his hair, and I've no idea why but I absolutely *knew* what was going on in his mind. He was thinking to himself that he'd have to go and find a practice target for himself without letting me know. Well, I had to put a stop to that, by jove. I didn't want him hacking someone to pieces willy-nilly when I had a nice little waitress all lined up; someone I could quite easily, I was certain, lull into our web; someone whose demise I could supervise.

'Look, John. Tell you what. Let's put the whole thing out of our minds for the moment. Let's you and me go to the pictures or something. Let's sleep on it. We can have another talk about it in the morning. You never know, something dead simple might occur to us in the night. It sometimes does happen that way, you know. Okay?' I knew I would be able to think more clearly, anyway, now that Farrell and his nocturnal grunting had moved back into Ma's room.

Reluctantly, Farrell nodded.

'That's my boy,' I told him.

If my life depended on it I couldn't tell you the name of the film we went to see. All I can tell you is that it was an American 'action' film wherein the hero gets into a multitude of unlikely scrapes and gets out of them in an unlikely way, screwing a succession of blonde Hollywood clones along the way before returning, a better man, to his wife and kids in somewhere like Oregon. But, since Farrell had chosen it, I had to be gracious. 'Good, that, wasn't it?' I said as we drove home.

'Yeah,' Farrell agreed, preoccupied as he had been since our lunchtime conference.

'No one can make those sort of movies like the Yanks,' I commented.

'Yeah,' Farrell said again.

And that was the extent of our conversation until I parked the car and the two of us went into the house. Immediately Farrell went into the sitting-room and slumped into an armchair, slinging one leg somewhat rudely over the arm. I'd hoped to get through the evening without having to revert to the subject of Kranze: I like to give everything I think of time and space. I hate being crowded or forced into making decisions. But I knew this wasn't to be the case now, so there was only one thing for it. Take the unicorn by the horn.

'What's eating you, John?'

'Thinking.'

'I thought we agreed to – '

'Can't stop thinking.'

'Well, you're just going to have to.'

'Can't.'

'Try harder,' I said. 'Anyway, I'm off to bed,' I added, knowing he would follow my example. He always went to bed when I did, almost as if he was frightened there might be no bed for him if he didn't. I started to walk out of the room.

'Marcus?' Farrell called after me.

'Yeah?'

'Could you find someone for me to try it out on?'

'Don't talk stupid, John.'

'I'm not talking stupid. Could you?'

How could I do such a thing? 'Of course not.'

'You could, couldn't you?'

Boy, was I appalled! 'No I could not,' I answered, stressing each and every word.

Farrell didn't protest further. What he did do was give a shrug, and that shrug told me a multitude. It was as though he had said aloud, 'Okay, fuck you, I'll go and find someone myself', which was the last thing I wanted.

'Look, John, let's do as we agreed. Go to bed and sleep on it.'

'You'll think about it then?'

'If it makes you happy – I'll think about it.'

We went upstairs together. 'You really will think about it?' Farrell asked at the top of the stairs.

'Yes. I promise. I'll think about it,' I promised. 'Goodnight and sleep well.'

''Night, Marcus.'

I half closed my door.

'Marcus?'

'Yes, John?'

'It's the only way,' Farrell told me.

Bless him, he'd taken the words right out of my mouth.

TWENTY-ONE

I used to ask myself, 'Why the hell do they do it?' And, 'Why do they put up with it?' when I read in the papers about them being abused, beaten up, knifed, shot, and some of the women even raped. I'm talking about the teaching profession, of course. Why in the name of God do they persevere, vainly attempting to drum some knowledge into the minds of thugs and layabouts who don't want to learn in the first place. Don't even want to be in school, the half of them. And even if they aren't being attacked, it must be soul-destroying for them to see those blank, uninterested faces lined up before them and know that the majority just want to get out, join the jolly old dole queue, smoke their pot and mug their betters when they need cash. Those were my thoughts exactly when I told Farrell that, with great reluctance, I'd agree to 'his plan' to kill Kranze – and started trying to educate him in the art of murder. Talk about people with learning difficulties! Some of it was my fault, I have to admit. I started out on the wrong premise: that Farrell had been slightly refined by his sojourn with me. 'Killing is an art,' I told him and knew by the vacant look he gave me that I was in for a rough ride. 'An art,' I repeated. 'You know what I mean?'

He shook his head.

So, it was really a case of laying a foundation on which to build. I should have known, though, that I'd be wasting my time. Farrell was one of life's most basic creatures. His senses had long since lost contact with his imagination. He saw what his eyes showed him, heard what his ears picked up, smelled what his nostrils inhaled and that was really all there was to it as far as he was concerned. Really basic. So, when trying to teach him how to kill someone I had to adopt an attitude that would appeal to him. I concocted a gladsome array of reasons why Miranda should be removed from this earth: expansions and variations on the theme I had started all those weeks ago in Fortnum's. In the end, the poor girl was a far more devious and dangerous Mata Hari than Dietrich had ever portrayed, and she was definitely Kranze's henchwoman to boot. It wasn't all that difficult to convince Farrell of this since, if he thought about women at all, he saw them in a very poor light; tricky customers they were, in his eyes, capable of the most appalling treachery. Why he felt this I've no idea. Maybe Miranda's very funny psychiatric nurse friend could have found out, given the chance, but I certainly wasn't about to try. His current attitude suited me to a tee.

'To tell you the truth, John, I suspect he's going to use that woman to get at me.'

'I thought he was going to use *me* to do that,' Farrell pointed out, sounding a bit too disappointed for my liking.

'Maybe both of you, then,' I said. 'No. Hang on,' I went on, making out that I was suddenly thinking all this, like it had never entered my head until that exact minute. 'You're right, John. That's what he's up to. He *is* going to use – try and use – you to do for me and then he's going to use Miranda to get you.'

Well, that was a red flag to a bull. 'Think I'm going to let some woman get me?' Farrell demanded ferociously, getting very hot under the collar now that his peculiar Celtic masculinity had been tampered with. 'Not fucking likely.'

'You must never underestimate the enemy,' I warned him in a voice of grave experience, choosing the word 'enemy' with care since it was this concept of Miranda I needed to implant in the compost of his mind.

'There's the *two* of us and only *one* of her,' Farrell pointed out logically.

'Yes, but it'll be *you*, you alone, John, who has to – well, rid us of this meddlesome priestess.' I should have known better. 'You alone who'll have to kill her,' I simplified.

'Yeah, but *you're* going to show me how, aren't you?' Farrell asked, somehow managing to make my participation the solution to any problem that might arise.

I wasn't about to argue the point.

After several days of intensive training I decided that teachers put up with all the shit thrown at them just to experience the ethereal satisfaction of finally getting one dimwit to learn one simple lesson. I also decided that Farrell was primed and ready to carry out his 'mission', as we'd started calling it: it appeared to give him a new status. A man with a mission. It certainly sounds better than an aimless turd.

The plan was dead simple. It had to be if Farrell was to accomplish it. No frills on this particular escapade. Indeed, it was just about an exact replica of the way I had disposed of the interfering Sharon, even down to the selection of the knife. Farrell was impressed and, I think, flattered, that he was to use the same knife as I had used. It became a sort of sacred implement, and on more than one occasion I found him fondling it. He took great pride in that knife. He honed it and polished it. He removed it from the rack and gave it a special place in one of the drawers, bedding it down on a piece of green felt he'd found in the cupboard under the stairs.

I went over and over the precise sequence of events. I choreographed the movements, basing them on those movements that had been danced by myself and Sharon. I explained how vital speed was. No hanging about. Knife in, knife out. No 'Excuse me, madam, but would you mind if I shoved this into your vital organs'. I impressed on him the need for cleanliness. We didn't want a lot of cleaning up to do later, did we? No, we didn't. We rehearsed spreading the plastic sheeting on the floor, and I made him explain to me why we did this. 'To catch any blood,' he told me.

'That's not what I mean, John. You can't tell bloody Miranda it's there to catch blood.'

'Oh. No,' Farrell said with a charming, disarming grin. 'It's 'cause we're having the kitchen decorated the next day.'

'That's it. You'll remember that?'

''Course I will.'

'I hope so.'

Even now I had to laugh at the antics we got up to when it came to putting the body in the black industrial waste bag. Feeling a total prat I'd bought one of those blow-up dolls in Soho, one of the more grotesque breed beloved of those unfortunates who prefer rubberised sex to the real thing. The wretched thing kept twisting itself into shapes that would have done the Kama Sutra proud, and both Farrell and I were pissing ourselves with laughter by the time we finally got the entire monstrosity into the bag. No sooner had we done it and stood back than Morag (as we'd christened her – as Farrell had christened her, to be more precise) exploded with just about the loudest bang I've ever heard. That really finished us off. We collapsed on the floor, rolling over and over in hysterics.

It was the perfect note on which to end the education of John Farrell.

If only hilarity and merriment could last! Later that night, alone in my room, I got down to the serious business of reworking my time-scale. To help me I got out my big desk diary, turned to the back page, and started to write down all that still remained to be done.

Remove Miranda.
Tell Kranze I'd located Speed and get his reaction.
Hear from the Blow Job Queen details of heist.
Tell Birt about heist.
And then . . . .

That's what I wrote: '*And then . . . .*' and I enjoyed writing it. I read through my notes. Removing Miranda, I felt, was not going to present a problem, but everything else seemed to hinge on that call from Stuart Bean. The call to tell me what I had to do, where I had to be, what the scam was all about. I really could not put very much else in motion until the details of this were made clear to me. I sat back and tried to visualise everything falling into place. The timing was so vital. Absolutely critical. But how much warning would Stuart give me? I reckoned the minimum I would need was one week, and even that was pushing it a bit. Dare I phone him and try and pressure him into giving me the information I needed? Would the cocksucker get suspicious if I did? I meditated on this. I could, of course, tell him some story about my having to go away on work shortly before the twenty-ninth and that for everything to go smoothly I simply had to know what the deal was – he wouldn't want me accidentally messing his plot up just because I'd been kept in the dark, would he? I hoped not.

So, despite the hour, I called him, creeping quiet as a thief downstairs so as not to disturb Farrell. 'Ah, Stuart, how are you, mate?' I asked cheerfully. 'It's Marcus,' I said when there was a daunting silence on the end of the line. 'Sorry to call so late, but it's important.'

Stuart cleared his throat. 'Something wrong?' he asked, and I could tell from his tone that he'd been asleep, probably sent to bed early by Mum so he couldn't watch late-night nasties on the telly.

His voice also gave me the impression that there had better not be something wrong.

'No, nothing wrong, exactly,' I said.

Stuart hissed like an adder.

I went on quickly. 'It's just that I really do need to know what the score is as soon as possible. I have to go out of town for a week or two, on work, so – '

'You agreed the twenty-ninth, Marcus,' Stuart told me, keeping up his Hissing Sid impression.

'Oh, yeah. Don't worry about the twenty-ninth. I'll be back for that. It's just – '

The serpent seemed pacified. 'Yeah, you're right. Should fill you in.'

'That's what I thought.'

Stuart said nothing.

'Just so I don't make any stupid mistakes and land you in it. Can't see you being best pleased with me if I did that, eh?'

'You could say that.'

'And who in their right mind would want Stuart Bean telling them they'd been naughty?'

At last I got Stuart to cackle. 'When do you have to go away?'

'That's the trouble, Stuart. I don't actually have the dates yet. Could be any day. Depends when this author is available. Could even be as early as tomorrow.'

Stuart digested this. 'We better meet.'

'I'd say so.'

'If it *is* tomorrow, can it be in the evening – that you go?'

'Guess so.'

'Come round in the morning then,' Stuart told me, and hung up abruptly.

With Stuart's cockney menace still ringing in my ears, there was no way I was going to get much sleep. So, I figured, why not get Kranze out of his cradle and tell him something to give him insomnia. Fair's fair, when all is said and done.

'Hiya, Helmut,' I said cheerily. 'It's Marcus.'

'I know who it is,' Kranze told me, clearly disgruntled. 'Do you know what time it is?'

'No, I don't, I'm afraid. Tell me.'

'It's after one in the morning.'

'Ah. Good. Still early. Wouldn't want to wake you up.'

Kranze growled. 'Why do you ring me at this hour?'

'I ring you at this hour to bring you glad tidings. That's why I ring you at this hour. Now, if you don't want to hear my tidings of great joy, I'll – '

I didn't have to spell out what I'd do. 'Tell me,' Kranze said, and his attitude had changed.

'You sure you want to hear? It'll keep till later if you like.'

'Tell me.'

'I located your beloved wee friend.'

'Where?'

'Say thank you.'

Kranze steamed. 'Thank you. Where?'

I decided to play with Kranze for a while longer. I wouldn't have dared anything so risky face to face, but on the phone and with twenty-odd miles between us I was filled with some sort of courage. 'Tell me this first. Why are you so desperate to see him again? I mean, it's not exactly as if you two have much in common, is it?'

'I've already explained to you why,' Kranze said.

'Yeah, but that was bullshit. Look, matey, I know you. There's no way you'd allow yourself to get so hung up on a drip like Speed. What's your real game?' It was the strangest feeling. Although I couldn't see Kranze's reaction and although he didn't speak immediately, I knew I had him on the run. Well, maybe not actually on the run, but going at a pretty good clip nonetheless. 'You still there?'

'I want to use him,' Kranze admitted.

'Like you used me, eh?'

'I didn't use you, Marcus.'

'Not bloody half you didn't.'

'You were caught because of errors *you* made, not because of any errors *I* made.'

I should have guessed it. Kranze was going to bamboozle me again. Or try to. I decided to let him think he had succeeded. 'Use him for what, Helmut?' I now asked.

I just knew Kranze's watery eyes glinted. I knew he was smiling confidently to himself. 'Just a small errand I need run,' he told me.

'Oh, your shopping?'

'Not quite.'

'What then?'

'I'll tell you in time, Marcus.'

'No time like the present, they say.'

'They, whoever they are, invariably get it wrong.'

I'm sure I heard him give a quiet laugh, but then he cleared his throat so I could have been mistaken. I was dying to tell him I knew exactly why he wanted Speed alias Farrell or vice versa. God, it would have been simply terrific. But the reaction to *that* I would most definitely want to see. So I behaved myself. 'Not going to tell me then?'

'Not at this precise moment, Marcus. Now, where can I find the boy?'

'Boy? Shit, Helmut, you must be getting old. I suppose all the police look young to you now too, do they?'

'Marcus, where can I find John?'

'I can tell you where he is but I wouldn't go looking for him if I were you.'

'Just tell me.'

'Cardboard city. You know, near the Festival Hall.'

'Ah,' Kranze sighed, and then after a minute's pause asked, 'and why shouldn't I go looking for him there?'

'No skin off my nose if you do, Helmut, but don't come crying to me if you're mugged or knifed or chucked in the Thames. Can you swim?'

I never did find out if Kranze could swim or not. 'Maybe you have a point,' he conceded finally. And then, 'Perhaps you . . . ?'

'Look, I said I'd try and find the creep, and I found him. I'm not going to go chasing after him again.'

Another short pause and then Kranze tried to tempt me. 'If you could bring him here one more time I would feel perhaps obligated to let you know why I am so anxious – '

'To use him?'

'You would find it amusing, I think.'

Oh, sure. Highly entertaining. Nothing like hearing how you're being used as a sacrificial lamb to raise a merry smile. I had to admire Kranze's nerve, though. He would have done it, too: told me that he needed Farrell to eliminate me. Only when the time was right, though. Right for him, that is. He'd have told me just as the knife or whatever was about to be shoved between my shoulder blades and watched and smiled and taken the utmost delight in the whole procedure. Old Brutus had nothing on my pal Kranze. 'That a promise?'

'Oh, that's a promise.'

'I might want a slice of the action, see?'

'I'm sorry?'

'I might want to be involved in your little game.'

Kranze had difficulty concealing his glee. 'It will be my pleasure to involve you, Marcus.'

'Okay, then. I'll have another look for him one day this week and bring him along to you.'

Kranze breathed the air heavily from his lungs. 'Thank you, Marcus.'

'But it's the last time.'

'I agree.'

'Don't ask me ever again.'

'I won't have to, Marcus. I won't have to.'

If talking to Stuart had sent the sandman on a fool's errand, my conversation with Kranze made the poor sod redundant. I propped myself up in bed and sipped a Jack Daniels nightcap. I was doing pretty well, I told myself. I had Beany convinced I was going to help him. I had Kranze convinced I was going to help him. I had Birt convinced I was going to help *him*. And I had Farrell convinced that by killing Kranze (after a spot of practice on Miranda, of course) he would be helping himself. I patted my stomach, and said, 'Who's a clever boy, then,' to myself. I finished my drink and switched on the CD with the remote control. I lay back. I was feeling really great. At peace with myself. At peace with the whole fucking world. I closed my eyes and listened to Schwarzkopf sing about *Pace, pace*, which was appropriate. Tomorrow morning and my meeting with Stuart Bean. No, *that* morning and my meeting with Stuart Bean would be when the giant wheel of destiny would start turning. Irrevocably. With little me doing all the cranking.

I started to doze and in that wonderful, warm, fairyland of a time that overtakes you in the few precious minutes before you actually fall asleep I was no longer anything quite so pedantic as the slewer of wheels but instead a conductor, all decked out in my dickie-bow and tails, baton in hand, conducting with verve and brio wondrous music, better than Bruckner and Mahler and Haydn all rolled into one, while, on stage, my puppets obeyed the pulling of their strings, totally controlled by them. And somehow, don't ask me how, I pulled those strings even though I was conducting. One tiny tug and a small, fat, Germanic puppet with watery eyes spun round, or doubled up in agony, or lay prone on the floor, frozen, impotent. A jerk on another string and lo, across the stage came a gaunt and haggard creation, advancing slowly, each step filled with menace, that curious, all-devouring ominousness of someone who has been terrorised but suddenly, for no explicable reason, finds within himself the power, that totally seductive and overwhelming power, to gain revenge. Away in the distance *Pace, pace* sang Schwarzkopf again. Strangely, that was all she seemed to be singing, *Pace, pace*. Maybe that was all there was to the song. Or maybe she'd forgotten the words.

BOOK THREE

TWENTY-TWO

Stuart Bean's Mum had the washing-machine on full tilt when I arrived. It made approximately the same racket as a de Havilland taking off.

Earlier, before leaving home, I'd telephoned the office to say I'd be late since I had an appointment with my dentist. Actually, what I said was, 'Going to the electric chair,' but when that one fell on bewildered ears I explained. 'Developed some sort of abscess during the night. Killing me,' I said, and that brought about the correct reaction, a little oooh, how dreadful for you.

Stuart closed the sitting-room door firmly, even testing the handle to make sure it was closed tight. 'Sorry about that, your Lordship,' he apologised. 'Don't know why she does it. Regular as clockwork with her washing, she is. Has to be the same time on the same day every fucking week.'

'That's okay, Stuart. That's the way with ageing folk. Like to be regular. A time for everything and everything on time.'

Stuart liked that. He liked my understanding just about as much as he liked my distorted proverb. 'That's what makes you different to all the other shits, Marcus,' he told me, not implying, I'm sure, that I was a shit. 'You understand things.'

'Way I was brought up. Got to try and see both sides of the story. That was always my Dad's philosophy.'

The washing-machine started its dry-spin programme and the walls of the sitting-room shuddered. 'Jesus Christ!' Stuart bellowed, and leapt out of his chair, making for the door. I stopped him.

'Hey, Stuart, it's okay, mate. Really. Doesn't bother me in the least.'

'Fucking bothers me,' Stuart growled, but came back to his chair and collapsed into it. 'Tell you what bothers me more. Can't get her away from it once she starts. Can't get her to do two things at the one time. Know what she's doing now?'

I didn't, of course. I raised my eyebrows.

'She's sitting on a fucking chair watching that fucking thing going round and fucking round like it was the fucking telly or something.'

I couldn't resist it. 'Delicately put,' I told him.

'Try and get her to make you a cup of tea while the washing's on and you might as well – '

'Probably better than watching some of the crap they have on the telly anyway,' I interjected.

And then, suddenly, the din ceased. The machine had completed its cycle. The silence was – I won't say shattering, but it was certainly just about as deafening as the whirring and clanking had been. Stuart heaved an enormous sigh. 'Thanks be to fuck. Right. We've got about ten minutes before it starts again,' he told me, and sat up in his chair, leaning forward, folding his arms and resting them on his knees. Automatically I found myself sitting up straighter, as one does when about to receive some vital, world-shattering information. 'Okay, Marcus. This is it. It's a Securicor van. There'll be four of us. You, me and two others who you don't need to know. All you have to do is stay in the car, keep the engine running, and get us out of there as fast as you fucking can.'

I nodded. 'Fine.'

'You don't leave the car. No matter what happens.'

'Okay.'

Stuart looked pleased that I had accepted his statements with such calmness. 'Anything you want to ask me?' he wondered.

I pretended to think.

'Ask if you have something on your mind.'

I knew exactly what I wanted to ask, but I had to sort of sneak it out, just in case it wasn't the sort of thing I should ask at this juncture. I put on a worried expression, which, as I had hoped, Stuart picked up.

'Come on, Marcus. What's eating you?'

'Nothing's eating me exactly. It's just – ' I hesitated.

'Just what?' Stuart demanded.

'Look, Stuart, I'm a very meticulous sort of person. I like to plan everything down to the last detail. Cut out chances. Give myself the *best* chance possible of succeeding in whatever it is I'm doing.'

Stuart nodded gravely, impressed, no doubt.

'You want me to get you away from the scene safely, don't you? That's my only function, as I see it.'

'That's your job,' Stuart told me.

'Okay, I want to give it my best shot. Don't want you saying later that it's *my* fault we're all banged up in Strangeways for fifty years.'

Clearly Stuart didn't want that either, although I have to confess I partly guessed that even without my tipping off Birt the job would turn out to be a disaster. Why? Because this would be at least the third Securicor raid Beany had attempted and he'd been well and truly stuffed at all previous attempts. 'You still haven't told me – ' he began.

'I need to know where the job is taking place. Where *exactly*. So I can plan an escape route. Drive over that route several times before the twenty-ninth. Drive over it at the same time I'll have to drive over it on that day. See if, like, there's likely to be any traffic jams at that time. See what buses might be on the route which could hold me up. Time myself. Find short-cuts. Check out one-way streets. All that shit. Be a right bitch if you pull it off and I drive you into some fucking cul-de-sac, wouldn't it?'

It was quite a long speech. Longer than Beany could take in all at once, anyway. He sat there, staring at me. I could see his brain ticking over as he tried to recall everything I had said and digest it. And asking Beany to do two things at the one time was – well, like asking his Mum to do the washing and boil a kettle simultaneously. Maybe he'd inherited this defect. Who knows?

Eventually, though, he'd thought about it long enough to appreciate what I'd said was logical. He nodded. 'You're right, Marcus,' he said approvingly. Then he got up and went to that hideous, black-ash unit along the wall, opened a drawer and took out a small notebook, flicking through the pages as he walked to the window, holding the book sideways towards the light. I expected him to read to me any minute. But he didn't. He took his time memorising the information he and I required, and then shut the notebook with a snap, and returned it to the drawer. I've no idea why the fool went through this little charade. It could simply have been that he wanted to keep me on tenterhooks, but the more likely explanation is that he was one of those inadequates who feels if he doesn't appear to be speaking off the top of his head the listener will think he's a moron. As if such a thought would cross my mind.

Anyway, he sat down again and started to talk, or rather recite the information, as a prologue – to whet my appetite, I should imagine – telling me that we could lift half a million. In dollars, as if that made it better.

'Very tidy,' I said.
'Know where the Saudi Arabian Embassy is?'
'Not off-hand. Haven't had occasion to go there much recently.'
'Charles Street,' Stuart advised me.
'Ah. That runs parallel to Curzon Street, right?'
'Right.'
'Okay. I know where we are now.'

'On the twenty-ninth of every month they ship dollars, in cash, from the embassy to the bank.'

'You're sure? Always on the twenty-ninth?' I asked, wondering about February.

Beany scowled. He didn't like being doubted. 'Of course I'm fucking sure.'

'Sorry. Sorry,' I muttered quickly, holding up both hands by way of apology. 'Of course you'd be sure.'

'The van – the Securicor van – always takes the same route.'

I had my doubts about that one, too, but I wasn't about to incur Beany's wrath a second time. If I did I suspected the only thing I'd be driving was my own hearse, if you'll excuse the Irishism. 'Fine,' I said.

It was curious to watch Beany get warmed up to his subject as he explained where and how they were going to hold up the van. He even gave way to a bit of play-acting, holding what looked like a bloody bazooka in his hands and firing. Not that I cared. I now knew all that I needed to know. All that Birt would need, that is. I let him ham it up for a while longer, seeing as how he was enjoying himself so much. Then, when the last round seemed to have been fired and Beany took a rest, I asked. 'And where do you want to be taken to?'

He hadn't quite come down to earth. 'What?'

'After you get the half million – where do I drive you to? Need to know that if I'm to plan our escape route.'

Amazingly, Stuart hadn't thought about that. All that had been entertained in his mind was the job, the getting his stubby, nail-bitten fingers onto the loot. 'You do know where you want to go, don't you?'

He snapped at me. 'Yes. I fucking know. 'Course I fucking know.'

I waited.

'Back here.'

I sucked in my breath.

'What's wrong with that?' Stuart demanded.

'Nothing if you don't mind being caught with the loot on the premises, like they say. I mean – hell, Stuart, you've got a reputation for doing the odd security van job. Don't you think the filth *might* just wonder if you've been involved in this one, too?'

Stuart knew I was right, but it hurt like hell for him to admit it. So he didn't. 'Fuck the filth,' he said belligerently. 'If I say back here I mean back here.'

'Okay,' I said nonchalantly. 'You're the boss.'

'And don't you fucking forget it.'

'As if I would.'

I never thought I'd find myself feeling gratitude towards a bloody washing-machine, but when daffy Mum restarted her entertainment, just about drowning out any possibility of further conversation, I could have whooped for joy. Even the Blow Job Queen couldn't compete with old Mr Zanussi. Hence, that was about the size of it as Stuart stood up and guided me once again towards the door. 'I'll be in touch,' he told me.

'Yeah. And I'll take a scout round, like I said, and find the best way for us to get the hell out of there. Half a million,' I said with fake wonderment. 'In dollars,' I added, shaking my head, and left Beany to his dreams.

I must have been overacting, looking as miserable as a lost spectre, when I put in an appearance in the office that afternoon, because two people, the receptionist and one of the girls from publicity (Janette or Janine or something of that ilk) said I looked 'really awful' – just the sort of thing that would have cured me if I hadn't been faking. Once inside my office, though, with the door shut, I was able to buck myself up, and that forlorn, abscess-ridden expression was replaced by my more usual sunny mien. Not that *that* lasted too long. The image of Stuart Bean's thuggish and menacing face soon put a stop to any elation I was feeling at having found out the nature and location of his heist. It was as though it only *now* dawned on me what a potentially dangerous situation I had got myself into. I would be 'dead meat' as the old lags have it, if Beany ever got so much of a whiff of suspicion that I had grassed on him. I suddenly became worried about how far I could trust Inspector Birt. I don't mean that he'd double-cross me or anything: that wicked concept never entered my head. But there was the small matter of tact, of arresting me, possibly, and of being able to have me released without Stuart putting two and two together and getting four for the one and only time in his life. There was also the gorilla Wilson to consider. I could see him being the vindictive villain of the piece, dropping me right in it without Birt even knowing.

I folded my hands behind my head and leaned back. It was then I noticed that the plant Camp Carl had given me had started to wilt, and for some curious reason this struck me as somewhat ominous, although the plain fact of the matter was that there was nothing more sinister to its deterioration than that I'd neglected it. I remedied that forthwith, using the water that would, normally, be used for making my coffee which I'd trained the cleaning woman, a buxom Trinidadian called Jessie, to leave ready for me each day in return for a few quid at the end of each week. The plant sucked at the water as greedily as a parched wolf, making strange, almost human noises as it consumed it.

Yes, Wilson, who I'd enjoyed mocking, was going to be a bit of a bugbear, I thought. But there was nothing I could do about him just now. Nothing I could think of, at least. And I certainly wasn't about to let *him* interfere with my plans no matter how much of a danger he represented. Anyway, I felt confident enough to feel that if he *did* try any trickery I would be able to explain it away to Beany. It might be quite hard for you to believe but there's a singular sort of snobbery that is part of a criminal's baggage. The word of an inspector would be treated with cautious respect, the word of a mere sergeant would tend not to be swallowed, even put down to that individual's lust for promotion, his desire to gain Brownie points, even his perverted sense of humour: nothing like compromising the innocent to give a sergeant a good titter. And I'd probably have to bank on Beany subscribing to this view.

Anyway, there was no point in dwelling on something that might never happen. There were far too many other things for me to deal with before any such mishap might occur.

I stayed closeted in my office for the rest of that day, not even venturing out for lunch, but accepting the offer of a cup of soup which one of the design girls volunteered to get me. Not that I drank the slimy muck.

And come five o'clock I was ready and, I thought, able to put the next phase of my plan into operation.

Miranda came out of the staff exit at twenty to six. I'd timed it to perfection, walking past the exit just as she emerged. 'Hiya,' I said. 'Just coming to see you.'

She was, naturally, delighted.

'Yeah,' I went on before she could speak. 'Come to arrange that date we spoke about.'

She looked even more delighted. 'I thought – '

'That I'd forgotten?' I interjected. 'Typical.'

'No, I – ' She got beautifully flustered.

'Just joking. Anyway, look, I've got to go to Colombia tomorrow so I won't be around for a week but I wondered – could we fix a definite date for next Wednesday? Not tomorrow, next week?'

I was a bit miffed that she wasn't impressed by my fictitious flight into Cocaine Country. I'd expected a small gasp of admiration at the very least. But then it dawned on me that the silly cow probably thought Colombia was somewhere up the M6, the Milton Keynes of Lancashire maybe.

I could see she was disappointed that our proposed meeting was so far away, but to her any date was probably better than none, so she smiled a simpering smile and said, 'I'd really like that.'

'Good. And you won't be towing that psychiatric nurse along with you, will you?'

She broadened her smile. 'Charlotte? No.'

We chatted for another few minutes, me bantering, her coyly twinkling, fixing the time and place for the date (here, outside Fortnum's at six forty) and deciding on a nice dinner at a destination I would choose but keep secret. 'Well,' I said when I'd had enough. 'I better push off. Next Wednesday, then?'

'Yes,' she confirmed, and then said something that struck me as a little bit odd. 'I'll be thinking of you, Martin.'

It was strange for two reasons. First, obviously, she got my name wrong – but that was a bonus in case she spoke of me to anyone. But the second reason was what interested me. The 'I'll be thinking of you' bit. True, on the face of it there's nothing all that peculiar about it, but for some reason she made it sound – shit, I don't really know. Made it sound really important, I suppose. As if she *really* meant it.

But it wasn't until the following week that I learned just how right my unease about those few words had been.

On the way home I stopped by a DIY store and picked up plastic sheeting to cover the kitchen floor and a pack of tough, black, industrial waste-bags.

'How you doin'?' I asked Farrell, putting my shopping on the kitchen table.

'Okay,' he told me, and then, in an unexpectedly calm way, he asked, 'That the stuff for when I kill that woman?'

With equal serenity, I replied, 'That's it.'

Farrell nodded. 'Doing it soon, are we?'

'Next week. If that suits you.'

'Been thinking,' he now informed me, and I didn't like the sound of that one bit.

'Oh?'

He nodded.

'You're not having second thoughts on me, are you?' That didn't seem to register. 'You haven't changed your mind, have you?'

'Oh, no.'

Thanks be for that.

'I just – ' Farrell began and then went over to check whatever potage he was boiling in a pot.

'Just what?'

'I want you to be there when – when, you know, when I do it.'

'Of course I'll be here when you do it,' I told him.

'I mean right here. In the kitchen. With me.'

'No problem.'

He stopped stirring and glanced at me, giving me a winning smile. 'Thanks,' he said.

'My pleasure,' I answered, and thought now would be a pretty suitable time to mention: 'Zanker wants to see you again.' There was no reaction. 'Alone, I think,' I added. Still nothing. 'Anyone home?' I asked.

'I hear you,' Farrell told me. 'Why?' he asked, using the spoon to stir again and transmit his simmering agitation to the cooking.

'*I* don't know why. Probably going to tell you how to get rid of me,' I said with a chortle.

Farrell didn't seem to think it was funny. 'When?'

'When what?'

'When do I see him?'

'Oh. Whenever. Whenever you and me decide the time is right. We're in the driving seat, you see.'

That cheered him up a little. He turned and gave me another smile and with some satisfaction I noted a tiny gleam in his eyes.

Nonchalantly I strolled across to the calendar on the wall and pretended to consider possible dates, finally coming up, surprise, surprise, with, 'What about, let's see – what about Friday the twenty-ninth? How does that grab you?'

Farrell shrugged.

'Gives us a couple of weeks. Bit more actually. Okay?'

'Okay.'

A civilised enough way, I thought, to discuss retribution and the terminal removal of the enemy.

After we'd eaten (nothing more exciting than cauliflower cheese, I regret to say) I decided there was no time like the present and went to telephone Birt. 'Any chance you could nip over and see me this evening, Maurice?' I asked.

'Is it important?'

'Not to me,' I lied.

'Can't you tell me on the phone?'

'No.'

'Then it *is* important.'

'Not to *me*,' I lied again.

Birt sighed. 'Very well. What time is it now,' he asked himself, and answered, 'Twenty to nine. I'll be there in – let's say about half nine.'

'Right. And listen. Listen good. This *is* important. Come alone. *Don't* bring Wilson. Not even to wait outside in the car. I'll explain why when I see you.'

'I don't – '

'Just do what I ask, will you? For once. I won't speak to you if Wilson is within ten miles of us.' Then a funny thought struck me. 'Hey, you think I'm up to something, don't you? You think I'm going to bump you off. That's it, isn't it?'

'Don't be ridiculous, Marcus,' Birt protested, but I could tell by his tone that *something* along those lines had been filtering through his mind.

I started to laugh.

Birt hung up abruptly.

I was still laughing when I got back to the kitchen. 'Want to hear something really funny?' I asked Farrell.

'What?'

'Just been on the phone to Birt. I have to speak to him about something. And you know what? Silly sod thinks I might be planning to kill him too!'

Farrell didn't see the funny side of it. 'Are you?'

''Course not. If there's one person I *need* alive and kicking, it's old Birty Boy.'

'So why's it funny?'

'Forget it.' I was getting a little angry with Farrell for spoiling my humour, and I admit to being overly gruff when I ordered him to go upstairs and stay quiet and out of sight when Birt came. 'Not a fucking squeak,' I warned him. 'I'm going to tell Birt you've left here. Gone back to your squat. Gone back to your bad old ways. And I don't want you making a liar out of me,' I concluded righteously.

So, it was a squeakless Farrell upstairs and a suave, sophisticated me downstairs when Birt arrived promptly enough. 'This better *be* important,' he told me.

'Why? Having it off with some little blonde WPC were you?'

Birt gave me a disgusted look.

'Not outside the realm of possibility,' I suggested. 'You didn't bring Wilson, did you?'

'You asked me not to.'

'You didn't?' I persisted.

'No, I didn't.'

'Good,' I told him, and my smile patted him on the top of his head.

I took him into the kitchen. The importance of the meeting merited the sitting-room but now that Farrell was using Ma's old room, and that room being directly over the sitting-room, the chances were that Farrell would drop something, or topple over himself and alert Birt to his presence. So, the kitchen it had to be. I went to the fridge and took out a can of lager for myself. 'Want one?'

Birt shook his head.

'Ah, no. Driving yourself this time, aren't you?' I sat down.

'I'm listening,' Birt told me.

Cheekily I cocked my head. 'Can't hear a thing,' I told him.

'Don't get smart with me, Marcus.'

'Touchy tonight, are we? I must really have taken you away from something out of the ordinary.'

'Just tell me what it is you say is so important.'

I opened my lager and took a long, leisurely swig, smacking my lips and going, 'Aaaah,' when I'd finished. 'Right. To business. This robbery I was telling you about. It's a goer as we old lags say. Four people involved. Me as the driver of the getaway car. Stuart Bean. And two others who I'm not being told about.' I took another sip of my lager. 'It's the usual old Securicor van job. Going to net us half a million in dollars!'

Birt frowned. 'Dollars?'

'Yeah. You know. That green crap the Yanks use for currency.'

'Just dollars?'

'So I'm told. At least, that's all that was mentioned.'

Birt was clearly puzzled. 'Dollars,' he repeated to himself.

'Go on,' I urged him. 'Ask me. Don't be ashamed you can't figure it out,' I said.

'Tell me.'

'Saudi embassy. They ship dollars from their embassy to the bank same day same time every month.'

'Do they now?' Birt asked, interested.

'They do. Don't know the time, though. I can tell you the day, though, if you're interested.'

'So tell me.'

'Friday, the twenty-ninth.'

'Four of you?'

'Four of us. I just stay in the car and whisk them off to never-never land when the job's done.'

I knew what Birt was thinking. He was thinking, firstly, that he should alert the Saudi Arabians and have the delivery cancelled. But he was also thinking about the kudos attached to arresting armed robbers. He was thinking about that pretty feather in his cap when Beany and his mates were once more behind bars. He was maybe even thinking about a few shares in the oil fields the Arabs might slip him. Some fat chance of that. And then he was thinking how tricky it could be if the robbery was stopped at the embassy, or anywhere on the route from the embassy to the bank. The risk of innocent bystanders getting in the way of stray bullets and all that sort of thing. Nothing like some gawping yob getting shot by mistake to take all the glamour away from a successful arrest and, instead, have accusations of police incompetence levelled at you. And he was thinking how much simpler it would be if he and his jolly band could be waiting at the drop-off point, pouncing when the gangsters felt they had got away with it.

'Where do you take them?' he asked.

'Ah, well, now, you see, we've something else to talk about before I give you *all* the information.'

'Like what?'

'Like me. Don't want to find myself banged up again with that horrible lot, do I? Common gangsters. So you and me, Maurice, we've got a little deal to make.'

'A deal,' Birt said as though he was considering it.

'A deal,' I told him. 'Dead simple, really. You just wait until I've dropped them off and driven away before you – what's the word? – before you nab them.'

Birt inclined his head. 'That's possible.'

'And you don't come looking for me, either. None of your smart-arse double-crosses.'

Birt gave me a wicked grin. 'As if I would.'

'Yeah, tell me about it. Anyway, try it and you'll never get what you're really after.'

'Which is?'

I paused significantly. 'Helmut Kranze,' I said finally.

It was extraordinary. There he was, Inspector Maurice Birt, sitting there opposite me, with a serious armed robbery solved and in his lap, yet the mention of Kranze's name made it all pale into insignificance. I think it was only then that I fully appreciated the full depth of Birt's loathing for Kranze. The *full* extent, I say, since I'd seen many signs of it before, of course. It'd be easy enough for me to load you down with all the jolly old clichés: the blood ran from his face, his eyes smouldered, his hands twitched, venom seeped from every pore; his voice, when he spoke, was a whisper choking with passionate detestation. That sort of jazz. But, you know, just about each of these was true in Birt's case apart from the bit about the eyes and the venom. His eyes remained totally *dis*passionate and were all the more frightening because of that. 'Want him, don't you?' I asked after a wait long enough for Birt to benefit from his emotions. 'We have a deal then?'

Birt nodded. He nodded slowly, almost reluctantly. But he nodded and I knew that was as good as his word.

'Well, you won't believe this, but Bean wants me to drive them all back to his place,' I said, and from the incredulous look on Birt's face I felt it better to repeat myself. 'I knew you wouldn't believe me, but I swear to God it's true. Crazy, but true.'

Birt kept watching me.

'Now, that's what he *told* me. Whether he comes to his senses or not in the meantime, I can't tell. He *might* change the drop-off point. I've no way of knowing, but he's *got* to tell me eventually where exactly I have to go if he *does* change his mind.' I stuck out my chest and let my voice do the swaggering. 'I've got to prepare the escape route, you see.'

Birt still stared.

'From Charles Street – where the embassy is,' I explained as Birt's brows furrowed, 'to Beany's place. Got to get every street and corner worked out – *and* do some dummy runs. *That's* an idea,' I said. 'Why don't you come along on one of them? Pick your spot. A good spot where no one, except maybe your mate Wilson, with luck, will get hurt, and from somewhere I can take off.' I was quite pleased with that. The thought of taking Birt along as I planned my route appealed to me as quietly ironic. But then: 'No,' I said, rejecting the idea. 'Better you wait till we get to the actual drop-off spot so I can drive off naturally.' I was glad I thought of that. 'But do come along for one of the planning rides,' I added brightly.

That wasn't what Birt had in mind. 'When do you think you'll know if Bean *does* change his mind about the drop-off?'

'Your guess is as good as mine,' I said, and then thought I might as well show a bit of bravado. 'I can try and find out now if you like,' I remarked with just the right touch of nonchalance.

'Now?' Birt asked, taken aback.

'Sure. Why not? I can give Bean a call and see what he says.' I stood up. 'Need to know myself anyway. Anything else you want to know while I'm on the phone?'

Birt shook his head. I think he thought I was having him on – about actually phoning Bean.

'Okay,' I said, and went to the phone.

My heart sank when his Mum answered. I suspected she only dared touch the machine if Stuart was out. 'Oh. Ah. Mrs Bean? Is Stuart there by any chance? It's Marcus here.'

'In the – ' She said something that sounded like 'casbah'.

'I'm sorry?'

'In the loo.'

'Oh. Right,' I said and then, stupidly, asked, 'Will he be long?'

'Long as it takes,' Mum told me, and you had to admire her erudition.

'You mind if I hang on?'

'Suit yourself,' Mum said but then hung up on me.

I wandered back to the kitchen shaking my head. Birt was grinning, pretty smugly, I felt. 'That was his Mum. Daft old bitch. Told me to hang on and then hung up. Stuart's in the loo.'

'Oh, sure,' Birt said.

'I'll try him again in a tick.'

I didn't have to. Stuart called me, much to Birt's chagrin. He was in good form, it seemed, so getting all that crap out of his system must have done him the world of good. He apologised profusely for Mum's fucking awful manners.

'No bother,' I told him. 'Listen Stuart, I'm really sorry to bother you like this but – well, I've been thinking. I was a bit pushy the other day and maybe I forced you into a bad decision about – about taking you directly back to your place.'

Stuart was benevolent. 'Don't you bother your head about that, pal. Made up my mind long before we had our natter. You just go ahead and plan your route from where we start to here. Okay? Just allow for a couple of quick stops along the way to let the others out.'

'You're sure about that now, Stuart, are you? I don't want to have everything nicely timed and then find out there's been a last-minute change.'

'There won't be any changes,' Stuart assured me.

'Okay. That's all I wanted to know.'

'Getting the buzz already, are you?'

'Yes, I am, as a matter of fact. How did you guess?'

'Easy. Always happens when the day comes close. Best buzz in the world, isn't it?'

'Best I've ever had,' I fibbed.

Stuart hooted like a coot. 'Enjoy,' he roared, and the phone clicked dead.

'No change,' I told Birt, glad to see he wasn't quite so smug any more. 'Just that I have to make a couple of quick stops on the way back to Bean's to let the others out.'

'That means they'll divvy up in the car,' Birt said, mostly to himself. 'Divvy up?' I asked scathingly. 'The old movies have really got to you, Maurice. Divvy up indeed!'

Then Birt shook his head. 'Maybe not. Maybe – ' He stood up abruptly. 'I've got to go.'

'What is it? What's happened? What have you thought of?' I fired the questions at him.

Birt stopped by the front door. He turned and gazed at me. 'You watch yourself,' he said. 'I'd bet a hundred quid to a penny that Bean is planning to do a runner.'

'Huh?' I asked, not quite following.

'He'll dump the other two saying he'll di– share out the cash later. But my guess is he'll head straight for the airport. That means he'll either get you to drive him or he'll let you take him home and then go there by himself later.' Birt put an almost fatherly hand on my shoulder. 'If he asks you to drive him to the airport, don't.'

'Okay, but why?'

'Because I don't want to find your corpse in the carpark at Heathrow, that's why.'

'Oh. Right.' I must have sounded like a dullard to Birt, but actually I was quite shocked. It really hadn't occurred to me that the Blow Job Queen would be quite that treacherous. But it made sense, of course.

'Just make any excuse you like but *don't* take him there,' Birt warned.

'I heard you.'

'And let me know if there *are* any new developments.'

'I will.'

'About this *or* about Kranze.'

'Of course.'

I watched him go down the road. I was quite touched by his concern. I even had a twinge of regret that I was going to use him. But that's life, I suppose. That's the way the cookie crumbles, the way the dice falls.

''Night, John,' I called as I passed Ma's room.

The response sounded mighty like a fart.

'Yeah, same to you, mate,' I said.

TWENTY-THREE

Farrell actually got up before me, so I expect he was feeling the excitement although it didn't demonstrate itself in any other way. He was quiet to the point of surliness, calm to the point of saintly serenity. But he must have been churning up inside. It was a big day for him, after all.

'Big day today,' I said as I came into the kitchen and the smell of fresh coffee, which is still, I think, the most seductive aroma in the world. 'How d'you feel?'

He gave a small grimace with his lips. 'Okay, I suppose.'

'Sure you are. Listen, there's nothing to it,' I assured him with the voice of experience. 'And I'll be with you all the time to give you a helping hand.'

'I'm okay, I said.'

'You said you *supposed* you were okay. Not quite the same thing.'

'I *am* okay then. All right?'

'All right. All right,' I said.

We drank our coffee in silence. I don't know what he was thinking, but I was thinking maybe I'd bitten off more than Farrell could chew, which didn't exactly make a brilliant start to the day. That's why I said, 'We can still call the whole thing off,' with a ridiculous temptation to sing the words – probably would have, if I could have remembered the tune.

Farrell shook his head.

'You don't *have* to do it, you know. You don't have to do *anything* you don't want to.'

'I know.'

'Okay. Look, I'll get home early in the afternoon and help get things ready. Then I'll nip back into town and pick up Miranda.'

'I can get everything ready,' Farrell told me.

'Yeah, I'm sure you can. But it doesn't do any harm to have things checked. Just to make sure,' I said, thinking the last thing I was about to do was trust Farrell to have everything ready. Christ alone knows what I'd have found. 'You just take it easy today.'

Farrell nodded his agreement.

'And better not go out.'

Farrell shook his head in agreement.

'Now I better get going.'

Farrell nodded again, acting the strong silent type, perhaps. I hoped so.

I need hardly say that I got nothing done that day, workwise, so no aspiring novelist had to suffer the brunt of my criticism. But just to allay suspicion and to prove that I did, sometimes, put in an appearance, I made a point of having a special word with Nick Putty about Mr Pekwangi's liberation of the veldt or whatever. 'Not bad, is it?' I asked.

Nick agreed. 'Not bad at all. In fact, I partly guessed it would be pretty good after you said you liked it,' he said with a smirk.

'Meaning?'

'Meaning just that.'

'It's my job, isn't it? Weeding out the dross?'

'Oh, indeed. And now that the Kranze book is ready, perhaps you'd take this one on and see it through, would you?'

'If you like.'

'I would like.'

'Your wish is my command. Might entail a trip to South Africa,' I added sarcastically, looking for a perk.

Nick just snorted and started talking about how it might be worthwhile for me to do some background reading on the area, but I wasn't really listening. The idea of a trip to less-dark Africa appealed – it would be an ideal break when all my private chores were finished. And God knows I would deserve a rest when I rid the world of Kranze. I cut in: 'You know, Nick, it might be a help to meet the author before I start work on the book. You know, try and get a feel for what –'

'I know what you mean, Marcus, but it's out of the question,' Nick told me.

'Yeah. Of course. You would,' I said, giving Nick a shy smile as though his reminding me that he was, after all, an editor of some note, had put me subtly in my place.

It gave me something to deliberate on when I got back to my own office anyway; and made the morning pass that much quicker, which was even more important.

I went home at lunchtime. The house was totally quiet. No TV on. No music from the radio in the kitchen. Unusual, that, since Farrell seemed incapable of functioning without the aid of some electrical entertainment. 'Anyone home?' I called, still standing in the hall.

'In here,' a voice from the kitchen told me.

Farrell had been busy. The plastic sheeting was laid out on the floor, covering every inch of it. He'd actually made a better job of it than I had when I experimented on Sharon. The black rubbish bag was neatly folded on the worktop, with the knife I'd used on Sharon lying on top of it. 'Great,' I enthused. I thought I better enthuse because Farrell was sitting on the floor, in the corner near the fridge, not exactly looking the part of a potential murderer. 'What you sitting there for?'

Farrell shrugged.

My guiding spirit warned me to make light of it. I sat down beside him, squatted beside him, actually. 'You've done a terrific job,' I told him. And then, loading my voice with compassion and understanding, I asked, 'You sure you want to go through with this, John?'

He took his time about answering, and I had this dreadful sinking feeling. I also had the feeling that I must have been out of my mind to ever imagine anything would go smoothly with Farrell as a partner. Which was probably why I felt such relief and felt so elated when Farrell finally said, 'Oh, yes. Just – just getting my mind ready, too.'

That shouldn't take too long, I thought. Not that there was much there *to* get ready. 'Sure, mate. I understand.'

'I'm doing it right, amn't I?'

Amn't I? I shuddered. 'You're doing it perfectly,' I answered. 'Just one small thing, though. You don't think that, maybe, leaving that bag and the knife sitting there where she can see them might just give her a spot of the old anxiety, do you?'

I had hoped Farrell might see the funny side of that statement but I should, I suppose, have known better.

'I'm not *leaving* them there,' he said grumpily.

'Oh.'

'Just wanted you to see I had them ready.'

'Oh.'

'I'll put them away now,' he said, and heaved himself upright. I stood up too. 'Well, I can see you've got everything well and truly under control this end, John, so I'll be off.' I went to the door. 'Nothing you want to discuss before I go?' I asked over my shoulder.

'Uh-huh.'

'Okay, then. See you later.'

I was just getting into the car, reminding myself to make sure and get petrol, when Farrell came running out of the house. You can imagine what the sight of that did to my heart. 'What's happened?' I asked, going towards him.

'Nothing's happened. It's just – you couldn't, you know, let me have – '

'Shit. Of course, John,' I said. And that just shows you how easy it is to get distracted and forget things. I'd fully intended to let John have a few of his special sweeties. In fact, I wanted him to take them. If those jellies were all they were cracked up to be, he should have all the courage he needed to commit the foul deed I had planned.

I went back into the house with him, and got him his jellies. Eight, I gave him. And I also poured him a stiff brandy with the advice that he take that first, just to buck him up.

'Don't like mixing,' he said.

'What d'you mean – mixing?'

'Drink and them,' he said, holding out his hand to show me the temazepam capsules.

'Oh? Why not?' I enquired innocently.

'Make you crazy, mixing them.'

'Well, it's up to you. Can't stay here arguing about it. Personally I can't see what difference it'd make to mix them just this once.'

And I left him sitting there, half hoping he'd agree with my conclusion and take the lot.

I had to get a shift on now as I was running late. Luckily most of the traffic was coming out of the West End and not into it. There's a garage just this side of Chelsea Bridge and I filled the tank with petrol there, cursing the bearded Sikh for taking so long about figuring my change: how bright do you have to be to work out that eighteen quid's worth of petrol gives two pounds change from a twenty-pound note? Probably just smuggled in and still thinking in rupees, I thought. Luckily, though, there were a few parking spaces in Jermyn Street so I had the time to compose myself before leaving the car and walking back to Fortnum's.

Miranda wasn't there when I arrived at the staff exit. I waited. And waited. Twenty minutes later I was still waiting, and getting very jittery, I can tell you. I felt like a pillock standing there so I strolled down the street a bit, window-shopping as far as anyone watching was concerned. I did this a couple of times, getting more and more worked up, all sorts of calamitous ideas rushing through my head. I decided to give her another three minutes. Not a sign of her. I was just about to go back to the car and drive home when this short, chubby woman of about forty came hurrying down the street and accosted me. Well, I thought she was about to accost me. She stood in front of me, eyed me, and asked, 'Are you Martin?'

I was so uptight that I very nearly told her that, no, I wasn't fucking Martin, but fortunately didn't. I said, 'I'm sorry?'

'Are you Martin, waiting for Miranda?'

What the hell was going on? 'Well, yes, as a matter of fact I am.'

'I thought I'd missed you,' the woman said. 'I'm Miranda's friend, Charlotte.'

'Ah. The nurse. Yes – she did mention you.'

'Could we – ' She looked about her. 'Could we go somewhere? I – '

'What's happened to Miranda?' I asked.

'Could we – please – I – '

I could see that Charlotte was getting both agitated and distraught and I didn't really want to be seen on the street with a hysterical psychiatric nurse on my hands. 'There's a café in the arcade,' I said, but didn't make a move to go there.

'Could we – '

I gave in. 'Sure. Let's go,' I said, thinking, God never shuts one door but He slams another one in your face.

She clearly had something of import to tell me, but equally she didn't want to say anything until we were in the seclusion of the café. I didn't push her. Not until I got her settled at a table with a cup of espresso in front of her. 'Right. What's going on?'

She started to sob, which was an ominous start, I felt. But I'm very good at dealing with women when they're sad, and if it wasn't for the morons at the next table who kept looking at me as if *I* had made this Charlotte cry, I'd have been in my element. I sat opposite Charlotte, so I stretched out and took her hand in mine. That really opened the floodgates. I gave her my hankie, and told her to keep it after she'd wiped her eyes and blown her nose in it: I didn't want her snot in my pocket, thank you very much.

'I'm sorry, Martin. I'm sorry,' she said, making a genuine effort to pull herself together.

'Just tell me what's happened,' I said, like a priest prising sin from a penitent.

'It's Miranda. She's been killed,' Charlotte blurted out, and switched on her lachrymatory taps again.

Well, blow me down! I have to laugh now, but at the time it was anything but funny. I honestly thought some interfering bastard had got in before me and murdered Miranda. God, I was furious, so it was with passion that I exclaimed, 'Oh, my God!'

But it wasn't quite like that, apparently. Miranda had been knocked down three days previously, by a drunk driver. She died before they could get her to hospital. 'Oh, dear God!' I said.

It was then that Charlotte started reeling off the litany which stunned me, telling me things about her friend which were quite incredible. Like, 'Miranda told me all about you, Martin', and, 'She just couldn't wait for you to come back from your trip to Colombia', and, 'All she ever spoke about was you', and – and this was the stunner – 'She confided in me all your plans for a secret wedding – she told me *everything*, you see'.

I was gobsmacked. All I could say was, 'She did?'

'Oh, yes. All about those wonderful places you took her and how you treated her like a queen.'

News to me. 'It was nothing.'

'It was to poor Miranda,' Charlotte said, sniffing and playing with one of her dangly earrings.

Poor Miranda, my arse. I should have guessed that anyone who had a psychiatric nurse as their bosom friend would be a bit off their head. 'I loved her so much,' I said with appropriate wistfulness and sadness. 'Oh, I know you did. And she knew too, which was so wonderful. That's why I had to come and try and catch you this evening. I wanted you to hear the sad news from me. Her best friend. That's what she'd have wanted.'

'That was very kind of you, Charlotte,' I said, and gave her hand another squeeze. Then, to take her down a peg or two, I decided to tell her something Miranda hadn't told her. 'She told me she was married, I – '

Charlotte gave a small, womanly, conspiratorial smile. 'She told me she told you that. She – '

'Was she – married?'

Charlotte shook her head. 'She desperately wanted to be,' she told me, slipping into her psychiatric garb. 'But I think you were the only one who – '

'Don't,' I pleaded, looking up at the ceiling, blinking like mad as though trying bravely and desperately to restrain the tears.

'Oh, I'm *so* sorry, Martin.'

I withdrew my hand from her clasp and rubbed my forehead, taking short, sharp breaths like, maybe, I was about to faint.

'Are you all right, Martin?'

Bravely I said, 'Yes. Yes. I'm fine. The shock – it's just hit me, I think.' I shook my head in disbelief. 'We had such wonderful plans,' I confided.

'I know. I know. She told me.'

I'd love to have known what plans the stupid Miranda had told her about, but this wasn't the time to enquire. Time was ticking by. Farrell would be getting all het up, and if he *had* taken the brandy and all the jellies, Christ alone knew what he was up to. 'Tell me, Charlotte, do you drive?'

She gave a surprised look. 'Well, yes, but I didn't bring – '

'Could I ask you an enormous favour?'

'Of course, Martin.'

'Would you be so kind as to drive me home? I just don't think I could – '

'Of course I will.'

'I'll have a taxi take you home,' I promised.

'Don't you worry about that.'

I didn't intend to.

So, Charlotte drove me home.

Don't tell me anything about the art of improvisation. That night I proved I was a dab hand at it. Mind you, Charlotte did make things quite ridiculously easy.

I didn't have to try and persuade her to enter the house: clearly she was the sort of female who once she'd made up her mind not even an act of God would change it. She *insisted* on coming in. To see me safely indoors, she said. Okay, girl, I thought, have it your own way. And so as not to disappoint her, I leaned on her shoulder and allowed her to steer me into the house, like I was one of the geeks she was used to dealing with.

Once inside, the excitement overtook me somewhat and I started to shake, the same sort of trembling, I remembered, as had overwhelmed me just before my first major sexual experience, which I won't go into just now. I expect everyone's had those *fornicatio tremens* anyway.

The nurse in Charlotte (the non-psychiatric bit, that is) said it was delayed shock, and who was I to argue? 'Must be,' I agreed.

'Have you any brandy?' she then asked.

'I think so,' I answered feebly, which was only being truthful since I didn't know if Farrell had left any.

'That's what you need. A good stiff brandy.'

'It's in the kitchen – if there is any,' I said, and we moved in that direction, Charlotte patting my back like she was trying to get me to burp, me clinging to her as if my poor old legs were about to give out at any minute. 'You'll have to excuse the mess, though. Got the decorators coming in tomorrow.'

Charlotte tutted. 'Don't you worry your head about any mess,' she said, and leaned across me to open the kitchen door.

When the late Miranda had been the object of my attentions I had, in my mind's eye, visualised this scene a number of times. It was to have been a very calm and dignified drama. A ritual. A sort of sacrifice, I suppose. Me, I saw, sitting at the kitchen table, behaving rather like the instructor at some Method Acting class, watching intently, and making notes of errors on which to reprimand my student later – when the curtain came down, so to speak. Regrettably, I hadn't taken Farrell into account, and it certainly hadn't entered my reckoning that he would have become quite so dedicated.

I found some brandy and was just taking the first sip when Farrell came into the kitchen. He looked at Charlotte, he looked at me, and then he looked at Charlotte again. Then, abruptly, he turned on his heel and stormed out of the kitchen, leaving me with my mouth open, and Charlotte looking pretty bemused, I can tell you. It was a miracle I recovered my wits as quickly as I did. 'My cousin,' I explained. 'He's a bit – you know,' I added, tapping the side of my head to indicate a mild lunacy. 'I better – ' I was out of my chair and out of the kitchen before my psychiatric Mother Teresa could object.

Farrell was in the hall, hugging himself and shaking his head as though truly demented.

'What the hell – ' I began.

'It's not *her*,' Farrell told me. 'It's not the one you told me to look at in that café.'

It crossed my mind to point out that Messrs Fortnum and Mason would be most distraught to hear their establishment referred to as a café, but what I said was, 'I *know* it's not her. She couldn't make it. This is a stand-in. She'll do just as well, won't she?'

'Won't be the same,' Farrell told me, peevishly.

'For Christ's sake, John, it doesn't make any difference.'

'Does.'

'It doesn't. She's a friend of the other one,' I heard myself say, as if that was some sort of logical argument.

Amazingly, to Farrell it was. 'Oh. She's the other one's friend, is she?' he asked.

'*Yes*. Taking her place. You know, a substitute. You know, Cantona off, Vinnie Jones on,' I said, aware that the analogy was totally crazy and unlikely but hoping it might just penetrate Farrell's skull and make sense.

It did. 'So there's no difference then?'

'None whatever.'

Farrell beamed at me. 'Just thought you'd made a mistake.'

'I don't make mistakes, John. Not if I can help it.'

'I know you don't. That's why I didn't want you to – '

I couldn't stand there listening to Farrell's serpentine explanations, not with Charlotte probably getting all hot under the collar. 'Look, I'm going back in there. Give me a couple of minutes and then you come in again and I'll introduce you. Okay?'

Farrell nodded.

'Okay?' I asked again.

'Yes. Okay.'

'He says he's okay,' I told Charlotte when I got back into the kitchen.

'He just has this thing – a phobia, I guess you'd call it – about meeting new people.'

Charlotte smiled understandingly. 'I understand,' she told me.

'He'll come back in in a minute and I'll introduce you. Then he'll be fine,' I said.

Alas, introductions were the furthest thing from Farrell's mind when he came back. The kitchen door flew open, and in he came like a rampant bull, charging across the kitchen, lunging at Charlotte with the knife raised high above his head. So much for my calm and dignified drama. But, in retrospect, it was probably the best way for things to happen since Charlotte hadn't the chance to let even a squeak out of her before she was dead; had no time to react in any way at all apart from plastering a slightly puzzled look across her face.

But the violence of Farrell's attack took my breath away. He just wouldn't stop. Even after Charlotte was on the ground with all semblance of life well and truly slithered out of her, Farrell kept on stabbing her. Time and time again he plunged the knife into her fleshy body, giving little grunts with each jab, a bit like he was leading up to orgasm, really, which I found a little disconcerting. I think he must have stabbed her some thirty times before I managed to pull him off. And then I had to struggle to get the knife away from him. Not that he didn't want to let go: it was as though he *couldn't* let go, as if the knife had been grafted to his hand. Eventually I did, though. I dropped it on top of Charlotte's body. I took Farrell in my arms. I held him. I comforted him. I consoled him. I praised him too, and after some ten minutes of us standing there like a couple of lovers, he calmed down. I guided him to a chair and sat him down. It was another ten minutes before either of us spoke. 'Did I do okay?' Farrell asked in much the same tone as he usually asked me if he'd cooked a meal okay. It was interesting that he no longer even glanced at the body. And it didn't seem to be a conscious decision. I wondered if maybe he'd forgotten about Charlotte lying there, forgotten that he'd just turned her chubby body into a sieve.

'You did great,' I told him.

Astonishingly he yawned, and said simply, 'I'm knackered.'

'It's been a long day for you.'

He nodded.

'Why don't you go on up and take a kip?' I suggested. 'I'll clear up,' I added, and surprised myself since I know I had adapted to his tone, and 'clearing up' could just as well have meant the dishes.

'You sure you don't want a hand?'

'No, that's okay. I'll manage.'

Farrell stood up and stretched. He gave another yawn, too, followed by a short, breathy snort.

'Eh, John, you better take your clothes off.'

He looked at me, puzzled.

'The blood. There's quite a bit on you. I'll need to burn them.'

'Oh. Yes.'

He stripped, folding each garment carefully and placing it on the floor. And then, naked and demure, he stepped over Charlotte without a look, and toddled upstairs.

I shook my head in wonderment. I also stripped naked since blood had got onto my clothes when I'd hugged Farrell. There was actually something quite sensuous about clearing up in the nude.

I checked the pockets of all my clothes and Farrell's and when I'd removed everything I put the stained clothing in a bin-liner. Then, I parcelled up Charlotte in a couple of rubbish bags. One I pulled over her head and down to her waist, the other over her feet and *up* to her waist, overlapping them, and tying them in place with a length of that plastic-coated string you buy on a roll and use for – shit, just about anything, I imagine. Even gift-wrapping corpses, I suppose. I put her handbag into the bin-liner with our clothes, and then folded up the sheeting which covered the kitchen floor, putting that into the bin-liner too. Finally, I washed the knife thoroughly and returned it to the rack.

It was all pretty strenuous and tiring. When I'd finished I poured myself a brandy, reminding myself that it was just what Charlotte had said I needed. I sat at the table and sipped, looking forward to a shower and some clean clothes.

I had no bother dragging the remains of Charlotte to my car. My house was the last in the row and because of that had a garage attached to it with a door leading into the kitchen. Very handy. So, with a bit of pushing and shoving, into the boot went Charlotte. The other bag, the one with the clothes, I didn't take with me. I'd deal with that tomorrow, I thought. One thing at a time.

The imp in me said I should dump Charlotte's body in the same place as I'd deposited Sharon's, but that would be asking for trouble, so I resisted the temptation. I chose Wimbledon Common instead, hiding her under some fairly dense shrubs from where even the Wombles wouldn't spot her unless they were particularly looking for her. I didn't, of course, leave her in the rubbish bags. I emptied her out, letting her flop to an interesting position, and took the bags home with me, putting them, also, into the bin-liner for burning.

Farrell was downstairs again when I did get home, looking quite chipper, as if he'd had a good rest. 'Feeling okay?' I asked.

'Feeling fine,' he answered. 'She gone?'

'Oh, yes. Well gone,' I told him.

'I'd have helped if you'd called me.'

'Yeah, I know you would. And thanks. But I figured you needed the rest. I managed okay.'

Out of the corner of my eye I noticed Pissquick make one of his ever decreasing visits, slinking in through the cat-flap that Ma had installed, at some considerable expense, I might add. Chelsea cat-flaps must be designer cat-flaps to justify their horrendous cost. Not your common or garden Tooting-Bec cat-flaps by a long chalk. I don't know who was feeding the brute: I did when our paths happened to cross and he bullied me into dishing up something for him, but we didn't seem to meet all that often. Maybe he'd become a Buddhist or something, and was doing the rounds of the neighbourhood with his Whiskas bowl, just biding his time until he went to Ma's where he knew he could stuff his fat gut till he burst. But his disciples must have filled his begging-bowl that evening for he gave us both the most casual of glances, and then crouched as if to pounce on something, his belly flat to the ground, the tip of his tail flicking like an adder's tongue. The dreadful thought struck me that there might be an up-market mouse in the kitchen and I felt myself get really queasy. I hate rodents of any kind. Really *hate* them. Quite honestly, rodents petrify me, and anyone who keeps any member of that species as a pet needs their head examined, in my opinion.

'Think you'll be able to manage the same with Zanker?' I asked Farrell bluntly, more to distract myself from Pissquick's activity than to shock Farrell or get any lucid answer from him.

He nodded, and continued nodding as he took his time about saying, 'Yes.'

'We've no problems, then. Tonight was a lesson well learned.'

'Yes,' he said again, and now we both watched Pissquick who suddenly sprung into action, leaping across the floor, skidding on the cushion-backed linoleum, and coming to an inelegant halt by crashing into the wall. He rebounded smartly enough, and took to teasing something with his paw, growling and making the sort of noise a Tube train does when it's coming towards you through a tunnel.

'Oh, shit!' I exclaimed. 'What's he got, John?' I asked, just getting ready to make a leap for the top of the table.

'Dunno,' Farrell informed me, implacably unmoved.

'It's not a bloody mouse, is it?'

'Dunno.'

I could feel my knees automatically drawing themselves up, taking my feet off the floor. 'Can't stand mice,' I confessed.

'Only wee things,' Farrell told me.

Pissquick clouted whatever it was he was playing with, and it skittered across the floor. Before I could make out what it was he had lunged at it and towered over it with total feline menace.

'Do me a favour, John. Get it off him, will you?'

But Farrell didn't seem to hear. He was fascinated by Pissquick's antics which, by this time, had become more and more frantic, as, indeed, was my state of mind. 'John!' I heard myself shout.

Farrell looked at me.

'Get that thing away from the cat, will you?'

Farrell continued to stare at me.

'And if it's a mouse, throw it out – *please*.'

Farrell gave me an odd look. 'You're scared,' he informed me.

'Yes. I'm bloody scared. Satisfied?'

'Didn't think anything scared you.'

'Well, now you know.'

'Didn't think – '

'Look, would you just get up and take whatever it is away from that damn cat and get rid of it?'

Farrell heaved himself to his feet, and walked towards Pissquick. He bent down. I cringed. Pissquick yodelled, and defended his catch by spitting and clawing at Farrell.

But Farrell, to his credit, and my amazement, was unperturbed. He simply grabbed Pissquick by the scruff of the neck and removed his toy, and then stroked the cat by way of apologising for being a spoilsport.

'What is it?' I demanded from the other side of the room.

Farrell took a good look. 'Dunno. Just a thing.'

'A thing?'

'Yeah. A thing.'

He sauntered across the kitchen and put the thing in the bin, out of Pissquick's reach.

'You sure it's not a mouse?'

'No mouse. Just a thing. A metally kind of thing,' he told me and came back to the table, sitting down and resuming the exact position he'd been in before he'd wrestled with Pissquick. 'Your mother rang,' he announced.

'Did you answer it?'

Farrell shook his head. 'There's a message.'

'Make us a cuppa, will you?' I requested and went to the phone, dialling Ma's number. 'Oh, Ma? You rang.'

'Darling! Goodness, do you know what hour it is? I'm in bed, dear.'

'But not asleep.'

'Not now, no.'

I could hear her pounding the pillows behind her head so I guessed this was going to be a long one. 'Is it all right?' she asked.

'Is what all right?'

'Didn't you get my message?'

'I didn't listen to your message, Ma. That's why I'm ringing you.'

Ma paused to try and work out the logic of that. 'I simply wanted to know if you could come down for the weekend either this week or next.'

'Oh. Yeah. That'd be nice.'

'Which, dear?'

'Sorry?'

'Which weekend?'

'Oh. Next.'

'The thirtieth?'

'Exactly. The day after the twenty-ninth.'

Ma tittered, thinking I was being smart. Of course she had no idea of the significance of that date.

'That will be lovely,' she said.

'I'm sure it will. I'll be down first thing Saturday morning.'

'Wonderful. I'm so looking forward to showing you round.'

'Yeah. I'm looking forward to seeing the love nest.'

I could tell by the drowsy sound in Ma's voice that she had settled back for a long chat now that I'd woken her. 'So, tell me, darling, how are you?'

'I'm just terrific. Ma?'

'Tell me *all* the news.'

'No news, Ma, I'm afraid. Nothing exciting happening at all. Just work and more work.'

'Oh dear. There must be *some* exciting news?'

''Fraid not, Ma.' Farrell crept past me on the way up to his room. ''Night,' I said automatically.

'Pardon, dear?'

'No. Not you, Ma. I was saying goodnight to John.'

'Oh. He's still with you then?'

'Just for a little longer.'

'You're so kind to him, darling. I hope he's at least making himself useful about the house?'

'Oh, he is, Ma. Believe me, he is,' I said, refraining from mentioning that he'd just filled the poor Charlotte full of more perforations than a Tetley's tea bag.

'Well, that's something at least.'

'Look, Ma, sorry. I'll have to go. Got something cooking on the stove and I think it's just boiled over. See you next week. Love you.'

'I love you too, darling.'

As I sat alone in the kitchen, just resting, I felt an extraordinary feeling of elation. By the time I visited Ma in her near Bath darling of a Queen Anne house, everything would be over. I would have completed my task. I would be king of the castle, and there wouldn't be a soul alive who knew a damn thing about it.

I let Fauré's Requiem put me to sleep that night. I played it as a tribute to Charlotte. I felt she deserved a little memorial for being such a good sport – and for being in the right place at the right time, as far as I was concerned.

TWENTY-FOUR

Farrell was up bright and early the next morning, and joined me in the kitchen for breakfast. I had to admire him. It really was as though nothing had happened. He was taking everything in his stride, although there were dark lines under his eyes so I suspected that perhaps his night's sleep hadn't been the greatest. 'Sleep all right?' I asked.

'Okay,' he told me.

Up popped the toast. 'Got to tell you that you did really well last night,' I said, scraping the toast with butter.

'Did okay, didn't I?'

'Certainly did. Didn't need me there at all in the end.'

'Funny feeling, isn't it?'

'What's that?' I asked, putting the buttered toast on the table and fetching some Fortnum's marmalade from the cupboard.

'Killing someone.'

'Oh, that. Different.'

I didn't really want to discuss the gory details over breakfast, but Farrell was keen, and in the end we got quite chummy about it, treating it as an incident that merited a review of sorts. I let Farrell do most of the talking, listening intently so that I could spot any flaws or even wavering in his comments: all grist to the mill for the next stage of my plan. My only disappointment was that Farrell hadn't seemed to *enjoy* it all. He'd done it, sure, but it was a chore for him rather than an entertainment. But he'd learned from it, and that had been the ultimate object of the exercise.

'Think they've found her yet?' he asked.

I shrugged. 'No idea. Shouldn't think so.' I looked at the clock. 'Put the telly on and you'll find out.'

He gave me a blank, uncomprehending stare.

'The telly. If they've found her there's bound to be some mention of it on the news.'

It was probably a sign of our times but now that the television had been mentioned Farrell's attitude changed completely. Suddenly he was alight. His eyes danced. His shoulders straightened. His voice was perky when he asked, 'The telly? You think it'll be on the telly?'

'Bound to be.'

He was up from the table and switching on the box like a shot. He walked backwards to the table, keeping his eyes glued to the screen, to the newsreader who was rambling through the same crap we'd been hearing for weeks: Major and Blair sniping at each other, the Bosnians and the Croats sniping at each other, the Palestinians going one step further and blowing some Israelis to kingdom come. The drought too was still causing havoc: potato and dairy produce prices were rocketing, and the good folk in Yorkshire were going bananas about hosepipe bans, their petunias and lobelia wilting. I'd just about given up listening when suddenly the newsreader changed his tone as is appropriate when reporting something as intimate as death. 'News has just come in that the body of a woman has been found on Wimbledon Common. Police are not commenting at the moment except to say they are treating her death as suspicious.'

'There you go,' I said to Farrell.

He was clearly disappointed. 'That it?'

'That's it, for the moment.'

'Mightn't even be her.'

I sighed. 'How many bodies d'you think they're likely to find on Wimbledon Common? Don't grow on trees, you know.'

'Could have said a *bit* more.'

'They will. Don't worry. They're always cagey to begin with.'

'Could have said a *bit* more,' he said again. He was like a starlet who'd been waiting to see his first major screen appearance only to find his dramatic efforts had been left on the cutting-room floor.

'Bet you what you like it'll be headlines this evening.'

'You think?'

'Sure to be. Unless they drop another bomb on Nagasaki or something.'

He gave me another of his blank stares.

'Forget it,' I said. 'Just wait until the evening news and you'll be up there with the greats.'

'You mean they'll talk about *me*?'

I couldn't believe it. He'd asked the question as though that was exactly what he wanted. 'I bloody hope not,' I said. 'They'll give more details about their discovery, that's all. They *can't* talk about you since they don't know you did it, do they?'

'Oh. No. That's right.' He cheered up a bit.

'You've outwitted them,' I went on, rubbing in the compliments.

'Yeah!' he said breathlessly.

'Who's a clever boy, then?'

'*Me*,' Farrell said, like Mummy dear had praised her favourite little brat.

'Yes, you.'

Anyway, I'd had enough of this puerile carry-on. And the news was over. And I'd finished breakfast. 'I think we'll go for a bit of a drive this morning,' I said. 'Just cruise about a bit. Clear our heads.'

'Yeah,' Farrell agreed, looking pleased. Clearly just about everything was going to please the dope from now on.

I hoped everything was going to please me also. I wanted to do a little tour of Mayfair, suss out Charles Street and the general area. I also wanted to burn the bits and pieces left over from last night. And I wanted to see Stuart. I needed another small favour from him, and if I could get him in the right frame of mind (into which I hoped my industriousness would put him) he might oblige without too much dithering.

So, after we'd tidied up and left the kitchen looking spick and span, we set out. My spirits were high and I felt just a tiny bit reckless with the bin-liner and its compromising contents in the boot of the car. That *should* have been the first thing I dealt with but I thought, no, leave it, maybe I could get good old Beany to take care of that for me, too.

We spent the rest of the morning driving up and down, in and around Mayfair. I used the Saudi Embassy itself as my starting point, returning there each time I'd completed one particular route away from it. We must have gone up and down, where it wasn't one-way, every street leading from and to the embassy. You name it, we cruised it: South Audley Street, Curzon Street, Berkeley Square, Fitzmaurice Place. The lot. I got a good *feel* for the area. I decided I'd settle down with my map that night and work out my exact route.

At lunchtime I bowed to Farrell's request and had a McDonalds.

Or rather, *he* had a cheeseburger and I settled for a milkshake. Mad cow's disease I didn't want, thanks.

Then on to Stuart Bean's, where I left Farrell in the car. We got there just after two thirty – a bad time to call, his Mum informed me. She said, 'Won't like being disturbed, he won't. Not while he's watching his racing,' but she let me in anyway, giving me a shifty look over her shoulder as she pushed open the sitting-room door as much as to say, 'Don't fancy your chances, matey.'

A race was just finishing. A sprint by the look of it. Stuart was sitting on the edge of his chair urging his wager home, I gathered. But the nag didn't quite make it. Got nowhere near it, in fact, and so, without a welcome, I had to listen to a harangue about the incompetence of some jockey I'd never heard of, about the dishonesty of the racing industry as a whole, and about those 'pricks on Channel 4' who kept telling punters that such and such a horse was going to win but never did.

'That's racing for you,' I pointed out philosophically.

But Stuart was in no mood to be either philosophical or even sporting. His horse had been pulled and that was an end to it. Worst of all, as it turned out, it was the first leg of a treble so his whole bet was out the window, giving him nothing to look forward to, and shattering his interest. That suited *me* just fine. At least I got his attention. The more so when I told him, exaggerating slightly, that I'd worked out the perfect route from the Saudi Embassy to his place.

He turned down the sound on the television, and faced me with a smile. 'Wish there were more like you, Marcus,' he said wistfully.

'Not having trouble with the others, are you?'

'Shit, no. They do what they're fucking told. Just no go in them, know what I mean?'

'No job satisfaction, eh?'

Beany hooted at that. 'God, Marcus, do you have a way with words! That's just it. No fucking job satisfaction. Want a lager?'

'No. No thanks. Got someone waiting for me in the car. Can't stay long. Actually, Stuart, I need another favour.'

Stuart's face clouded over momentarily, assuming the countenance of a godfather, or what he *thought* a godfather should look like. 'Name it,' he said.

'Well, two things, actually. First, I've got some – some stuff in the car I need disposed of. Permanently. I don't mean for resale, Stuart,' I said as I thought I spotted him making a quick calculation of possible profit. 'I mean burned. Totally destroyed. Not a trace left.'

'Got it with you?'

'In the car.'

'Leave it here. It won't be around more than an hour.'

'Thanks. You're great. Now the other thing. It's a bit delicate.' And that was no more than the truth, because I didn't know if Stuart was into the supply of drugs, and if he wasn't – well, those who weren't could be, I knew, very touchy about it. 'You know just about everyone who's worth knowing,' I began.

'Fuck the flannel, Marcus. What is it you want?'

Here we go, I thought. 'Heroin. Pure heroin.'

Stuart narrowed his eyes. 'How much?'

'Just enough for – ' Again I hesitated, but I was in up to my neck already so it was sink or swim. 'Enough for someone to have a lethal overdose.'

The nice thing about dealing with remorseless, conscienceless thugs is that nothing fazes them. 'When do you want it?'

'Soon as poss.'

'Now?'

I blinked. 'That'd be just dandy.'

Stuart nodded and went to the phone. 'Go take a leak,' he told me. 'Down the passage, last door on the right.'

'No problem.' And it wasn't. I was dying for a pee.

When I got back to the sitting-room Stuart had finished on the phone. Just about. All I heard him say was, 'And send Davey round with it. Got another little earner for him.' He looked up at me. 'That stuff you want rid of. Portable?'

'Oh, sure. Just half a bin-liner.'

'And in the car?'

'Right.'

'Okay. Sit.'

I sat. I waited, twiddling my thumbs.

Stuart didn't speak for a while. He did glance at the television from time to time, particularly while the following race was being run, and as the hacks galloped past the post he winced, so I guessed the second leg of his treble was up, making that first loser all the worse.

Then his Mum came into the room and said Davey was at the door for him.

'Tell him to come in, Mum.'

'In here?'

'Yes. In here.'

Davey was about sixteen, I'd guess. A weedy youth of the sort you'd suspect was suffering from rickets, if anyone suffers from rickets these days. He had the worst acne I'd ever seen on a lad, and, of course, picked at it constantly. He looked at me with considerable suspicion until, 'Give,' Stuart said, and Davey handed him a little plastic bag. Then Stuart said, 'Wait outside,' and obediently Davey left the room.

When he'd gone Stuart tossed the little bag into my lap. 'Know how to use that stuff?'

'Yes,' I lied. 'How much do I owe you?'

Stuart shook his head. 'I'll think of something,' he said with a grin.

I grinned back. 'I bet you will.'

'Okay,' he said, standing up. 'Give that other stuff to Davey and then forget about it.'

'Glad to. And thanks.'

Stuart became affable. 'Like doing favours for friends,' he told me. 'And I should have that car for you in a couple of days.'

'Fine.'

I still had the heroin in my hand and Stuart nodded towards it. 'Put that away, and mind how you go with it.'

'I will,' I said, putting it in my shirt pocket. 'And thanks again.'

'No problem.'

Outside, leaning against the wall, still picking away as if his life depended on his decapitating every zit on his face, Davey was waiting. He pushed himself upright and got into his stride in a single economical movement. 'Nice,' he said when we got to the car.

'Bit old now,' I said off-handedly.

'Old ones are best. The new stuff's all crap.'

I didn't argue.

'Gonna get me a Porsche, I am,' he told me.

'Nice,' I said since I knew he'd understand that.

'The best.'

'If you say so.'

'Gonna get me this Porsche and a house in Spain,' he now informed me, and you have to admire his ambition.

'Nothing like aiming high,' I said.

'Gonna do it,' Davey insisted, as if I was questioning his ability.

'I'm sure you are,' I agreed, opening the boot and giving him the bin-liner.

'This everything?' he asked.

'That's the lot. Make sure you – '

'I know what to do,' Davey told me coldly.

'Yeah. Sorry.'
'Want to keep my head on my neck, don't I?'
'Huh?'
'Forget it.'
'Oh. Stuart.'
'Yeah. You don't make a mess of things when Mr Bean gives the orders.'
'I gathered that.'
'You working for him?'
'I'm working *with* him actually.'
That gained me a dozen Brownie points. 'Must be okay then, you must.'
'Oh, sure, I'm very okay. Very, *very* okay.'
'See you around.'
'See you.'

You might think I was either very trusting or very stupid to allow Stuart Bean and his ragamuffin to dispose of anything quite so incriminating for me. And yes, I was trusting but I wasn't stupid. The one thing I could be absolutely sure of was that Beany would dispose of the bag and that would be the last anyone would hear of it. It was a question of reputation and status, you see. Beany's very existence depended on his doing 'favours' for people. If he agreed to do something and messed it up, his status would be severely dented. And, of course, if he tried to use any of the favours he did as leverage with those forces of security – if he grassed, in other words – it wouldn't just be his status that took a bashing. It had, though, nothing to do with honour. It was all based on fear, terror more like: his reputation as a hard man was all that Beany had, and no way in the world would he do anything or say anything to have that taken away from him. And like any so-called hard man there was a whole band of up-and-coming hard children ready to take his place, to dethrone him, if they possibly could. No, I was confident everything would be fine in the hands of the Blow Job Queen. He'd swing, as the old lags like to say, remembering the jolly times when people were hanged, rather than land a mate in it, bless his cotton socks.

'They've been talking about her,' Farrell informed me as soon as I got into the car.
'Who?'
'The news. About her.'

'Oh? What've they been saying?'

'Just that they've found her and haven't identified her yet.'

I smiled to myself. I haven't mentioned, and I hadn't told Farrell, that I had removed all identification from Charlotte's bag before putting it in the bin-liner. I did this as an act of devilment, giving the flatfeet a chance to earn their pay. 'Be much more about her on the telly this evening,' I said.

'Hope so,' Farrell hoped.

'And in the rags tomorrow! They'll have the time of their lives. Nothing to excite the rags like a body on Wimbledon Common.'

'That where we're going to put Zanker?'

The question took me by surprise. 'Naw,' I said. 'Won't be any need to shift him. If he kicks the bucket in his own home there'll be nothing to connect us to his journey to the great big Bundesrepublik in the sky,' I replied. And then, in one of my mischievous moods, I asked, 'Want to nip over and see him now?'

Farrell was full of surprises that afternoon. 'Yeah,' he said, and gave a kind of chirring sound, and smiled broadly.

I shook my head. 'Sounds like you – '

'Just want to have another look at him,' Farrell interrupted and explained.

'Like an undertaker – size him up for the coffin?' I asked morbidly.

Farrell loved that. 'Yeah, just like that.'

But we didn't go to see Kranze. Far too risky, in my book. It would have been just like Kranze to pull some wizardry out of the bag, bamboozle Farrell, and land me right in the shit. One more visit to Kranze was all I would allow Farrell. On the twenty-ninth. After that, there wouldn't be much point in visiting Kranze, I hoped. Unless we took a bunch of flowers with us.

I changed the subject. 'How come you never tried heroin, John? I mean, you seem to have tried everything else.'

'Crazy shit,' Farrell pronounced the drug.

'Yeah, but I thought you might have *tried* it. Once even.'

'No way.' Then he looked at me. 'Why you ask?'

I dismissed any seriousness in my question. 'Just wondered. Never been into anything but hash myself. Just wondered what made someone like you – an expert, so to speak – draw the line.'

Farrell didn't feel like continuing *that* conversation, so I tried another. 'Given any thought to what you're going to do when all this is over and you leave me?'

He hadn't. He shook his head. 'No.'

'What would you *like* to do?' I asked, not that it mattered or had any significance.

'Dunno.'

'Go abroad?'

He gave me a wistful smile. 'I wish.'

'You'd like that, eh?'

'Sure would.'

'Well, you know, John, life is full of little surprises. If everything goes according to plan I might just send you on a little trip,' I said, and could barely stop myself laughing at my brilliant choice of words.

'You'd do that for me?' Farrell asked.

'I said I *might*.'

I could, of course, have *promised* him his trip but I didn't want to fill his head with inessentials. He'd have started dreaming about Spain, probably: like young Davey, everyone I met seemed to want to go to Spain. 'Like to go to Spain,' Farrell told me now, as though he'd been reading my mind.

'Spain? Why Spain?'

'Hear it's great.'

'I'm sure it is. I was thinking of a rather longer trip,' I couldn't resist saying. 'Ever heard of the Paradise Islands?'

Not surprisingly, he hadn't. 'Uh-huh.'

Maybe it was just as well I couldn't pursue this line of chat any longer. We'd arrived home.

'That was a *most* satisfactory day,' I said as I passed Farrell a bottle of wine to open.

I'm sure he agreed although he didn't say so. All he was interested in was the news on the television, so we took the wine to the sitting-room and settled down to watch, just catching the tail-end of *Neighbours* as we sat down: cretins. Australian cretins.

I was seeing and hearing it all over again. It could easily have been Sharon instead of Charlotte except for a few minor details: the spot where the body was found and the number of wounds. But the rest was all but identical. The unidentified body of a woman had been found. She'd been brutally attacked and stabbed, and hidden in some shrubbery. Police were appealing for witnesses to come forward. And then they put up one of those little film clips, giving the police themselves the chance to come forward, and who popped up? Inspector Maurice Birt, that's who, and very pretty he looked too.

Farrell and I looked at each other and simultaneously made the identical grimace, which made us giggle. Birt, meanwhile, was doing his piece to camera. Sombre and a mite angry, he announced that this was one of the most vicious attacks he had come across in all his years in the police force. Then, concerned, he told us that whoever was responsible for this outrage could easily strike again. Next it was his paternal tone, asking *anyone* who saw *anything*, no matter how insignificant it might seem, to contact the police. And, finally, he answered a few innocuous questions. No, the woman had not been identified yet. No, there was no sign of a sexual attack. Yes, robbery *could* have been the motive. Yes, a description of the woman would be released as soon as he deemed it advisable. Yes, the police were following several lines of enquiry. And that was that. Birt was wiped from the screen and into oblivion.

'Think we should tell him?' I asked, joking, of course, and, for once, Farrell was on my wavelength.

'Be a laugh,' he said, and started laughing as if to prove his point.

'Yeah,' I said, 'and then we'd be laughing all the way to Brixton.'

'Be nice, though, won't it? Seeing how he gets on,' Farrell remarked.

It wasn't the word I'd have chosen, but I got his drift. 'Very nice,' I agreed. 'Have to be really careful, us two, though.'

'Oh, yes.'

By the time *The News at Ten* on ITV came round, Birt had identified Charlotte. Charlotte Adams, she was, which I already knew from her driving licence and Barclaycard. She was forty, a psychiatric nurse, unmarried, living alone with her arthritic mother in Chigwell. She was attached to some hospital, the name of which escaped me, and had been last seen leaving the hospital at around five o'clock. She had in her possession at the time one handbag – a large one with a shoulderstrap, black leather. It was therefore now possible that robbery *was* the motive. The handbag had not yet been found. They also kindly showed us a photograph of Charlotte, taken, I would think, a couple of years earlier, and in it she looked a lot better than in the flesh, so maybe the psychos she'd been dealing with had taken their toll.

Farrell asked, 'That her?' and he sounded genuinely surprised.

'That's her. Can't you tell?'

And then he said a remarkable thing. 'Didn't see her, did I?'

'What d'you mean – you didn't see her?' I asked, still amazed.

'Didn't look at her,' Farrell explained. 'Didn't want to look at her. Had nothing against her, did I?'

'No,' I said, thoughtfully. 'I suppose not.' Now I started worrying again. Would he be able to go through with it all? The fact that he *knew* Kranze, would that stop him doing – I needn't have worried.

'Won't be the same with Zanker, though,' Farrell interrupted my thoughts.

'Oh, why's that?'

'I know I know him. But I hate him too, so I do.'

'That's all right then.' I made as if that was an end to it, and then shoved in, 'If you're absolutely sure.'

'I'm *absolutely* sure,' Farrell told me, getting 'absolutely' out by spacing the syllables.

'Good.'

And so I was feeling good when I went to bed that night. Nearly absolutely good, but not quite. I'd phoned Birt just to say how gorgeous he looked on screen but he wasn't available, which didn't altogether surprise me. I'd put quite a lot on his plate. And there was more to come. Much more.

TWENTY-FIVE

I got hold of him the next morning, though. Birt, I mean. I phoned him from the office, early. 'Saw you on the box last night,' I told him. 'Very nice you were, too,' I added.

'It's no laughing matter, Marcus,' Birt told me curtly.

'Who's laughing? Tell the truth I'm worried. What with this to deal with, how does that leave us on the twenty-ninth? I don't want you abandoning me at this stage and leaving me up to my neck in it.'

Birt snorted. 'You won't be *abandoned*,' he told me sarcastically.

'No. Okay. So I won't exactly be abandoned, but I don't want some moron put in charge who doesn't know the ins and outs of our deal.'

'We have a deal?'

'You know exactly what I mean,' I said, in no humour for games. 'I can just as easily get Bean to call the whole thing off, you know. All I've got to say is that I heard you're onto him.'

That shortened Birt's cough, I can tell you. Suddenly he was nice as pie again. 'Marcus, don't worry, will you, for heaven's sake. Your – your escapade is cut and dried and it's all under control. The other – well, the other will take time. A great deal of time by the looks of it.'

'No luck then?'

'Nothing.'

'Life's tough at the top, ain't it?'

Then, and I could hear the smile in his voice, Birt asked, 'I don't suppose you'd anything to do with it?'

'Sorry, chum. Can't help you out on this one,' I answered, trying to give a hint of levity, which wasn't all that easy.

'Pity.'

'And don't you go trying to pin it on me, either.'

'As if I would.'

'Tell me about it.'

'Just wishful thinking,' Birt said. 'But it wasn't your style, was it, Marcus, eh?'

'Meaning?'

'*No* style. Too brutal. No finesse.'

Oddly enough, that remark quite pleased me. 'Sounds like some right maniac to me.'

'There's maniacs and maniacs.'

'Get away! Anyway, as long as you're okay for the twenty-ninth, I'm not really bothered about who's been puncturing who on Wimbledon Common.'

'I told you not to worry.'

'That's when I *do* worry.'

'Well, just don't.'

'If you say so.'

'I do.' I thought that was the end of the conversation, and was about to hang up, but then Birt said, 'There are some similarities, you know.'

'You've lost me.'

'In this murder and Sharon's.'

Was he just taunting me or was he . . . 'Come off it, Maurice. You don't think I'd be so *fucking* stupid as to – '

'Oh, no. Just thinking aloud, that's all. A knifing. No apparent reason. Killed elsewhere and dumped.'

'Oh, she *wasn't* bumped off on the Common, then?'

'Oh, no. Anyway, enough of that.'

'You can say that again. You know, I've just realised what a dangerous little man you could be.'

'Oh. deadly, Marcus. Deadly.'

'Well, that's tough on whoever did it.'

'That's what I meant.'

And that *was* the end of our chat. It left me in an unaccustomed frame of mind: worried when I knew full well I had nothing whatsoever to worry about. Not yet, at any rate. I went through everything in my mind. *Had* I made any mistakes, I wondered? I couldn't, for the life of me, think of any. I'd been my usual meticulously careful self. There was nothing whatever to connect me with Charlotte. We'd only met a couple of hours before her demise. We'd been as inconspicuous as any other couple in the café, except when Charlotte had started crying and I gave her my handkerchief. Shit! The handkerchief! Could they trace that? Hardly. It had been clean. One I had bought myself in Marks and Sparks ages ago. Millions of them gathering up snot all over the United Kingdom. But would someone connect that weeping creature with the peppered body on Wimbledon Common? Most unlikely. The chubby thing that had sobbed in the café was nothing like the younger version in the photo. And even if some interfering creep dying to get his name in *The Sun* really *did* spot a resemblance and tell the police, why the hell should that lead the flatfeet to *my* door? It wouldn't. Yet . . . the more I thought about it, the more I seemed to be able to conjure up grim possibilities of detection.

I gave Camp Carl's plant a good soaking in water, and told myself I was being paranoid. Fortunately, I believed myself. That was simply it. I was being paranoid. So then I switched my mind to thinking about all the things I had to do in the next couple of days, and sang 'Onward Christian Soldiers' to myself, just those three words of it, I mean. And I felt much better for it. Maybe I'd found a patentable cure for paranoia.

And that was all that happened of any interest on that Monday.

Tuesday didn't augur much better to begin with. I'd planned to put in some sterling work for my employers over the next few days since I would have to take leave on the Friday, and evenings, I'd discovered, were the best time to get Farrell's attention: something, I imagine, to do with his jellies of the night before having had the time to make their way out of his system, leaving his brain, addled though it might be, more receptive to my instructions. And I certainly needed it to be pretty well receptive if he wasn't going to cock everything up. I *was* asking quite a lot of him, really. But Svengali asked a lot too – and got it, which must have been nice for him. And maybe that was the answer to getting through to someone like Farrell: ask for a lot more than you should rightly hope him to achieve, and be pleasantly surprised. Anyway, there was no going back now, and, to tell the absolute truth, there was an element of the suicidal intrinsic to my plan. There was, I think (or am I being just too clever, too introspective?), some demon inside me which hinted failure would be even more exciting than success. A masochistic demon, evidently. One with a self-destructive bent, perhaps. It was as though, despite all my careful planning, despite my taking every precaution *not* to get caught, I really didn't give a hoot if I *was* caught. I'm sure that's true. It would explain why I enjoyed the whole escapade so much, wouldn't it? Although some might say what I was doing was dastardly (no one, I know, would actually say *that*, but it's a terrific word, I think), it genuinely never struck me as so being. It was a game. A fantastic game, but no more than that. If I won – smashing; if I lost – tough. No McEnroe tantrums for me should I net the final ball. I was more the polite Stan Smith of the game and would accept defeat with charm and a pat on the back for my opponent. That's what I told myself anyway. Mind you, as you've noticed, I'm a pretty glib liar!

Farrell was already glued to the TV when I set off for work, and by my reckoning he'd be stuck there for the rest of the day, watching those hideous cartoons they shove on to get infants out from underneath hapless parents' feet, but waiting avidly for each newscast, waiting, just as eagerly for me to come home so he could tell me all about it.

And, to be fair to myself, I did put in some good work. I sorted out quite a few manuscripts, seven in all. Five consigned to the Return With Thanks tray, two to be given further consideration: what appeared, at first glance, to be an intriguing thriller about a meek little man driven to murder by circumstances beyond his control (as the blurb would without any doubt put it), and a historical novel by a woman from Perth who at least had done her homework – not, as I had once come upon, writing of someone in the Elizabethan court using a pop-up toaster. That's the absolute truth, you know. Had me in stitches for days. That was before I'd been in prison, and I'd shared the preposterous gaffe with Camp Carl first. I thought he was going to have a seizure, so hard did he laugh. 'Oh, my God! Oh, my God!' he kept saying over and over, as though those three words were the only means he had of getting his breath.

'Great, isn't it?' I asked.

'Oh, Marcus, you've simply *got* to get *that* published. Couldn't you get it slipped through? Think – just *think* – of the Dragoness's face when the reviews came out!'

It was very tempting. 'You going to get me another job?'

'If only I could,' Camp Carl told me, and I guessed what sort of job he'd like to get me.

But I still regret not having had the guts to at least *try* and get that book slipped through, especially since whether the Dragoness had fired me or not would have been irrelevant as it turned out.

It was probably thinking about all this that made me, on the spur of the moment, decide to ring Carl and ask him out to lunch. Needless to say he accepted, and his company was high relief after my diligent morning. 'It's so *good* to see you, Marcus,' he said, and he meant it.

'Good to see you too, Carl,' I answered, and *I* meant it.

We had a pub lunch, a ploughman's lunch – the nearest, Carl said, he'd ever get to a ploughman.

'Didn't know you were into the earthy types, Carl.'

'At my age, ducky, you're into anything you can get.'

Friendly banter. That's how I'd describe our lunchtime conversation. And it was just what I needed, even though I was aware that underlying all the campery there was a yearning in Carl's mind. I really think the poor old chap was honestly in love with me. Nothing too strange in that, given his propensity. What was strange, though, was that in the most curious way I was flattered. My instinct was to be repulsed, but I wasn't. Not with Carl. I mean, I'd never have actually done anything with him, but he was such an intrinsically *nice* person that it was rather like an honour to have him interested. And I'm not going to even try and explain that.

'How's your mother?' Carl asked out of the blue.

'Ma? Ma's fine. Why d'you ask?'

Carl gave me a puzzled look. Then he smiled. 'I don't know. It just seems the right thing to ask.'

I laughed. 'Like I said, she's fine. Married life seems to suit her. I'm going over to see her this weekend.'

'Good.'

'Why good?'

'Don't keep asking me why I say things, Marcus. It's most irritating.'

On impulse, I asked, 'You want to come with me?'

I thought for a moment Carl was going to cry. 'God, Marcus, you're the sweetest man I ever met.'

'I'm only asking if you'd like to come to my Ma's for a weekend. It's not a proposal, sunshine,' I said.

'I'd love to. Really love to, but I can't,' Carl told me.

'Ah-ha. Got a heavy date, have we?'

'That's about the size of it,' he answered, but I knew he was lying. He didn't want to come to Ma's because he believed she would disapprove of him and that this disapproval would be taken out on me. I'm sure that was it. I knew also that there would be no point in trying to make him change his mind, so I decided to make light of it, just so he wouldn't be embarrassed.

'What's the size of it?' I asked. Adding, as I held out my hands, moving them further and further apart, 'This size? This? This?'

Carl gave an almighty, high-pitched whoop of a laugh. 'The last one – like that,' he said, putting his own hands about two feet apart. 'I hope.'

'I wish you luck,' I said, smiling.

'Need more than luck, I will, dear heart. Half a pound of Polyfilla and a dozen new joints is what I'll need.'

'Nothing wrong with you as you are, Carl,' I told him, and he really appreciated that.

'Thank you, Marcus,' he said sincerely.

We'd finished our lunch and beer by then. As we left the bar and stood on the pavement Carl turned to me and asked, 'Everything *is* all right, isn't it, Marcus?'

'Everything's fine, Carl.'

'I'd hate – I'd hate to see you – '

'Get into trouble again?'

Carl nodded.

'Don't you worry your pretty little head about me, pal.'

'That's just it. I *do* worry about you. God alone knows why, but I do.'

'Thanks.'

'Look, *if* – if you ever have problems – you know, if – oh, shit, if you ever need anyone to talk to – '

'Don't worry, Carl. You're number one on my list of counsellors.'

'I hope you mean that.'

'I do. Believe me, I do.'

And so we parted. I watched him walk away with that short-striding, mincing walk of his and had this feeling he was walking out of my life forever.

I was exhausted when I got home. I'd really concentrated all the afternoon and read the whole of the thriller. Although we'd have to change the title (*Tarts Aren't Always Jam*), the story itself was gripping. A nice holiday book. A beach book. An airport book. A profit-making book, which was the exception mostly. And being so tired I was peeved to find Farrell still in the sitting-room, his eyes fixed to the television, and not a sign of a meal being prepared. He didn't even look up at me, but he did say, 'Hiya.'

'Hiya,' I answered, and went straight to the kitchen to get myself a drink. A neat Jack Daniels with loads of ice. 'Any news?' I enquired when I came back to the sitting-room.

Farrell shook his head.

'Nothing? Nothing at all?'

Farrell shook his head again.

'You mean to say you've been stuck there in front of that goggle-box all day and there's no news whatever?'

'Nothing,' Farrell said in a surly tone.

'You could at least have cooked something.'

'Couldn't.'

'Why not?'

'Might have missed something.'

'You just said there wasn't anything.'

'Might have been if I went to cook.'

'But there wasn't, was there?'

'Might have been.'

'Well, would you like to cook something now?' I asked, and then changed my mind. 'Forget it. You stay there. I'll fix something,' I told him, thinking stardom was getting to him.

Well, as Ma always says, 'Why keep a dog and bark yourself', and I wasn't about to slave over a hot stove just to feed my Jellybaby. Especially since I wasn't all that hungry myself. I rooted around in the cupboards and found, very much to my surprise since I'm sure Ma wouldn't have bought them and I know I didn't, a couple of cans of ravioli in tomato sauce. And that was what we had. Just that, Farrell devouring most of it. With relish, I might add. The way Oliver Twist might have gobbled his first plate of pottage, I suppose. But Farrell didn't come back for more. When he'd finished he just put his plate on the floor beside his chair and kept watching the television. Well, no way was I about to tolerate this. Neither *Coronation Street, EastEnders,* nor *Emmerdale* was about to be given viewing space in my home. Somewhat peevishly, I switched off the box.

'What'd you do that for?' Farrell demanded.

'There certainly won't be any news now before nine o'clock.'

'So?'

'So if you think I'm going to sit here with you and watch the crap that's on between this and then, you've got another thing coming. Besides, I want to talk something over with you.'

If looks could kill, the one Farrell threw at me would have left me stone dead. There certainly had been a change in his attitude of late, and not a change I was all that keen on, either. Getting far too big for his boots, he was. And what really irked me was that I had to pander to him. I needed him, damn it. For the moment.

When the silence between us had run to a couple of minutes, Farrell asked, 'What do you want to talk over?'

'A lot of things.'

'Like what?'

Before I could answer that, the phone rang. It was Stuart, sounding on top of the world. 'Got you your car,' he told me.

'Oh, great. What sort?'

'BMW. Exactly like your own. Same model. Won't have any bother driving that, will you?'

'No,' I agreed, 'none.' Then, 'How did you know what model BMW I drove anyway?'

'My job to know. Why d'you think I sent Davey out to the car with you?'

'Oh.'

'Knows more about cars than anyone I know, does Davey.'

'Oh.'

'And that delivery you left?'

'What about it?'

'It's gone, as you asked.'

'Thanks, Stuart.'

'Yeah, some kids I know set fire to a load of tyres and your bag happened to fall in.'

'Great.'

'Not a trace of anything. I made sure Davey checked.'

'Great,' I repeated. 'So, what happens now?'

'How do you mean?'

'When do I pick up the car, for one thing?'

'You don't.'

'Oh?'

'You come here eight thirty sharp on Friday morning. The car will be here. We all get in and we're off.'

'Off to see the wizard,' I heard myself say.

'What?'

'Sorry. Nothing. So that's it then? I come to you at eight thirty on Friday and Bob's your uncle?'

'And Fanny's your aunt,' Beany added with a chuckle.

'We do the job, back to your place, dropping the others off along the way, and then I vamoose.'

'Got it in one.'

'Sounds perfect.'

'It will be perfect. Better be.'

'As you say, Stuart, better be.'

'Then we lie low for a bit and in a week or two you'll get your share.'

'Nice.'

'The whole thing should be over in a few hours.'

'As quick as that?' I asked, surprised although I shouldn't have been.

'No hanging about on this one. Leave here eight thirty. Do the job nine thirty. Back here latest ten thirty – eleven at the latest. You can be back at that posh desk of yours in the afternoon if you want.'

'Sure have everything planned to a T, haven't you, Stuart?'

'Got to. Fucked up on a couple of other jobs by not planning right. Not going to fuck up on this one, I promise you.'

'I certainly hope not. Jesus, another stint inside would just about kill me, Stuart.'

'Nothing's going to go wrong if we all of us do like we should.'

'I'll certainly do what I'm supposed to,' I assured him.

'I've no worries about you, mate.'

'Worries about the others?'

'No worries,' Stuart told me, changing his tone, indicating, I felt, that the mysterious others were shit-scared of Beany and would have walked through fire to avoid his wrath.

'Okay, then. See you Friday.'

'Yep.'

After that I didn't feel like talking anything through with Farrell. I decided instead to appease him. 'Look, John, sorry I was snappy just then. Getting a bit het up, I suppose. Big day looming and all that. You watch the telly as much as you want.'

'Thought you wanted to talk?'

'It'll wait. Wait until tomorrow, anyway. How about that? What say we go out for a Chinese tomorrow evening and have a right good heart to heart, eh?'

Farrell liked that idea. 'Yeah,' he said with enthusiasm, and with similar enthusiasm he switched on the TV again.

'I'm off to bed,' I told him.

He nodded.

'Need an early night for a change,' I tried, but got the same reaction, another disinterested nod. 'You can wake me up if there's anything really exciting on the news.'

He nodded a third time.

'Only if it's really interesting.'

'Okay, I heard.'

'Just won yourself a medal,' I said, and left him to *The Bill*.

But there wasn't, it transpired, anything world-shattering on the news. Nothing that struck Farrell as being so, anyway. He didn't bother me for the rest of the evening, and I had a pleasant time by myself, myself and a joint or two, and Cesar Frank. And thus Tuesday came to a conclusion.

Wednesday followed a similar pattern – almost. I didn't, of course, meet Camp Carl for lunch. I didn't have any lunch at all, unless you can call an egg-and-cress sandwich from the local deli and a mug of coffee lunch, and I ate and drank these while I worked my way through the historical novel from the madam in Perth. If Babs Cartland writes her stuff for shop assistants, Gloria Denhap-Calanar was slightly more up-market, writing for manageresses – the sort of girls Marks and Spencer like to think they attract. She went to town rather on the split infinitives, and there were unwanted adjectives by the cartload, but apart from these and the regular passages wherein the author decided she was A Writer and got well and truly carried away, it was a jolly sort of book; a romp through the period when James the Sixth and First was astride the throne, the sort of book that would make its female readers yearn to be seduced by the foppish courtiers that littered the pages: lace cuffs and buckled shoes and cod-pieces and all.

'Doing well,' I told Nick Putty just before I went home. 'Two possibles in one week. That must be some kind of record.'

'Sounds good to me,' Nick said. 'Or else you're losing your discerning touch.'

'No fear of that. Incisive as ever, I am. Rapier sharp.'

And that's just what I needed to be when I got home: rapier sharp. I'd barely got in the door when Birt called at the house. Luckily, some sixth sense warned me it might be him, or someone equally unwelcome, and I'd time to get Farrell out of the kitchen (where, thanks be, he'd taken up duty again) and upstairs with the usual warning not to make a sound. But with pots simmering on the stove and the table set for two I had to take Birt into the sitting-room – after I'd allowed him into the house, of course. 'This is a surprise, I thought you'd be off scouring Wimbledon Common still,' I said, taking a quick glance about the room to make sure Farrell hadn't left his untidy trademarks anywhere.

'That's being taken care of,' Birt told me smugly.

'Ah, by the lesser gods.'

'Precisely.'

'Have a seat.'

Birt sat down.

'Now, what can I do for you?' I asked affably.

'Tell me about the developments.'

'On which front?'

'Both. Your little dabble in armed robbery, and Kranze.'

I chuckled. 'I like that, Maurice. My little dabble in armed robbery. Very tastefully put. Well, what can I tell you? I've got to be at Bean's place at eight thirty on Friday morning. He's got a car for me. A BMW. Same as mine. Then off we go to Charles Street. We do the job – I think he said nine thirty. I mean he *did* say nine thirty but whether he meant *exactly* nine thirty or not, I don't know. Then back to his place, dropping the other two off *en route* – as I think I've already mentioned.'

Birt nodded. 'And you've picked your route?'

I now nodded. 'That I have.'

Birt waited a few seconds for me to speak, and when I didn't, he said, 'Well?'

'The route? Oh. Easy. Charles Street to Fitzmaurice Place. Left into Berkeley Square. Straight ahead to Grosvenor Street. Left through Grosvenor Square. Straight ahead to Upper Grosvenor Street. Out onto Park Lane. And away.'

Birt had been nodding all through this, and he continued to nod for a while after I'd finished, looking for all the world like one of those appalling nodding dogs some idiots put in the back windows of their cars. Then he said, 'Clever planning,' and I was just sunning myself in this compliment when he added, 'Pity you won't be able to put it to any use, Marcus.'

'Oh? Why not?' I asked, keeping my cool with some difficulty.

'We're going to hit you as soon as there's the slightest move on the Securicor van.'

I was flabbergasted. 'You can't *do* that,' I told him.

He got quite uppity. 'And why not?'

'Why not? Why fucking not? I'll tell you why not. Because the only way I'm going to survive this is to get Bean – at the very least Bean – away from there safely. It's going to look like a right set-up if you grab *them* and let *me* go,' I said.

'Maybe I wasn't planning to let you go, Marcus,' Birt said.

I could tell he was taking the piss, and I wasn't in the mood to have the piss taken. 'Right,' I said. 'Forget the whole thing. I'll call Bean and have him cancel everything.' And when Birt gave me his don't-be-so-silly look, I added, 'I mean it, and don't you think for one minute that I don't.'

Birt decided that taking the piss wasn't a good idea. He became serious. 'I can't run the risk of letting Bean get his hands on the money.'

'Okay. Grab the other two masterminds and let Bean and myself slip off,' I suggested. '*That* shouldn't be a problem. You can pick him up later. Even have someone waiting when I get him home. But you've got to give me the chance to get clear out of there and have it look as though I was dead lucky to escape.'

Birt thought about this. And finally he agreed. 'All right. But you've got to stick to the route you've given me.'

'Of course I'm going to use that route.'

'No changing your mind for any reason.'

'I won't.'

'That way,' Birt went on, almost forgetting me and working things out aloud, 'that way I can see to it that you get a clear run and we can follow you at the same time.'

'What d'you mean follow? For Christ's sake. If you start following me and Bean twigs it, I'll have to keep on driving and *not* take him back home. Forget about the following. I'll take him home and you nab the sod there. It's my head on the block here, you know.'

Birt thought some more. Maybe he was trying to figure out if I was up to some trickery, but he must have concluded that I wasn't. 'Very well,' he said finally. 'But you muck me about, Marcus, and it'll be the last act you ever perform on this earth.'

'Oh, dearie me,' I said, my cheek emanating from my relief.

He gave me a scathing look, but one which warned me that he

really would do something drastic to me if I pulled a fast one.

'Look, stop worrying. I'll stick to my part of the deal. Just you make sure you do and we'll all be happy.'

'You better or you'll regret it,' Birt told me.

'*You* better or I'll be dead,' I reminded him.

I thought that was that, and that now Birt would go, but it wasn't to be. 'Now, what about Kranze?' he asked.

'Oh, Kranze. Well, to be honest, I haven't been thinking too much about him recently. I want to get this robbery out of the way first, if you see what I mean.'

'I *want* Kranze,' Birt reminded me.

'Yes, I *know* you want Kranze,' I said, and then I thought I might as well tell him the good news. 'What I *have* found out is that Kranze wants Speed to help him get me.'

For a second or two Birt remained frozen. And then he burst out laughing, as though the possibility of my demise was quite the funniest thing he had ever heard. '*You*?' he spluttered. 'Kranze wants to get *you*?'

'So I understand.'

'Oh, dear Lord,' Birt said, still laughing and now wiping his eyes with a rather dirty hankie.

'I'm glad you're amused,' I said coldly.

'Amused? Marcus, this is the funniest thing I've ever heard,' he told me, so I hadn't been wrong.

'Not to me, it isn't.'

'Well, no, I can see it wouldn't be.' The more serious side of my allegation seemed to strike Birt now. 'Do you mean he's going to try and kill you?'

'Guess so.'

'And how does he propose to do that, do you suppose.'

'Use Speed. John Speed, his soul-mate.'

'Ah. And where's *he* now?'

I shrugged. 'God knows. Gone back to his squat, I should think.'

'And he told you that Kranze was – '

'Not in so many words,' I said. 'He doesn't *have* that many words in his vocabulary to begin with, and Kranze is far too crafty just to come out and say it. My guess is that Kranze will try and manipulate the stupid arsehole into a situation where he gets rid of me without even knowing what he's doing.'

'And you? What do you propose doing about it?' Birt asked, narrowing his eyes.

'Not a lot at the moment. Probably, when this other thing is over,

I'll see if I can't find Speed again and see what I can find out. Maybe persuade him that I'm a nice sort of fellow. Find out what Kranze is definitely up to, anyway.'

'And you won't, of course, try any funny business on your own?'

'Sorry?'

'You won't go and smite Kranze without telling me first,' Birt said, and it wasn't a question.

'Smite Kranze? Oh, I like that. That's really poetic. No, I won't try and smite Kranze without letting you know. In fact, I've no intention of smiting Kranze whether I let you know or not. I just want the shit legally and forever behind bars again. That's what I want. No bloody good to me if he's smitten. I want him to *suffer*.'

Birt must have believed me. I was so convincing I almost believed myself. 'Right,' he said, and stood up at last. 'As you say, let us get this other matter out of the way first and then we can *both* concentrate on what Mr Kranze is up to.'

'Herr Zanker,' I corrected.

'Whatever.'

I walked him to the door. 'Hope you catch that other maniac soon,' I commented.

Birt stopped dead in his tracks. He turned and looked really hard into my eyes. 'We'll catch him all right, Marcus. Never you fear.'

'Nothing to do with fear, Maurice. A question of health, really. Not *healthy* to have some nut like that going round stabbing people to death.'

'You'd know all about that.'

'Yes,' I said with a grin. 'I would.'

Birt opened the door, and then stopped again. 'Tell you something that really puzzles me, Marcus.'

'What's that?'

'I'm genuinely puzzled why I don't hate and despise you.'

'Me? Why on earth would you hate and despise *me*?'

'Frankly, because you're just about the most unscrupulous person I've ever met.'

'Come off it, Maurice. I made a mistake. I paid my dues and all that. *And* you know full well I'd never do anything like that again.'

'I wish I could believe that.'

'Believe it. Even if I am unscrupulous, as you say – which I'm not, by the way – I'm not fucking stupid. Think I want you breathing down my neck for the rest of my life? No way, José. My criminal life is well and truly behind me.'

'I hope so.'

'Hope's a tricky thing, Maurice. Faith is what you need. Have faith in me.'

Birt gave me another hard look, and grunted, 'Huh,' and then off he went, giving me a wave without turning round, a sort of back-to-front Nazi salute.

'Okay. The coast's clear. You can come down again,' I called to Farrell from the foot of the stairs.

Nothing. Zilch. Silence. I went quietly up to Ma's old room and peeped in. Farrell was sound asleep, lying on his back, one arm thrown across the second pillow.

It's a curious thing about sleep, isn't it? Have you ever noticed how people change when they're asleep? All those lines that the specialists call character lines seem to be momentarily erased. All hardship and mirth and worry gone. So it was with Farrell. He looked innocent. Vulnerable. Gentle. A child again, almost. Ah, well, he'd grow up again pretty damn quick by the time I was finished with him, and no mistake. And when I'd done with him, I'd see to it that he had the sleep of a lifetime, if you'll excuse the expression.

TWENTY-SIX

I'm not going to take you step by step through what happened on Thursday, *day*time Thursday, that is. Enough said that the pressure was now really on and I was loving every minute of it. I felt born again, if not particularly Christian.

The only significant thing I did was trot along to one of those drug addiction centres, you know, the places where addicts can go to get free advice and free needles, which is very nice for them, I'm sure. I hung about outside until I saw a couple of likely lads emerge – pale, haggard youths, semi-skinheads, one of them clutching just what I wanted. I sidled up to them, looking timorous as a church mouse. 'Eh, what's it like in there?' I asked.

'What you mean, what's it like?' one of them asked in return, a hint of the brogue, no less.

'You Irish?'

'What if I am?'

'Just – well my Dad's from Ireland. Galway,' I explained, hoping for a sort of national bondage and sympathy. No such luck. National identity and love of one's fellow countrymen (albeit a fake like myself) went out the window once Auntie Heroin moved into the house.

'So what?'

'Look, forget it. I need – I don't want to go in there, that's all. Someone who works in there knows my Dad. You know. You wouldn't give me that,' I asked, indicating the syringe in his hand, 'and nip back and get another one for yourself?'

'Fucking wouldn't. Piss off. Go get your own fu – '

'I'll buy it off you,' I interposed quickly. 'A fiver?' I suggested.

The eloquent Paddy exchanged glances with his comrade in arms, and he nudged his head towards heaven. 'Tenner,' Paddy said.

I sucked in my breath. I hesitated. 'Okay, a tenner.'

'Let's see it.'

I took a tenner from my pocket.

Paddy One looked at Paddy Two, who nodded, and the deal was struck. I got my needle and the two Paddys got their money, and went back into the centre with the sort of greedy grin only a one hundred per cent profit can create spread across their potato faces. I wished the sods AIDS under my breath and scarpered.

There was just one other thing I did before going home that I think you should know about. I drove to Kranze's home in Cricklewood. I didn't go in. I stopped the car a few houses away, looked at my watch and then drove off as quickly as was reasonable without arousing suspicion or the blood level of some overzealous traffic cop to Kilburn, through Regent's Park, on to Euston Road, over Waterloo Bridge to the Elephant and Castle, and to Stuart Bean's pad. I looked at my watch again. Twenty-nine minutes. Not bad. But I'd been lucky with the traffic. Still, eight o'clock tomorrow morning shouldn't be any busier.

After that I drove home at a leisurely rate, even allowing some daft woman driver to pull out in front of me without biting her flipping head off.

Farrell was a bit despondent when I got home. There was, in his opinion (although he didn't know how to express it) a conspiracy against him. He was being purposely, he felt, kept in the dark, from which I gathered there'd been no update on the police activity with regards to solving the murder of Charlotte Adams RIP.

'Look, John,' I began reasonably. 'They only give out information when they find out something new or when they want help. If they've got nothing new, nothing new to go on, they stay quiet. They're not going to pop up on screen every ten minutes saying the same thing over and over. Makes them look like the incompetents they are, and they really hate that, you know. And they've no idea you're sitting here mad keen to hear their every word, even if it is what they said umpteen times already.'

'I *know* that,' Farrell snapped at me petulantly, turning the bubble and squeak he was making in the pan, and whacking it with the slicer. 'But they should have *found* something new by now.'

'Oh, really? Like what? Like it was you who did the dreadful deed? That suit you? That what you want?'

'No, but – '

'But nothing. Just be glad they seem to be stuck for the moment. Just you think of it this way: you, by the grace of God, John – what's your middle name or don't you have one?'

He had the grace to blush. 'Hamish.'

'Heck. Didn't know you were Irish,' I said, adding quickly, 'A joke, John, a frigging joke,' as he got ready to launch some displaced patriotic garbage in my direction. 'As I was saying, you, John Hamish Farrell, have made the police look like right twits. Made the greatest police force in all the whole wide world look like prats. Now, *that* should put roses in your cheeks.'

Not roses, but something else blossomed in John Hamish Farrell: pride. 'Yeah,' he said in awe of himself, 'you're right, Marcus. Made them look really stupid, haven't I?'

'That you have, sunshine.'

And all of a sudden it was a chirpy, pride-filled, amenable Farrell who dished up the supper – gone, thanks be, the surly brute who would have been anything but receptive to the lesson I was about to give him. But I waited until he'd digested his food first. And shared a joint with him. *And* buttered him up some more, telling him that I felt really fortunate to have someone as co-operative as him to help me during these stressful times. When he was relaxed and properly grateful, I began.

I began by expressing my admiration, in appropriately sober tones, for the way he had handled what I called 'the removal of Charlotte'. I had been impressed, I said, lying through my teeth, at his coolness, his dedication, his speed, his agility, his real professionalism. He'd never had this sort of crap heaped on him before and grew probably six inches as I spoke. There was a jaunty slant to his head, a straightness to his shoulders, an almost haughty glint in his eyes by the time I'd finished. Fine. So far so good. But, I now impressed on him, that was only a practice run. The true test of his talent was coming tomorrow when he dealt with Zanker. This was to be the act that made a man of him. Raised him to certain heights not achieved by many mortals. He lapped up that rubbish also, nodding, pursing his lips, accepting the enormous honour that I was bestowing on him. He couldn't have been more pleased if he'd been asked to join the Freemasons – not that he'd have had a clue what that bunch of whackies were all about.

'The situation is this, John. I'm going to drive you to Zanker's house tomorrow morning. Early. We have to be there about five to eight. I'm going to leave you there. You just go in as if you'd called to see him – he's been asking me to arrange another meeting with you anyway, so he'll be over the moon to see you.'

'You're not coming in?' Farrell asked with a tiny note of panic.

'Can't. Got something else on. Besides, you don't *need* me any more, John. You can do this one all by yourself. You're brilliant, you know. You really don't need me there to hold your hand.' I stopped and waited to see if there was any further objection. There wasn't, so on I went. 'Like I said, you go in and – well, you know exactly what you have to do. Okay. When you've done it you walk quietly out of the house. If Mrs Zanker tries anything, just threaten her with the knife and she'll back off for sure. On the way out – I don't know if you noticed – there's a stand in the hall with a couple of overcoats on it.'

Farrell looked blank.

'Well, believe me, there is. Take one of those coats and put it on. That'll hide any blood you might get on your clothes. Okay so far?'

Farrell nodded.

'You walk out of the house and walk quietly up the street. No running. No fuss. Just a nice steady walk. You go to the tube station – I'll point it out to you in the morning. You get the tube to Marble Arch. You get off the tube at Marble Arch and walk down the Bayswater Road to that squat where I first came to see you. You go in there and wait until I come and pick you up. And that's it.'

'Why can't I come back here?' Farrell asked.

'Because I think Birt will suspect *me* of dealing with Kranze. So the first place he'll come is here. And I don't want *you* here when he does come. I'm just looking out for your safety, John,' I said. If you believe that, I thought, you'll believe anything, honey.

He believed it. 'Thanks, Marcus.'

I made him repeat everything I'd said, and he did, almost without a fault. 'Again,' I said, and he repeated it all again. 'When will you pick me up at the squat?' he asked when he'd finished.

'As soon as I possibly can. I'll definitely be there some time tomorrow evening. Might be latish, but I'll be there. You have my word on that.'

'And I can come back here then?'

'Sure you can come back here then,' I assured him expansively. 'Shit, where else could you go? Besides, I'd be lost without you to help me around the place now, wouldn't I?'

He was delighted. 'S'pose you would.'

'Sure I would. I promised you right at the beginning that I'd take care of you, didn't I? Well, that's just what I'm going to do. I always keep my word, John. Especially to my pals.'

Farrell got all doe-eyed again. 'We *are* pals, aren't we, Marcus?'

''Course we are. Till death us do part, as they say.'

'That's nice, Marcus.'

'That's how it is.'

'That's nice,' he said again.

I'd had enough of the flannel so I got down to business again. 'Just a couple of other things. Minor things, but don't forget them. First, try not to get carried away. Just do the job, don't *over*do it, okay? When he's dead, leave him.'

'Right. I've got that.'

'And for heaven's sake take the knife away with you. Shove it in your pocket. Make sure you don't leave it in the house.'

Farrell frowned and I thought we'd hit a snag. 'I can use the same knife, though, can't I?'

I was glad he'd mentioned that. 'Well, no, actually, you can't, John. With all the new-fangled techniques they have, the police *might* just be able to tell it was the same knife as the one you used on Charlotte, and we don't want them to make that sort of connection, do we?'

'They can do that?' Farrell was amazed.

'I'm not sure, but I think they possibly can. So you see, another knife would be better, wouldn't it?'

'Yes,' Farrell agreed, 'yes. Much safer.'

'*Much* safer,' I stressed.

When I didn't say anything else immediately, Farrell asked, 'Is that it?'

I smiled beatifically at him. 'That's it.'

'Just stop when he's dead and take the knife away with me?'
'You've got it in one.'
'No problem.'
'I didn't think there would be, John. Got complete faith in you, I have.'

He gave me a sad and rueful smile. 'First time in my life anyone has.'

'That's 'cause nobody's ever bothered to get to know you like I have,' I said.

'That's why we're pals, I suppose.'

'That's exactly why we're pals.'

Bloody hell, he'd have us married off if I let this go on, so I brought him down to earth with a bump. 'Now, I've got to go and phone Zanker and tell him I'm bringing you round in the morning.'

Farrell went very white all of a sudden. 'Do you have to tell him?'

I patted his hand. 'Yes. Don't worry. Trust me. I've got to tell him so he won't suspect anything. If you just turn up out of the blue he'll think it's very odd, won't he?'

'Might, I suppose.'

'He really would, John. All I'm going to do is say that I found you again and that you would like to visit him once more before you go back to Glasgow.'

Farrell gave a little jump. 'I'm not going back to Glasgow, am I?'

'No, John, you're not going back to Glasgow.' Jesus, it was like talking to a three-year-old. 'I'm just going to tell Zanker that you're going back to Glasgow. I wouldn't send my worst enemy back to Glasgow. It's just a ruse – a trick – to make sure Zanker is ready and willing to let you come round at that hour.'

'Oh, I see. A trick. I thought, maybe you were sending me back – '

I squeezed his hand as a great sadness came over him. 'I told you. You're going back to the squat first. Then I pick you up and you come back here, and we live happily ever after.'

'Okay. Yes. I get it.'

'So I can phone him now?'

'Yes. Phone him now.'

'You can listen to everything I say, if you like.'

Farrell did just that. He pulled his chair close to the kitchen door and sat down, watching me as I went down the hall to the phone. I dialled, and as I waited for it to be answered I gave him the thumbs up.

Farrell nodded, and winked, and returned my signal.

'Ah, Helmut, my dear chap. I trust this time is more suitable than when I last called.'

'More civilised,' Kranze told me.

'That's what I am if nothing else. Civilised.'

'Is that what you phoned to tell me?' Kranze asked. His idea of a joke, I think.

'Oh, among other things.'

'What, may I ask, other things?'

'You may ask.'

'What other things?'

'Our friend. I beg your pardon – *your* friend,' I winked at Farrell just in case he got the wrong idea, 'your friend, Johnny Go Lightly. I've been speaking to him again.'

Kranze was silent.

'You still there?'

'I'm here. And what was said?'

'Do you want the good news or the bad news first?'

'Marcus, don't – '

'Answer the question,' I insisted, smiling at Farrell, who was enjoying this as much as I was, it seemed. Beaming, he was, my little ray of sunshine.

'The bad news,' Kranze said reluctantly.

'The bad news. You're sure now? You're sure you want the bad news first?'

'Yes, Marcus, I'm sure.' Talk about your ice-cold tone.

'Well, the bad news is that he's going back to Glasgow to live.'

That took the wind out of Kranze's sails with a vengeance. 'He told you that?'

'No, I'm making it up. Of course he bloody told me that.'

'When is he going?'

'Tomorrow morning. Something about going home to Haggisland to be with some girl he'd once been pretty intimate with, if you catch my drift.'

'Tomorrow morning,' Kranze repeated for his own benefit.

'Yep. So it's bye-bye birdie as far as he's concerned, I'm afraid.'

If I didn't know better I'd have said there was something very akin to desperation in Kranze's voice when he told me, 'I've got to see him before he goes, Marcus.'

I kept him waiting now.

'Did you hear me, Marcus? I've got to see him before he goes.'

'I heard you the first time. You haven't asked me what the good news is yet, have you?'

Now Kranze got really angry. It was a new experience for me, and I thoroughly enjoyed it. 'I'm not about to play any more of your ridiculous games, Marcus. If you've got something to tell me, just – '

'Ask me what the good news is,' I said patiently, almost as if I was talking to Farrell himself.

I heard Kranze take an enormous deep breath. I swear I could *feel* the effort he was making to control himself come hurtling down the telephone line. 'What – is – the – good – news, Marcus?' he asked, almost choking on the words.

'Well, the good news is this,' I answered chirpily. 'The good news is that I've persuaded him to come and see you before he goes.'

Kranze laughed quite literally with relief and, I imagine, delight.

'When? What time? Marcus, you're a friend indeed. Tell me.'

'Tomorrow morning. Early, I'm afraid.'

'That doesn't matter. Just tell me.'

'Around eight. He has to catch his train sometime near eleven. I think that's what he said. Anyway, I told him I'd pick him up and give him a lift over to you before I go to work.'

'You are most kind, Marcus,' the old hypocrite informed me.

'Kindness personified. But I can't hang around. I'll just dump him with you and then I have to take off. Some of us have to work, you know.'

'I understand,' Kranze understood, and I understood just how thrilled the bastard must be feeling: his handmaiden to himself, and me, the victim, actually volunteering to stay out of the way while the plot was hatched.

'Doesn't matter whether you understand or not, Helmut. I can't afford the time to stay dithering about waiting for you two lovebirds to say farewell, goodbye, *ciao*, *arrivederci* and all that. I'll bring him over, dump him on your doorstep, and then it's toodle-pip.'

'I won't forget this, Marcus.'

'Frankly, I'd prefer if you did. *Auf wiedersehen*.' And I hung up, and to my surprise I found I was sweating. 'Phew,' I exclaimed.

'You did that great,' Farrell told me.

'Not bad, was I?'

'Had me believing you,' Farrell said in what I suppose was a compliment.

'Really? Oh, well, that's all right, then. If I had *you* believing me I must have been convincing.'

'Had me believing every word you said.'

'Great.' I followed Farrell into the kitchen and watched him put his chair back in place. 'Want anything?'

He shook his head.

I poured myself a glass of orange juice and swallowed the lot in one prolonged gulp. Then I rinsed the glass and put it back in the cupboard, tidily. I pointed to the knife rack, and said, as casually as I could, 'Choose one.'

Farrell made a terrific song and dance about choosing the knife he would use, taking each one down in turn, testing the sharpness of the blades with his thumb, gripping them in his palm, the way I remember Gary Cooper fitting a Colt into his hand and saying something about a man having to *wear* a gun, not carry it. Or maybe it was pint-sized Alan Ladd. Or the frightening Jack Palance. 'Make up your mind, will you?'

'That's what I'm doing.'

I sighed. 'I was hoping we'd both get a good night's sleep.'

'This one.'

'You're sure?'

'Yeah. This one.' He'd chosen a thin-bladed, stiletto-like knife, useful for taking the flesh of fowl off the bone.

'Okay. Put it on the table there. That way you won't forget it in the morning.'

'I'm not going to forget it,' Farrell told me, aggrieved.

'Not if you leave it on the table, you won't. It'd be just like us two to go rushing off to Zanker's and find that you'd left the knife behind. Look like a great pair of wallies then, wouldn't we?'

Farrell placed the knife carefully on the table. Very carefully. Almost as if it was loaded and liable to go off at the slightest touch. He then stared at it in a mesmerised kind of way, only looking away when I said, 'Come on, pal. Bedtime for the two of us.'

Obediently he followed me up the stairs.

'What is life to me without thee,' Kathleen Ferrier sang in her haunting contralto.

I wondered how knights of old felt the night before an important joust. I wondered how matadors felt the night before facing a particularly courageous bull. I wondered how astronauts must have felt the night before they were sent whooshing into the unknown. I wondered how a condemned man felt the night before they sent lethal voltages into his body. I wondered how the Blow Job Queen was feeling on the eve of the great heist that he was definitely going to pull off and be the envy of his tiny underworld. I knew how I felt. On top of the world, that's how I felt. Relaxed and calm and in control and on top of the fucking world.

TWENTY-SEVEN

Both Farrell and I were appropriately sober, sombre and sedate on that fateful Friday morning. Yet the atmosphere was not charged as you might expect. There was a peacefulness, a serenity that only the total acceptance of destiny can bring. We moved about the kitchen as though to the strains of a stately pavane, and breakfast took on the aspect of a predestined, Oriental rite. Kismet reigned.

We ate our toast and drank both orange juice and coffee in silence, as though to speak would break some mysterious thread that linked us invisibly to the infinite. We were, I suppose, lesser gods about to perform those duties which would elevate us to heights undreamt of. And when we'd finished, we washed the plates and mugs together, making of this simple act a symbolic ablution. At least I did; what Farrell made of it God alone knows. All that mattered as far as I was concerned was that he was calm and in control of himself. Indeed, I had never seen him *so* in control, and this gave him a dignity and a purposefulness that was wonderful to behold. It was Farrell who said, 'I'm ready when you are, Marcus.'

'We have a few minutes yet,' I answered. I had timed everything and I didn't want to diverge from this. We would leave the house in seven minutes, and not a second before. And this gave me time to say something that I really meant, in a strange sort of way. 'I'm very proud of you, John.' And I wondered if the early Christians said much the same to each other as they waited to be sacrificed. 'Got everything?'

'Yes,' Farrell said quietly, producing the knife, showing it to me, holding it out to me laid across both his palms, before returning it to his inside pocket.

'And you know exactly what you have to do?'

'Yes.'

'No questions?'

'No.'

'Do you need anything?' I asked.

Farrell hesitated before answering that one. No doubt he'd have loved a jelly or two, but even this longing was overridden by his determination to make the best possible job of killing the man who had so humiliated and betrayed him. 'No,' he said finally. 'Not now.' Then he thought for a moment. 'I will need something afterwards,' he added reasonably.

'I'll bring something when I come to pick you up at the squat,' I promised.

Farrell shook his head. 'I'll need something immediately afterwards,' he told me.

'Oh. You want me to give you some jellies now to be taken afterwards, is that it?'

Farrell nodded.

'You won't take them before – '

'I'll need them *afterwards*,' Farrell insisted.

'Okay, John. I know I can trust you,' I lied.

So (rather surprisingly, without any qualms) I gave him a handful of Temazepam. I also gave him what valium tablets were left in the bottle, and I threw in a miniature Remy Martin for good measure, just in case he wanted to make a proper cocktail of it. I watched him stow the lot away carefully in his jacket.

Then we had another short silence, a time for prayer if either of us felt like praying. 'Time to go,' I said. And we left the house. Well, something else happened before we actually went out. Something that affected me quite badly. As I opened the connecting door to the garage Farrell called my name. I turned. And Farrell, without warning, took me in his arms and embraced me. He also kissed me on the cheek. And for some reason I felt compelled to kiss him back, and the awful spectre of Judas suddenly loomed over me. For one split second, for even less than that, I wanted to call the whole thing off. I wanted to confess to Farrell that I was using him, that by doing what I had so carefully orchestrated he was condemning himself. That if he did it he would be doomed. It was disconcerting to discover that even for that fraction of time I had a conscience. 'John,' I heard myself whisper in his ear. He stood back. The embrace was broken. Any sense of remorse was whipped away from me. 'Let's go,' I said, and quickly now we left the house, got into the car, and headed for Cricklewood.

It was a glorious morning. For the first time in ages it had rained overnight, and the air had a clean, fresh feel to it. You could smell things again, smell them as they should be, not the parched, arid smell that I had got used to during the drought. And, again, silence seemed to be in order. We didn't speak once on the journey. Nor did I put on the radio. On the contrary: it came on automatically when I switched on the ignition and I consciously turned it off.

Traffic was still fairly light. In an hour people would be choking to death on the fumes of a million cars as executives and plumbers, lawyers and lackeys made their way to work. But not yet. All of them taking those extra few moments in bed; all of them rushing to work at the last minute.

So, in no time at all we were in Cricklewood. We were driving down the street where Kranze's house stood, a small street, once probably quite elegant, bourgeois even, but going to seed now, slowly, sadly.

I parked just up the road from Kranze's house, and for a couple of minutes we just sat there. Then, 'Will I go?' Farrell asked.

I gave him a smile. 'Ready?'

He smiled back. 'As much as I'll ever be.'

'And you know exactly what you have to do?'

'Yes. When I'm finished I leave the house after I've put on one of the coats that are in the hall. I walk to the tube – '

'Shit,' I interrupted. 'I never showed you where – '

'I saw it,' Farrell said in an oddly matter-of-fact way. 'I walk to the tube and go to Marble Arch. I walk down Bayswater Road to the squat. And I wait there until you come to get me.'

'That's it,' I said proudly, proud, really and genuinely proud of my student. Instinctively I held out my hand, and Farrell shook it, and there was a change in that also. It wasn't the limp, wet touch of old. He gripped my hand and shook it firmly, confidently.

And then he was out of the car, walking towards Kranze's house, striding towards it. He never looked back.

And I imagine some of you will be thinking what a right, blundering twit I was. Asking yourselves, what about Brünnhilde, that gorgoness who was allegedly Kranze's spouse, that ugsome harridan who protected Kranze as though her life depended on it – which maybe it did, come to think of it. Had I forgotten about her? Well, no, I hadn't, as it happens. Not by a long chalk. She, the dear lady, was very much part of the plan. It would be she, I hoped, who would be able to identify Farrell to the police. She, who would tell the police how this young man arrived at the house to see her husband, who had been welcomed into their home, who had repaid such kindness by knifing her husband to death. How he *alone* had knifed her husband to death. Oh, no, that escapee from the libretto of some Wagnerian orgy was very much considered, and very much a leading player. So, I hope that sets your minds at rest, and makes you remorseful for having doubted my precocity.

I reached the Old Kent Road at quarter-past eight, and parked my car in one of the parking spaces provided for some flats, careful not to leave it in one of the Disabled Only slots. Then I walked the rest of the way to Stuart's, arriving at precisely eight twenty-nine. I noticed a BMW identical to mine except in colour parked near the stairs that led to the upper storeys, and presumed it was the getaway vehicle. It looked fine to me. And I took the stairs two at a time, arriving at Stuart's door dead on eight thirty. I pressed the bell.

Stuart himself opened the door, a transformed Stuart. Stuart the gangster, I imagine he thought of himself. Stuart dressed in black jeans and a black polo-neck. A hard-faced, menacing Stuart with no trace of the Queen about him.

I was the first of the merry band to arrive, but I'd barely settled into the chair Stuart indicated by nodding his cropped head than the doorbell rang again, and off he went. When he returned he had Bill and Ben with him, gorillas, enormous brutes as wide as they were tall, and they were very, very tall. They dwarfed Stuart. They dwarfed me. They'd have dwarfed King Kong if he'd been in on the job. Both of them walked with the stiffness of the musclebound, but agility wouldn't have been their forte. They exuded such an impression of strength that even the sight of them would have crushed the opposition, I felt. It certainly made me keen to watch my Ps and Qs. The one I thought of as Bill wore one of those camouflage jackets, a round-necked, dark-blue pullover, jeans and boots. Bovver boots, I think they're called – Doc Martins with steel toe-caps, excellent for kicking someone's brains out. Ben was into leather, and creaked as he moved, the way those ghastly leather sofas you see advertised in the Sunday supplements creak when you sit on them. Indeed, Ben didn't look unlike an overstuffed settee. We all gave each other a perfunctory nod. It was all we could do, since Stuart was busy as a bee, ignoring me, for which I was grateful, but dishing out 'shooters' to the goliaths. I know they were shooters because that's what Stuart called them. 'A shooter for you. A shooter for you. A shooter for me,' he said, like he was dealing out cards before what he hoped would prove an interesting and profitable session of poker.

And those, as far as I can remember, were the only words spoken, apart from, 'Let's do it,' which was Stuart's way of setting things in motion.

Next thing we were in the BMW (indeed the one I'd seen parked at the foot of the stairs) and driving at an approved rate through the building traffic. It struck me that maybe Bill and Ben were dumb and this (and the nerves which were slowly tying my stomach in knots) made me start to giggle. Stuart, sitting beside me, gave me a glowering glance, but then, getting it wrong, smiled at me. 'Good, eh? The buzz?'

I nodded. 'Great.' I was about to add facetiously that it was something to tell the grandchildren, but caught my tongue in time. Stuart might just have taken it as a slur on his sexuality and I didn't want to have him clobbering me. Even less getting the two boyos in the back clobbering me.

So, in silence again, we buzzed down Park Lane and arrived in Charles Street at nine twenty. What happened thereafter is still a bit of a blur.

I remember driving towards the Saudi embassy in a perfectly calm frame of mind, looking idly about for a parking place. I remember, too, that the Securicor van was outside the embassy. Then, without warning, Stuart bellowed, 'Stop,' at me, and I stopped dead, braking so hard I can recall Stuart being thrown forward. Then Stuart and his gigantic cohorts had their doors open, balaclavas on, shooters at the ready, and were dashing across the street towards the van. It was as if I was not really there, as if I was viewing all this farce from a considerable distance, as if it had nothing whatever to do with me. It was an old silent movie I was watching, a black and white, 1930s' gangster film in slow motion. Everyone had suddenly become bionic, moving in grotesque languidity. I recall an elderly woman strolling along with a freakish chihuahua on the end of a golden-coloured cord. She must have seen what was taking place, but she totally ignored it, giving, even, the impression that heists were something she was witness to every day of her life. Incredibly, the violence now being meted out to the security guards didn't look like violence. It looked staged. It looked absurd. It looked funny. And then all hell broke loose.

In the twinkling of an eye the street filled with armed police. They didn't come running into the street. They just appeared, and with their arrival everything speeded up. There was a ferocious bang and Ben went down, clutching his leg. Another crash and Bill returned fire from his shotgun. Everyone was shouting, and in my head something like the Horst Wessel song was being sung.

The next thing Stuart was beside me in the car, roaring, 'Go, go, fucking go,' and believe me, I went. 'What about – ' I managed to get out of my mouth as I gunned the BMW down Charles Street and turned, almost on two wheels, into Fitzmaurice Place.

'Fuck them,' was Stuart's advice, so I forgot them, and instead thought about that bastard Birt breaking his word.

I must say he had done his job well, though. A police car came hurtling towards us, going the wrong way in Berkeley Square. Under normal circumstances I'm certain it wouldn't have done what it did: swerve to one side, giving me the right of way.

'Frightened the shit out of that bastard,' Stuart told me.

I agreed. 'Teach him!' I said.

And that was about as exciting as it got. It wasn't until we were back on the Old Kent Road that Stuart really let rip his frustration. 'Fuck, fuck, fuck it,' he said to himself, and to me, I suppose. 'Bastards,' he said, although whether this applied to the police or to Bill and Ben I've no idea. 'At least you've done your job, Marcus.'

'Well, you know me.'

'Christ! What the fuck went wrong?' Stuart asked himself aloud.

I wanted to say, 'You fucked it up again, matey,' but needless to say I didn't. I did say, 'Must have raised the alarm in the embassy.'

Stuart shook his head. 'Couldn't be that. They'd never have got there *that* quick.'

'Maybe they've got a squad on special alert every time the embassy moves its money?' I suggested helpfully.

'Could be,' Stuart said.

'Must be,' I added.

We arrived at the turn-off for Stuart's flat. 'Pull over there,' Stuart ordered, pointing to a small timber yard.

I did as I was told.

Despite the overnight rain the yard was still very dusty, and I raised a cloud of it as I skidded to a halt. When it cleared young Davey was standing there by my door, opening it, and getting into the driving seat as soon as I got out. Another cloud of dust rose as he spun the car and drove off, leaving Stuart and myself standing there. And now that the sublime heist was over, other thoughts of other things swamped my mind. 'That it, Stuart?' I asked.

Bless him, he looked thoroughly woebegone. 'That's fucking it, pal,' he told me.

'Look, I'm really sorry things didn't work out.'

'You did okay.'

'Yeah, well, at least *you* weren't picked up. I suppose the other two will keep their mouths shut?'

'Too fucking right they will.'

'Then you've nothing to worry about, have you. Live to fight another day, as they say.'

Stuart gave me a look which told me that was more or less what he'd been thinking. 'Listen,' I said as we walked out of the yard. 'Next time, why don't you and me form a partnership. You know, do it together?'

Stuart quite liked that idea. 'We might just do that,' he said.

'Good. Well, I better toddle on then.'

'Yeah,' Stuart agreed. 'And thanks, Marcus. You're okay.'

'Any time,' I told him, and went back to my own car.

I sat in the car for a few minutes, letting what adrenaline had been raised subside. It had all, in reality, been a big let-down, nothing as exciting as I had anticipated. Armoured robbery, I decided, was definitely not my cup of tea. It was for morons. For cretins. And with that decision made I wiped the entire chaotic incident from my mind.

I was home shortly after eleven thirty, and with a certain amount of trepidation I entered the house by the kitchen door. I half expected to find Farrell there, covered in gore, a gibbering wreck, telling me of another failure to add to the day's work. But he wasn't there. The house was as quiet as a morgue. So now I'd something else to worry about. Where was Farrell? Had he gone back to the squat? More importantly, had he dealt with Kranze? Or had he botched it up, been caught, and was now in some stinking police cell getting ready to cry his heart out, spill the beans, and land me right in it? There was one way to start finding out. I telephoned Kranze's house. The phone rang and rang but no one answered. That, at least, augured well, unless Kranzey Boy had taken the missus up to the shops for a bit of his favourite bratwurst. Only time would answer that one. The next way of checking would yield more solid evidence. Go to the squat and see if Farrell was there. But first . . .

I went up to my room, taking with me a pudding spoon and a bottle of vinegar. I lit a candle, a candle in the shape of Santa Claus that Ma had lit in my room on the Christmas Eve before my incarceration. Then I tipped most of the pure heroin Stuart had so obligingly provided onto the spoon, added some vinegar, and held the spoon over the candle. When it was cooked, if that's the word, I stuck the needle into the mixture and sucked it into the syringe, just about filling it. If that wasn't lethal, God knows what would be. I then wrapped the syringe in a sock and stowed it away in the inside pocket of the leather jacket I proposed wearing. I changed into an old pair of jeans, took a quick snifter of Jack Daniels, put on the leather jacket, and away was I.

To my utter, unadulterated delight, Farrell, the little darling, was in the squat. Zonked, I might add. I'd presumed he'd go to the same room in which I'd first found him since he'd always shown himself to be very much a creature of habit, and my presumption was correct. There he lay, on his back, his mouth open, a strand of saliva trickling ingloriously from the left side, in a daze brought on by the temazepam and valium I'd so kindly given him. More to the point, he was wearing an old overcoat I hadn't seen before. Quietly, so as not to disturb him, and tentatively, so as not to disturb myself, I opened the coat. Even in the dim light of the room I could make out a healthy splattering of blood on Farrell's clothes. I felt a very pleasant giddiness: at least I now knew *something* had happened. Whether or not my stoned hero had actually disposed of Kranze was still to be discovered. I gave him a little prod. 'John?' I called gently. No reaction.

Strangely, there was something so awful about the place that, for a moment, made me loath to wake him. To most people squalor is just a word, applicable more, I think, to shanty towns in Latin American countries. But this was squalor of a high order, and not in Brazil or Bolivia, either. The stink was horrendous, and the whole place shuddered with little pattering noises as if rats were sequestering the building: and you already know how I feel about rodents. Somewhere upstairs a child whimpered, and it really sounded as if they simply didn't have the energy to cry properly.

I gave Farrell a firmer prod, and a louder, 'John?' and he opened his eyes: just. 'It's me, Marcus,' I told him.

For a second he looked puzzled. He looked at me as though I was, perhaps, the figment of some nightmare he'd been having. And then, slowly, it dawned on him who I was. He smiled a tired smile. 'Hey. Marcus,' he said, and tried to sit up.

I put my hand on his shoulder and eased him back down onto the urine-reeking mattress. 'Told you I'd come and get you, didn't I?'

'Yeah,' Farrell said, or rather he pushed air from his lungs and let the pressure of it say, 'Yeah.'

'Well, I'm here.'

Farrell smiled again and nodded.

'Everything go all right?' I ventured.

'Did just what you told me.'
'Everything I told you?'
'Everything.'

I sat down on the mattress and held his hand. He was starting to fall asleep, and we stayed there, holding hands for a while. 'John?' He opened his eyes.

'Just want to sleep, Marcus.'
'Sure,' I said.
'Just want to sleeeeep.'
'Sure.' I gave his hand a squeeze.

Somewhere, in another room, in another world, really, Pink Floyd's *Dark Side of the Moon* started playing: '... someone inside my head but it's not me,' the song went. Someone inside my head but it's not me, I said quietly to myself. Good, that. I pushed up the sleeve of Farrell's overcoat, the sleeve of his jacket, the sleeve of his shirt: my jacket, my shirt, actually. He didn't budge. I rubbed his arm and found the vein I wanted no bother. I unwrapped the syringe from the sock and inserted the needle into the vein. Slowly, with some reverence, in fact, I injected the lot.

To say that I felt remorse would be pushing it, but I did feel *something*, although I can't for the life of me define it too clearly. I was sorry to be losing him: I mean, you don't go through what Farrell and I had been through without having some kind of bonding. But, on the other hand, his usefulness was done and I had always regarded him as disposable, so any grief I felt was tempered by the thought of the damage he could do to me if he wasn't to go to that great opium den in the sky. Nonetheless, I was pleased he wasn't going to suffer; was, in fact, departing this earthly mayhem in a manner which I felt would be ideal for him. A bit like Bing Crosby keeling over while playing golf, or Tommy Cooper collapsing with the sound of laughter still ringing in his ears. What better way for an addict to leave us than in a state of total, obliterating, mind-boggling stupor? Besides, as I looked about the fetid place I felt I might just be doing Farrell the biggest favour of his life.

I wiped my fingerprints off the syringe with the sock, put the sock in my pocket, and fixed the syringe firmly between Farrell's fingers, making sure *his* dabs were on it. And then, in a gesture of brotherhood and goodwill, I kissed Farrell on the forehead, just to let him know, in whatever paradise awaited him, that there was nothing personal in all this. It was life proving once again that it was a bitch.

I was on my way from the room when I remembered the knife, and I was back searching my dear John Hamish like a shot, telling myself, 'See what shit sentimentality can land you in if you're not careful?' Bless him, though, he'd remembered that too, and I felt a renewed surge of gratitude towards him. It was in his inside pocket, still sticky with blood. I wiped most of that gore off the knife, using Farrell's shirt. Then I popped the knife into the sock which had wrapped the syringe, and shoved the lot into my own pocket.

Farrell was making strange, disagreeable gurgling noises by now. At least, his insides were, and I didn't really want to witness his retreat. I honestly couldn't stay there and stand to see him suffer, if suffer he must. I don't like to see anyone suffer. An unnecessary brutality, I think.

I went quickly to the door. I stopped, and turned, and took one last look at John Hamish. I gave him a wave, too, just to send him on his journey.

I drove meditatively home, stopping at the Serpentine to chuck the knife away, watching the ever-expanding circles it created with something close to fascination. The circles in the mind, I thought. The circles *of* the mind, I thought. And as the circles were swallowed up and vanished into the vastness of the river, so, too, did all my energy seem to be consumed and evaporate.

But that's always the way, isn't it, when you've achieved your goal, your ambition, achieved something great? The glory of it belongs totally and utterly to you. But with that possession there comes a terrible void, that emptiness that leaves you feeling nothing but loneliness and sorrow, but mostly sorrow.

Just as confession, repentance, absolution and the generosity of God wash away the sins of the sinner, so does a hot Radox bath, a glass of Jack Daniels and a decent joint remove that jaded sadness I was talking about.

The first thing I did, though, on my return home was to phone the Kranze residence again. I still got no answer, so *then* I rolled my joint, poured my drink and filled my bath. I smoked, drank and lounged in it, letting the warmth and luxuriousness of it all ease my aching nerves and raise my spirits. It was after five before I could drag myself out of it, and since I was planning on going out that evening I slipped into my dressing-gown and slippers. I then threw the few things I would need for my visit to Ma into a bag and carried it downstairs with me. I fixed myself an omelette, a plain one, using four eggs, adding a few drops of soda water to make it fluff up nicely. I carried it and a glass of wine into the sitting-room and switched on the television, and fed and wined myself as the fiends from Ramsay Street bickered and certainly removed me from any wish ever to visit Australia. And I'd just eaten the last of my meal when the news came on.

Poor Charlotte had had her day, but our blundered heist got top billing. Even the thousands of victims of ethnic cleansing had to play second fiddle to us, if you don't mind. 'Police this morning foiled an attempted armed robbery in central London,' we were told. 'Two men have been arrested and are helping police with their enquiries,' we were further informed. 'Two other men are being sought,' which was nice to know. It also meant that Stuart Bean was still on the loose, so I wondered what had gone wrong there. Maybe Beany wasn't quite as thick as he looked, I was thinking when the newscaster shattered my illusions by saying, 'We've just heard that a third man has been arrested in connection with this morning's attempted robbery of a security van in Central London.' Ah, well. Can't win 'em all. Couldn't win any of them as far as Beany was concerned, it seemed. There was no mention of any goings-on in Cricklewood, though, and it can't have been too long after the news ended that I dozed off.

At eight o'clock almost to the dot Inspector Maurice Birt played a really shitty trick on me. The doorbell woke me. I *thought* it was the doorbell I'd heard but wasn't sure so I didn't get up immediately. Then it rang again. Rather groggily I made my way down the hall to answer it. There was Birt, looking grim and unpleasant on the doorstep, and a few yards away was Wilson, also looking unpleasant, but that wasn't unusual for him. Before I could say a word, Birt started. 'Marcus Walwyn, I'm arresting you in connection with an attempted armed robbery. You don't have to say anything – ' And then he stopped. He stopped because I was actually reeling, swaying, probably about to faint. Birt grabbed me, helping to steady myself. 'I was just joking, Marcus,' he said with an asinine grin on his face.

'Fuck you, Birt,' I said with all the venom I could muster.

'I thought it was very funny,' he told me.

'Oh, very fucking funny. Jesus, you frightened the shit out of me.'

'That's what I wanted to do.'

'Well, you did it. Sadistic fucking bastard.' I turned on my heel and went back to the sitting-room, still, frankly, shaking with the fright of it all.

Birt followed me in. I think he was concerned I was about to have a heart attack on him, because he became very conciliatory. 'I didn't really mean to, eh – '

'Well, you did. Frightened the bloody shit out of me.'

'All right. I apologise. It was tasteless.'

'You can say that again.'

'I apologise. It was tasteless,' he repeated with a winsome, winning smile, and the relief of it got to me and I gave a short guffaw.

'You're a bastard,' I told him.

'Quite legitimate, in fact. But I take your meaning.' He settled himself comfortably in the chair opposite me.

'What the fuck were you playing at, arriving with your hit squad outside the embassy? I thought we had an arrangement,' I snapped, still angry.

'Sorry about that. We couldn't take any chances,' he replied apologetically.

I nodded towards the television. 'I see you got the other three.'

'Oh yes. All wrapped up and cosy. They're not saying much, of course. Saying nothing, in fact. But we expected that.'

'So, that's *one* you owe me.'

Birt made a little mewing noise. 'Not quite,' he said.

'What does that mean? Not quite?'

'It means that we're – how shall I put it? – all square?'

'And how do you figure that out?'

'Let's just say *you* owed *me* that one.'

'How come?'

'Do I *have* to explain?'

'Yes. Yes, you *have* to explain.'

Birt sighed. He studied his nails. He looked at me again. 'Put simply, Marcus, if I had argued with a little more vehemence, if I'd *wanted* you to spend the full life sentence inside, you wouldn't, believe me, be sitting here enjoying your wine and toasties.'

'Balls,' I told him vulgarly. But it was true, I knew. 'Old Harry Rutherford, my new stepdad, by the way, found the cock-up somewhere down the line and *he* got me out.'

'With a little help from me. Or rather, from me because I didn't offer any hindrance. But no matter. Let's call the slate clean, shall we? For old time's sake?'

'Call it anything you like. I still reckon you owe me, but – for old time's sake,' I stressed with heavy sarcasm, 'I won't hold you to it.'

'Most generous.'

'Too generous. But that's the way I am. Generous to a fault.'

'I'm sure. Anyway, there's a massive search under way at the moment for the driver of the getaway car – oh, we found that, by the way.'

I raised my eyebrows, hoping young Davey had been nabbed.

'Burned out. In Stepney.'

'Stepney?' I asked, as if interested.

'But as I say, there's a search on for the driver but I doubt we'll ever come up with a suspect. No one saw *him*, you see. And I'm sure only Bean really knows who he is.'

'And Bean won't be saying.'

'No. Bean won't be saying. More than – '

'Yeah, I know. More than his life is worth.'

'Quite.' Birt stretched and stifled a yawn. 'It's been a long, hard but successful day,' he said. Then he spotted my overnight bag, and frowned. 'Going somewhere?'

'Oh. Yes,' I said casually. 'To Ma's new house for a couple of days.'

'Ah. Tonight?'

'In the morning. I'm allowed to leave town, I suppose?' I asked cheekily.

Birt was effusive. 'But of course. But of course,' he told me, spreading his hands to indicate my absolute freedom.

'Well, that's something, I suppose.'

'And coming back?'

'I told you. In two days. Less, in fact. Be back late Sunday night.'

'I see. And then, maybe we could . . .' Birt stopped talking and let the beguiling, pleading tone he had used take over.

I pretended not to understand. 'Could . . . ?'

'Get on with the other matter?'

'Oh, *Kranze*! Yeah. I suppose.'

Birt didn't like me only supposing, but he accepted it with grace. 'Good,' he said, and stood up. 'After that, I *will* owe you. Won't that be nice?'

'Be lovely. Just lovely.'

'I thought you'd feel that way.'

'Believe me, I do. You going now?'

Birt nodded. 'Yes. Off home. Off home to my sad little dwelling, my cold and lonely bed.'

'My heart bleeds for you.'

'I know it does, Marcus. That's why I'm *so* fond of you.'

'Yeah.'

I didn't even bother to get up and see him out. I didn't move until

I heard the door close behind him, and only then did I allow myself to breathe with any semblance of normality. And with that same breath I cursed Birt. Not for coming round and waking me. Not even for the repugnant joke he had played on me. But for bringing up the matter of Kranze again, and settling that name firmly in my mind just now. It meant one of two things: either my first fear was grounded – Farrell had made a botch of it, possibly dismembered someone I'd never heard of, leaving Kranze alive and kicking; or Kranze was dead but hadn't been discovered yet. I badly wanted to believe the latter was true, but that mischievous demon was at me again, telling me that, alas, the former was the more likely. It all added up to anything but peace of mind for me that night. Nothing helped, not even my beloved Mahler, who tried valiantly. I had quite the most dreadful night I'd had in years, a night of fretful dozing, a night filled with the cries of demented whiffmagigs. Sighs and moans that had been familiar in prison. A night of turmoil.

Bleary-eyed I watched the dawn take hold through the window. Another day. That was the wondrous thing about being alive. There was always another day. Anyway, I was getting away for a day or two, and Ma would certainly cheer me up. She could do that even when it wasn't her intention. I showered and practised witty sayings to spoil her with. I heard her tinkling laugh. Good old Ma. And Harry. Pedantic, reliable, boring Harry. Even he seemed a lively enough prospect at that particular moment. I shaved with care, making sure not to cut myself since Ma really hated nicks on a man's face – it was a sign of narrow-mindedness, she claimed, but how she came to that conclusion only she could tell. Or couldn't. I dressed with care also, choosing a navy-blue Italian shirt with the hint of a red line running through it, a pair of Daks, and my favourite Gucci loafers. I felt much better by the time I got downstairs, which was just as well, otherwise I might not have coped with what was in store for me.

TWENTY-EIGHT

The Sun had a dandy headline, I thought:

MASSACRE IN CRICKLEWOOD.

Inspector Birt came barging into the house before I even had the chance to make myself a morning cup of coffee, pushing past me when I answered the door, going straight into the kitchen, and flinging the newspaper on the table. 'Read that,' he said, visibly shaken.

I read it to myself: MASSACRE IN CRICKLEWOOD. I then read it aloud: MASSACRE IN CRICKLEWOOD. It sounded better out loud so I said it again, 'Massacre in Cricklewood. So? Want some coffee?'

'No. I don't want coffee. It's Kranze.'

I was making my way to the percolator when he announced that, and I made as if he'd struck me. I stood stock still. 'Kranze? *Our* Kranze? Jesus. Who's he killed now?' I asked, and went forward again, and started brewing my coffee.

'It's Kranze, Zanker, who's been killed.'

I swung round. 'What?' I asked incredulously. Goodness me, was I aghast.

'Kranze has been killed,' Birt said.

'You mean he's *dead*?'

'People usually are when they're killed.'

'I just can't believe this. How did it happen? I mean, a car crash, a fall, a – '

'Christ, Marcus, he was murdered.'

Oh, I was appalled. '*Murdered!*'

'Hacked to death.'

'Oh, dear God!' I moved over to the table and sat down.

'And his wife,' Birt appended.

'Not poor Brünnhilde too?'

'Who?'

'Brünnhilde. His wife. I always thought of her as Brünnhilde. Kranze's missus.'

'Lisa. Lisa was her name.'

'And she's dead too?'

'He was dead when we got there, she died a few hours later in hospital.'

'This is frightening,' I confessed. 'Really scary. When did it happen, do you know?'

Birt nodded. 'Early yesterday morning. Got that from Mrs Zanker before she died. Got a description of the killer too.'

'Well, that's something.'

'That's why I'm here, Marcus.'

'Oh, sure. Me, I suppose. The killer looks like me, eh?'

'Nothing like you. Very like that man Speed.'

'John?' I gasped. 'Naw. John wouldn't – '

'Where is he, Marcus?'

'Jesus, I don't know. Haven't seen him in weeks. Could be back in the squat, I suppose. Could be back in Scotland. Could be anywhere.'

'That squat – where was it?'

'Just off the Bayswater Road. God, this is really crazy.'

'Where off the Bayswater Road?'

'I can't remember that. Not the name of the road. It's – let me think – one, two . . . the fifth turning down from Marble Arch. There's a row of boarded-up houses. It's the second of those, I think. Why would John *kill* Kranze, though? I just can't see it. I simply cannot see it.'

'I'll be back,' Birt told me, and left the house in a hurry.

I thought he meant he was going away and would be back later, but that wasn't it. He had a confab with Wilson and another moron, and then returned. 'I'll have that coffee now.'

I gave him a stare.

'Please,' he added.

'Pleasure,' I said. Just because tragedy had struck didn't mean I was going to let Birt forget his manners. I got up and poured us each a mug of coffee. 'You know, I'm still shaking, Maurice.'

Birt watched me.

'I mean I know I – we – wanted to get the old bugger behind bars and all, but to have him – hacked to death, is that what you said?'

'Butchered would be a better word.'

I shook my head. 'Dreadful. Terrible. How did you find him – and his wife?' I asked, keeping a slightly disinterested tone in my voice.

'Neighbours heard Mrs Zanker shouting for help.'

'Ah. Neighbours. Where *would* we be without them? Jesus, Maurice, it's really piling up on you now, isn't it. First that woman on Wimbledon Common, then Beany's fiasco of a robbery, and now this.' I shook my head. 'Where *is* it going to end?'

Birt didn't answer. He sat down and started sipping his coffee, not even noticing it was sugarless and black. 'That woman – ' he said and paused.

'Lisa?' I asked innocently.

Birt grimaced. 'Not Zanker's wife. Charlotte Adams,' he said, and drifted off into thinking again.

'What about her?'

'She was near as be damned butchered to death too.'

'Ah, you think whoever killed Kranze was – what d'you call

them? – a copycat killer? Could be.'

Birt was getting irritated with me. 'No, that's *not* what I mean. I'm just wondering – '

'If the same person did *both* killings?' I looked doubtful, but said, 'It's possible, I suppose. Seems like anything's possible in this fucked-up world. Be handy for you if it turned out that way, though, wouldn't it – kill two birds with the one stone, if you'll excuse the phrase?'

Before he could answer (if he was about to answer at all) Birt's little intercom thing crackled into life. Instantly he got up and went trotting outside again: very confidential, all these inter-police messages are. Not for the ears of plebs like you and me. I turned to the paper and started to read. Lurid was hardly a strong enough word for it. All the stock words and phrases were trotted out: a 'maniac' (later to be described as a 'fiend', an 'enraged psycho' and a 'demented thug') had hacked to death an elderly couple in a quiet street in Cricklewood. I'd just got to where the details of the number of stab wounds inflicted and, it appeared, their precise location, when Birt came bounding in again. His face was an odd grey colour but he was busy, busy, busy. 'Got to dash,' he told me, but not before another swig of his coffee. 'Found Speed.'

'At the squat?'

'Yes. Not much good to us though.'

'Oh?'

'Overdosed. Needle still in his hand.'

'Poor bastard,' I said with considerable feeling. 'Never know if it was him who did it now.'

'We'll see.'

'Listen. I'd appreciate it if you could tell me what happens with John's body. I quite liked the poor chap. Think I might go along to his funeral. You know. Bring a few flowers. Something like that. Wouldn't want him to go off all on his own. Must be terrible that, mustn't it – getting buried in that cold, cold ground and nobody there who gives a damn?'

I think Birt was quite impressed by my undoubted Christianity. His voice had a reverend touch to it when he said, 'Of course I can let you know if that's what you want.'

'Thank you.' I stood up and went with him to the door. 'Be nice to think I'd have him waiting up there for me when I finally turn up my toes. He might just be the one to do the trick and get me in.'

'I think, Marcus, you'll need more than John Speed to get you in through the pearly gates.'

'Every little helps, Maurice. Every little helps.'

Then something struck Birt. 'Ah – you're going away today, right?'

'In about ten minutes, I hope.'

'And coming back tomorrow night?'

'That's right. Why?'

'Oh, nothing. Just in case. Just – well, you knew Speed better than any of us.'

'Oh. That's true enough, I suppose, but I didn't know him *that* well. Nobody gets to know a drug addict *that* well, do they? Unless it's another needle-freak, I suppose. They're a secretive, lying bunch, in my experience. Bit like the Masons, really,' I concluded with an enigmatic grin since I suspected that Birt, like so many of his colleagues, might have had his trouser-leg over his shoulder at some time or another.

But Birt got into his car without a murmur, so maybe I was wrong. I shut the door for him, and watched as he muttered something to his driver. He wound down the window. 'Enjoy your weekend,' he said, making it sound as if it was the last weekend I might enjoy for some time to come.

'Oh, don't worry. I intend to. You enjoy yours, too.'

'I will,' Birt said so sincerely it sounded like a promise.

I stood back as the engine started, giving Birt a nod and a smile as he waved: a small, ceremonial wave like the Pope's, and it was probably this that inspired me to bless him, using an image of the jet-setting Pontiff we currently have to suffer to get my blessing affable but reserved. 'Happy hunting,' I told him.

It was only when I got back inside that I discovered the old skinflint had even taken his newspaper with him.

Visiting one's mother might seem at first glance an odd way to celebrate what was, in my estimation, the perfect murder, but I happen to enjoy my mother's company, and the wacky way she has of seeing life. I set off in high good humour.

It didn't last long though. About seven hundred and fifty yards to be more precise. There I was, tootling along minding my business, my Ps and Qs, my road manners, when, from a side street came this van which whacked straight into my front wing. It was so unexpected that I sat in the car for quite a few seconds before leaping out, ready to have a right go at the nincompoop who'd just about wrecked my precious car. When I saw the size of the bugger, though, I decided that caution certainly was the better part of valour. I just stood and gaped at him, letting him take the initiative. To his credit he was in a bad state, and properly apologetic. I didn't want the police dragged in, did I? Well . . . Come on, mate, he'd lose his job if . . . The usual palaver of someone scared gutless of some shitty boss just waiting to fire him knowing there were a few thousand unemployed bastards just waiting to leap in and take the job. I don't honestly know what made me ask, 'You married?' but I did.

'Yeah, mate. Got kids, too. Three of 'em.'

'Who's going to pay for this?' was my next question.

'I – ' bloody Fangio began. 'How much d'you think it'll be?'

'A grand, I'd say. Maybe more.'

'Oh, shit.'

'You're insured – I *suppose*?'

'Yeah. Oh, yeah. But if the boss – '

'Yeah, I know. If the boss finds out you'll lose your job.'

The poor sod nodded.

'Well, you're going to have to explain that somehow,' I pointed out, nodding towards the damage to the van.

'Can say some fucker – sorry, mate – some bastard ran into it when it was parked.'

It was definitely an indication of my well-being that I said, 'I suppose you could.'

'And your insurance would pay for yours. I mean, look, you could say the same thing, couldn't you?'

'I'd hope to think of something a bit more erudite and original,' I told him, and then said. 'Go on. Piss off.'

So, you see, despite what you might think, I'm not all bad. Couldn't have his wee missus and three bairns on the breadline, could I?

But now I had to take the car to the garage, and with the wing all bashed in it was all but impossible to drive. So I called in the Fourth Emergency Service, and saw about hiring a car which my deal with the AA allowed.

Come to think of it, maybe I *am* close to being all bad since I felt more sorrow seeing my beautiful BMW being towed away than I had done seeing poor John Hamish having the celestial breakdown service do their bit on him.

Ford Mondeos are not what I'd call my cup of tea. They smack of the less-than-successful commercial traveller, the type who always hangs his jacket on that little hook over the back door, and keeps the driver's window open, rain or shine, so he can drum his fingers on the roof of the car to give the impression he's in a desperate hurry to clinch some terrific deal. But it was a Mondeo they gave me, and it went, so I wasn't complaining, and despite the unfortunate start to my weekend I really did enjoy my couple of days near Bath.

Ma was in sparkling form: witty and gay, and making above-average outrageous gaffes and predictions that had me in stitches.

Mind you, there was another reason why the damage to my BMW hadn't altogether ruined the weekend. I'd made my own contribution to ethnic cleansing before I left Chelsea: Pissquick in a cardboard box, tied and dumped in the boot. Catching the bastard hadn't been all that easy, so when I finally collared him my triumph was all the greater. The wily old sod smelt a rat, I'm sure of it. He also smelt the sardines in the can I opened, though, and sardines were sheer nectar to Pissquick. Keep your smoked salmon, your calf's liver, your poussin: I swear to God if a can of sardines was opened within a radius of five miles Pissquick would sniff it out, make a beeline for it, and be hollering for his share before you could say John West. For a beast brought up by Ma to appreciate the finer things in life, it always struck me as a peculiarly plebian dish for him to drool over. I can only presume it had something to do with his heritage, his roots. Once a moggy, always a moggy, I guess. Anyway, when I started looking for him, he was nowhere in sight. I opened the kitchen window, opened the sardines, and lo, within seconds, there he was, tail erect, green, avaricious eyes agleam, hightailing it up the pathway.

What I really wanted to do was get him in with the promise of the fish, but then grab him and box him up before he had the chance to get even one mouthful. Just to teach him the consequences of greed, you understand. But grabbing Pissquick was like grabbing at straws. He was the Carl Lewis of cats, lithe and speedy. One minute he was at my feet. I was reaching for the cardboard box. In the split second I took my eyes off him he was up on the worktop, devouring the sardines. So *now* I *did* teach him the dire consequences of greed. I grabbed him by the scruff of the neck and bundled him, head-first, into the box. Jesus! You'd have thought there was a snowy tiger in there, the racket he made, clawing and screaming, and, no doubt, telling me in cattery what an utter bastard I was. *That* made *my* day, I can tell you.

I arrived at Ma's just before lunch, still humming the tune of the Sonata for Horn and Harp by Louis-François Somebodyorother that had been on the radio for the final miles of my journey. Ma must have been watching out for me because I hadn't even brought the car to a full stop when she was out of the house and running towards me, her arms outspread, ready to envelop me in a huge, maternal embrace. 'Hiya, Ma,' I greeted her, and let her hug me.

'Darling,' she said.

As we stood there, locked in love, I saw Harry come out of the house. His grave face told me he had read or heard about Kranze, and he was definitely wondering if I'd had anything to do with it. His nasty mind worked that way. Ma, of course, wouldn't know a thing about it. She never read anything unpleasant in the papers, and she had trained her mind to switch off automatically if something 'not nice' came on the television. So, such things as riots, mayhem, murder and catastrophe never got access to her consciousness, while pretty things like Wimbledon, Ascot and Jean Muir fashions gained entry with sublime facility and were devoured with an avariciouness that would do credit to a marauding panther.

Anyway, while Ma busied herself in the kitchen with a welcoming saucer of cream for Pissquick, I decided to have a heart to heart with Harry and ease his aching soul. I began by saying, 'I take it you've heard, Harry?'

'About Kranze? Yes.'

'And if I know you, which I do, you're wondering if I had anything to do with it. Right?'

Harry reddened, but he admitted such a thought had crossed his mind.

'Well, you needn't worry. I assure you I had nothing to do with the departure of Mr Kranze. In fact, between you and me, I had a visit from Inspector Birt, and *he* told me he's pretty sure he knows who *did* do it.'

'Oh?'

'Yeah. Some druggy Kranze had abused in prison.'

'But it's been *years* since Kranze – that's not his name, is it?'

'Zanker,' I provided.

'*Years* since Zanker got out of prison.'

'Well, they've long memories, these chaps, it seems.'

'Birt's arrested him?' Harry asked.

'Well, not really. Chap was dead as a dodo when they found him. Overdose, apparently.'

Harry couldn't avoid giving me a sly look. 'Convenient,' he commented.

And then Ma told us lunch was ready and we trooped into the

dining-room: a really pretty room which Ma had decorated, or had *had* decorated in the best possible taste, as the late lamented Kenny Everett might have said. It had pale-green walls ('Always green for a dining-room, darling,' Ma used to say. 'Reminds one of spring salads, and the delicious fresh fruits of early summer, doesn't it?'), the floor sanded and polished with a scattering of real Chinese rugs.

I wanted to forget Kranze, so I told Ma about my trip to South Africa, omitting the fact that Nick Putty had totally ruled it out.

'South Africa!' Ma exclaimed, giving Harry an irritated glance as he tucked into his smoked salmon without cutting it up into small enough pieces for her liking.

'Only a maybe,' I pointed out.

'Still – South Africa! When would you have to go?'

'*If* I go it could be as soon as next week,' I lied.

'So soon?' Ma suddenly became alarmed. 'Oh, you will be careful, Marcus, won't you?'

I didn't quite get the drift of this. 'Sorry?' I said, and stood up to take Harry's plate and my own and put them on the sideboard. 'Why careful, Ma?' I then took her plate and added it to the others: stacking, you see, is very *infra dig*, something that really upset Ma since only the very commonest of folk stack plates one on top of the other as they remove them from the table.

'Well, I mean, they're all – all – well, all *black* out there, aren't they, dear?'

'Most of them. Africans have a tendency towards the ebony.'

'Well, then, you know what I'm talking about,' Ma said, and started dishing up the noisettes of lamb en croute.

'I believe the Mau Mau are a thing of the past, Ma,' I said, 'aren't they Harry?' I asked, feeling obligated to draw my new stepfather into the conversation: politeness is not dead, you see.

'I believe so,' Harry said, and passed me the Georgian gravy bowl.

But Ma wasn't impressed. 'I know they've *told* us that, dear,' she said. 'Peas? But I believe they're a bit like those Irish ones, aren't they? The Mau Mau and the IRA?'

'That's supposedly all over now too, Ma.'

'Whatever,' Ma dismissed that faction since she found it difficult to tolerate any organisation that used mere letters as a form of identification, believing to do so meant they had something to hide. 'I mean, they're telling us they're a thing of the past now too, aren't they, and then up they pop just when you least expect them.'

'It's not quite the same thing, Ma.'

'Well, of course, you know a lot more about international politics than I do, dear – no, not for me, thank you,' Ma said, rejecting the sauté potatoes. 'But it would be more than I could bear if anything happened to you out there, darling.'

Pudding was fresh raspberries and cream, and very good they were too, so succulent and tasty that they removed the threat of any lurking Mau Mau from Ma's mind, and the possibility of a trip to Bermuda which Harry, in a moment of weakness, I suspect, had suggested, took over. 'Just to get away from the *dreariness* of England in the winter, darling.'

'You're being spoiled, Ma,' I said.

Ma giggled. 'I know. Isn't it lovely?'

And after lunch Ma went for a lovely little nap – without Harry, so I suppose she might have got forty winks. That left Harry and me together. I wasn't best pleased. I'd seen Harry in action in the courts, remember, seen how he got witnesses to admit to things I'm convinced they had sworn never to divulge. I didn't want to get enmeshed in any probing he might feel inclined to instigate. However, it didn't come to that. Harry decided he wanted to keep away from me also, perhaps expecting contamination as a possibility. He chose an alternative – a spot of gardening: a few roses to be deadheaded, raking up the few leaves which had already fallen from the autumn trees, an agapanthus to be touched and told how very pretty it was.

I watched him meander round his garden, looking for all the world like a harmless retired military type for whom war was a necessity and retirement something to be painfully and aimlessly wandered through. I just hoped all this fresh air and country living wasn't going to blunt his ability. One never knew, did one: I might have to call on his services yet again if I'd overlooked anything. I was *sure* I hadn't, but over-confidence is what kept Her Majesty's fun farms ticking.

Which reminded me: Pissquick was still in solitary. Maybe suffocated. He wasn't, though. I might have guessed. That dumb bastard would have survived just to spite me. I let him out, and within seconds you could tell he now owned the place.

Ma and I went to Mass on Sunday morning, in Bath. During the consecration, which I felt was a mite inappropriate, Ma whispered to me that it was just like old times, wasn't it?

It was, in fact. Very old times, though. Times before I had even left school, before I had started work, before Dad had hanged himself, before Kranze had come into my life and all that this represented. And maybe that's why this particular Mass was one of the most pleasing I had ever attended. I did, truly, feel rejuvenated when it was over. I felt like a new man. I felt that what was behind me *was* behind me, and that the future was nothing if not the promise of peace and tranquillity. I should, alas, have remembered that the adage 'Promises are made to be broken' has a nasty way of becoming the truth.

When I think about it now it seems to me that when it came time for me to leave Ma and Harry to their rustic lifestyle, our parting, if not such sweet sorrow, was oddly melancholy. There was, for some unknown reason, a finality about our goodbyes. They weren't those cheery see-you-soons, those be-in-touches, those slightly glib *au revoirs* one bestows on those one is about to see again in the very near future. I remember distinctly that each of us said 'Goodbye'. It should have told me something.

And as I drove back to London it struck me that I was driving into a storm. A great, black, cloud-laden storm. One that would consume me. It was an extraordinarily powerful feeling. It was also a premonition but I didn't know it at the time.

So, too, probably, was the sign plastered on a billboard on the outskirts. THE END IS NIGH, it told me. And all I thought of that was 'The end is always bloody nigh'. From the moment you're born the end is nigh. The only thing that happens as you go through life is that the end gets nigher. That brought a smile to my face, a smile which, I regret to relate, would be wiped away in a very short while.

TWENTY-NINE

I'd barely stepped into the house when I knew something was wrong. Or, rather, that something was not right rather than something wrong. There's a subtle difference, I think. The first thing I did was stand absolutely still, and listen. Maybe I had been burgled;

maybe I was *still* being burgled, and I didn't want to come face to face with some yob of a housebreaker wielding a crowbar. I could think of better ways of having my face rearranged. But there wasn't a sound. All was definitely quiet on the western front. I didn't put on the light: I crept out of the kitchen, into the hall, and again listened. Not a dickie-bird. I switched on the hall light. Everything seemed to be in order. I plucked up courage. I went from room to room. Nothing out of place. I stood outside my bedroom door and said aloud, 'It's all getting to you, chum.' And then I went back downstairs, into the kitchen, and fixed myself probably the stiffest Jack Daniels I'd ever allowed myself in my entire life. A couple of gulps of that and I was feeling a lot better. I was about to take a third when it hit me, and I very nearly threw up. Everything in the house was too much *in* place. It hit me like a sledgehammer. Which led to the unpleasant realisation that someone had been in the house while I was at Ma's, had presumably gone through everything, but had made the error of being just too damn tidy about the job, and putting things back not where I had them but where he or she *thought* they should be: an inch to the left, a millimetre to the right. And, having been smitten by this brainwave, I had to go through the house and check everything all over again. I can tell you I was really bugged when I couldn't actually put my finger on anything. But I knew, I knew, I *knew* someone had been in and searched the place. Some home-coming that was.

But *who* had been the intruder? That was the most puzzling part of it. My first thought was crazy: that the Blow Job Queen had found out I'd grassed him and had sent someone round to plant a bomb or something like that under me. I nearly set off for a third tour of the house looking for explosive devices when the stupidity of it all struck me. It was most unlikely, even if he had uncovered my shameful secret, that Beany would have had the time, let alone the opportunity, to organise a hit. In any case, blowing up the victim wouldn't be his style. Far too lenient a punishment for the hard man Stuart to indulge in. No, Beany Boy would want his victim to know he was suffering, and he'd want to see him suffering if that was at all possible. Beany would wait to get me if he ever found out. Wait ten, fifteen years if necessary, using those years to formulate quite the most appalling end for me that his limited brain power could design.

It had to be Birt then. But why would he come like a thief in the night to search my place when he could quite simply come to the door with a warrant and take as long as he liked scouring the house

– and not a thing I could do to stop him? It didn't make sense. And even if it was he who had been in, what the hell was he looking for? I had no connection with Charlotte Adams. I was driving a getaway car when Kranze and his good lady got their comeuppance. And even though there was the slimmest of slim links between myself and Farrell (or Speed, as far as Birt was concerned), Birt couldn't have gleaned any information from him unless, unbeknownst to me, Birt had the knack of communication with the dear departed. It is ludicrous, I know, but I was so frustrated I even gave this possibility my serious consideration.

I took what was left of my drink up to bed with me. I undressed and lay naked on the bed. I balanced the cold glass on my navel. I tried desperately to find another suspect, but no matter how hard I tried I kept coming back to Birt. Okay, I thought, and put my drink on the table and got a pad and a ballpoint pen from my desk. Returning to bed I propped myself up comfortably and used my drawn-up knees as a lectern. Okay. Let's accept the obvious: it *was* Birt. Now what? I wrote down: What was he looking for? And under that I wrote down the only answer I could come up with: Clues. But what clues, for Christ's sake? I ripped out the page I'd been writing on, and started all over again:

(1.) Birt came to the house and searched it: Fact.
(2.) Looking for? Clues.
(3.) Clues to what? My involvement in murder.
(4.) Whose murder?   (a.) Kranze and Frau.
                              (b.) Farrell/Speed.
                              (c.) Charlotte.
(5.) What clues could he possibly find linking me to any of their deaths?

I took another sip of Jack Daniels. A car pulled up on the street outside, and I froze, my heart suddenly thumping like it was trying to crack my ribcage. But then a rather boisterous, drunken individual yelled something decidedly bawdy, and the car took off again at well over the speed limit. Dickheads. My heart-rate slowed. I defrosted. I went back to my meditations, mentally calling forth the protagonists in a fruity sort of voice like the one used when they announce the winners on *Come Bloody Dancing*.

(6.) Farrell/Speed. Can't be any significant clues. Even if by chance there still remained something in the house to link me to Farrell, so what eh? He'd been living here. I certainly didn't deny that. Birt had met him here.

The squat? Anything there? Had I been spotted? Maybe. Did it matter if I had been seen? Not one whit. I'd simply gone to see if he was okay when I didn't find him here at Chelsea. He was fine when I last saw him. Spaced out, sure. But when wasn't he? How was I supposed to know he'd taken an overdose? No medical expert I.

(7.) Kranze/Zanker. Driving car in Charles Street at time of murder. Been seen by Birt's men doing same. Had someone spotted me dropping Farrell off near Kranze's house on the morning of the murder? A possibility. Soon talk my way out of that one. Yes, okay, I'd dropped the sod off, but how was I to know he was going to use the Krauts as pincushions? Besides, Birt knew I was arranging meetings between Farrell/Speed and Kranze/Zanker. I'd most assiduously kept him informed. Indeed, at a push, it could be said Birt *encouraged* me to arrange those meetings. Be interesting to see how Birt wangled *his* way out of *that* one.

(8.) Charlotte. Zilch. Unless there'd been video cameras in the arcade as we'd made our way to the café when we met? Possibly. But I hadn't walked *with* her. I'd stayed in front of her. Birt knew I used Fortnum's regularly, so my cutting through the arcade would be pretty natural: her being behind me just one of those inexplicable coincidences life seems to be full of. Wimbledon Common? No one saw me there. I was positive of that. As positive as I could be, at any rate. Maybe I'd dropped something there? No. Been careful not to bring anything I *could* drop.

I got up from the bed and carefully lit the faithful Christmas candle and burned all the notes I'd made, including the original page that I'd discarded. When they'd burned completely I ground up the ashes with my finger and blew them out of the window. Then I rubbed my hands (out of the window, too) just to make sure every iota of ash was removed. Then I stood back and stared out, letting the cool night air drench my naked body in calmness. I was definitely in the clear. I really had done it. I just wished I could have been that infamous fly on the wall to see Birt's misery when he'd searched the house and found sweet Fanny Adams. I had a nice little chuckle to myself, and was still chuckling when two cars, one clearly following the other, came slowly down the street, almost stealthily, and stopped outside my house.

Inspector Birt was all smiles and saintliness when I opened the door.

'Marcus!' he exclaimed as though both surprised and delighted to find me at home.

'Maurice!' I exclaimed, imitating his tone.

'May we come in?'

'Both of you?' I asked, eyeing Wilson as though I suspected he might be bringing some quite unmentionable venereal disease in with him.

'This time, yes, Marcus,' Birt told me.

I stood to one side. I shut the door behind them and led the way to the sitting-room. 'You'll have to excuse – ' I fluffed out the skirt of my dressing-gown.

'Oh, please. Please. Don't apologise. Who would have expected visitors at this late hour?'

'Nobody civilised, that's for sure,' I retorted, and opened the sitting-room door.

'Nobody civilised,' Birt repeated, and cackled as though the slur amused him greatly. He didn't go into the sitting-room, though. 'Ah,' he said. 'The kitchen, I think, Marcus.'

I raised my eyebrows, and my pulse-rate rose, too. 'The kitchen?'

'If you please.' He gestured for me to lead the way. 'It's always more friendly, I find. A kitchen. Nothing quite like a group of friends gathered about a kitchen table, don't you think?'

I didn't, particularly, but, 'Oh, sure. A great leveller of humanity a kitchen table is,' I replied.

'Quite. A great leveller. Something quite earthy. Homely. I mean, it's difficult, wouldn't you say, to get on your high horse when surrounded by pots and pans and unwashed dishes?'

'Depends how slovenly you are, doesn't it? Personally, I wash up immediately after eating. It's called hygiene, I believe.'

'Hygiene,' Birt said. 'Yes. You're right, of course. But then you'd have more time for *hygiene* than us poor working folk. Eh, Wilson?'

Wilson nodded and gave a supercilious smirk.

'Well,' I said. 'Some of us make it, and some of us don't, I guess. You've *almost* made it, Maurice,' I went on, and then volleyed Wilson's smirk back at him. 'Others never will. Coffee?' I asked, as I wandered over to the percolator.

'No. No, thank you, Marcus.'

'It's no bother. I mean, I'm wide awake now and I could use one.'

'Please. Do have one yourself. We won't. I don't expect we'll be staying all that long.'

'Please yourself,' I said, but I didn't make coffee for myself either. I came back to the table and sat down with them. I looked from one blank face to the other. 'Okay. You've got us all round your earthy table. Now what?'

'I need your help, Marcus.'

I'd heard that one before. I gave him a charming smile. 'Oh? You know, that's precisely what you said just before you nailed me for killing Sharon.'

Birt looked surprised. 'Did I? Did I really say that?'

'Yes, you really did.'

'Extraordinary.'

I sighed. 'You want help?'

'Yes. Oh, yes. Just some loose ends to be tidied up. Let's begin with Farrell,' Birt said and watched me like a hawk.

Well, come on, I wasn't falling for that one. 'Who?' I asked, screwing my face into lines of utter bewilderment.

Birt slapped his hand lightly on the table. 'How silly of me. You wouldn't know, of course. Speed. John Speed. His real name was John Farrell. John Hamish Farrell, in fact.'

'You don't say.'

'I do. Oh, I do. But you couldn't have known that, as I said. We'll call him John Speed then, shall we? For convenience. Your convenience, Marcus. Now, you had him here for a while, right?'

'You know full well I had. You met him here.'

Birt nodded. 'That's right. That's perfectly right. So you knew him – well, let's say, *reasonably* well. I mean, you'd have noticed any little habits he might have had. Any little quirks. I like that word – quirks.'

'Probably.'

'Yes. I accept that. Probably. Tell me, Marcus, was he left- or right-handed, can you remember?'

I felt a tiny nerve near my temple start to judder so I put up my hand to cover it, using the action to rub my forehead and help my concentration. 'Right,' I said finally.

'*Right*-handed?'

'Yes. Right-handed.'

'You say that as if you're positive. Are you positive, Marcus?' Birt was needling me.

'Yes,' I said calmly. 'I'm positive. He was right-bloody-handed.'

'Hmm. That's the first of my small problems, you see. We know you're correct. Speed definitely *was* right-handed. So how did he inject himself with a fatal dose of pure heroin in his *right* arm?'

I felt the muscles in my stomach tighten. 'How should *I* know? You're the experts.'

'It would have been virtually impossible for him to do it,' Birt told me.

Virtually impossible, I thought. And then I thought, Harry Rutherford could make something of that in court. And then I thought, perish the thought that he'd have to. I pulled myself together. '*Virtually* impossible means possible,' I pointed out.

'But you see, Marcus, the angle was all wrong. I said "virtually" because it would have been possible if he was a contortionist, but we've no evidence he was that. Would you like to know what I think?'

I said nothing since I knew he was going to tell me one way or the other.

'I think,' Birt said he thought. 'I think someone injected the poor bastard with that lethal dose. It wasn't self-administered. Someone knowingly put that needle in the arm of John Hamish Farrell and knowingly killed him.'

'That's what you think, eh?' I asked.

Birt nodded. 'That's what I think.'

'Well, all you have to do is prove it and you're home and dry,' I told him.

'Oh, no. I *then* have to find who did inject Farrell, and then *prove* that he did it. Oh, no, Marcus, there's a long way to go yet.'

'Well, I'm sorry I can't help you.'

'Pity. Pity. Which leads me to another thought that's been crossing my mind.'

'Oh?'

'*If*, as we now suspect, someone killed Farrell, do you think it might be possible that this same person somehow managed to persuade the unfortunate drug-addicted Farrell to kill Kranze? Someone, maybe – well, almost certainly – someone who wanted Kranze dead?'

'Oh, come off it, Maurice. You couldn't *persuade* someone to murder someone else,' I said, pooh-poohing the idea as nonsense. But as Birt's eyes continued to bore into me I adopted a childlike innocence. 'Could you?' I asked.

'That's exactly what I thought, Marcus,' Birt told me affably. 'I thought, nobody could be persuaded to do such a terrible thing.'

'But something changed your mind?'

Birt sucked in his breath. 'Not changed my mind, exactly. Opened it to the possibility that the *right* person *might* be able to present murder in a light different to the way normal people would regard it.' He drummed his fingers on the table. 'Remembered something you told me – '

'*I* told you?'

'Yes, you told me, Marcus. Years ago now. Something you'd read in Kranze's book – you do know I've read the book, too?'

'No, I didn't as a matter of fact.'

'Oh, yes. While you were inside. Read your copy of the manuscript, in fact. Borrowed it, you could say, since I returned it. Anyway, I remembered it when I read it for myself in that manuscript and then I remembered it again the other day.' He stopped talking and watched me.

'I'm all ears.'

'"Murder can be a very pleasurable exercise" – does that ring a bell, Marcus?'

'Not off-hand.'

Birt raised his hands in the air. 'Now, that *does* surprise me. I was certain you'd remember that. No? No matter. The point is, I wondered if someone very cunning hadn't presented murder as a very pleasurable exercise to the – well, the somewhat witless John Farrell. Maybe even not as a pleasurable exercise. An exercise in revenge, perhaps.'

'I suppose it's possible.'

'Oh, I think it is. I think it was. I mean – look,' Birt spread his hands. 'What have we got? A simple man like John Farrell. Not only simple but addicted to drugs. A man who – as you yourself told me – hated and loathed Kranze, or Zanker, as he would have known him. Oh, I do believe it would have been a simple enough task for someone clever to persuade John to have a go.'

It wasn't, believe me, difficult for me to fill my voice with anger when I said, slowly and coldly, 'Let me get this straight, Birt. You're saying I tricked Farrell into killing Kranze and then I killed Farrell myself. Is that what you're saying?'

Birt threw up his hands again. He donned an affronted expression. 'No, no, no, Marcus. I'm saying no such thing. I'm saying *someone* devious and cunning and clever, someone who *also* wanted Kranze dead might have been able to persuade Farrell to do the job for him. That's all I'm saying. Not that *you* had anything to do with it.'

I relaxed. A mistake. 'So,' Birt was saying immediately, 'Can you think of anyone, barring yourself, who might have wanted Kranze dead – and Speed, of course. A third party?'

'You're still saying I wanted Kranze – '

'Well, you did, didn't you?'

'No I did not. Shit. Look, we were publishing his book. The book

I discovered. It could have made my name in publishing. I wanted Kranze alive.' It was a stupid argument. I knew that as soon as I'd uttered it. I suspect Birt knew it too, but he let it pass, so I answered his original question. 'Knowing Kranze for the shit he was he probably had hundreds of people who wanted him dead.'

Birt sighed deeply. He gave a small, tired laugh. 'I suppose you're right. He wasn't a very nice man.'

Something about hearing Kranze described as 'not a very nice man' got right up my nose. 'He was a fucking shit,' I shouted, and regretted my outburst immediately. I calmed down. 'As you say, he was not a very nice man.'

'And you can't, off-hand, think of anyone who might have hated him as much as Speed?'

'Me,' I said with a grin.

'Besides you, Marcus,' Birt said patiently, and returning a fraction of my grin.

I shook my head. 'Apart from yourself, no,' I said cheekily.

Birt clasped his hands behind his head, leaned back and closed his eyes. He stayed like that for a few minutes, while Wilson and I glowered at each other. Then in one swift movement Birt had his hands on the table, using them to push him from his chair and onto his feet. 'Back to the drawing-board, I'm afraid,' he said to Wilson.

The two of them walked towards the kitchen door, Birt saying as he went, 'Thanks for your help, Marcus.'

'Sorry I couldn't do more.'

'So am I. So am I.'

He had reached the door. Suddenly, without any explanation, he stopped and turned, came back to the table and sat down again. He gestured, in a vague, off-hand way, for me and Wilson to sit down again also. When we were seated he said, again with no explanation, 'The woman we found stabbed to death on Wimbledon Common, Charlotte Adams – she didn't ever come here, did she?'

'Here? To this house? Of course not. Why would she?'

'You didn't know her?'

'No. I didn't know her.'

'She was a nurse,' Birt said quietly, possibly intending just to think it.

'A psychiatric nurse, actually,' I pointed out.

'Oh, you know that much?' Birt asked, not pouncing on it as if I'd just made a really incriminating mistake, just asking me.

'Yes. It was on the news. And in the papers. One of them, anyway.'

'That's right,' Birt confirmed.

'Same paper suggested it might be one of her psycho patients who did it,' I told him.

Birt pointed a finger at me. 'That's right, too. I read that. *You* think it was . . . one of her patients?'

'I never speculate,' I told him loftily.

'*I* think it might have been,' he informed me. 'A psycho. Not necessarily one of her patients, but a psycho. A truly mad person. An insane person.'

He wasn't going to get me this way. 'You're probably right,' I agreed.

'But that's just more guesswork, unfortunately,' Birt admitted with a sigh.

I said nothing. I just cocked my jaw and looked at him, letting him take whatever tack he wanted.

Again he spoke as if to himself. 'She was never here,' he said.

'She was never here,' I repeated.

'And you never met her?'

'I never met her.'

'Not even briefly?'

'Not even briefly.'

'No contact with the poor woman at all?'

'No contact with the poor woman at all.' But by now I'd had just about enough. 'Look, Birt, what the fuck are you playing at? What the – '

My words stuck in my throat. Slowly, like an aged magician whose joints were seizing up but who wanted to perform just one more sleight-of-hand, Birt took a small plastic bag from his pocket and laid it on the table. There was something inside the bag. I couldn't quite make it out. 'What's that?' I asked coolly, although by this time I was feeling anything but cool.

'Have a look,' Birt suggested.

'Can I pick it up?'

'Please. By all means,' Birt said affably.

I picked it up and studied the object through the plastic. It was an earring. A dangly earring, and I recognised it instantly as identical to the ones Charlotte had been wearing. My hands let me down and started to shake. I stretched out my arms full length and held the little bag up to the light. 'Looks to me like an earring,' I said, and put the bag back on the table.

'An earring,' Birt said, nodding.

'That's right. An earring,' I repeated with aplomb. And then I lifted the bag again and put on my very best *Antiques Roadshow* accent.

'Indian, I'd say. Very much twentieth-century. Of poor quality. Attractive, of course, but, as I say, the quality is poor. The embossing – here and here – very crude. Jaipur, probably. Made strictly for export to the European market. Of little value, I'm afraid. Pretty enough in a subcontinental way, but worthless.'

'Anything else you can tell me?' Birt asked, pretending to be totally enthralled.

'I'm no expert on ladies' jewellery,' I told him.

'I thought you were doing very well.'

I gave him a condescending smirk.

'Go on,' Birt urged. 'Try and tell me some more.'

It never ceases to amaze me how the mind works. Up to that point I truly had no idea about the full significance of the earring in the bag. Certainly it was the same as the ones Charlotte had been wearing, but so what? There was still nothing, as far as I could tell, to connect me with Charlotte or this wretched piece of tat. And then Pissquick came through my head, on the scrounge, no doubt. And suddenly everything clicked in my mind. The incident with the supposed mouse filled my consciousness, and before I could stop myself my eyes flicked to the rubbish bin where Farrell had deposited Pissquick's plaything. When I looked back at Birt's face he had an impassive expression, but there was that tiny light of success in his eyes. 'Must be thousands of them around,' I heard myself say. 'Hundreds of thousands, probably. They were, you see, my dear Birt, very fashionable at one time. I think even my Ma had a pair once.' I smiled. 'Until she realised the error of her ways.'

Birt returned my smile. 'Oh, threw them out, did she?'

I shrugged. 'Possibly. *I* don't know. Am I my mother's keeper, I ask you. I'm not in the habit of keeping a check on Ma's cast-offs. Could try Oxfam. Most of the stuff goes there. Hers and mine.' I gave Wilson a bit of an up-and-down look. 'Come to think of it,' I said, and left it at that. There was silence for a few seconds, and then I thought I better show some sort of interest, so: 'What's the significance of it, anyway?'

'It's one of Miss Charlotte Adams' earrings.'

'So?'

Birt didn't answer. The merlin, it seemed, was getting a new lease of life, becoming ever more sprightly. He took quite a collection of little plastic bags from his inside jacket pocket and proceeded to spread them out on the table, one after the other, like he was dealing cards, carefully, making sure I got none of the aces, watching me all the while.

I felt my throat go dry. My palms were sweating. Under the table I wiped them on my dressing-gown before leaning forward and moving each little bag a fraction the better to view them. I hadn't a clue what they were – the contents, I mean, of course. Or rather, I did *know* what they looked like but couldn't for the life of me fathom their significance.

I looked up at Birt. 'Supposed to mean something to me?'

Birt shook his head. 'No. Probably not. Just fibres, mostly. A little dried leaf. A spot of mud.'

'Very decorative.'

'The trouble is – oh, how come there's a Ford outside the house? Changed cars, have you?'

It still didn't click. 'No. As a matter of fact some moron ran into me just after you left the other morning. The BMW's in getting a facelift.'

'An accident. Oh dear. On the Chelsea Road, was it? A van, perhaps, that caused the damage? Driven by a burly chap, close-cropped hair, plaid shirt, very working class?'

Then it clicked, I can tell you. 'Your – ' was all I got out before Birt nodded, and said, ''Fraid so, Marcus. One of my lot. I don't know about the facelift but your car has certainly had a thorough examination.' He paused. He smiled. He went on, 'Now, all these little bags contain evidence taken from your car.' He pushed one bag forward. 'That's fibre from clothing. It matches precisely the clothing Charlotte Adams was wearing when we found her body.' He pushed another little bag under my nose. 'That leaf – would you believe its twin was still clinging to the sole of one of Charlotte Adams' shoes.' Another bag came my way. 'That mud, now *that* was on the other shoe. Tucked up under the heel. Amazingly,' he pushed another bag across the table, 'this piece of mud, which is identical in every possible way to *that* scrap of mud, was found under the brake pedal of your BMW.'

There wasn't a lot I could say, really. I felt my head reeling as I tried desperately to find some even *reasonably* plausible excuse for these items being in my car. But nothing would come. 'How do you explain that, Marcus?' I heard Birt ask, and for some reason his voice was all echoey and seemed to come from quite a distance.

I was still bending over the bags when Birt pulled another trick from the hat. Two more of his wretched little plastic bags, would you believe.

'How many more of these have you got?' I asked.

'Just these two,' Birt said simply.

Inside both bags were different lengths of plastic-covered red cord, and before I could stop myself my head jerked up and my eyes were fixed on the reel of plastic-covered red cord hanging by the kitchen door. Slowly I turned my head and faced Birt. He was nodding. Not smugly, though. Not even looking very pleased with himself. Sadly, I'd say. Even a tinge ashamed. He coughed. 'That,' he said, pointing to the shorter length of cord, 'we took from the end of that reel over there,' he told me solemnly, pointing in the direction I had mistakenly, foolishly looked.

'Been a busy little beaver, haven't we?'

'Yes. We've been busy, Marcus,' he agreed. 'As I was saying, *that* we took from the end of the reel over there, and *this* – ' he indicated the bag with the long piece of cord '– this,' he explained, 'is a length of cord we found beside the body of Charlotte Adams.'

I blustered. 'There must be miles and miles of that cord – ' I began, but Birt held up a patient hand. 'The end of *that* one matches the end of *that* one. The fibres match. Forensics prove that they match.' He was now speaking very slowly. 'So *that* piece there was once joined to that piece *there*.'

I could feel my entire body sagging involuntarily. I leaned back in my chair. I felt my head jerk as I gave a small, snorting laugh. I looked at Wilson. 'Not going to say "gotcha" this time?'

Birt said, 'No need, is there, Marcus?'

I gave him a kindly smile. 'No need. No need at all.' I started to gather up the bags for him. 'Tell me, how did you – '

'You won't like to hear it,' Birt warned me in the friendliest possible manner.

I shrugged. 'Tell me anyway.'

'Your friend Kranze got you again.'

'Kranze?' I was flabbergasted.

'In a manner of speaking,' Birt said. He collected the bags and put them back in his inside pocket. 'You told me you were going away for two days – when I was here the other morning, the morning I informed you Kranze had been killed. Now, I've no explanation for this. Maybe it's just experience. Maybe it's what's known as gut feeling, but your reaction to his death just was not right. Don't ask me what was wrong with it. I don't know. It wasn't right and that's an end to it. So, during your two-day absence I got hold of the editor-in-chief of – '

'Nick? Nick Putty?' I asked.

'Nick Putty,' Birt confirmed, keeping the same tone as though he hadn't been interrupted. 'From him I got the manuscript of Kranze's book, and I spent those two days rereading it.' Birt looked up at me, his voice apologised when he said, 'Things just fell into place. That business about there being no harm – indeed it being advisable – to have a practice run before killing someone. You'd done that with Sharon before killing Darren. I began to wonder if Charlotte Adams had been a practice run. I thought, quite honestly, for you, Marcus. But then I began to wonder if it wasn't a practice run for Farrell since all the indications are that he killed Kranze. But Farrell, you see, would never in a million years have thought of practising murder. Someone had to put that idea into his mind. Kranze certainly wouldn't have. Nobody else had read the manuscript. That left you. But, you know, I still couldn't make myself believe you were insane enough to put yourself through all this horror again.'

I gave a derisory snort: me? insane? *moi*?

'And I'll tell you something else,' Birt went on, as I stifled an improvised yawn and tapped my mouth. 'This afternoon, when we came here to search this house, I was still convinced – no, I was hoping against hope – that we'd find nothing. That my suspicions of you were wrong. That you'd be in the clear. Instead – ' Birt patted his inside pocket. 'So you see,' he concluded. 'It was Kranze, through that damn book of his, that put me onto you.'

A voice from far away said, 'Even from the grave.' It gave me quite a turn when I realised the voice was my own. And Birt, damn him, nodded and repeated, 'Even from the grave.'

I know full well it was my imagination, or some acoustical clown playing tricks on me, but just for one split second I could have sworn I heard Kranze's distinctive, mocking cackle, and I can only think it was the sound of it that made me hysterical. Suddenly, with precious little to laugh about, I was rocking back and forth in my chair roaring with mirth: real and genuine glee, quite as if what was happening to me at that instant was the most comical thing in the universe. And I laughed myself to the point of exhaustion, tears rolling down my cheeks, blinding me. I didn't see Birt stand up. I didn't see Wilson stand up either, but I felt his shovel-sized hand grip my arm. And in the twinkling of an eye my mood changed. I became furious. I jerked my arm away and the look I gave Wilson must have been pretty venomous because he recoiled for a moment before lunging for my arm again. Then I heard Birt say in that calm, phlegmatic voice of his, 'Leave him, Wilson,' and I remember smiling at Birt, wiping away my tears and smiling at Inspector Maurice Birt.

He returned my smile. 'Ready?' he asked politely, the smile leaving his face almost unwillingly.
'Ready,' I replied. 'Oh, just one thing.'
Birt inclined his head to listen.
'Mind if I make a phone call?'
'Just the one,' Birt told me.
'Oh, yes. Just the one.'
Birt walked in front of me, Wilson behind me, as I went into the hall. It struck me suddenly that Birt was an old man, his shoulders rounded, slouching. I wanted to tell him to stand up straight, but I didn't. I picked up the phone, and dialled. Birt, with manners, kept his back to me almost as if that position would prevent him eavesdropping. Wilson, the ignoramus, watched intently, probably noting the number I called.

The phone seemed to ring for an age before a tired and grumpy voice said a hoarse, 'Hello?'

'Ah, Harry. Sorry to disturb you so late. It's me, Marcus. D'you want to hear the bad news or the bad news first?'

There wasn't a lot else I could say, was there?

THIRTY

I was in prison. On remand, as they call it, and feeling pretty pissed off about it, too. I'd denied everything during my interrogation, of course, denied it all so vehemently I just about convinced *myself* I was being nothing but honest. Anyway, only escapees from asylums and complete arseholes admit to any crime, even if the evidence is well stacked against them. But I was polite about it, even affable, just saying, 'No comment,' when appropriate, and, 'You've got that all wrong, Inspector,' and, 'No, that is simply not correct,' as Birt and the gloating Wilson tried to get me to confess just so they could have it recorded for posterity.

But they charged me nonetheless: one count of murder – Charlotte's, would you believe. I know they were hoping to get me on a conspiracy charge, or aiding and abetting, or something in connection with Herr and Frau, but they must have been told they'd no hope of making that stick because they didn't pursue it. They never even mentioned poor old Farrell, which I thought was a shame.

Maybe they felt they had enough on their plates. I did feel bad, though, about the way they neglected the poor chap.

And, alone in my cell now, I was also depressed. Not *depressed* depressed. Just feeling down. I'd had a letter from Ma that morning, and it lay unopened on my cot. I was curious to know what was in it, but at the same time I didn't want her haranguing me, even ever so sweetly. But eventually curiosity won, and I started to read what she'd written.

She was, she wrote, most upset about my situation, and added some trimmings. That took up the first six lines of the letter. The other four pages were all about something that had upset her a great deal more. She'd been shopping. Back to the cheese counter in that fancy food hall. Forced to take a ticket with a number on it and wait in a queue like a bumpkin until her number was called before they would serve her. Ma really had expected things to change for the better after her spat with the manager on the day I took her shopping when she'd just returned from honeymoon. Ma did *not* enjoy having her remonstrances treated lightly. 'Can you imagine, darling,' she wrote. 'Me, your own mother, standing there, clutching a scrap of coloured paper, waiting for some impertinent missie to call me – by *number*, no less. I have *never* been so humiliated. I mean, who do these people – ' by whom Ma meant anyone who had even so much as a thimbleful of what she called non-Anglo-Saxon blood in their veins '– think they are? We let them come into the country, save them from famine and pestilence, and before you know it they're treating us like – well, like convicts, dear, aren't they? I am *not* a number. Oh, dear, I've just thought. I'm so sorry, darling. I didn't mean . . . Well, at least I understand what you must be going through when they call you down for your supper.' Wasn't she just terrific? She certainly cheered me up no end. I was still grinning to myself when my cell door was banged open, and I was told to get my arse down and get my tea.

I could use a cup of tea. Even that black, stewed concoction, thick enough to trot rats on, appealed. I got to the door and heard a familiar voice yelling, 'That's not fucking tea. That's fucking piss.' Stuart Bean, no less. My heart stopped. I wanted to retreat to the nominal safety of my cell. But the screw was watching me and the last thing I wanted was for a screw to get any hint I was avoiding someone. So, out I stepped onto the gallery, and came face to face with Beany. The look he gave me, or I imagined he gave me, made the hairs on the back of my neck stand upright as a Rhodesian Ridgeback's. He walked towards me. He put his arms about me, pinning *my* arms to my sides. He lifted me off my feet. He whirled me about and I had visions of suddenly being jettisoned onto the tiled flooring some twenty feet below. And then I heard him saying, 'For fuck's sake, mate. I didn't know you were here.' Then he released me and to my overwhelming joy it was a beaming Stuart Bean, an amicable Stuart Bean, a delighted Stuart Bean who gazed up at me.

I beamed back. 'Didn't know you were here either,' I said.

'Buggers got you too, then?'

'Like you say – the buggers got me. Not for our little job, though.'

'No?'

'No. Got clean away with that, I did,' I told him, knowing he'd be proud of me for escaping.

'What then – if I'm not being nosey?'

'A little matter of assassination, Stuart.'

Stuart's mouth dropped open as he assimilated that information. And then, in a thrice, he'd forgotten about it. Indeed, in that wonderfully optimistic way that full-time criminals have of overlooking the long penal years lying ahead of them, before they even know how many of those years there will be, Stuart had taken me by the arm, and was saying, 'You know what we're going to do when we get out? I'll tell you. We're going to sit down together, just you and me, mind, and we're going to plan a job the likes of which no one's ever seen. A real job. Something to set us up for life. You'll drive. I'll do the robbery. In, out and away. And only you and me knowing a fucking thing about it. What you say?'

He was so enthusiastic I was loth to deflate him, but, 'I think the only thing I'll be fit to drive by the time they let me out, Stuart, is a zimmer,' I told him.

Stuart gave me an elbow in the ribs. 'Be able to get you a good one of those cheap,' he said, with a huge grin.

'With a turbo?' I asked.

'And wing mirrors,' Stuart added.

'And disc brakes?'

'And rearwheel drive.'

'And sun roof?'

'And stereo, CD, the lot.'

'Fog lights?'

'Convertible.'

'Cocktail cabinet?'

'A *stretch* zimmer,' Stuart said, and we couldn't think of anything else.

We were having a great time. We were laughing our heads off but not out loud. Quietly, intimately, not sharing our small, ridiculous pleasure with those other bastards.

Then it was lockup, and Stuart left me. 'Don't you fucking forget now, pal. You and me.'

'I won't forget, Stuart.'

He winked and walked off, and I got the impression he was much more at home here than in his own flat with long-suffering, moribund Mum, surrounded by those ghastly home-made flowers, and irked by the continuous clanking of the clamorous washing-machine. I'd have felt the same myself, I shouldn't wonder.

Night. I lay on my bunk, listening to the humming/crackling noises that insects and small animals make, that prisoners, sleeping and dreaming, also make. It was oddly comforting. It was the sound of men still on remand, not yet condemned, still hopeful. Eternally, optimistically hopeful, some of them.

Then a quite ridiculously giddy mood swept over me. I sat up. Out loud, but not too loudly, in a sing-song, hickory-dickery dock kind of voice, I called, 'Ha-a-ar-eee? Oh, Haaa-a-ar-eee? Are you the-e-ere? Come on now, Harry. Jump to it. Pull your socks up. Put your thinking cap on. Get those little grey Poirot cells busy. I know you can get me out of this if you put your mind to it. I simply *know* you can.'

And the odd thing was that I did know it. I was totally and utterly convinced that if I could just cajole Harry (with the odd shove and push from Ma, of course) into defending me yet again, I would walk free, my tail at as high an angle as ever conceived by Pissquick.

'Twas just a pity he couldn't hear me.